4/14

D0455263

RANSOM RIVER

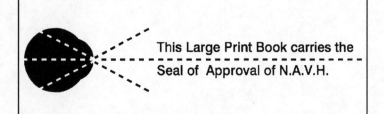

This Large Print Book carries the
Seal of Approval of N.A.V.H.

RANSOM RIVER

MEG GARDINER

THORNDIKE PRESS
A part of Gale, Cengage Learning

Detroit • New York • San Francisco • New Haven, Conn • Waterville, Maine • London

LIBRARY OF CONGRESS CATALOGING-IN-PUBLICATION DATA

Gardiner, Meg.
    Ransom river / by Meg Gardiner — Large print ed.
        p. cm. — (Thorndike Press large print thriller)
    ISBN 978-1-4104-5031-9 (hardcover) — ISBN 1-4104-5031-7 (hardcover)
1. Large type books. I. Title.
PR6107.A725R36 2012b
823'.92—dc23   2012023333

Published in 2012 by arrangement with Dutton, a member of Penguin Group (USA) Inc.

Printed in the United States of America
1 2 3 4 5 6 7 16 15 14 13 12

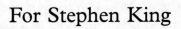

For Stephen King

1

Then

The night was meant for shooting stars. Before the shadow rose, or the sirens moaned, the sky was cut by a meteor shower: ice on fire, streaks of light that tore the air. Maybe meteors would crash into the mountains, Rory thought. Or into West River Elementary School. Or into the Chevron gas station downtown. That, she thought, would cause a supermassive fireball. That made sneaking out at one in the morning worth the risk.

Or it should have.

In her bedroom, in the dark, she tied her Converse All Stars. Outside the window, the sky boomed at her, looming and endless and pounded white with stars.

The house was school-night quiet. She turned her ear to the closed door but heard nothing — no TV, no talk or laughter from her mom and dad's room. Pepper was in his dog bed in the kitchen. Everybody was asleep.

Beyond the window a voice whispered. "Rory."

Seth pressed his hands to the screen. His eyes swam with starlight.

"Getting my stuff," she whispered back.

She shoved binoculars into her backpack and slung it across her shoulders. The Power Rangers felt like a shield, even though the bright plastic might shine under the streaking light of a meteor. As if a falling star could read *R. Mackenzie* written in black marker across the pack and aim for her. But maybe. Like her dad said sometimes, *Don't look back. Something might be gaining on you.*

Seth stretched on his toes to look in her window. "Hurry up."

She stuck the flashlight in her sweatshirt pocket. She slid the screen open, boosted herself onto the sill, and jumped out.

The air was chilly. She crouched beside Seth on the grass. In the night he seemed nothing but blond hair and a crazy smile. Beyond the lawn and avocado tree and her mom's tomatoes, beyond the cinder-block back wall, the countryside seemed to murmur at them.

Ransom River, most of it, was the other way, out her front door. The city, popula-

8

tion 172,000 according to the poster in her fourth-grade classroom, had fallen asleep. Streetlights kept watch, like a giant skein of Christmas lights. Farther away, over the mountains, Los Angeles was a smudgy yellow glow in the sky. Like the post-thermonuclear scene in *Terminator 2: Judgment Day,* which her parents didn't know she had secretly watched at Seth's.

She hunkered like a commando and pointed north, at black hills that swallowed the stars. "We can see best from the Pinnacles."

Seth snickered. "This isn't a jailbreak."

"My parents will *kill* me if they catch me sneaking out."

Mom would look worried and disappointed. Dad would get the black-cloud face and call her sternly to attention on the carpet, saying, *Aurora Mackenzie, this is preposterous.* And she would flush and stutter *sorry* and hide in her room.

Not tonight. They ran across the cool grass. At the back wall Seth jumped, grabbed the top, and pulled himself up. Rory was a step behind.

And from the dirt road on the other side of the wall, headlights caught Seth and outlined him in the night.

He froze. The headlights belonged to a

9

heavy vehicle, maybe a hundred yards away, bouncing slowly toward them. It looked like a delivery van bumping in their direction along the dirt path.

Seth hesitated only a moment. In a hard whisper he said, "Come on. We can make it before they get here."

Rory grabbed his leg. "Wait."

There was no reason to run in front of a big old van at one in the morning. Except Seth Colder wanted to do it. It was a dare. The van rattled toward them. Seth glanced down at her, and the look on his face seemed like a promise. This was an adventure. Rory boosted herself up.

The van's headlights popped to brights. They lit Seth up like a paranormal creature.

Rory jumped back down and yanked on his leg so hard he fell to the ground. They bungled to a heap on the grass. On the far side of the wall the van ground to a stop. Its door creaked open.

"Crap," Seth said.

Rory huddled to her feet against the wall. "We can't get in trouble for being in my own backyard. It's my house. It's Mackenzie property."

"What if it isn't the UPS guy?"

The engine gargled. Gingerly, Rory stood on tiptoe to see over. Her blood turned to cold water. The van was stopped a few yards away on the dirt road. In front of it a figure stood silhouetted, feet planted wide. Just standing there. Looking.

She crouched back down. "What does he want?"

"What does Freddy Krueger want?"

Her skin seemed to zing, like she'd touched an electric socket with wet fingers. "Tree house."

She'd never seen Freddy Krueger, but Seth had three big brothers and snuck along whenever they did things. Freddy Krueger had knives for fingers and killed teenagers. She ran low along the wall to the avocado tree. Its leaves were dark and slick in the starlight. She dashed underneath it with Seth hard at her side. Outside the wall, the van rumbled.

"Who is he?" Seth said.

"Don't want to know."

She shimmied up the tree trunk. Seth squirreled up behind her. They clambered into the tree house and crouched on the creaking planks and peered out through the leaves. The headlights of the van caught the upper reaches of the tree.

"Think he can see us?" she whispered.

Seth shook his head.

The figure stood silhouetted in the headlights. He moved like a lump, splitting the beams. He turned in a slow circle and paused, facing the tree.

"Oh," Rory said.

"We didn't do anything," Seth said.

"Like Freddy Krueger cares?"

They held still, hands curled over the edge of the open tree-house window. And Rory saw more lights, in the farther distance.

At first she thought a shooting star had blazed to the ground. Far, far along the county road that pushed into the foothills, near the freeway to Los Angeles, hot white lights burned the night. But it wasn't a flaming meteor crater. It was big road spotlights, like construction crews used when they fixed highways in the dark.

And those lights were surrounded by flashing red and blue.

"Seth," she said.

He looked. After a moment, he shrugged. "Don't know."

But she did. Police and fire trucks. Maybe ambulances. They were parked under big spotlights out near the highway. Like there'd been a huge wreck.

"This is freaky," she said.

Seth turned back to the Freddy guy on the dirt road. "He's looking for something. Or someplace."

She leaned close to him. His Ninja Turtles T-shirt hung loose on his skinny shoulders. The figure in the road seemed to be backing up, toward the van.

Then, from beneath the tree, came a bad, bad sound. *Yap.*

She spun and leaned down through the trapdoor. "Pepper, shh."

Below her the little dog put his paws on the trunk of the tree. His tail wagged in the moonlight. He barked again.

"Pepper, no," Rory said.

Seth yanked on her sweatshirt. "Be quiet."

She pulled back into the tree house. The man in the headlights stopped. And walked toward them again. They ducked.

The man's breathing was hard, like a mummy wheezing through its wrappings. His footsteps were slow and uneven. They heard him stumble and grunt.

"Fuck," he said.

Rory's ears went hot. Seth had stopped moving.

The man groaned. He was right there, just beyond the wall. "Fuck it all."

With a click, the beam of a flashlight veered and shone through the tree-house window.

"He knows we're here," Rory said.

Pepper kept barking. The flashlight

paused. They heard Freddy hawk and spit on the dirt, something wet and nasty.

And they heard a siren float on the air. Far away, maybe out by the hot white lights and red police alarms near the freeway.

"Is he after us?" she said. "Why would he be after us?"

"You're the genius. You tell me."

She hit him in the arm. "Don't be stupid."

He looked at her. "Don't worry. I got ya."

"What does that mean?"

He looked hurt. "You know. I'll protect you."

She was bigger than him. Right. She wanted to hit him again, just to stop being afraid. She wanted him not to move away from her even an inch.

Freddy's footsteps faded. They heard grunts and a groan and a thud.

"What's he doing?" Seth said.

Rory peeked and saw the flashlight next door, swinging like a light saber. "He climbed into the neighbors' backyard."

The van sat on the dirt path, idling. Rory said, "This is too weird."

Below the tree, Pepper began a low, sad moan. It was his sound when he was frightened. Through the leaves of the tree, Rory saw the flashlight dim. Freddy was sneaking between houses to the street out front. *Hunt-*

ing, she couldn't help thinking.

"What does he want?" she said. "To rob houses? Kill people?"

"How should I know?"

"Don't get mad."

But she knew why he sounded angry. 'Cause his dad was a cop, and he got it all the time. In the far distance, the siren wailed.

"What if he comes back?" she said.

"Lay low."

She thought of Pepper running loose. Did Freddy Krueger murder dogs? She stood up. "No. The house. Let's get in my room."

She swung through the trapdoor and slid down the tree trunk. A moment later Seth hit the ground beside her. She whistled for Pepper.

Freddy's swinging flashlight wavered across the wall of her house.

"He's coming back. Hurry," she said.

She thought she heard the door to the garage creak open. She called Pepper again but he bolted for the kitchen door. She heard his dog door swing as he pushed through it. She sprinted to her bedroom window with Seth beside her. She jumped and squirmed a knee onto the sill.

She stopped. Her room was dark, but a bright yellow stripe leaked under the door.

The lights were on in the hall.

Footsteps hurried past the door. Her mom's voice. "What the hell?"

Farther away, maybe in the kitchen, came a crash, like a table had fallen over. Her dad called out, "Samantha, stay there."

Rory hung on the windowsill. A voice deep inside her head whispered, *Leave.*

She jumped back down onto the grass. "Let's get out of here."

She slid the window and screen closed. She and Seth ran across the lawn and herked themselves onto the top of the concrete wall. The old van idled on the dirt path, lights blazing. Seth leaped into their glare and landed and ran.

In the house, more lights turned on. Behind closed blinds, a shadow hurried across the living room. Rory jumped, awkwardly. She crash-landed in front of the van.

From the field, from the dark, Seth hissed, "Come on."

Her breath clapped out of her. She put a hand against the van and wobbled to her feet. Back at the house, a man's voice rose sharply. A meteor streaked overhead, pointing the way into the field and the wide night.

They ran for five minutes. They ran until Seth grabbed her sleeve and said, "You trying to get past the city limits sign?"

She stuttered to a stop. She could barely breathe.

She knew they were in trouble. She knew it while they huddled beneath an oak tree, eyeing the night. She knew it an hour later when they went back to her house and she crept in her window. The neighborhood was dark and still. The van was gone. Her house was quiet. But things weren't right.

She knew it. She just didn't know what was wrong.

Not then.

2

Twenty-four hours would have changed everything. If Rory had been slower, if she had taken a breath and waited, she wouldn't be here. If she'd torn up the place, gotten drunk, mooned the moneymen, seduced a border guard, she would have missed the flight home. She would have arrived twenty-four hours later and skipped this grief.

"All rise."

But no.

Rory hadn't paused, not even to give a middle finger to the bean counters. Others had pleaded or even cried. Rory had cleared her desk. She said, "This will kill people." And she walked.

The bailiff stood before the bench. "Superior Court of California, County of Los Angeles, is now in session. The matter of *People versus Elmendorf and Smith*. Judge Wieland presiding."

In the jury box, Rory stood with her peers. Back row, chair number seven. She'd finally been chosen for a team.

Morning sunlight prismed through the windows. The courthouse was surrounded by an acre of lawn, and the third-floor courtroom looked out on palm trees and the civic center and the River Mall. A blue sky glazed the view. The rocky hills of the inland ranges sawtoothed the horizon, charcoal and brown.

The door to chambers opened and Arthur Wieland entered, black robe rustling. Sunlight shone on his white hair and rimless glasses. He ascended the bench.

Noisily, everybody sat. The courtroom was full. It was day three of the trial but the air still had a buzz. Outside on the street, news vans lined up nose-to-tail. Eager reporters stood on the sidewalk talking to the camera.

Rory took out her notebook and pen. To her left, Helen Ellis smoothed her brown wool skirt. To her right, Frankie Ortega plunged his hands into the pocket of his hoodie. In front of her, Daisy Fallon gazed yearningly at the prosecutor. Daisy had confided the first day, "He's *hot*." Daisy had texted her friends about his hotness. Daisy had, Rory figured, already decided to vote guilty.

The bailiff tucked his thumbs into his utility belt. He was a totem pole with a Tom Selleck mustache. Though he wore an L.A. County Sheriff's uniform and his belt bristled with weaponry, his job consisted of standing still, for hour upon hour, staring at the courtroom. How he bore the tedium Rory couldn't imagine. Create a TV cop show about the guy, it would be called *Stultified.*

Welcome to Ransom River.

In Ransom River, nothing happened. That was the line. Everybody was quietly hardworking, and all the tattoos said *Mom,* even the gangbangers'. The unofficial city motto was "Look away — nothing to see here."

Except the Ransom River Superior Courthouse had become center stage for a spectacle of murder. And Aurora Faith Mackenzie had been plucked from the voter registration pool and thrown into it. Juror number seven on the teen burglar execution trial.

Twenty-four hours. If she had waited, even long enough to spit on the corporate hacks who slashed the funding for Asylum Action, she would have had an out. *Please excuse me from jury duty. I'm overseas, assaulting heartless pricks.* But cast adrift in Geneva and nearly broke, she'd grabbed the only escape route she had: her return airline ticket. She'd tried to out-distance her anger and dejection. So she ran straight ahead and in the wrong direction. Home. Where a jury summons waited.

Juror number seven. Caucasian female, age twenty-nine. Slight, angular, with what her parents called Black Irish looks. Today she'd dressed conservatively, at least compared to her Peace Corps days. V-neck sweater with a tank beneath, hipster khaki jeans, boots. The press was getting an eyeful. The jurors' names had not been made public, but a courtroom artist had sketched each of them, and one journalist had described her as having "night-sky hair and blue eyes with a challenging gleam."

She'd rolled those eyes at that.

Beside her, Helen Ellis adjusted her bifocals. "They look so excited."

She was eyeing the public gallery. The crowd was Southern California exurban: women in mom jeans or in mom-jean shorts. Men in *Tijera Sand and Gravel* shirts. Ranch workers in denim. At least today nobody wore T-shirts with an agenda. No *Justice!* shirts, no *Self-defense is our right.* The first day of the trial several people had shown up in pro-defendant attire. Judge Wieland had put a stop to it. No shirts with messages, he decreed. No disruption from the gallery. Violators would be ejected.

He'd clamped the lid down. Still, the atmosphere hovered between edgy and *We're going to Disneyland.*

"Bring on the popcorn vendors," Rory said. And maybe the Reaper, dancing up the aisle playing his scythe like an electric guitar.

Because the heart of this show was death. And its emissaries were the defendants. Behind the defense table, they took their time sitting down.

Charged with murder, they were standing tall. Wearing civvies, they looked every inch the cops they were.

Jared Smith shifted his shoulders inside the jacket of his suit as though it was too snug and his tie was choking him. He sat forward, like a plow. Like he expected other people to move aside for him.

Lucy Elmendorf didn't look at him. Sober and drawn, she sat with her hands laced together on the table.

Helen Ellis leaned heavily toward Rory. "Check out Lucy's husband."

Neil Elmendorf sat in the second row. Though his expression was stoic, he hunched, as though flinching. He seemed sandblasted with humiliation.

"Telling, don't you think?" Helen said.

Rory didn't respond. Elmendorf had put distance between himself and his wife. Maybe that lessened the anguish. After all, the man had to watch Lucy stand trial for murder. More than that, he had to endure her sitting beside the lover she'd been romping with when the gunfire began.

And Rory wondered again why the defendants hadn't had the sense to screw around in a motel across the county line. If Officer Lucy Elmendorf had handcuffed Jared Smith to a vibrating bed in Bakersfield instead of playing Bad Cop, Really Bad Cop at Smith's house in Ransom River, the victim might still be breathing.

And Rory wondered again how Smith and Elmendorf thought they could prove self-defense when they'd shot an unarmed sixteen-year-old kid in the back from point-blank range.

Traffic on River Boulevard was light. This city didn't really have a rush hour. Or rather, it did, at six a.m., when half the population hit the road to drag their asses onto the freeway and over the pass and into Los Angeles to punch a clock. Now, mid-morning, the lights were green and the dark gold Blazer was rolling along at thirty-four

23

miles per hour, just under the speed limit.

Sylvester Church saw the courthouse ahead. Again.

"Steady," he said.

Behind the wheel, Berrigan frowned. "I heard you the first time. And the seventeenth."

"And you'll hear me the next twenty times, if I have to keep telling you."

The light ahead turned red. They stopped. Across the intersection, outside the courthouse, news vans were parked. Reporters and camera crews stood idle. Church scanned the cross street, the road ahead, the side mirror. No cops.

But there were undoubtedly CCTV cameras in the vicinity. They'd passed a bank ATM a couple of blocks back. He didn't know whether the surveillance cameras there would be aimed at the street, but he had to assume this vehicle had been caught on video.

Like the two defendants on trial up at the courthouse.

"Lamebrains," Church said.

Berrigan frowned at him. "Who?"

"Drive."

Berrigan was nervous. Church didn't like the fact that it was so obvious.

Church was also nervous. But he hid it.

He erased all tells from his face, his voice, his posture. Years at the tables in Vegas had trained him well.

He glanced in the back of the Blazer. The rear seats were down, creating one big open space behind darkly tinted windows. The glass kept the sunlight from reflecting off the toolboxes and their cargo of weapons.

The light turned green. Berrigan eased away from the intersection toward the courthouse. Church unbuckled his seat belt.

"Around to the back."

He set the timer on his watch. It began counting down.

3

Judge Wieland peered down at the prosecutor. "Mr. Oberlin, call your next witness."

Assistant District Attorney Cary Oberlin stood, reading his notes. He was deliberate and calm. He reminded Rory of a carpenter who carefully takes one nail, then another, and exactingly hammers them into a board. Slowly, point by point, he intended to nail the defendants to the wall.

"The People call Samuel Koh," he said.

Today he was going to use a heavy hammer. Rory girded herself.

The victim in the case had been killed by a single gunshot to the cervical spine. He died instantly and awfully. And the courtroom was about to see what that meant.

Prospective jurors had been questioned about it during voir dire. *Could you look at graphic crime-scene photos of the body?*

Rory had said yes. She'd seen blood

before. She'd seen gore. Still, she braced herself.

She wasn't alone. In the front row of the public gallery, the victim's father stirred. And when Grigor Mirkovic stirred, the whole courtroom seemed to shudder.

Mirkovic sat surrounded by minions. Bodyguards, lawyers, personal assistants. He was banty and grim. His presence crackled like static electricity, itching, causing unease.

Grigor Mirkovic had a reputation and seemed to thrive on its impact. He sneered at reporters who asked him about his sketchy business background. Or about his millions. Or about his criminal connections. Such innuendo was beneath contempt, he told them.

It was all about Brad, he said. Brad, his son, his golden boy, his beautiful young man. Obrad Mirkovic, who would never attend the senior prom or walk across the stage at his high school graduation. Brad Mirkovic, who had been shot dead on Jared Smith's patio at two in the morning, with Lucy Elmendorf's fingers gripping his tangled hair.

In the courtroom, Grigor Mirkovic's walleyed glare never wavered from the defendants. The filthy cops who killed his boy, he called them.

But his anguish couldn't alter certain realities. Starting with the fact that Brad Mirkovic had died because he broke into Jared Smith's home on a dare.

The night he was shot, Brad had driven with friends to Ransom River from Beverly Hills, high on weed, cruising for kicks. They decided that improvisational burglary was their ticket to fun. It was a fatal decision.

According to the defense, Jared Smith was awakened by the sound of men climbing through his kitchen window. And Officer Jared Smith, who had an impeccable record as a Ransom River Police Department patrolman, had defended himself, his home, and his guest, Officer Lucy Elmendorf, with a legally registered handgun. He confronted Brad Mirkovic, informed him he was a police officer, and told Mirkovic he was under arrest.

Mirkovic, according to the defense, resisted. And Jared Smith, fearing for his life and the life of Officer Elmendorf, fired his weapon.

That story had problems. The first of which was Samuel Koh.

Jared Smith claimed that Brad Mirkovic had brandished an object he reasonably believed to be a gun. In the urgency of the moment, confronted in the dark by thieves, outnumbered and about to be overpowered, he responded with deadly force.

Everybody bought it. Until it turned out that Samuel Koh, Jared Smith's neighbor, had a video surveillance camera mounted under the eaves of his house. The camera angle captured not just Koh's backyard but Smith's. The camera was motion activated. It had never caught anything more threatening than a coyote loping across Koh's grass. Then it caught the shooting of Obrad Mirkovic.

Koh came through the heavy wooden doors of the courtroom, neat and tired in his gray suit. He passed through the gate to the witness stand and was sworn. He waited, face pinched.

Rory felt for him. Going up against two police officers had taken a toll. Attitudes about cops and authority were sharp undercurrents in the case. In voir dire, the most unsettling questions hadn't been about death, but power.

Do you have relatives in law enforcement, Ms. Mackenzie?

No, she'd said. Thinking: *Almost, once. But not anymore.*

Could you send a police officer to prison for the rest of his life?

Yes.

They believed her. They didn't even strike her for being a lawyer.

She figured she'd been chosen for the jury because she had only cursory knowledge of the case. When Brad Mirkovic died she was six thousand miles away, trying to erase Ransom River from her memory.

Now she was about to see the evidence. Maybe even the truth. If she glimpsed it, then no matter what the cops thought, or the victim's father, or the media, or the other jurors, she had to call it. She wondered if that made her the court jester.

At the prosecution table Cary Oberlin held up a DVD. He said in his mild, leaden voice, "Mr. Koh, can you identify this disc?"

Koh leaned toward the microphone. "It's mine. It contains a recording from the CCTV camera outside my house."

Koh's pained eyes said what his testimony probably would not: He wished he had never looked at the video. He wished he had never installed a camera on his back porch. Then he would feel safe. Then nobody would have threatened his life anonymously over the phone, or set his car on fire while he was in the supermarket.

He would not have seen Brad Mirkovic die.

Berrigan nudged the Blazer past the court-house at a steady twenty-five miles per hour. The sun glared off the hood. Church eyed the scene as they passed.

"Nice and easy," he said.

The courthouse took up the entire block, with a back exit one street over. That door was a fire exit: It would be locked from the outside but not barred. It could be opened from the inside. And when they needed that door, they'd be inside heading out. At speed.

Berrigan gripped the wheel like it was the only thing keeping him from blowing out an airlock into space. Though Berrigan was wearing gloves, Church bet the man's knuckles were as white as gristle.

Berrigan signaled and turned to head around the block. He was sweating. That worried Church.

Church himself had showered and scrubbed his skin hard and shaved and trimmed his nails and run a clipper over his head so his hair was a quarter inch long. He didn't want DNA left behind. As long as he didn't bleed, he was okay.

He was wearing new clothes bought from Walmart, the store's own brand. He had

31

another set of clothes in a duffel bag, for later, when he was done with this thing and could shed his shirt and pants and burn them, along with the Blazer itself.

But Berrigan was sweating. He licked his lips and touched his shirt pocket. Inside it a squarish shape was outlined.

"You brought smokes?" Church said.

Berrigan quickly put his hand back on the wheel. "I'm not gonna smoke until —"

Church reached across the Blazer and dug the cigarette pack from Berrigan's pocket. A mostly used-up pack of Winstons.

"Jesus, you been pushing cigarettes out of this thing, straight into your mouth? You probably left spit all over it." He shook his head. "Pull over."

"It's for good luck," Berrigan said. "My thing, I always keep a pack in my pocket, for luck."

"And how's that worked out for you so far?"

That shut him up.

Berrigan eased the Blazer to the curb behind the courthouse, directly outside the back exit. Church got out, opened the back door, and reached inside for his toolbox.

"If we want to get out of here alive, we need more than luck," he said. *Idiot.*

He grabbed the toolbox and headed along

the sidewalk. He passed a trash can, crumpled the cigarette pack, and threw it inside.

Berrigan caught up. Side by side, they walked toward the front entrance of the courthouse. The sun was shining. Traffic was light. Church stared straight ahead and felt the morning sharpen to a point.

Samuel Koh hunched toward the microphone. "When I watched the video, I realized what it had recorded. I copied it onto the disc and took it to the police."

Cary Oberlin entered Koh's DVD into evidence. Then he prepared to play it for the court. The room grew hushed. Rory held her pen suspended above her notebook. The sun streamed through the windows behind her.

In the front row of the public gallery, Grigor Mirkovic stood up. Face blank, he turned and marched down the center aisle. His entourage seemed caught flat-footed by the unexpected move. They scrambled to their feet and followed him.

Helen Ellis watched them go. "Goodness."

Frankie Ortega's hoodie was drooping over his forehead like a monk's cowl. He pushed it back. "Whoa."

Mirkovic threw open the doors and swept

into the hallway and out of sight. The minions disappeared after him. The static electricity, the building unease in the courtroom, snapped, relieved as if by the crack of lightning.

Rory realized she was holding her breath. She exhaled. She couldn't blame Mirkovic. Who could stand to watch footage of his own child being shot to death, in grainy, slow-motion detail?

The heavy wooden doors creaked shut. Against the murmurs of the crowd, Judge Wieland banged his gavel.

"Order," he said.

The crowd quieted. Wieland nodded at the prosecutor. "Proceed."

Oberlin pressed Play.

Church and Berrigan strolled toward the front entrance of the courthouse. Jackets zipped, shades and caps on, steady, relaxed. Two workmen coming to perform repairs. From forty yards away, Church could see everything perfectly.

This was the Criminal Division. In earlier times, a couple of decades back, a man could walk straight into a courthouse without being stopped or searched or monitored. Access to the justice system for all. Now, with street gangs and paramilitary policing and a state security apparatus that pulled in millions by bleating *Homeland Security* and whispering *terrorism,* criminal courthouses put up barriers. Especially courthouses where douche-ass cops were on trial for murder.

Church licked his lips and tried to swallow. His throat locked. Beside him, Berrigan kept pace. The man seemed to have a hitch in his step.

"Easy," Church said.

Outside the courthouse was a sign: WEAPONS CHECKPOINT. Little pictures of every sharp object and firearm you had to leave behind. Inside the doors, milling aimlessly in the empty foyer, were two security screeners. County employees but not sworn deputies, guys in their sixties wearing blue blazers and gray slacks and cheap ties. They were loitering between the X-ray machine and the metal detector. Plexiglas partitions on either side of them, so people coming in had to funnel through the middle of the building.

Church and Berrigan had two ways into the courthouse. One: a door on the left side of the building's glass front. It was locked, with NO ENTRY signs on it. Exit only. Everybody leaving the courthouse came through that door. It was outside the foyer's

Plexiglas security box. Church could wait for a lawyer to breeze through it, some guy distracted by a phone call, maybe headed to the mall for coffee. Grab the door before it shut. Then he could sweep inside and completely bypass security. That would give him a head start on Homer Simpson and Ned Flanders at the weapons checkpoint. By the time they saw him, he'd be past them. But to do that he needed luck. Needed an unobservant lawyer coming this way. And there was none.

Then a group of men slammed through the door into the daylight. Men in suits, surrounding a smaller, strutting man in a suit. Church nearly tripped. He recognized the guy. Grigor Mirkovic.

Mirkovic, right there. Small and nasty and powerful and vivid.

And with his goons holding the door open. Church sped up.

Berrigan grabbed his arm. "Christ, don't run."

Church checked himself. Yeah. Don't draw undo attention. He forced himself to walk casually.

Mirkovic and his posse swarmed down the sidewalk to a waiting SUV. And the side door shut behind them.

Dammit.

That left the second way into the building: directly at the security screeners. Right through them.

Church said, "Code names only."

Berrigan nodded.

Would Berrigan bolt? Church assessed the man's walk, the tremor in his hand, the pale look on his face. The guy was shit scared. But no — he wouldn't run out on this. Not in this lifetime.

Church's balaclava was in the inside pocket of his jacket but would have to wait. "I'm going in straight ahead," he said. "Peel off. Go round to the back door. I'll let you in."

Berrigan kept walking, toolkit in hand. Church turned and ambled through the front entrance. He set his toolbox on the X-ray conveyor belt and strolled to the metal detector.

The video began to play. In grainy, gray-blue light, it showed Samuel Koh's backyard and fence and, beyond that, Jared Smith's house. A clock was running at the bottom of the screen, reeling off the seconds: *2:03:02 a.m.*

At Smith's house, Brad Mirkovic burst through the kitchen door, off balance, arms wheeling. He looked back.

Lucy Elmendorf, clad in a T-shirt and panties, came at him through the door. There was no sound, but her mouth was moving. It looked to Rory like she was saying *Stop.* He didn't.

Jared Smith was right behind her, in his boxers, with his service weapon.

Outside the courtroom, noise rose abruptly, echoing.

Rory glanced up. For a moment she wondered if her parents were outside. They'd said they might stop by.

The doors of the courtroom swung open. But it wasn't her dad who came through.

Two men stormed in. They wore balaclavas. They wore green fatigue jackets and leather gloves and pants tucked into their heavy black work boots.

They had shotguns in their hands.

4

Rory froze.

One man slammed the door shut. The other dropped a toolbox to the floor and shouted, "Everybody down."

The bailiff turned in seeming shock. His hand jerked toward the gun holstered on his hip.

The gunman leveled the barrel of the shotgun and advanced at him. "Drop your weapon. Drop it *now.* Get on the floor."

The bailiff held poised, hand near the holster.

The gunman charged him. And with one jarring motion he created the scariest sound known to modern America. He pumped the shotgun.

Rory felt it like a shock behind her eyes. People screamed. In the jury box, Helen Ellis jumped. Frankie Ortega sprang upright, eyes wide like a rabbit's.

The gunman descended on the bailiff,

voice booming. "Throw your weapon on the floor. *Now.*"

The bailiff tossed the gun to the floor, raised his hands, and dropped to his knees.

Rory's heart thundered. In the public gallery people stood and pushed toward the aisles, clambering over others who sat stunned.

At the back of the courtroom, the second gunman swept the barrel of his shotgun across the room. "Sit down. Right now, and shut up."

He was slight and twitchy. The gun barrel panned the room and stopped at a man on his feet in the aisle. The guy shrank back. People sat down.

"Hands in the air. Everybody. Do not touch your phones."

Twitchy dropped his own toolbox to the floor with a clatter. From inside it he produced a Club steering-wheel lock. He jammed it through the handles of the courtroom doors, extended it, and locked it.

The first gunman stood over the bailiff. "Hands behind your head."

The gunman was built like a stove and had a voice so raspy it sounded charred. The bailiff laced his fingers behind him. The gunman picked up the man's gun and took

40

his Taser. He bound him with his own handcuffs and ripped the police radio from his shoulder. Then he turned to the judge.

"Off the bench. Get down here."

Somebody was sobbing. Helen Ellis said, "Oh Lord God, oh Jesus." Frankie began to wheeze. Rory's vision pulsed. Bright, thumping, neon, unreal. Un-*what-the-hell*-real. The blood roared in her ears.

It said, *Get out.*

Somehow. Now. Get out of the courtroom. The window behind her — they were on the third floor but if she could open the window they could escape to safety along the ledge outside. She looked over her shoulder.

"Hold the fuck still."

She turned. The first gunman stood in front of the jury box. She held still. So did the barrel of his shotgun, aimed at her face.

For an endless moment the gunman faced her, as though daring her to move. Behind the black balaclava, his eyes were flat.

The shotgun could be loaded with buckshot or with slugs. It made no difference. He was ten feet away. For a crooked second, she pictured the courtroom being swept by forensics techs, and another murder trial — for the people clustered around her like eggs

41

in a carton. *Exhibit A,* a diorama with red strings pinned to it, fanning out from the point of origin and ending in seats and windows and the wall. *Shots fired.* She fought the urge to vomit.

Then he raised the barrel, stepped back, and called over his shoulder. "Reagan. Clean 'em out."

The twitchy second gunman stepped forward. "Everybody empty your pockets." He pulled a plastic supermarket bag from inside his jacket. "Give me your phones. Do it now."

Frankie's wheezing intensified. His eyes were wide and he looked twelve years old.

"Phones, right now. Hand them over." Reagan stalked along the courtroom aisle holding open the plastic bag, like it was cell phone trick or treat. "Do not try to be a hero. Do not try to call for help. If you do, you'll die."

People passed their phones to the aisle or simply threw them to the floor near him. A woman broke into loud sobs. One young man stood shaking.

"I'm a reporter. I'm not a part of this," he said.

"You're what?" Behind his balaclava, Reagan seemed to snort. He turned to his confederate. "Nixon. Listen to this clown."

Nixon. Reagan. They'd gone with off-the-shelf code names, Rory thought. Tricky Dick turned and lowered the shotgun at the young reporter's chest.

"Did you say you're not apart? I can make that happen."

His index finger hovered near the trigger. The reporter cringed.

Nixon turned back to the crowd. "Purses, backpacks, satchels, toss all your possessions to the center aisle."

Hesitantly, most people looked at him.

"Immediately."

Rory jumped again. So did half the room. Helen Ellis emitted a choked cry.

Frankie's shoulders lifted. He was struggling to inhale. He fumbled manically in his sweatshirt pocket.

Rory grabbed his forearm. "Careful."

He looked near panic. "Can't breathe."

Rory held his arm. "It could look like you're pulling a weapon."

He nodded tightly and brought out an inhaler. Helen Ellis kept repeating, "Oh God God Jesus, help us."

In front of the bench, Judge Wieland stood with his hands raised. "You have no right to do this."

His voice had a quaver but came out strong. Nixon and Reagan ignored him.

"This is a court of law, and these are the people of the State of California. Let them go," Wieland said.

Rory's throat tightened. Wieland hadn't lost his composure. He was acting like the captain of a ship, trying to hang on to the tiller and get people to the life rafts as water poured over the decks.

She recalled the Marin County Courthouse attack in the seventies. Black-and-white photos: the judge with a sawed-off shotgun duct-taped to his neck. He was taken hostage by radicals seeking to break the Soledad Brothers out of prison. It was a spasm of "revolutionary" violence, terrifying and pointless. The judge had been shot dead.

"Shut your mouth," Nixon said. "Keep it shut."

What did these men want?

Nixon nodded at the jury box, at Frankie. "Throw that thing here. Hands in the air."

Frankie shook his head and gripped the inhaler. "I can't . . ."

Nixon lunged forward. People screamed and climbed over each other, fighting to get out of the aim of the shotgun. Frankie shrank back and raised his hands but held on to the inhaler.

Rory shouted at Nixon, "No."

44

She pulled Frankie against her. Yanked him almost onto her lap, gripping his sweatshirt, and tried to get both of them onto the floor.

"Shut up and hold still, everybody." Nixon held poised right in front of the jury box. His chest rose and fell. His gloved hands gripped the gleaming barrel of the gun.

Frankie shuddered. Rory held him. He was hot, he was barely breathing, he was all she had, human connection, maybe the last seconds of a life she thought would be completely different.

"Out of the jury box, all of you," Nixon said.

Motion, clatter. Sunlight poured through the window onto the backs of people streaming out of the jury box.

Digging her fingers into Frankie's sweatshirt, Rory stood up. Nixon was staring at her.

She said, "He has an inhaler." Her voice cracked. "Asthma. He needs it."

The gunman seemed to think about it. Finally, he nodded and indicated the inhaler with the barrel of the gun. "One shot."

Jesus, why'd he have to use that expression?

Frankie's eyes shone with fear. He looked about to rabbit, to bolt, suicidally, right through the window. He needed air.

Rory nodded and released Frankie's arm. His hand flew to his mouth. Gulping, he pumped the inhaler.

Nixon said, "Toss it here."

Shaking, Frankie stole a second pump. Then he tossed the inhaler to the gunman. Nixon caught it and put it in his pocket. Rory could swear that behind the balaclava he was smirking. Bastard.

She edged down the steps. Her leg ached, the one with the pins in it. She joined the rest of the jurors in front of the bench. Helen Ellis was swaying. Frankie's wheezing eased.

At the defense table, Jared Smith and Lucy Elmendorf were bent forward, foreheads on the table, hands locked behind their heads. The gunmen must have instructed them to do it, though Rory hadn't heard it. The tabletop had been swept clean. No pens or pencils or anything that could be used to stab the gunmen.

Nixon looked around. "Everybody listen. You will do exactly as we say. You will not hesitate. You will not hold back. You will not scream or cry out for help, and if anybody has held on to a cell phone" — he reached into his pocket and pulled out a small electronic device — "we will find it, and we

46

will punish you."

Nixon raised the device like a police officer waving his badge. Reagan held his gun at port arms, aimed at the ceiling.

"Well?" Nixon said.

"Here."

A man scrabbled in his pants pocket, pulled out a phone, and tossed it on the floor like it had bitten him.

"Anybody else?" Nixon said.

Nobody spoke up. He pushed a button on the device and walked up the aisle.

"Okay." Crying, a woman pulled a phone from her bra.

He grabbed it. "You do what we say, and you'll survive. Play Rambo, you won't."

He stalked to the defense table and climbed on top of it. "Everybody on the floor. Facedown, hands behind your heads."

People began dropping to their knees. But one of the defense attorneys, a ravenish man named Pritchett, edged back from the table, hands in the air. "Tell us what's going on. What do you want here?"

Nixon turned his head, slowly, and lodged a stare at Pritchett. Without a word he swung the butt of his shotgun and cracked Pritchett in the face. People gasped. Pritchett staggered back, legs like bamboo. He crashed into his chair and toppled, hand to his bloody forehead.

Nixon swung the shotgun back up, finger on the trigger. "Any other questions?"

The lobby of the courthouse was empty. Two lawyers strolled in and stopped chatting. The weapons checkpoint was unmanned.

"Hello?" one said.

A moment later, she heard banging sounds. The noise came from beyond the checkpoint, around a corner. It was repetitive and heavy. Like shoes kicking wood.

The lawyers glanced at each other and, with a shrug, went through the metal detector. It rang but nobody came running. They rounded the corner. The banging grew louder. Down the hall, a closet door shook with each thud. The lawyers glanced around. The administrative offices for the courthouse were in the opposite direction at the far end of the hall, behind closed doors.

"Hey, anybody here?" she said.

The kicking got louder and was accompanied by muffled shouts. The lawyers jogged down the hall to the closet.

It was locked, the key broken off in the door.

"Anybody in there?" the lawyer called.

The kicking resumed, and more desperate

shouting. The lawyer pulled out her phone. Her colleague dropped his briefcase and ran down the hall toward the administrative offices.

The lawyer called 9-1-1.

5

One by one people dropped to the court-room floor. Frankie Ortega lay down, breathing like a wheezy metronome. Rory held still. A voice within her said, *Stand up. Don't get on your knees.* Around her, shuffling, crying, people prostrated themselves. *Don't let them shoot you in the back.*

Pritchett, the defense attorney, lay collapsed by his chair, his face creased red with blood. Atop the defense table, Nixon swept his gun barrel slowly across the courtroom. He looked like a tank turning its gun turret. A wire of anger and fear heated in Rory's chest. Nixon's gun veered toward her. *We've lost.*

She dropped to her knees and stretched out on the floor, facedown.

She laced her fingers behind her head and rested her cheek against cold stone. Two feet away, the court reporter stared at her. The woman's eyes were wet. In a staccato whisper she began reciting the Hail Mary.

"Faces *down*," Nixon said. "Stare at the floor."

People placed their foreheads against the stone. Rory heard heavy breathing, whimpers, the percussion of a woman's charm bracelet shivering against the tile. She heard a small airplane buzz overhead, and traffic on the street. In the hall: nothing.

Didn't anybody know what was happening?

From the table, Nixon said, "Stay exactly as you are. Do not roll over. Do not raise your heads."

Across the well of the court, the defense attorney breathed in broken, wet gasps. The court reporter murmured, "Holy Mary, mother of God, pray for us sinners . . ."

Behind the woman's prayer, Rory heard another voice.

"One. Two. Three."

It was Reagan. His footsteps scuffed across the floor.

"Four." He paused. "Stand up."

A cry. "No. Please, don't . . ."

"Stand up."

Nixon's voice boomed out. "If you are tapped on the back, stand up."

"No, please . . . *no.*"

Nixon jumped down from the table. His

boots hit the floor. "He touched you with the barrel of his weapon. He didn't shoot you. But if you lie there mewling, you're going to get hurt. Now *stand up.*"

Rory heard a man clamber to his feet.

The court reporter opened her eyes, desperate. "Now and at the hour of our death, amen. Hail Mary, full of grace . . ."

Nixon's voice again, slow, metallic. "One. Two. Three. Four."

A choked cry.

"Stand up," Nixon said.

Shoes scraped the floor.

Reagan's footsteps moved again, inching across the courtroom. "One. Two. Three. Four."

Nixon: "Stand up."

Fabric rustled.

"Pray for us sinners . . ."

"One. Two. Three. Four."

The barrel of the shotgun tapped Rory between the shoulder blades.

Her breathing faltered. Behind her closed eyes, the view burst with yellow stars.

"Stand up," Nixon said.

She pushed to her knees. The court reporter watched, her expression brimming with relief and pity. Rory climbed to her feet.

Reagan stood in front of her. His eyes

52

were hazel. His skin, the bare ring of it visible beneath his balaclava, looked pasty.

Amid the crowd massed on the floor, three other people stood with their hands raised. A man in his sixties in a red-checkered shirt. Prosecutor Cary Oberlin. And Judge Wieland.

Nixon nodded at the door to Wieland's chambers. "You four. Walk."

Stepping cautiously over people on the floor, they picked their way toward the door. Rory went last in line, hands raised. Nixon trailed her. Reagan stood to one side and urged the four past him, like a gun bull guarding a chain gang.

Where were they going? Were the four of them being released? If so, would they be given a message to take to the world outside?

She didn't think they were being released.

She walked. Ahead, the older man in the red check took care to avoid juror Daisy Fallon, who lay crying in his path.

Nixon said, "Speed it up."

Oberlin got about ten feet from the door to chambers. Reagan wiped his nose with a gloved hand. Judge Wieland drew even with him.

Rory saw a blur of blue to the left, off her shoulder. A swift movement, somebody sitting up. Then fumbling, a grunt. She turned.

A man from the public gallery was sitting upright, unzipping his Dodgers jacket. His eyes were spiked with panic. He yanked the jacket open and reached inside.

Things went clear and smeared all at once. Beneath the jacket, the man wore a searing yellow *Justice!* T-shirt. He was breathing hard enough to blow out candles on a cake. He drew a handgun.

He raised the gun and aimed at Reagan. And fired.

Orange flame flashed from the barrel. The report cracked through the courtroom. Screams erupted. The pistol rose in his hand with recoil.

Reagan spun and raised the shotgun. The man in the *Justice!* shirt leveled his handgun. He fired.

Reagan fired.

At such close range, it sounded like the world coming apart. The roar of the blast reverberated through Rory's chest. A dark form dropped to the floor. The man in the *Justice!* T-shirt pitched backward onto a young woman. His gun clattered to the tiles.

Nixon ran across the room, stepping on people. He bellowed, "Do not touch the weapon."

No chance of that. People shrieked and

crawled away from the *Justice!* man, mouths wide, hair falling in their faces. The man was dead. His eyes stared at the ceiling and his yellow shirt glistened red with blood. Rory stumbled back.

How did he get a gun into court? How did any of them?

Nixon grabbed the handgun from the floor. "Everybody shut up and hold still."

People cowered, sobbing. The air swirled with cordite. Nixon turned in a slow circle and took stock.

Judge Wieland was down.

The *Justice!* man had fired at Reagan but missed and caught the judge in the shoulder. The man in red check knelt near Wieland. He tentatively put a hand on the judge's shoulder. Rory dropped to a crouch and inched forward to his side.

Wieland gazed up at her with surprise in his eyes. Rory felt the world seem to tilt and slide away. He was bleeding profusely. Without immediate medical care, he wouldn't stay alive for long.

The man in red check said, "What do we do?"

Rory turned, lips parting. Nixon loomed above her.

He grabbed her by a handful of sweater, fingers twisting into the fabric and into her hair. She cried out.

"Up."

He dragged her away from the judge. She struggled for balance, knees sliding along the stone floor.

"On your feet," Nixon said.

"Let me —"

"Up."

He lifted her by the scruff of her sweater. She flailed to her feet. He pointed at the man in the red shirt. "Move it, pops."

The man looked up with shock and complete loss. "But . . ."

Nixon swung the barrel of the gun toward him. The man threw his hands in front of his face.

Nixon pointed at Cary Oberlin. "You too. Come on. Now."

Then he shook his head at the dead wannabe hero in the *Justice!* shirt. He turned sharply toward Reagan. "Fucking idiot —"

Outside the main doors, noise. Voices in the hallway, footsteps, the squawk of a radio. The door handles rattled.

Reagan and Nixon turned toward the doors.

A man in the hall called, "Open up."

More rattling sounds. "Sheriff's Department. Open the doors."

Beyond the windows, the first of the sirens floated on the morning air.

6

Nixon snapped his fingers at Reagan. "Get 'em out. Hurry."

Reagan waved Rory and Oberlin and Red Check toward the door to chambers. "Go."

Judge Wieland lay breathing shallowly, his face white. Blood soaked his robe, dark and sparkling against the black fabric. He caught Rory's eye. She found her feet unable to move.

She turned to Reagan. "We've got to get him help. You —"

He shoved her toward the door to chambers.

Nixon lumbered ahead, opened the door, and ducked into the hall. A second later he returned, eyes narrow, and shut the door behind him.

"They're outside."

Reagan said, "No. God, what . . ."

"Shut up."

Sirens strengthened. The main doors

rumbled again, rattling the Club steering-wheel lock. Something heavy — a shoulder or foot — hit the door.

From outside, a man shouted: "Open up. What's going on in there?"

A moment later, the phone at the court clerk's desk rang. And, more distantly, another phone, in Judge Wieland's chambers. Then a cell phone stuffed inside Reagan's plastic supermarket bag.

Nixon grabbed a chair from the defendants' table, dragged it to the chambers door, and jammed it under the doorknob.

Reagan twitched. "No. We gotta get out of here."

Nixon said, "I know."

The chambers doorknob rattled and turned. But with the chair jammed against it, the door wouldn't budge.

On the far side a man said, "Wedged shut. Get a crowbar."

Outside the main doors, harsher: "This is the Sheriff's Department. Open the doors or we'll break them down."

The sirens grew loud outside. Rory heard them as the sound of deliverance.

Reagan grabbed Nixon's arm. "We need to move. Come *on,* man."

Nixon held up a hand. Then he raised the shotgun toward the ceiling and fired.

People screamed. Plaster exploded and pebbled down.

Nixon tightened his grip on the shotgun and stalked down the aisle to the main doors. He planted his feet wide.

"Touch the doors again and people will get shot," he called.

Plaster dust drifted around Rory's head. The banging and rattling of the chambers doorknob stopped. In the courtroom, the air seemed freighted.

From the hallway, more distant now: "Is anybody injured in there?"

Nixon looked at the dead *Justice!* vigilante. He didn't even glance at Judge Wieland. "One down. His own fault. If you want to keep casualties to that number, you stay away from the doors."

From beyond the windows came the heavy blat of rotor blades. A helicopter was approaching. Rory had an unobstructed view of the street, the parking garage, and the mall. Two Ransom River PD cars raced up, lights popping.

Jerkily, Reagan ran to the window. "They're swarming us. What . . ."

Nixon turned. "Get away from there."

Reagan's shoulders spasmed up. "We need a lookout, we need a way out . . ." He pressed a hand against the window and peered at the frame. There were no shades, no curtains, and, on that side of the building, no ledge outside.

"Get away from the window," Nixon said.

Reagan turned his head, hand still pressed to the glass. Though his face was obscured, Rory swore he seemed confused.

This was not good.

More police cars pulled up outside. Officers jumped out and ran into the building.

Nixon yanked Reagan back from the window. "They see you, they shoot you."

"We can't stay here," Reagan said. "Oh, man."

Nixon stalked back to the center of the room. He pointed to Rory. "Against the window."

He snapped his fingers at Red Check. Or tried to. The sound was muffled by his glove. "You too."

Heart drumming, Rory walked to the west-facing window that overlooked the front entrance to the courthouse, the street, the mall, and the parking garage.

"The judge needs help, bad," she said. "Let him go. Somebody can carry him out and —"

Nixon shoved her. "Forehead to the glass. Hands flat against the window, level with your face. And shut up."

She pressed her palms to the window and leaned her forehead against the glass.

Outside, through the glare of her own reflection, the morning gleamed. Five police cars had pulled up outside. With their lights spinning, it looked like a carnival ride, lurid and out of kilter.

From the corner of her eye she saw Nixon shove Red Check against the window to her left. Reagan pushed Cary Oberlin against the window to her right. She heard a sharp cry as Nixon grabbed another person from the floor.

"Stand there. Forehead to the glass. Don't move," Nixon said.

Rory breathed. In the glass, her see-through reflection did the same. She saw, in the V-neck of her sweater, the turquoise stone in her silver necklace. She saw herself swallow.

Nixon and Reagan rounded up enough people to block all — what were there, nine? — windows in the courtroom.

On the floor behind her, the volume diminished to a vicious hum. The air seemed charged, but the pitch of fear had changed. Whatever this was, whatever it had started out to be, it was now a siege.

The sirens continued to come. She waited. Somebody would be appointed spokesman.

If they were wise. Were they? Were they competent? The cop she had known best on the Ransom River police force certainly had been.

Police cars kept arriving, black-and-whites. They turned sideways at either end of the block, barricading the road. Officers jumped out and stopped traffic. Outside the River Mall, pedestrians paused on the sidewalk and stared and pointed.

Moms with strollers. Elderly mall walkers in their mom jeans and sun visors. A cop jogged toward them, radio to his face, and brusquely waved them back.

Her gaze clocked each of the people on the sidewalk. She was hoping not to see her parents. *Please, don't let them be here for this.*

And yet she felt a catch in her throat and a low, sad longing. She wished her mom could pull her around a corner, laughing her melancholy laugh, saying, *Don't be silly. Get your keester out of there, kid.* Her mom, calm and practical and no-nonsense after thirty years of teaching at Ransom River High School. Samantha, who hugged hard, as though the earth's gravity had evaporated and she had to anchor Rory.

Her eyes stung. In her mind her dad appeared, stern and warm, his hair too gray, his arms tanned and strong from a life spent working outdoors. He seemed to shake his head and say, *Let her go, Sam. World's a big place and she needs to get started if she's going to see it.*

Her eyes welled. She wanted to wipe them but didn't dare move her hands from the glass. She blinked and tears fell to her cheeks.

Get out. That's what her dad had always told her about Ransom River. Half the folks who lived there might think it was paradise, but for her it had become a landscape of strip malls and stagnation, bullies and heartbreak.

And when she said, *How come you and Mom don't leave?* he'd say, *We're old. It's different.* Then he'd grin, a sideways smile, a smile that wanted to be careless but always had something behind it. And when she called him on it, he'd quote Satchel Paige: *Don't look back. Something might be gaining on you.*

She had tried. She thought running, training, being strong, getting an education, keeping her eyes wide open, and always having one foot on the gas, one thumb out to hitchhike out of this town, would take care of her.

She'd gotten nowhere. Something had

been gaining on her all along. And here it was.

She gritted her teeth and fought the need to let her shoulders jerk. *Don't give them anything.* Pull down the shades. Don't let them see a crack they can exploit. She squeezed her eyes shut to stop any further tears.

Outside, a news crew packed up their van. Everybody jumped in and they floored it — straight across the street into the mall's parking garage. The van's back doors were open. The cameraman sat in the rear, filming.

The police perimeter took shape. The phalanx of patrol cars retreated from the curb directly outside to a safer distance. Uniforms and plainclothes officers now stood behind their vehicles. A policewoman jogged toward the shoppers outside the mall, one hand on her utility belt to keep it from bouncing. She urged them back.

The officers outside looked sharp in the morning sun, moving with dispatch, their uniforms dark blue against the green grass. So close, tangible, separated from her by millimeters of glass and a hundred feet of air, right there.

That's not who she saw. Not who she could almost feel, who was whispering in her memory.

The tears welled again. *Hell.*

Behind her, barely visible, a ghostly reflection from the glass, Nixon grabbed Reagan's sleeve. He leaned close and shook it, as if to get Reagan's full attention.

She leaned against the window, exposed, surrounded, motionless, and her mind filled with a knife-edge of a voice. *Don't go quietly.*

Of all the people surrounding her, the one she longed overwhelmingly to see was a man who might not even know she was alive. She forced herself to stare at the officers below. Her necklace, the turquoise stone, shone back at her. Seth had given it to her. Of all the things she had lost, all she had jettisoned when she went away, that was one thing she'd kept. Given to her on a hot night when things were good, when the world had opened up and shown her she could breathe, that there was a rapture to being alive. And all it took to light the sky was one person.

Just one, Seth Colder, the joker, the wild card, the school friend who grew up to show her what was what, that love felt as brilliant and sharp as the blue knife of an acetylene torch. But that was long gone. Burned out, swept away.

She resisted the desire to touch the necklace. What was this surge of sadness and longing? She was on the verge of losing it. Thinking of *Seth,* for Christ's sake? Cut *that* out, Rory.

Except that as she stared out the window, listening to the gunmen mutter and argue behind her, she couldn't stop thinking: *Seth would know what to do. Seth would know how to end this thing.* Seth had been a cop.

A bullhorn voice emanated from the hallway. "This is the Ransom River Police Department. Put down your weapon. Open the doors and come out with your hands behind your head."

They thought there was only one gunman inside.

7

In the hallway, Lieutenant Gil Strandberg lowered the bullhorn. Since the shotgun blast, nothing more had been heard from Judge Wieland's courtroom. Nobody had answered his order to surrender.

The Ransom River PD and two bailiffs had set up a perimeter at the end of the hallway twenty yards from the courtroom door, out of the line of fire. In the parking garage across the street, snipers were maneuvering into position. Their rifles had scopes that would provide a direct view into the courtroom. Other officers were reconnoitering the courthouse roof. They would place microphones and try to listen in. He had ten channels of chatter on the radio, people running around outside, officers trying to clear civilians from the street. He had two security guards who didn't know what the hell had happened, except that they had apparently let a man armed with a goddamned shotgun into a murder trial.

A uniform jogged up, radio whining. "County Clerk's office is getting the courthouse blueprints. Should have them in ten minutes."

That was barely a start on what Strandberg needed. "Find out the strength of the glass in the windows. In case we have to go in that way."

SWAT was headed in this direction, and a hostage negotiator.

Neither of those specialties had been employed in Ransom River in the last year. Strandberg didn't know whether that meant they were rusty, eager, or both. He didn't know anything except that this morning had turned from dull to deadly.

"What about the door into the court from the judge's chambers?" he said.

"Wedged shut. We might be able to force it."

"Wedged with what?"

"I don't know."

Strandberg shook his head. "Nobody touches that door until we have more information about what's happening inside."

"What does the guy inside want?" the uniform said.

"Hell if I know."

Strandberg wondered how much time they had.

At Leticia's Taqueria on Wilshire Boulevard, the TV mounted above the counter played a news channel nonstop. Night, morning, noon, it showed violence and corruption, hurricanes and drunken senators and naked celebrities. When the jerky images and breathless audio first interrupted normal coverage, nobody bothered to look up. This was Los Angeles. Los Angeles TV news would interrupt coverage of the Second Coming for footage of supermodels fighting in an alley.

The reporter's voice cut through the restaurant's background noise. "The police won't tell us what's happening inside the Ransom River Superior Courthouse, but we have reports that shots have been fired."

Seth Colder stopped eating. He turned to the screen.

The news crew was huddled inside the parking garage across the street from the courthouse. The reporter slid in and out of view, a youngster who couldn't get the frightened excitement out of her voice.

Seth thought, *Enjoy the rush, sweetie. It sours quickly.*

"All we know is that an incident is in

progress in the Criminal Division, where Ransom River police officers Jared Smith and Lucy Elmendorf are on trial for the murder of teenage burglar Obrad Mirkovic."

Seth wiped his hands on a napkin. He forgot his coffee.

He hadn't been through the doors of that courthouse in two years, but nothing about it had changed. And what he saw, from the shoulder-mounted news camera inside the parking garage, brought him to a standstill.

The Ransom River PD was there in force. Patrol units and unmarked cars with antennas on the back, officers positioned behind them. They'd barricaded both ends of the block.

The reporter said, sotto voce, "There. The courtroom windows."

The camera zoomed in. Seth forgot that he was in L.A., that he was mountains and valleys and a lifetime away from Ransom River.

Hostages stood pressed against the windows of a third-floor courtroom. Men and women were crowded against the glass, hands up. They blocked any view of the courtroom interior.

He knew that police snipers would be moving into place. In that garage, certainly.

71

The news crew would get yanked any second. If the cops were smart.

If, that is, the cops realized where the news team was broadcasting from. And if they weren't too busy to shut off the feed. And if some idiot commander didn't decide the news team's footage provided the PD with a useful vantage point. The authorities needed to shut that news crew down. Letting it broadcast live was dangerous.

Because Seth knew he was looking at Judge Wieland's courtroom. And like all busy Superior Court judges with full dockets, Wieland was adept at juggling. He would lend his ears to the case being tried in front of him while he signed motions with one hand and checked his e-mail with the other. He had a big screen on his desk, and it was wired for speed.

Anybody in that courtroom could watch the same TV broadcast Seth was looking at. If they did, they could stay one step ahead of the cops.

Rory swallowed hard. *Hold it together.* Behind her in the courtroom, crying continued. At Judge Wieland's desk, the phone rang and rang. But she couldn't hear Wieland, didn't know if he was still breathing, whether anybody was able to offer a human touch as he lay struggling. Reagan and Nixon paced nearby, arguing in jittery undertones. Rory slowly, slowly turned her head so she could see them.

"We got to do it, and now," Reagan said.

"No."

Nixon took a phone from his pocket. At first Rory thought he was checking the time, but he scrolled through a couple of buttons, as if he was looking for messages. With apparent frustration he put it away.

". . . just go, the two of us," Reagan whispered. "We could . . ."

Outside the window a helicopter lowered briefly into view. Engine noise droned through the room.

Nixon tightened his grip on Reagan's arm. ". . . losing proposition. We leave by ourselves, we die. No. The plan is the plan."

"Then what are we going to do? There's . . ."

From the hallway a new voice blared through the bullhorn.

"This is Sergeant Ray Nguyen of the Ransom River Crisis Negotiation Response Team."

Hostage negotiator. Rory held her breath. Reagan flinched.

And glanced at the doors. He muttered, "If we surrender —"

"No." Nixon shook him by the arm. "Do you not fucking understand the consequences? If we — Jesus Christ, surrender? Not just the payment we'd . . ."

"I'm here to listen to you and to try to make sure everybody stays safe. So can you tell me please, who am I speaking to?"

Reagan pulled his arm free. "I understand, you dick. If we don't draw him out, we —"

"Shut up," Nixon said. "We stick to the plan or we lose."

Reagan barked a hard nonlaugh. "Plan? It's already blown. Now what?"

Nixon turned and crossed the courtroom. Rory couldn't tell if he had a destination or simply wanted to get away from Reagan. And Reagan's fear and Reagan's questions.

Outside in the late morning sun, police officers were positioned behind their vehicles. The news van had sidestepped the order to evacuate and taken up a position inside the parking garage. Down the street in the distance, an enormous vehicle rolled toward them. Some gigantic RV, painted in the white and blue colors of the Ransom River Police Department. It was a mobile command center. Maybe SWAT. Maybe a food truck with margaritas for the mall visitors. Jesus, would SWAT storm the courtroom? If they did, would they even know how many opponents they faced?

Nixon's voice came louder than she expected. "Hey, police."

Rory turned her head another couple of inches. Nixon stood back from the main doors about ten feet. Reagan hustled to his side.

"What's —"

Nixon lifted a hand to silence him. He raised his voice. "Hey, cops."

The bullhorn answered. "This is Sergeant Nguyen. Who am I speaking to?"

"The guy who's gonna tell you what to do," Nixon called out.

After a pause, Nguyen continued calmly. "Okay. Can you tell me what's happening in the courtroom? Does anyone need medical attention? Is everybody safe for now?"

"Shut up. *Shut up.*"

The air in the courtroom abruptly felt too warm. It smelled of aftershave and cordite and sweat.

Quiet. After a second, when the bullhorn didn't repeat its expression of concern, Nixon shouted, "Here is a list of my demands."

Dammit. *My* demands. Nixon deliberately wanted to mislead the police into thinking there was only one attacker inside. Why?

Maybe to deceive the authorities in a way

that would help him escape. With hostages. Maybe to ambush any cops who rushed the courtroom expecting resistance from a single gunman. To take out as many officers as he and Reagan could before they went down themselves.

"Got a pen?" Nixon shouted. "Write this down."

Rory looked again at the parking garage. There had to be cops in there. They had to be watching the courthouse. However, with hostages crammed against the windows, those cops couldn't see the two gunmen.

But they could see her.

The scene at the perimeter was crowded and chaotic. Police black-and-whites blocked either end of the street outside the courthouse, and uniforms pushed back any civilian who lingered too long near the building, playing lookie-loo. The cops had no sawhorse barricades but had strung yellow police tape to mark the danger line. The crowd pressed close, angling for a good view. Noisy, confused, some with their hands to their mouths, others on tiptoe, they peered at the courthouse, trying to see the mayhem. Which, frankly, wasn't obvious from street level.

A Los Angeles television news crew toughed it out and barged through the crowd, the cameraman and reporter forging past people. When the police turned their backs, the news crew ducked beneath the yellow tape so they could get footage of the swarm. The reporter grabbed sound bites from people. Witnesses to horror.

"Cops drove up like an invasion . . ."

"Heard there was shooting inside . . ."

"Those poor people against the windows. My God, like fish in a barrel . . ."

The reporter got a one-on-one with a man who was near tears. The guy kept putting his hand to his forehead and waving at the courthouse. Great visuals.

In the background, off to the side, the cameraman noticed a young woman pushing her way to the front of the crowd. Her face was strained with shock. She was in her late twenties, a perfect Southern California beauty. A stunner, actually. Sleek black hair that shone almost blue with the sun. Eyes to match, feline and hot. A nose ring. A sleeveless red T-shirt, unbuttoned to show creamy and perfectly augmented breasts.

Honey shot, his instincts screamed. He tapped the reporter on the shoulder, trying to refocus his attention from Angsty Man to the frightened beauty.

"What the hell?" the beauty said. "What's going on?"

An older woman said, "Terrorist attack on the courthouse."

Honey Shot put a hand to her head. "Oh my God."

"I heard shooting. I heard the gunfire,"

the older woman said.

The man behind her added, "It's the Mirkovic trial. They've got everybody trapped in the courtroom."

Honey Shot gaped at the courthouse, openly horrified. "No."

"Yeah, look which courtroom it is. That's the Mirkovic trial."

"Oh Jesus."

Finally alerted by the strength of her reaction, the reporter turned to her. The cameraman refocused. Honey Shot looked near tears.

"You sure? You goddamned sure?" she said.

The crowd nodded. She let out a harsh cry.

The reporter said, "Miss —"

"My cousin's in there," she said.

Everybody's attention clicked toward her.

"My cousin's a juror on the Mirkovic case. Is this for real?"

"Miss, what's your cousin's name?" the reporter said.

She pressed her hands to her head. "Rory Mackenzie."

"Number one," Nixon shouted. "Defendants Jared Smith and Lucy Elmendorf will

plead guilty to the murder of Brad Mirkovic."

Surprise rippled through the courtroom.
At the defense table, Jared Smith said,
"What?"

"Two," Nixon called. "Both defendants
will sign a confession to the murder. This
confession will describe their crime in full
and complete detail. It will include a statement admitting they took Brad Mirkovic's
life with deliberation and malice afore-
thought."

So he knew the California Penal Code
definition of first-degree murder, Rory
thought. Good for him. Did he realize he
was on the hook for felony murder himself,
because Reagan had killed the *Justice!* vigilante?

"Three," Nixon shouted.

Christ, these guys loved to count.

"The defendants' confession will be read
live on all major networks. It will be read in
full. And the defendants' signatures will be
shown on-screen, so everybody knows
they're authentic."

After a second, Nguyen said, "Okay, let
me make sure I got all that."

Nixon shifted his shotgun, almost cradling
it. The sun caught the barrel, a strange, dull
light, like the glint of a reptile awakened

from beneath a warm rock.

Nguyen said, "You want the defendants to sign a confession and —"

"And I want five million dollars in gold bullion."

A long, long pause on Nguyen's end.

Nixon shouted: "That's five million U.S. dollars' worth of gold bullion as calculated at the close of market yesterday."

"That will take some doing, but —"

"And a helicopter, and safe passage to Mexico."

Nguyen paused again. Rory wondered who he was, with what experience and what authority.

Finally, he said, "I'll see what I can do. In the meantime —"

"No meantime. Now."

Nixon turned and paced. He rubbed his forearm against his forehead, as though to wipe off sweat, despite the balaclava. Reagan intercepted him.

"What are you —"

Nixon raised a hand to silence him, turned, and paced back to the doors. "That's a helicopter large enough to carry the pilots and five passengers, plus the lifting capacity to haul the bullion."

After a moment, Nguyen said, "I'm going to need some time to see what we can do.

But I'll need you to do something for me, all right? Can you let me know if everybody's okay in there?"

Rory breathed against the window. How did hostage negotiation work?

She had spent years with a cop and hadn't learned a thing about crisis negotiation. Years with Seth, a man who drank the Kool-Aid of police work like it was the river of life, and not once had she asked him how to rescue captives from a locked room where they were imprisoned by violent men with guns.

Of course, Seth had been a cop who took on the coloring of violent men with guns. He had worked undercover.

But she knew one thing: Hostage negotiation shouldn't work like this. Not like Nixon screaming demands but failing to give Nguyen a time limit. She didn't negotiate many deals, but she knew not to ask an open-ended question, hoping for yes. That betrayed weakness and poor planning. She knew so from selling her Barbies to her cousin when she was seven. Failing to institute a deadline was a bush-league mistake. As was failing to spell out the consequences if the cops failed to meet Nixon's demands.

She'd also learned that from the Barbie

transaction with her cousin. Who had pushed her into the sticker bushes by the creek and run off with the entire collection. Rory knew from bush-league mistakes.

What in hell was going on here?

Reagan caught Nixon and put a hand against his chest. Quietly, he said, "What about the girl?"

Nixon brushed his hand aside and continued to pace.

The girl.

Four people had been tapped on the back with the shotgun. Three men and her. She didn't like the odds that the gunmen were talking about somebody else.

In the parking garage across the street she saw the news van, in the shadows. And she saw shadows she didn't think had been there earlier.

She inched her hands up the window. Slowly, gently, she spread her fingers against the glass.

9

Seth stood at the counter in the taqueria, eyes on the TV, phone in his hand, waiting. Instinct told him this thing in Ransom River was more than big. This thing at the courthouse was about to erupt into the realm of the very bad.

Traffic on Wilshire was busy. The autumn sun cut through the window and caught him. He scrolled through his contacts and hovered over his dad's number.

On TV, the news crew that was hunkered down in the parking garage zoomed in on the courthouse. Sirens in the background. The focus blurred and sharpened on the image of hostages pinned to the courtroom windows.

Seth's hand slowly fell to his side. He forgot about calling his dad. His dad was fine. His dad was retired and wouldn't go within two miles of the courthouse for fun or profit.

The reporter's voice was hushed. "This is Jennifer Warner-Garcia at the scene of a developing hostage situation at the Ransom River Superior Courthouse."

There on-screen, up against the glass, stood Rory.

Seth's nerve endings seemed to snap with sparks. It was Rory, no question. No doubt, not a chance he was imagining it. Two years since he had seen her, since he had touched her, since she had given him that fateful look and told him, *No more.* Two years that hadn't passed so much as scored him like a rusted knife.

When had she come back? Nobody had told him. Not her parents, of course — if her father approached him, it would be with a baseball bat. Her dad, the guy who wouldn't let a sparrow with a broken wing die on the forest floor, the guy who thought Seth Colder was a maniac with a death wish.

Seth had thought she would never set foot in Ransom River again. That she was gone for good.

Aurora Faith, what are you doing there?

He heard reporter Jennifer Warner-Garcia mention *gunman* and *shots fired.*

Rory looked beautiful. She was wearing the turquoise necklace he had given her. He thought, seeing it, that he might crack into pieces.

The hostages at the windows had their hands up, palms pressed to the glass. They looked like figures in a Navajo sand painting. Seth could guess what they'd been told: Hold still or get shot.

Though Rory was holding still, she seemed to thrum with energy. And he saw that she wasn't completely motionless. Her hands were moving. She put two fingers of her left hand against the glass. She shaped her right hand into a gun.

"Goddamn," he said.

Two guns.

Then she walked her fingers up the glass, as if they represented a little human figure. With her left hand she continued to press two fingers to the window.

Two gunmen.

The sparks beneath Seth's skin turned chill.

She was silently signaling the police that two armed hostiles were inside the courtroom. Obviously, Rory thought the cops didn't know how many attackers were inside. And she thought they needed that information to rescue her and everybody else there.

Rory paused and glanced to the side, as

though checking that nobody in the court-room had seen what she was doing.

"Watch yourself," Seth said.

She put one finger of her left hand against the window. Slowly, with her right, she drew letters on the glass, like a kid writing in condensation. *D-E-A-D*.

She paused. Again she put one finger against the window with her left hand. With her right, she spelled out *H-U-R-T*.

One dead, one injured.

The reporter didn't comment. Maybe she didn't see what Rory had done. She said, "We have no audio from inside the build-ing, but it's apparent that the hostages are in fear for their lives. We can see — it looks like nine people — against the glass. We can't view anything of the interior of the courtroom."

"Of course not," Seth said. "The gunmen want it that way."

He raised his phone and scrolled to a new number. It was time to take this to another level.

But he stopped, riveted by the sight of Rory, her necklace gleaming in the sun. She had gone very still. But her lips were mov-ing.

The reporter said, "The hostages in the Ransom River courtroom seem to be a microcosm of the people who make up this Los Angeles suburb. Women and men, young and old, black and white and Latino. We can't know what's in their minds, but it has to be terror. And . . . one woman seems to be praying."

The camera focused on Rory. She was speaking, whispering, to herself. Her lips moved clearly. Seth stepped closer to the screen.

"She seems to be reciting a prayer," the reporter said. "It's heartbreaking."

Rory, pray?

Seth watched her, feeling helpless. And then the last vestiges of heat poured from beneath his skin and left him shocked and empty. He watched Rory's lips.

Things I've never done . . .

She wasn't praying. Not Rory Mackenzie, who might believe but would never submit to the idea of begging mercy from a remote and capricious power. She was singing to herself.

He murmured, "Never much but we made the most . . ."

Seth couldn't believe it, and knew what she was going to say next. It was her favorite song, never fashionable, sad and harsh and beautiful. A little indie lullaby about loss and the thirst for love.

"Welcome home," he whispered.

Two years. No good-bye. No wave over the shoulder, no word that she had planned to move overseas, no postcards. And yet here she was, murmuring words he knew from a hundred nights in her arms.

I've come home . . .

Not her song. Their song.

He grabbed his truck keys.

10

Rory's hands felt numb. For forty-five minutes she'd pressed them to the window, and the blood was draining from her arms. A twisted quiet held the courtroom. Nobody tried to rush the gunmen. Nobody begged to be let out. Rory had stopped singing. Trapped, they were waiting for whatever came next.

She didn't know if the police had seen her hand signals. *Two gunmen. One civilian dead. One hurt.*

Behind her, Nixon paced like a buffalo. She caught him at the edges of her vision, shotgun resting across his forearms, masked face staring at his cell phone. He scrolled and texted and paused, perhaps to read incoming messages.

At the court clerk's desk, computer keys clicked. The clerk was typing up the confessions of Jared Smith and Lucy Elmendorf. Nixon had dictated it to her. The defendants had complained about this, but their counsel told them the law would disregard any declaration of guilt signed at gunpoint.

Rory listened for the sound of Judge Wieland's breathing. He had gone fearfully quiet. She risked turning her head.

Wieland lay on his back, bunching the wet fabric of his robe against his shoulder to keep pressure on the wound. He looked pale and vague with pain. Forty-five minutes without medical aid. A knot lodged in Rory's throat.

She opened her mouth to say something to Nixon. He saw her and jerked his head.

"Eyes out the window," he said.

"This is Sergeant Nguyen. Is everybody still okay in there?"

Nixon yelled at the doors. "Where's my gold bullion?"

"If we're going to talk about that, let's do it over the phone so we don't have to shout. Can you pick up the phone at the judge's desk?"

"No. You better tell me the gold's on its way."

"If we're going to arrange that, we need something from you," Nguyen said.

"When will it be here?"

Reagan jittered to Nixon's side. They whispered a moment. Reagan, twitchy, hissed, "Mexico? Don't like that."

"It's a stopgap."

"But it won't be the end."

"It will be for us unless we get out of here."

Nixon turned back to the door. "And get the networks here to broadcast the defendants' confession. I don't see any TV cameras outside."

"That might be workable. But for a broadcast to be arranged, we all need to work on an agreement. I understand that the defendants' confessions are being signed. That's major. So earn yourself some goodwill in return. How about you let some of the hostages go?"

"What part of *no* don't you get? You give me what I ask for; then we'll see who comes out."

Reagan muttered something. Nixon nodded.

"When's the helicopter getting here?" he called.

"We need some time to arrange a chopper that meets your requirements. I'll see what we can do. But while we're working on that, let's work on helping you and the other folks in the courtroom with you."

"I don't want to hear you're working on it. I want to hear you tell me exactly when the helicopter is going to land on that lawn outside," Nixon repeated.

"Then work with me. Fair enough?"

"No."

This, Rory thought, was a half-assed ransom negotiation. Her first, and it was simply piss-poor. Nixon wouldn't give an inch.

Nguyen said, "We heard gunfire earlier. You gain nothing by letting injured people suffer. If you want the helicopter, you're going to need to help me out —"

"Forget it."

"That's a tough attitude," Nguyen said. "Who am I talking to here?"

"The guy who needs his fucking helicopter and five million dollars," Nixon shouted. "And Fox Fucking News outside, ready to broadcast the confession to murder by these tools of the police state."

"Then give us something," Nguyen said.

Reagan waved an arm in frustration. He strutted up to Nixon, jumpy, like he was walking on hot coals. He hissed, "It's not working. They aren't budging."

Nixon stared at him for several long seconds. He turned toward the doors.

"Get the chopper here in the next ten minutes or I'll shoot a hostage," he said.

A woman cried out. The entire room

stirred, like birds challenged by a fox.

"Ten minutes — that's unrealistic," Nguyen said.

"Do it. Get me the chopper *now.*"

Nguyen said, "It'll take longer than that to get a heavy-lifting-capacity helicopter."

Reagan yanked on Nixon's sleeve and whispered, "That's not what I meant. Hell you doing?"

Low and sharp, Nixon said, "Getting us out of here. Sticking around is not an option. Don't you get it? The longer we stay, the more the odds stack against us. We go, and we go now."

Rory began writing on the window again. One small letter at a time. *Help. Hurry.*

She tried to stay present, to focus. On anything, even the song she'd been singing. *Welcome home . . .*

Home, as empty as ever.

She wondered where SWAT was and how many long-range rifles lurked in the shadows of the parking garage across the street. She wondered if her roomie was out there in the crowds behind the barricades, muttering about karma and worrying who would take care of the dog if Rory didn't come out alive. She wondered if her parents were there. The thought tightened the knot in her throat.

Get out, they'd said. They'd been concerned when she came home this time. Hell, she'd been concerned too. Out of work, the entire thing kicked out from under her and, awfully, out from under all the people who relied on the charity.

She had always believed the Japanese proverb: "Fall seven times, stand up eight." But she had run, and run, and ended up back where she started. Maybe it was a sign: Whatever her life was missing couldn't be found. And here she was, at the finish line.

Behind her Reagan paced skittishly. Nixon stood planted like a stump.

"Nine minutes left," he shouted. "Where's the chopper?"

From the hallway, Sergeant Nguyen, said, "Give us more time."

"You've had time," Nixon shouted. "You've had two hundred fifty years to impose the police state on us. And to let thugs and criminals run rampant while cops take bribes to look the other way. You've had all the goddamned time you need."

Holy shit, Rory thought.

"Get a chopper on the lawn or the roof of the courthouse right this goddamned minute," Nixon shouted. "I can hear a whole bunch of them outside. Tell one of them to land. You have ninety seconds."

11

Pressed against the yellow police tape at the perimeter, the crowd had grown nervous. The camera crew rolled continuously, catching the windows of the courthouse, the eerie no-man's land in front of it, the police officers who dashed anxiously from location to location. A mobile command unit, a huge gaudy RV, had rolled up and parked a block to the south. Overhead, three helicopters hovered.

The honey with the cousin inside tried to pace in a packed space. She weaved back and forth, turned in circles, pressed a hand to her ear while talking on her cell phone.

"It's crazy here," she said into the phone. "Unbelievable. No, I'm not making it up. Turn on your TV. Something's gone way to hell wrong and everybody's trapped in the courtroom including Rory. It's a nightmare."

She scraped her fingernails through her

gleaming hair. A vivid tattoo ran across one shoulder and down her left arm, parrot bright, some mythic battle, demons and angels. She looked on the verge of panic. No, that wasn't it — she looked like she was desperate to *do* something. To act. To help.

The reporter said, "Miss, what's your name?"

She glanced up from her phone call. After a second, she focused. "Nerissa Mackenzie."

"And your cousin —"

"If anything happens to her, oh God."

"It looks like some of the hostages are trying to communicate with the police."

She glanced at the windows.

"Does your cousin have a cell phone?" the reporter said.

Nerissa paused and slowly turned back to him. She seemed to take in the implications and instantly jumped ahead about ten steps.

"If I can get through to her, you can patch the call to the cops." Another quick glance at the courthouse. "It's a long shot. Look at her. They have her pressed to the windows where she can't move."

"But if her phone's in her pocket . . ."

"Yeah. Worth a try. We could find out what's really happening in there." She nodded at the cameraman. "Record it, so we get everything verbatim. No mistakes."

She hung up on her call without saying good-bye and scrolled through her contacts.

The reporter said, "Quickly — she's your first cousin? You live here in Ransom River?"

"L.A. Here visiting my mom. I'm an actor."

"Have I seen your work?"

"Video game — *Skywraith: Ascent of the Damned.* I'm the body model for a rebel fighter. And Butterfly Bombshell in Hollywood, the bar. I waitress and cosplay — role-play on duty. Catholic schoolgirl, usually."

"Okay." Fabulous. And how gloriously weird.

"I was coming to see the trial. If traffic had been better, I'd be trapped in there right now."

The cameraman turned to her. She straightened, flipped her hair over her shoulder, licked her lips. Eyes dazzling, her face riven with tension, she dialed a number.

To herself she murmured, "Rory, baby, please pick up."

Overhead, a hard thwapping motor drowned out all sound. A black helicopter swooped over the roof of the courthouse and slowed above the lawn.

Nixon's demand echoed through the courtroom. *Ninety seconds.*

The moment stretched. Reagan pushed Nixon and muttered at him. Rory caught, ". . . ultimatum, *idiot,* you . . ."

Nixon shoved him away and pumped the shotgun. The sound chittered across the room. Rory sensed more than saw the hostages cringe. A woman's crying turned jagged.

"Eighty seconds," Nixon cried.

Sergeant Nguyen came back: "The helicopter is on its way."

"Seventy-five seconds."

"It's coming. It's inbound. It needs clearance to land. You have to give the pilot time to approach safely."

"Seventy seconds."

In the reflection from the glass, Rory saw Nixon turn and look around the courtroom. The ghostly reflections of the hostages shrank back. They all knew what he was doing.

He pointed. "You."

A man said, "No."

"Stand up," Nixon said. He turned back to the main doors. "Sixty-five seconds."

"The helicopter is coming. You should be able to hear it," Nguyen called back.

Bullshit, Rory thought.

"Bullshit," Nixon said.

Rory could see distant choppers and hear one that seemed to be hovering high overhead, but it could not have had time to load up five million dollars' worth of gold bricks. Her stomach cramped. Whatever this was, it was coming, and fast.

Nixon's voice settled into a low rasp. "You at the far window there, yeah — you. Tell me what you see. You see a helicopter flying this way?"

A woman planted against a window to Rory's left said, "I don't know."

In Reagan's plastic supermarket bag, a cell phone rang. With Rory's ringtone.

Nixon's reflection darted right, then left. With the windows blocked by human shields, he couldn't see what was going on outside. He turned to Reagan. Snapping his fingers, he pointed at the bench and Judge Wieland's computer.

"Check to see what the news is showing."

Oh God.

Reagan ran up the steps to the bench, set his shotgun on the desk, hunched over the monitor, and clumsily pounded the keyboard.

After a second he straightened. Shook his head.

Nixon turned. He shouted at the doors: "You're bullshitting me."

Nguyen said, "It's inbound."

At the computer, Reagan shook his head more vehemently. He whispered, "Cops are just standing there. Not clearing a landing zone."

"Sixty seconds," Nixon shouted. "Get a chopper on the ground. Or you've got a kid who's going to regret answering his jury summons."

A man's voice, broken: "Don't shoot me. Please. I take care of my mom. I have little sisters."

It was Frankie Ortega. Rory felt dizzy.

She said, "I see the helicopter. It's landing."

It wasn't; it was barely visible, a copter easing its way over the roof of the courthouse, high up. But bullshit was all she had, so she'd better dish it with conviction.

"Don't lie to me. Fifty seconds," Nixon said.

"No," Rory said. "Can't you hear it?"

"Where?" Nixon said.

She hoped the other people lined up against the windows would get it and wouldn't falter.

"It's directly overhead. Up high. The TV crew in the garage can't get an angle to see it. That's why it's not on the news," she said.

The helicopter lurked at the top of the

101

view out the window. She could tell it had law enforcement markings on it. She could also tell it wasn't anything close to a heavy-lifting aircraft. She had no idea if the cops had actually sent it for them.

The sound grew louder, bouncing off the walls. Nixon shouted, "Thirty seconds. Hovering don't count. On the ground where I can see it."

From the end of the gun barrel, Frankie said, "Don't, man. I beg you."

Reagan was staring at the computer screen shaking his head.

"That's it. Ninety seconds gone," Nixon yelled.

"It's landing," Rory shouted. "You can't see it on the screen. But I can — it's landing on the roof."

Red Check, next to her at the window, said, "It's descending. For God's sake, you can't demand that it touch down before the cops have even had time to contact the pilot."

Nixon went silent. Rory held her breath. *Please spare Frankie. Please.* The sound of the engine blatted against the walls. She glanced over her shoulder.

Nixon stared at the windows, trying to see the copter. Reagan continued to stare at the screen. He shook his head. "They're not showing it."

"They probably know you have TV access," Rory said. "They want to keep everything covert. But it's there. Listen to it."

The noise of the helicopter grew louder.

Nixon shouted at the door: "That had better be it."

After a second, Nguyen said, "It's landing on the roof."

Rory didn't believe it. She really didn't. She thought Nguyen may have heard her shouting and gone with her bullshit, a desperate gamble.

After a moment, Nixon said, "We're leaving."

Relief bled through her. She turned around and saw Nixon pull the barrel of his shotgun off of Frankie. He stalked back down the aisle. Frankie steadied himself against a bench, one hand to his face.

Nixon strode to the middle of the courtroom. "Heads up. We're getting ready to depart. The three people who were tapped on the back earlier, come with me."

Rory didn't know what was about to happen. But if she and everybody else in the courtroom were going to emerge unscathed, it was going to require skill, luck, and a discipline Reagan and Nixon had so far failed to show. She figured she had a better chance of capturing Bigfoot.

Nixon shouted out the main doors: "You just got a reprieve. If you fail to carry through on your promises, that stay of execution will be lifted."

He beckoned Reagan. With his index finger he drew a diagram on the palm of one hand. To Rory it looked like he was drawing their exit plan. She would lay money that it involved surrounding themselves with the hostages. And she was taller than both of them. Anybody who wanted to reach them would have to go through her. Nixon and Reagan wouldn't even have to duck.

She didn't want to go anywhere with these two, not even past Go on a Monopoly board. An itch in the back of her brain told her it would be equally dangerous outside, with a battery of heavily armed cops facing off against men who seemed jumpy enough to shoot at dust motes and lint. And once they got outside, Nixon and Reagan would know she'd been bluffing about the helicopter.

Nixon waved at the chosen three and snapped his gloved fingers, a dull, muffled sound. "Come on."

Red Check and prosecutor Cary Oberlin walked toward him, looking uncertain and alarmed. Rory remained at the window, her hands touching the warm glass, because it had become familiar, and sturdy, even though it could burst in an instant.

"No," she said.

Nixon did a double take. "What did you just say?"

She was gambling. Coin toss on her life. She was convinced they wanted her — and they wanted her alive.

"What if I refuse to go?" she said.

At that, people roused. A woman cried, "Shut up!" A man on the floor called out, "Be quiet. You've been chosen."

She stared at Nixon. If her refusal drove him to threaten somebody else, she could still accede. But she was calculating that he wouldn't do that. Besides, letting others decide what happens to you is never a good choice. Fight it if you can.

Nixon stared back. Beneath the balaclava, the skin around his eyes was pale. Below his left eye was a scar. It was deep and ran vertically, like a tear track. One that had dried into gnarled white tissue, dead and hard.

The man on the floor reacted badly to Rory ignoring him. "They picked you. You have to go. If you resist they'll just choose somebody else instead."

She barely heard him; heard mostly the

whine and panic in his voice. *Not fair.* She felt loose at the knees and forced herself to stand still.

Nixon's lips parted. His aftershave wafted in the air. "No back talk. You're going."

"Why?"

She tried to put a demand into her voice. Nixon almost seemed to shake himself, to verify he wasn't imagining her obstinacy. Reagan was across the room, headed toward the door to the judge's chambers.

It was perfectly possible for him to grab somebody else, somebody more pliable, somebody as tall and fast, somebody who would shield them as they escaped, without asking questions. But she didn't think that was going to happen.

"Why?" she said, stronger.

Beneath the balaclava, Nixon's eyes were flat. He crossed the space between them in three strides.

He grabbed her arm and yanked her away from the window. He pulled her against him. He was hot, sweaty, his body odor mixing with the cologne. He grimaced. His teeth were chipped.

"Why? Because —"

The mist and dust and *crack* landed all at once. Nixon's head snapped to one side and he dropped in front of her.

The air in front of Rory was all at once empty — she could see straight across the room to the main doors — and blurred with something hot and sticky.

People screamed. She looked down. Nixon had collapsed in a heap. The side of his balaclava had shredded. His skull had shredded. A pool of dark blood spread across the stone floor. He had been shot in the head.

She backed up a step. People screamed and crawled away from Nixon, leaving an empty circle around her. She raised her hands. They were clean, but she felt wetness on her face. She touched her cheek. Her fingers came away stippled with blood.

The screams got louder. The blood pool spread toward her, as if drawn magnetically. She stumbled back another step. In the window a fractured hole had blossomed at eye level, surrounded by cracks and white crazed lines. A bullet hole, exactly where she'd been standing.

Nixon's head had been twelve inches from hers. They'd shot him, long range, right past her. She put a hand to her mouth and gagged.

Reagan stared at the sight of Nixon dead on the floor. He was framed against the door to the judge's chambers, gun in his hands, mouth open. He gaped at Nixon and, slowly, at the window.

He was still staring at the window when the door behind him burst open.

The door to chambers shattered, wood splitting. Behind it was darkness, but Rory saw shadowed forms and a battering ram in their arms. Then she heard a clatter and saw a small cylindrical object roll into the courtroom.

Before she could do anything, it blew.

The noise, the flat, overwhelming *bang,* filled her ears, her head, deafened her. The light ignited everything, white. She found herself smacked back against the wall.

Her ears rang. She didn't hear the next shots.

12

The room seemed to billow and shake. A high-pitched whine filled Rory's ears. Through fizzing white smoke she saw the thread-line light of red lasers. They sliced past her and lit on Reagan.

His jacket flayed, a burst of fabric and blood. His head jerked back and he dropped.

SWAT surged into the courtroom.

Figures in black tactical gear flowed through the smoke, guns drawn. Through the bathtub dullness in her ears, Rory heard voices.

"Police! Don't move."

A SWAT officer in a helmet and goggles and body armor came toward her, rifle raised, finger on the trigger. *"On your knees. Hands behind your head."*

She went down and stayed there like a penitent.

"Officer," she said.

He turned. She nodded with her chin. "Judge Wieland's been shot."

The officer glanced across the room. Got on his radio.

One by one the other hostages dropped back to the floor. Across the room, Frankie Ortega knelt, coughing. Lucy Elmendorf sat on the floor hugging her husband.

A SWAT officer checked Nixon for signs of life. Drew a slash mark across his throat with his thumb. Pulled off Nixon's balaclava. The dark pool of blood beneath the gunman's head seemed to crown him. Looked like his thoughts poured out, gone.

No back talk. You're going. Because . . .

His face was rough. A man in his forties, his features worn and creased. His eyes stared sightlessly. Rory looked away.

By Judge Wieland's side an officer knelt on one knee. He was holding the judge's hand and talking into a radio. Rory began to shake. Her vision blurred. She realized she was crying.

A cop shouted for the hostages to stand up. He told them to lock their hands behind their heads and walk out single file. By the time they got to the Department of Corrections buses outside, they'd been searched and cuffed with zip ties. The sun seemed too bright. Rory's knees felt like Silly Putty.

Helen Ellis tried to climb aboard the bus but wobbled. A cop gestured to the steps and said, "Please keep moving, ma'am."

Helen looked ready to crumble. "But we're not criminals."

"It's just procedure. Take care but get on board, please."

Rory said, "Procedure doesn't have to be spelled *asshole.*"

The cop eyed her coolly. "You've been restrained for your own safety. This will all be over soon."

Not soon enough. Not by a long, rocky mile. She helped Helen up the stairs.

The door to the interrogation room finally opened at 7:42 p.m. Rory checked her watch. They'd let her keep the watch. They'd even let her keep her belt. In this room she couldn't have killed herself for fun or money. If she'd taken off her boots and tried to beat herself to death with them, the cops behind the two-way mirror would have simply ambled in and laughed at her.

Noise flowed through the open door. Conversation, phones, television. In walked a woman with a disheveled ponytail the color of Mountain Dew. Her blue blouse was limp and wrinkled. Her badge was clipped to the waistband of her skirt.

"Aurora Mackenzie?" she said.

"Call me Rory."

"Detective Mindy Xavier." She looked a rugged forty-five. She gestured Rory to the worn plastic chair at the table. "Sorry it's taken so long. And for all the rigmarole."

Rigmarole. Rory guessed it was the technical term for plastic cuffs and aggressive pat-downs and a locked interrogation room.

"We had to make sure that there weren't any bad guys pretending to be hostages. You know, blending in with the rest of you and threatening everybody into keeping silent about it." Xavier closed the door. "Can I get you anything? Coffee?"

"I'm fine." Rory sat down. "What's the word on Judge Wieland?"

Xavier dropped a file folder on the table. "I don't know. Sorry."

Xavier scraped her own chair back and sat heavily. She looked frazzled. She examined Rory's face, seemingly for cracks.

"You okay?" she said.

"In one piece. When will I get a chance to clean up?"

"Excuse me?"

"When the first gunman was shot, I was close by. I got sprayed . . ."

Her voice chipped. She needed to stay calm. She could hardly bear having Nixon's blood on her clothes and skin. But she wasn't going to beg, not in a police station. She wasn't here to seek mercy from the cops.

Xavier eyed her sweater. She flushed. "Maybe I can find you a T-shirt."

"Even a grocery bag. Paper or plastic, I don't care."

Xavier stood, opened the door, and beckoned to a passing colleague. She asked for a clean T-shirt. Then she closed the door and sat down again.

She shook her head. "Sorry. Demanding day."

"Do you know who they were?" Rory said.

"We're investigating."

"Why did they attack the courtroom?"

"Investigating."

Xavier opened the file folder. Rory's driver's license was clipped inside.

Xavier uncapped a pen. "Tell me what you saw. What you heard. Take it from the top, and take your time. Don't leave anything out."

Get through this, Rory thought. *Just give them what they want and get home.*

"They came in through the main doors," she began.

She went through it. Moment by moment, step by step, trying to recall the choreography and the score. Xavier took only occasional notes. The CCTV camera near the ceiling probably had something to do with that. As Rory described the siege, her heart started to pound. Her leg throbbed, the old ache. The room turned stifling.

"Could I have a glass of water?" she said.

"Sure." Xavier glanced at the mirror. "At what point did the gunmen first indicate resentment of the defendants?"

The door opened and another detective stepped in, a man with placid Young Republican features and a frat-boy strut. He set a plastic water bottle on the table, pulled up a chair next to Xavier. Set down a laptop.

"Had you ever seen the gunmen before today?" he said.

"I don't know," Rory said.

"Really? Two men hold you hostage and you can't say whether you recognized them?"

He didn't offer his hand. Neither had Xavier, but Rory got the sense that if she had put hers out, Xavier would have taken it. This guy didn't give her that vibe.

"They wore ski masks," she said.

She unscrewed the bottle top, tilted the bottle to her lips, and gulped it down. She felt like her toes and fingers and teeth had curled. And she felt something else: fear.

Because, on the Ransom River PD's busiest day in twenty years, with three people dead, a major crime scene to process, and sixty-five witnesses to debrief, the department surely had no manpower to spare. Sending a second detective to deliver water seemed inefficient. And unlikely.

"The SWAT guys pulled Nixon's mask off," she said. "That's the only time I saw his face. And he was dead, with a gunshot wound to the head." A huge, gaping wound. "I don't know how he looked when —"

"Nixon?" he said.

"The gunman who was shot by the sniper through the window. That was what his accomplice called him. They referred to each other as Nixon and Reagan."

"And the only time you saw his face was when SWAT removed his mask."

"Yes." *And I'd been talking to him at the moment he turned dead.* She pressed her hand to her forehead.

"You all right?" Xavier said.

"Headache."

She drank some more water. The bottle had a chemical tang. She put it down. Her hands had developed a tremor. She clenched them to stop it.

Xavier gave her a sympathetic look. "I know it's been a hard day. But we want to get your recollections while they're fresh."

"I understand."

The man said, "At what point did the gunmen first mention their demands?"

She took a second. "I'm sorry — should I call you Detective Number Two?"

"Zelinski." He folded a stick of gum into his mouth. "When did the gunmen first make their demands?"

"When Sergeant Nguyen tried to engage with them."

"Not before?"

"Until Sergeant Nguyen came on the bullhorn the only thing they demanded was for four of us to stand up and head toward the door."

"Any guesses why they did that?"

"Guesses?" Rory looked back and forth between them. "Yeah, actually. I think they had an outside agenda. And I don't think they were working alone."

Zelinski looked at her thoughtfully. "Really. Why?"

She seemed to hear a creaking noise, like a pin had been pulled from a support beam below her.

"I think they were working with somebody on the outside. Nixon kept looking at —" She spread her hands. "Do you know his name? Something else I can call him?"

"Nixon is interesting," Zelinski said. "We can go with that for now."

She paused. She wasn't imagining the good cop, annoying cop routine. "Nixon kept handling his phone. I got the impression he was sending text messages. And I heard them arguing."

Xavier said, "About what?"

"Whether the two of them should flee on their own. Nixon wanted to take hostages with them. He said, 'We leave by ourselves, we die.' "

"He probably meant he wanted human shields. For good reason. Look what happened to him the second our sniper got a clean shot."

Rory shook her head. "It was more than that. He insisted that they take the people who got tapped on the back. He said, 'The plan is the plan.' "

They didn't react.

"Then Reagan suggested surrendering. Nixon shut him down cold. And asked if Reagan understood the consequences. That's the word he used. *Consequences.*"

"Yeah. Trial, conviction, execution," Zelinski said.

"I don't think that's what he was talking about. I think he meant that if he botched the attack, a third party would punish him for it."

"Really?"

"He got increasingly upset. Then he mentioned 'payment.' "

"Payment for what?" Xavier said.

"I don't know."

"When you were pinned against the window," Zelinski said, "did they tell you to pass along information to the outside?"

"What? No."

"They didn't direct you to make hand signs and give the police ideas about how many gunmen were inside and what weapons they had?"

"God no. The police thought there was only one gunman in the courtroom. I was trying to tell them there were two."

"The gunmen didn't want you to mislead the authorities?"

She just stared. "I provided accurate information."

Xavier had stopped writing. The ventilation system hummed. The fluorescent lights hummed. Rory's nerves hummed.

Zelinski said, "What kind of outside agenda do you think the gunmen had?"

"I have no idea."

Xavier looked pensive. "You grew up in Ransom River, didn't you, Ms. Mackenzie?"

What was this, a change-up pitch? "Born here."

"Ransom River High? Sports — is that where I remember you from?"

"Cross country and track," Rory said.

Xavier nodded. "I played basketball at St. Joe's."

Zelinski turned to her, head cocked. "Really, Mindy? You want to talk old times?"

She waved him off. "He's new in town. Doesn't know the ropes. You were a star."

"I did all right," Rory said.

"Better than that."

Xavier continued to stare at her. Waiting for her résumé, it seemed.

"I won State my senior year," Rory said.

Xavier said, "You have siblings?"

"Only child."

"Mackenzie sounds familiar."

"There's family in town."

She had cousins. And maybe Xavier remembered them from Ransom River High School football games. Boone had started at tight end, when he wasn't benched for fighting. Nerissa had been a cheerleader. She was rumored to be the one who seduced the St. Joseph's quarterback the night before the game, slipped Rohypnol into his rum and Coke, and then dumped him, stoned and naked, on a back road outside town.

The QB ended up in the hospital. St. Joseph's won anyway.

But Rory bet Xavier knew her cousins' branch of the family from their history of arrests. The air buzzed as if a scarlet *M* had lit up overhead. *She's a Mackenzie. One of them.*

"Small world," Xavier said.

Zelinski said, "Glad to know you could outrun me, Aurora. Glad it won't come to that." His smile was humorless. "Can we show you something?"

He opened his laptop and queued up a video.

Rory said, "You got footage from inside the courtroom?"

"CCTV system records all proceedings at the courthouse. Each courtroom has a camera."

He pressed Play.

The video was silent, grainy and gray. Prosecutor Cary Oberlin was conducting his direct examination of Samuel Koh. Oberlin waved his hand as he spoke. The stenographer typed on her machine. Judge Wieland studied his computer screen. In the jury box, everybody seemed attentive.

Then, soundlessly, people jumped. Oberlin turned and Wieland looked up, startled. Nixon rushed the bailiff.

Rory tried to swallow. The hum of the lights and ventilation system seemed to set her entire body thrumming.

On-screen, the gunmen forced people to lie on the floor. Nixon began to count aloud. Reagan moved among the crowd. When Nixon called *four,* he tapped a hostage on the back with the barrel of his shotgun.

It was random and chilling. Judge Wieland was tapped and drew a faltering breath. Reagan moved on, slowly. Nixon counted *four* and Reagan tapped the man in front of him, Oberlin.

Rory felt the detectives' eyes on her.

On-screen, Reagan stepped over hostages. *One, two, three, four.* He tapped the third man on the back.

Rory's stomach tightened. She knew what was coming next.

Except she didn't.

Nixon counted. Reagan walked. She expected him to continue moving slowly and randomly. But he didn't. He took large steps. Quietly, carefully, he covered twice the distance he had previously. He aimed straight across the courtroom. He stepped over half a dozen people. And when Nixon counted *four,* Reagan took an extra second to stare down at the person on the floor below him. He glanced back at Nixon.

Nixon raised his chin, a crisp, wordless *yeah*.

Reagan lowered the barrel of the shotgun and tapped Rory between the shoulders.

The humming in the interrogation room filled her head.

"What the hell?" she said.

Zelinski paused the video. "You saw that?"

"He picked me deliberately. What the *hell?*"

"Can you explain it?"

"No."

This was crazy. This was bad.

"Rewind," she said. "Show that to me again."

"It'll show exactly the same thing," Zelinski said.

"They *chose* me?" She turned to Xavier, lips parting. "Why did they do that?"

"You tell us," Xavier said.

The temperature in the room seemed to plunge. Rory felt so spooked that she forgot herself. And she did what no Mackenzie ever did: She spoke without thinking, without checking her cards. She spoke without understanding she'd been dealt a joker.

"Jesus Christ. I heard them muttering when I was up against the window — when they were talking about leaving, one of them said something about 'the girl.' They were talking about me." She looked at Xavier. "They chose me. They wanted to take me."

Zelinski said, " 'The girl'?"

"That's what they said."

He fast-forwarded through the video. "Show me where they mention you."

She watched, a tremor building in her arms again. "Stop."

The camera showed her pressed against the window. Behind her, Nixon and Reagan had their heads together. Their posture was aggressive and nervous.

"That's where they were discussing it all," she said.

Zelinski tilted his head and examined the screen. "You think they were after you. Not the defendants?"

"I'm telling you what I heard."

"You don't think they were after money?"

"They asked for five million bucks in gold. So maybe."

"Why did they demand bullion, do you think?"

"Shall I speculate? No dye packs. No serial numbers. You can melt gold down. Craft it into wedding rings and necklaces and little figurines of the Smurfs."

"You don't sound convinced."

"I'm not. I thought their demand for bullion was absurd on its face."

"Really?" Zelinski said.

"What kind of institution has five million dollars in gold bars lying around? How'd they expect to get it within a short period of time?"

"You interested in money, Ms. Mackenzie?" Zelinski said.

And when did you stop beating your wife? She kept her voice even. "I like to pay my rent and put food on the table."

"You're unemployed."

"The charity I work for lost its funding." She knew her cheeks were burning.

"Lucky that put you here in Ransom River with plenty of time on your hands, so you could fulfill your civic duty."

"Lucky? Asylum Action works — worked — to monitor refugees seeking political asylum. We followed up on cases where people were sent back to their home countries. Filed appeals. Fought deportations. Checked that people weren't put in danger."

"I saw your passport. Geneva?"

"Helsinki, London, then Geneva. Two years."

"You have any Swiss bank accounts?"

Xavier said, "Gary."

Zelinski took out another piece of gum, added it to the wad already in his mouth, and started the video again.

"What did the gunmen want?" he said.

Rory felt chilled. "I don't know."

"Did they storm the courtroom to kidnap the defendants?"

"Maybe."

"Then how come they chose four other people to go with them?"

Rory's lips parted. It stopped her dead. "I have no idea."

"You said they had an outside agenda. So you think they were coordinating with somebody outside the courtroom?"

"You've got Nixon's phone — you can find out who he was contacting."

Zelinski's mouth stretched into cold and toothy approximation of a smile. Rory thought, *Burn phone.* Prepaid, used only during the courthouse attack, and then dumped. And whoever he was texting probably did the same.

Zelinski leaned forward. "Outside agenda. I agree. But I can't help wondering whether you're part of it."

The room seemed obscenely bright. The hum from the lights and ventilation system sounded electric.

"No," she said. "What are you talking about?"

"Outside forces. Sounds completely plausible. The gunmen had confederates outside.

But they also had one inside."

"Not me." She heard the shock in her voice, and the note of panic.

Xavier said, "Show her the rest of the video."

Zelinski pressed Play again. The silent gray video showed Judge Wieland lying shot on the floor, gripping his robe in agony. On-screen Rory turned to Reagan, her face stricken. Her words didn't need a lip reader.

"We've got to get him help. You —"

Zelinski paused the video. " '*We've* got to get him help.' "

She said nothing.

"Not *you*," Zelinski said. "*We*. If I remember my grammar, *we* means the first person plural. *We* means 'our group.' It means *us*. And it means you're done."

This wasn't bad. This was crazy bad.

She said, "*We* meant all of us in the courtroom. Judge Wieland needed help. I didn't think about grammar; I just spoke."

Zelinski was leaning forward like a dog at the end of its chain. "You were speaking to somebody on your team. You were under pressure. You let it slip."

"No." And she finally got a grip on herself. She put her hands on the table. "I'm done talking until I speak with a lawyer."

Xavier looked gravely disappointed.

126

Slowly, with what seemed immense frustration, she shut her notebook. Zelinski, however, looked pleased. He looked like he had just won a jackpot on the slots.

"What was the agenda?" Zelinski said.

Xavier put her pen away. "Never mind, Gary."

She meant: no more questions. Rory had just invoked her right to counsel. But Zelinski didn't stop talking — he simply changed his questions into statements.

"Save yourself a long and agonizing process, Ms. Mackenzie. Tell us what the gunmen wanted."

She shook her head.

"Maybe you were bought off to throw the trial."

"Gary," Xavier said.

"I'm just speculating," he said. "Maybe you were getting paid to ensure that the defendants were convicted unjustly."

"Am I under arrest?" Rory said.

Neither detective answered, which was an answer. But Zelinski turned to the computer and pressed Play one last time. He fast-forwarded to the end, to the moment when Rory turned from the courtroom window and refused Nixon's order to go with him.

"What did he say to you?" Zelinski asked. "Because to me, it looks like a cozy conversation. It looks . . . intimate."

Rory sat like a stone.

Xavier stood. "You're free to go. But think hard about your next steps, Ms. Mackenzie."

"She's an attorney," Zelinski said. "She knows the score. That's why she lawyered up."

Rory bore their stares and the weight of their accusation. She refused to look away from Xavier. Finally the detective waved her toward the door.

"Go on," Xavier said.

She held still. "One thing," she said. "What time are the jurors expected in court tomorrow morning?"

Zelinski actually sat back in his seat.

"Excuse me, but I need to find out." She stood up and left.

13

The station was in overdrive. Phones rang. People looked harried. Xavier and Zelinski flanked Rory as she walked out, as though she might indiscriminately steal staplers or the WANTED posters from the walls.

At the main entrance Zelinski stopped. "Good luck not talking, Ms. Mackenzie. Have fun out there."

With the heat of his words on her back, she pushed through the doors into the cool night.

Into the center ring of a circus.

White lights overpowered the black sky. Headlights, spotlights, camera flashes, beams from shoulder-mounted television cameras. Overhead a news helicopter trained a spotlight on the front steps of the police station, pinning her. The shadows of palm trees cut across the scene like scimitars.

The media was massed on the sidewalk. Behind them, kept back by barricades, were the crowds she'd seen outside the court-house. They'd followed the sideshow here like rock groupies. All this scene needed was a souvenir stand, selling ball caps and com-memorative shotgun shells. *I was taken hostage and all I got was this lousy balaclava.*

The cops hadn't even given her the T-shirt.

The reporters saw her. Almost as one they turned — faces, microphones, lenses. Be-hind her the station doors clicked shut.

"It's one of the hostages," a man shouted.

"Over here!" a woman cried. "Miss, Ac-tion News!"

Rory faced the wall of lights. It seemed as if two hundred watts of white water was pouring down on her.

"Fox News Los Angeles. Miss, can we have a word?"

"What happened in the courtroom?"

Her breath frosted the air. Her car was two miles away, parked at the courthouse. To get to it she would have to swim through the reporters and the crowd.

"You! You were up against the window. Tell us what you saw."

"Did you witness the gunmen being shot?"

A shout of *"Hey —"* cut through the din. Beyond the spotlights, across the street at the edge of a park, a woman with strawberry blonde hair had climbed on a bus-stop bench. She waved her arms overhead. Rory felt a rush of relief and gratitude. It was her friend and housemate, Petra Whistler.

Rory squared her shoulders, aimed toward her, and waded into the press mob. Cameras swiveled to track her. Mikes jutted at her face.

"Why did the gunmen attack the courtroom?" a man said. "To kill the defendants?"

She raised a hand. "Not now. Sorry."

Directly in front of her a TV camera appeared. Its light burned a hot white spot in her eyes. She turned her head. From behind the cameraman a woman reached toward her.

"Rory."

She shaded her eyes. "Petra?"

The woman stepped forward, an apparition solidifying. Alabaster arms, feline eyes, coke black hair. A face so like her own.

"Rory, sweet pea, oh God," she said.

Nerissa swept her into an embrace. She cradled Rory's head against her shoulder and rocked back and forth, her voice breaking. "You're alive, you're alive, you're alive."

Rory felt like she'd been caught in a net. She felt the urge to scratch her cousin's eyes out and flee.

"Riss," she said.

"It's okay, baby doll. You're safe. You're free." She leaned back, cupped Rory's face in both hands, and laughed her cool, breezy laugh. *"Free."*

The crowd cheered. Riss shot both arms into the air and tilted her head back and yelled, *"Yes."*

The crowd began to clap in unison. Riss mussed Rory's hair and laughed again, silvery. The camera caught every instant of it.

"Miss Mackenzie," the reporter said.

Simultaneously Rory and Riss said, "Yes?"

More laughter. The light burned the night. It looked like the tunnel to bright death. Rory tented a hand over her eyes. Riss swept a stray hair from her forehead and lowered her chin, Princess Diana–like, and faced the camera.

The reporter said, "What was it like in there?"

"Hellish," Rory said.

Riss put an arm around her shoulder and squeezed and leaned her head against Rory's. Jesus Christ.

The reporter stuck the microphone in Rory's face. "Did you fear for your life?"

"It was a nightmare." She put up a hand. "Please, no more questions."

Riss said, "Give my cousin a break. She's

had a tough day."

Rory ducked around the reporter. The cameras and lights tried to follow, but she swerved into the crowd.

Riss clung to the sleeve of her sweater. "Hang on."

Rory kept going, trying to shake loose. Riss called to the reporter, "She'll feel better tomorrow. Call me."

Rory broke from the crowd. Riss pulled her to a stop. "Wait."

The laughter had abated. Her eyes looked dark. "Sounds like you had a wild ride in there."

"And I'm completely rode into the ground. If I talk anymore, I'm going to lose it. Bad."

Riss gave her a cool once-over. "I came down here to see if you were okay. Guess I didn't need to. You've locked it down as tight as ever."

Two years since Rory had seen her. Two long, peaceful years. No drama, no subterfuge, no fear.

She nodded tersely. "Thanks for coming, Riss."

Riss let a silence grow. "Sure. Right. Go home, bolt the door. But tomorrow you should talk to that reporter. It's never a good idea to turn your back on people who set the agenda."

Petra came jogging through scattered onlookers. When she saw Riss, she slowed.

Riss raised her chin in greeting. "Petra. It's like gym class all over again. I'll let you two get on with it."

She walked away. Petra watched her go, horrified.

An onlooker raised a cell phone to snap a picture. Rory grabbed Petra's hand and bee-lined away from the police station before the guy could post the photo as a status update or run to Vegas to hock it on *Pawn Stars.* She meant to keep her face blank and disappear from the scene without a further word. But Petra said, "Hey," and tugged her to a stop, and the next thing Rory knew, she was hugging her friend, hard.

"You don't know how glad I am to see you," she managed.

"Jesus, girl." Petra squeezed her tight. "You had me scared."

Rory clutched her, overwhelmed, embarrassed at her neediness, unable to let go. "Thank you so much. For being here."

"Hush." Petra leaned back and put a hand to Rory's cheek. The bangles on her wrists flicked with reflected light. She seemed cool and completely in control, but her palm felt hot.

"I thought I might never see you again. Goddamn it, Aurora. You make people do the strangest things. I actually prayed today. On my fucking knees."

Rory was shaking but nearly laughed. "I hope you got video. I'd pay hard cash to see that."

Petra knew how to say the right thing at any moment. She had a gift Rory lacked: She could talk effortlessly to any human being on the planet. Even when it was talk of near death. Petra could be outré and absent-minded to the point of dreaminess. She had a huge laugh that always seemed startled and delighted. She was a third-grade teacher at West River Elementary School. And she had opened her home when Rory got laid off and landed back on U.S. soil, broke, exhausted, and lost. She welcomed her with tequila and a banner that read, WHERE'S THE MONEY YOU OWE ME?

And right then, she was trembling. "You okay?"

"Nowhere close to it. But I'm not hurt. I just need to get out of here."

"Let's scoot. Couple of people waiting to see you." Holding Rory's elbow, she headed along the sidewalk. Her boot heels clacked on the concrete. "What the hell was Riss doing here?"

"Arranging for our close-up."

"Unbelievable."

Petra shot a hand in the air, whistled through her teeth, and waved.

Across the street, Rory's parents were huddled at the edge of the park, facing the police station. At Petra's whistle, they turned. A knot the size of a golf ball lodged in Rory's throat. She ran across the street.

Samantha Mackenzie's hand went to her mouth. Will Mackenzie grabbed her arm, and together they strode toward Rory.

For once Sam didn't smile. Didn't offer her slow, sweet grin. She swept Rory into her arms. "Thank God. Sweetheart, thank God."

"I'm fine," Rory said. "Absolutely fine."

Will wrapped his arms around the both of them. "Of course you are," he said. "It's that tough Mackenzie Highland blood."

She struggled to keep her voice even. "Thank God you guys didn't come to the courthouse this morning to watch the trial."

Samantha was small and tanned and hardy in the way of women who dug gardens and hiked the hills. Her face, creased with smile lines, looked drawn.

"All those times we worried about you overseas, who would have thought —"

"Sam," Will said.

Overhead the news helicopter droned with the subtlety of a chainsaw. Its spotlight drew a meandering circle across the ground.

"Let's go," Rory said, and nodded at the media. "Before the chopper picks us out as targets for the walking dead."

Her dad clamped an arm around her shoulder and led the group away from the police station. Sam slid one arm around Rory's waist and the other around Petra's.

"I can't believe the cops kept you so long," Will said.

"You must be starved," Samantha said. "You girls come over. I'll cook up a big mess of chili." Her drawl, as always when she was under pressure, intensified.

"I want to go home and take a shower," Rory said.

Her mom glanced up, concerned. Sam was always quick to look concerned. "Darlin', you need to eat."

Rory felt like she'd been in the path of a tornado. Somehow she was still standing, but a blunt and roaring force had stripped bark off the trees and reduced the landscape to splinters.

"Thanks. Really. But I need to wash this day off of me."

Her mom forced a smile. "Okay, sugar. You get home and see your new baby."

Rory glanced at Petra. Her friend didn't look up, didn't even react.

Her dad squeezed Rory's shoulder. "You want to talk about it?"

"Yes, but not now." She squeezed him back. "I'm sorry I worried you."

He stared straight ahead. Gathering his thoughts, she knew. Will Mackenzie rarely spoke off the cuff. He considered his words before speaking. The habit came, she thought, from years spent as a forest ranger. All that time among silent giants, trees that had centuries to live — what was the hurry? She sometimes thought that if he didn't have to, he wouldn't say anything at all. If you don't talk, nobody can pin your words to you later on.

Finally he shook his head. "If you think you were the one causing us worry today, you need to study up on logic."

She leaned against him. He kissed the top of her head. Then he looked over his shoulder.

"They after us?" she said.

"You never know."

They were a block from the police station. The street had quieted to near desertion. Rory felt a compulsion to pick up her pace.

The stars were out and the moon was up. Everybody's breath frosted the night air.

She felt watched from all angles, from the dark beyond the streetlights, from the recesses beyond corners and in the depths beyond trees in the park. A truck was parked on a cross street, lights off. In the cab, backlit by a streetlight, she saw a man's silhouette.

The wind brushed over her thin sweater and her skin shrank. She needed to get home, needed to get under hot water, needed to take off these clothes and burn them.

Detective Zelinski's voice whispered in her head. *What did the gunmen want?*

They wanted something from her. They hadn't gotten it.

And if they were working with outside forces, it meant somebody else was still out there. Still wanting whatever it was.

"I'm okay, I swear," she said. "I love you guys. But I need to get home."

And lock the door.

As the police station spit out hostages one at a time to cheers and paparazzi flashes, half a block away, protected by shadows, the truck sat idling at the curb. It was a heavy Mack truck with a winch on the back and RANSOM RIVER AUTO SALVAGE painted on the doors. It had an engine big enough to pull a crashed DC-7 out of a gully. And it had a police scanner under the dash. Boone Mackenzie hung his arms over the steering wheel and watched through a cloud of cigarette smoke.

Rory and her little buddy Petra and Uncle Will and Aunt Samantha. Walking down the middle of the street in the dark like they were four bowling pins, primed for a strike.

And his stepsister, walking away, but pausing to turn and stare. Like Rory was the Holy Grail. Like she was the living model for the voodoo doll Riss kept on the shelf back home.

Three weeks Rory had been back in Ransom River, and already it was starting again.

Cousin Aurora, with the sweet bod and the twisted heart. Who looked at him like he was transparent. Who thought she was too good for this town, swore she was gone for good, but here she was. She didn't look so smart now, did she?

Seven hours she'd been in the police station, talking to the cops. What did she know that took seven hours to tell?

The police scanner had caught stray chatter from the cops during the siege. Five million bucks in gold bullion. That's what the gunmen had demanded. Five damned million in shiny gold bricks. It didn't add up.

Five million and a helicopter ride to Mexico? It sounded like a joke.

He figured he hadn't heard everything on the scanner. This thing — the siege and then the shootout in the courtroom — it was big. Riss had started to tell him on the phone, before the TV crew interrupted her: Things had gone to hell in the courtroom, gotten crazy, a nightmare.

No, the gunmen had asked for plenty more than he'd heard about. And Rory had heard every word. She'd heard enough to talk about for seven hours. He took a drag from his Winston. Smoke lazed through the cab of the wrecker.

In the distance, in the trees apart from the crowd, a man moved. Casual and confident. From the shadows the man watched Riss walk away.

"Fuck me," Boone said. "No way."

Not the guy he ever thought he'd see here, and nobody he needed to talk to. He put the wrecker in reverse. Lights off, he drove away.

14

The sun cut through the blinds, low and gold. With a scratching sound the latch turned and the bedroom door burst open. Rory came awake in a rush. The dog bolted in, paws clattering on the hardwood, straight at her bed.

"Chiba, no," she said.

He skidded up, whining a welcome, and stuck his nose in her face.

He was a Husky–Australian shepherd mix, blue eyed and half-deaf because of neglect as a puppy. She'd found him abandoned one day when she was on a run. He was limping along a road outside of town, a bit like her. She took him home. He was now healthy, loyal, and crazy. He jumped around her and licked her neck.

She hugged him and buried her face in his fur. "Hello, you nightmare."

His tail battered the air. He always greeted her as if she'd been rescued from a mineshaft, and she appreciated the unconditional attention. With him she didn't need to put up her guard. Chiba had no agenda.

Petra appeared in the doorway, mug in hand, wearing a T-shirt and men's boxers emblazoned with *Polly wants a cocktail.*

"Coffee's hot," she said.

"Thanks." Rory fought her way out of the covers. She was stiff and sore.

"You turned your phone off, I presume."

Rory pressed the heels of her hands against her eyes. "How many calls?"

"Fifteen on the machine. Mostly people who saw you on TV. I left a vodka bottle on the kitchen counter. Feel free to add it to your coffee."

Under the slatted golden sunlight, the room looked less like a garret and more like a cubbyhole. Rory had unpacked some mementos. A brass Thai Buddha. Books — *The Great Gatsby, Bangkok 8, The Making of the Atomic Bomb.* Snapshots with kids from the school where she'd volunteered in Thailand, the girls bright and shy. A photo taken near Bulawayo, her kneeling next to young Grace. Grace, strong little arms squeezing Rory around the neck. A framed photo of her with her mom and dad. Another with her uncle Lee. He'd left Ransom River when she was a young girl, and she

143

missed his confidence and mischievous smile.

Chiba parked himself in front of her, tail wagging. When she ignored him, he put his head on her knee and groaned, peering up at her with the mournful eyes of a Goya martyr. Rory scratched the ruff of his neck.

Petra leaned against the door. "Your baby."

Rory didn't look up. "Thank you for keeping a poker face when my mom said that."

"Poker face? That's nothing. Outside these doors, you live a poker *life.*"

"Maybe someday I'll talk to her about it. But not now." She glanced up. "Besides, why shouldn't I play my cards close to the vest? It's how I was raised."

"You Mackenzies. You'd fit in at the NSA. For all I know, you're your own little spy network. Or international jewel thieves. You could have liquidated an entire Al-Qaeda cell and buried them in the orchard and I'd never know it."

"Plus we're terrible cooks."

Petra held her mug with both hands. "It's okay. If you want to talk about yesterday, talk. If you don't, don't. Either way, I'm here."

"Thank you."

She felt a swell of affection for her friend, and the tug of her nerves tightening. She stood and went to the window and raised the blinds.

Sunlight shone through the leaves of the avocado trees in the backyard. Petra's place was a two-story farmhouse near the end of a road dotted with funky old homes. The neighborhood was guarded by orange trees and weighty pines, and butted up against the dry foothills at the northern edge of the city. Beyond the back wall, empty fields of yellowed grass led to lemon and avocado orchards. Rows of trees curved neatly over hillsides, vivid green. Beyond, the mountains rose, rocky and blue, outlined crisply against the sky.

Rory said, "Remember my worst-case-scenario game?"

As a teenager, she used to panic at the thought of things going wrong. At the starting line before a race, she would nearly freak out. *What if I lose? Doom,* she thought. Shame. Expulsion from school. Poverty. Economic collapse, bread riots, flying monkeys attacking from the sky. Until, one day, about to vomit with nerves, she thought, *What's* really *the worst that could happen?* Would she be dragged to the center of the football field and burned at the stake? No. She'd have to look at some other runner's ass accelerating away from her. Big deal.

145

Since then, when faced with a challenging situation, she always asked, *Worst-case scenario?* And generally, the worst was not apocalyptic. Not slavery, prostitution, tattoos, or a job at the drive-through window at Arby's. Yet.

Of course, some scenarios had turned out worse than she'd thought possible. Briefly she heard a shriek of metal and had a vision of sudden endings — of plans, love, possibilities. She forced it away.

"When I got called to jury duty, I asked myself, what's the worst that can happen? And I thought, I'll have to decide the fate of two people charged with murder and bear the weight of that decision. I miscalculated."

"No reason 'taken hostage' should have come up on your worst-case dartboard," Petra said.

"That's not the worst case." She turned. "The cops think I was working with the gunmen."

Petra lowered her mug. "Girl, what the fuck?"

"They have video of the siege. And . . ." Her head pounded. "The gunmen chose people to go with them. Me. I thought it was random, but apparently not."

"What does that mean?"

"That's the problem. I don't know. And

I'm scared."

"The cops are scaring all the hostages, I'll bet. Rory, it's a dirty trick."

"I don't think so."

"They're hard-case cops. They think the gunmen were working with an inside man, so they try to frighten the shit out of all the hostages by accusing them of complicity."

Hard-case cops. Memory flickered again. Seth Colder, Mr. Once-upon-a-Hard-Case himself.

Petra said, "The cops probably have no clue what happened, so they accuse everybody to see if anyone freaks and confesses. It's a dirty, low-down trick. Christ, Aurora. Do you really think you're so special?"

Rory had to laugh. "Maybe not."

But she recalled the grainy courtroom video. Reagan, stepping across prone bodies, aiming straight at her.

She said, "Last night I put in a call to one of my old law profs. David Goldstein — he was my advisor at UCLA. I left a message telling him I need a referral to an attorney."

"You're an attorney."

"But not a fool. I need a criminal lawyer."

For a second she felt leaden. How could she afford to hire somebody competent, who might want several thousand bucks up front as a retainer? Sell her car? How much could she even get for a beat-up Subaru? *Fall seven times, stand up eight.* She didn't want to admit that she'd been knocked down again. More like bitch-slapped into a wall.

Petra crossed to her side. "It's going to be okay." She put a hand on her back. "Come on. Get coffee. The messages are on the machine. Including one from your aunt."

"What?"

"Your aunt Amber called. Worried, wants to know all about it."

Rory's mouth slowly fell open. "Every time I think I've considered the worst case, the world creates a scenario beyond my imagination."

Downstairs in the kitchen, Rory listened to the messages on the machine. Friends had called, and high school cross-country competitors. Former Peace Corps colleagues. A law school classmate.

"This thing is damned huge," she said.

"I thought you knew that."

The courthouse siege had to be the loudest thing to happen in Ransom River in decades. The city hated loud. Within Rory's memory there were few comparable criminal outbursts — the hijacking of a gasoline tanker, an arson fire that leveled an entire subdivision under construction, the armored car heist that put the city in the news when she was a kid.

"Do I want to turn on the television?" she said.

Petra gathered her lesson plans from the kitchen table. "You're the star of the day, whether you like it or not. Do you want to hear what they're saying?"

She had to expect media attention. It was Southern California, where live criminal confrontation got higher TV ratings than hockey. And why not? Shootouts were cheaper to film than game shows. No sets, no salaries, no releases for contestants to sign.

She downed her coffee and aimed the remote at the television. Then, reluctantly, she played the last message on the machine.

"Aurora, it's your aunt Amber. I saw you on the TV and talked to Nerissa. I can't believe you were in that courtroom."

Amber's voice was raspy. It sounded like Virginia Slims.

"Anyhow, I wanted to know all about it. You take care, honey."

Rory pressed Delete.

Petra said, "Told you. You're a celebrity."

"And she's hoping it'll rub off on her and her kids."

Petra gave her a tart look.

"You heard her — she talked to Riss. Who put on an Emmy-winning performance last night," Rory said.

"That was bizarre."

"That was calculated. Riss has an angle. Guaranteed. One that has her at the focal point." *And me in her sights.* "With Riss it's always win-lose. My rule is to treat her like she's a grenade with a pin that's been pulled."

It had always been that way. She tried to remember a time when it hadn't. Maybe when Uncle Lee had been around.

On the television, catastrophic music erupted. Orchestral melodrama. A fanfare of menace. A red title burst across the screen: *Courthouse Siege: Nightmare in Ransom River.*

It was a news special, recapping the attack. Rory shut off the TV. "I gotta get away from this."

"Where are you going?" Petra said.

"Running."

15

Then

"Hand me that wrench."

Rory dug through the toolbox. Uncle Lee waited with his hand out. She lifted the wrench and set it on his palm.

He grinned. "Thanks, princess."

She smiled, to the bottom of her shoes. Six-year-olds didn't usually get to tune up a car. But Uncle Lee was letting her help him with the El Camino. His grin made her feel like she could float.

The car was in the shed. The shed was like a little barn, on the dirt road out on the acreage her parents owned near the edge of town. The El Camino was her dad's car from when he was in high school. It was red and had muscles and he kept it in the shed under a tarp. He said it was going to be Rory's when she got her driver's license. That would be in ten years. She would be a *teenager.* The car was huge, and her dad was in the driver's seat, watching Uncle Lee turn the wrench.

The puppy ran around her feet, sniffing the dirt. She picked him up and he squirmed and licked her chin.

Lee tightened a bolt. "Where'd you find that thing, Aurora?"

"By the river. He was hiding under a cardboard box. Somebody left him there."

Lee heard the quiver in her voice and looked up. She swallowed. His eyes softened.

He shook his head. "Always collecting strays. That's you."

She bent and nuzzled the puppy and hid her face. After a second, she said, "His name's Pepper."

Her dad called from the car. "She wanted to call him Pokémon. I said no way."

Lee leaned over the engine and frowned at it like it was a bad dog. He made a circle in the air with his hand.

"Crank it, Will."

Rory's dad turned on the car.

With the hood raised, the noise was loud. Angry almost. Rory pressed the puppy to her chest and put a hand over his ears. The engine shook, like it wanted to jump out of the car. The fan belt squeaked and spun and the carburetor shimmied.

Lee nodded. He straightened and wiped his hands on a grease rag. He handed the wrench back to Rory.

"Perfect. You could make a fast getaway in this, princess."

She giggled.

Uncle Lee was a jack-of-all-trades. He said that meant he didn't have a boss. It meant he could do any job. Her dad said not every job was worth doing — or legal.

Her dad left the engine running and got out of the El Camino. He stuck his head under the hood and clapped Lee on the back.

"Got her. Thanks."

"No problem," Lee said.

Lee was bigger than her dad even though he was the little brother. He tossed aside the grease rag and got behind the wheel himself and gunned the motor. Rory put her hands over Pepper's ears again.

Her dad said, "Don't worry. We're going to keep this car tuned up for you."

From the driver's seat, Lee beckoned her with one finger, *Come here.* His smile seemed sneaky.

Rory set Pepper down and climbed into the passenger side.

"Close the door," Lee said.

She pulled hard and it creaked and shut.

He closed the driver's door. Leaned out the window.

"Will, put down the hood. I'll take her for a test drive."

Will lowered the hood and pressed it carefully shut, not slamming it. Lee gave him a salute and put the car in gear. He eased it out of the shed into the sunlight. It sounded to Rory like a space fighter, rattling and powering up.

Lee held on to the gearshift and nudged the El Camino over the rough gravel drive. He pulled onto the road and stopped. Looked at her and smiled again. He was good at smiling. It made her feel like something exciting was about to turn her day into a surprise. It made her heart beat hard in her chest. Like she was in on a secret.

"Want to drive?" he said.

She inhaled so loud it sounded like a gasp, like the movies.

"It's gonna be your car, your dad says."

"It's his car now."

"Yeah. He gets all the good stuff. I just help out," he said.

She looked up at him. He kept smiling.

"He got *you,*" he said, and tickled her. Then he said, "The car's yours. You oughta drive it."

She blinked. He patted his knee.

She scrambled onto his lap. He wrapped his arms around her. He was strong and always made her know she could trust him. They were a twosome, he said. Uncle Lee had kids of his own, but he always made special time for Rory. She didn't have brothers or sisters. She was an only. And he made her feel like she was his best friend.

The steering wheel was hot when she put her hands on it.

"You just hold tight and steer straight," he said. "Okay?"

"Okay."

He put his arms around her and touched the bottom of the wheel with two fingers. That was all. He pointed up the road.

"Know what that is?" he said.

"The national forest."

He laughed. It didn't sound funny, though.

"That's the horizon. That's a boundary. You gotta think about what's on the other side."

She nodded. She didn't know what he was talking about.

"Your dad says this'll be your car. He means it'll be here, and if you stick around, it'll be available. It's what's called a bribe," he said.

She shrugged. She didn't understand.

"It's bait," Lee said. "Crawl into the trap to get it, the trap snaps shut behind you. Boom."

She held on to the wheel. She waited for him to say something that made sense and didn't leave her feeling . . . worried.

"Out there," he said, "that's the world. That's the real deal. The Show. Ransom River, that's the hamster wheel. You understand?"

She nodded, though she didn't.

Lee laughed. "Lesson number one, Aurora. What people give you becomes a debt. What you take is yours. Claim it. Get your own."

He looked in the rearview mirror. It was too high for Rory to see, so she turned and looked out the back window. Behind them, Will Mackenzie had walked out to the end of the gravel drive. He stood in the road, hands on his hips, looking at the Elco.

"There's Dad," she said.

What she meant was *He'll get mad.*

Behind her dad, from the shadows in the shed, her cousin Riss walked out into the sun. She stared at the car. The stuffed bear in her hand dropped to the dirt.

Lee said, "Hold tight. Don't swerve."

Rory gripped the wheel. He put it in gear and jammed his foot on the gas pedal.

This time Rory gasped for real. The car accelerated and it seemed like it was a real rocket, and she was steering it with the road zooming underneath the wheels.

"No holds barred, princess," Lee shouted. "It's a circus out there. Lights and wild animals and walking the high wire without a net. Don't let 'em shut the cage door on you. Get out there and star in the show."

She nodded and held on to the wheel and felt the El Camino gain speed. Lee laughed. The wind furrowed the car and blew her hair around her face.

16

An hour, Rory figured. Just pound the trails. She checked the clock. Seven forty-five. She had to be at the courthouse at nine thirty.

She dressed for a cold-weather run. She clamped her gloves between her teeth, swept her hair back into a ponytail, and stepped out into a nippy morning that smelled of gardenias and jasmine. The plum trees near the porch rustled in the breeze. A chill sped up her back. The street was empty.

She paused, but only for a moment. She couldn't let fear cage her. *Do it.*

She whistled. "Chiba, come."

The dog rushed out the door and jumped in circles around her. With him bounding along at her side, she headed out into the early light.

Running cured almost everything. It eased pain; it exhilarated; it served as penance and validation. It turned *lone wolf* into a compliment. Running was objective — the stopwatch never lied. Races judged competitors on how long and hard they could run fast, not on a coach's decision to play favorites with the starting lineup. Running was pure.

It could do everything but get her out of this town for good.

Her breath frosted the air. As always since the accident, in cold weather her right leg ached and her hip felt stiff. She headed slowly out of the neighborhood, fighting the urge to limp. But after a mile she warmed up. She quickened her pace. Chiba loped alongside her. When she passed the orchards, she took the river trail.

Ransom River flowed out of the national forest in the mountains north of the city. The trail was a gravel frontage road above its banks. Below Rory, willows dragged slim limbs in the water.

In dry months, the river drizzled along the valley floor. But the autumn had been rainy, and now water rushed noisily over rocks and creek grass. After downpours the river would swell to a crazed muddy flood. To control it the city had concreted the riverbed for three miles and fenced it off. Along one stretch they'd driven the river underground into a storm drain and constructed a neighborhood over it. She could see it in the distance, overinflated beige houses with fourteen-foot cathedral ceilings and postage-stamp lawns, packed side by side. A *Poltergeist* neighborhood — cheap gaudy dream houses piled together, like in the movie. Maybe not built over ancient burial grounds, but still draining to the spirit.

She could run this trail blindfolded. She'd run it since she was fifteen. She loved it — and hated the fact that she was running it today.

For two years, she thought she'd made it out. She had grabbed a job by her fingernails and flown away without a look back. She'd healed. And Helsinki had been amazing. Lonely as hell, but beautiful. The summer sun rose at one a.m. and set at eleven p.m., and so she had run. At first, that's all she'd wanted to do. Run, all night long, through birch forests and along the harbor past the Russian Orthodox cathedral. Running helped her forget. It proved that she had recovered. It proved she could leave the rest behind. The part that snapped in the wind, sheets like ghosts.

The trail rose. She dug in. Chiba paced her. In the distance, somewhere downtown, the sound of a siren floated on the chilly breeze.

What the hell had the courthouse attackers been after?

Maybe they hated the defendants. Hated them for being cops. Hated them for killing Brad Mirkovic.

Brad was no Cub Scout. He'd had run-ins with the police and issues with drugs and alcohol. He was a punk. *P-u-n-k,* spelled out in diamond-flecked letters. So at first, public sympathy lay solidly with Jared Smith and Lucy Elmendorf. Spoiled son of a rich crook attacks a cop and his partner, in the cop's own home, and gets shot? Instant karma.

Then Samuel Koh walked into Ransom River police headquarters with a CCTV video that captured the killing, and things changed.

It became known that Brad Mirkovic had caught the defendants in bed. And that, on a double-dare, he decided to snap a souvenir photo of Smith and Elmendorf banging out a rhythm to beat the USC marching band. But he forgot about the automatic flash on his phone's camera.

In the screaming aftermath, Brad fled. He clutched his phone and the incriminating photo, and he ran to the kitchen and threw open the back door and staggered into Smith's backyard.

Which exposed Lie Number One in the

defendants' story.

Brad was outside when he was shot. Not in the kitchen. Not attacking Jared Smith head-on.

The police had not released images from the video. But based on its contents, Smith and Elmendorf were arrested and charged with murder. Soon after, the harassment campaign started against Koh. Then the dead boy's father gave a string of interviews claiming the "city political machine" planned to rig the trial. The case became a swamp of gossip and conspiracy theory.

Into all of that, the jury summons had pitched Rory headfirst. And then the courthouse had been attacked. None of it made sense.

She got to the top of the Pinnacles in twenty-five minutes. She didn't stop to enjoy the view of the city and the valley. She turned around and came down fast, letting the rhythm of the run drown out everything that threatened to overwhelm her.

When the road flattened she forced the pace. Chiba ran easily at her side, steady and relaxed.

She was a block from Petra's house when a black Suburban pulled alongside her. It slowed to match her speed. Its windows were tinted dark and reflected the glare of the morning sun. Gunning the engine, it screeched ahead of her and stopped.

Oh God. Rory pulled up sharply. She grabbed her keys and stuck them through her fingers like claws.

"Chiba," she said.

The Suburban's passenger door opened. Out climbed a man wearing a funereal suit over two hundred pounds of steroid-marinated muscle.

Rory backed up. *"Chiba."*

The man shook his head. "Don't, Rory. Grigor Mirkovic has a question for you."

17

Rory scanned the street. Aside from the black Suburban, it was deserted. Her nerves fired, an adrenaline Morse code tap-tap-tapping through her veins. Chiba darted to her side. She backed up another step.

Grigor Mirkovic knew her name and where she lived.

The stump in the black suit stood in the open door of the Suburban. "Mr. Mirkovic needs answers from you. Stop right there."

Rory turned and ran. Sprinting, flat out, zero to *hauling ass* in half a second.

"Not smart, lady," the man called.

Across the street was a house with the curtains open, TV flickering in the living room. She ran straight to the door and pounded on it with the flat of her palm.

"Help," she called. "It's your neighbor, Rory Mackenzie. Please."

Nobody answered. Inside, the television blared — the damned theme from *Court-*

She shot a glance over her shoulder. The man was walking toward her. Despite his bulk he moved with slick fluidity. His skin was tanned and shiny, his features so flat as to be vestigial. He looked like a six-foot night crawler in Armani.

The next house was a hundred yards away. Rory dashed for it, fumbling in her pocket for her phone. Chiba sprang happily at her side. The engine of the Suburban dropped into gear.

Grigor Mirkovic knew full well not to contact a juror from his son's case. He shouldn't have known her full name. And he should never have been able to find her address.

Ahead of her was a windbreak of tall pines. Beyond it, the road curved. A car rounded the bend. She dashed toward it, waving her arms.

"Stop. Help me —"

The driver's mouth went round with surprise. He swerved and raced away.

The Suburban pulled alongside her, cruising up the wrong side of the road. The Nightcrawler stood in the passenger-side doorframe, braced against the open door, and stared blankly at her across the roof of the vehicle.

"When Mr. Mirkovic asks a question, you don't run away. You listen. And you answer him," he said.

And fricking e-mail wasn't good enough for Mirkovic?

Grigor Mirkovic owned nightclubs and a construction firm in Los Angeles. He was in the cocktail and nail-gun and concrete business. He was also rumored to be in the labor business, smuggling people over the border. Mirkovic had immigrated to California himself, from Serbia, and had all the go-get-'em traits that turned poor boys into success stories. Especially poor boys willing to break the law, and do it well armed and without remorse.

And she knew that his men in the SUV weren't going door to door on his behalf, selling plywood and roofing shingles.

The Suburban paralleled her. Ahead, seventy yards away, a Civic was parked in a driveway. She knew the woman who lived there, Andi Garcia. Rory aimed for the house and groped her phone, trying to unlock it and call 9-1-1.

The Nightcrawler watched her, his face callous. Or bored. "Mr. Mirkovic has one question for you. Did you know the gunmen were coming yesterday?"

She didn't slow down. Her shadow fled

ahead of her like a spike.

"Who got to you? Jared Smith? Lucy Elmendorf's husband? The Police Benevolent Association?"

Breathlessly, she said, "That's five questions, you prick."

The driver's window buzzed down. A slab of meat sat behind the wheel, aviator shades pinging with the morning sun. "Run your mouth all you want, but this thing can chase you to Vegas."

Ahead, a brown Chrysler wallowed around the bend in the road. It was confronted head-on by the Suburban. The driver braked harshly.

The Suburban swerved across the road. The Nightcrawler ducked inside. The driver stepped on the gas and roared away.

Rory turned to the Chrysler, her chest heaving. *Thank God,* she thought.

Detective Xavier climbed out.

Xavier watched the Suburban whine out of sight around the curve in the road. She had the Chrysler's police radio in her hand. "Who was that?"

Rory couldn't believe it. The worst-case scenario was turning out to be a joke book. She put her hands on her knees and tried to catch her breath.

"They said they work for Grigor Mirkovic."

"What did they want?"

Chiba trotted over, his tongue hanging out, and nuzzled Rory's side. Some guard dog. She straightened. "Why are you here?"

Xavier was freshly repackaged for the morning shift. Her pantsuit was navy blue, her sunglasses flat gray. The gun on her hip was the color of a shark.

"Why don't you tell me what's going on?" she said.

Rory had previously invoked her right to counsel. Xavier shouldn't have been there. Shouldn't be asking questions. And if Rory started talking, Xavier could claim she'd waived her Fifth Amendment rights. But to keep silent would only make things worse.

"That Suburban drove up and a guy jumped out who said Grigor Mirkovic had a question for me. He wanted to know if the Police Benevolent Association has me on its payroll," she said. "I didn't answer. I ran."

Xavier put the radio away.

"How'd he get my name?" Rory said. "How'd he find out where I live?"

"Maybe you told him."

"Please don't." Rory tried to keep her voice calm, but heard the glittering, glass edge in it. "If he found me, he may have already found other jurors. Or Judge Wieland's family, or Cary Oberlin's."

Xavier hesitated for a moment, as though considering whether to press her advantage on a distraught and breathless woman. "Did they threaten you?"

"They weren't here to stick happy-hour coupons through mail slots. They said nobody ignores Grigor Mirkovic. When I ran they offered to chase me to Nevada."

"Because you know what it looked like," Xavier said.

Rory didn't want to play this game. "Tell me, Detective."

Her voice was clipped. Xavier glanced away. Looked back.

"Like yet another instance of bad guys having a strained conversation with you."

"It wasn't a conversation. They followed me. They intimidated me. I don't know them. I've never spoken to, written to, or spit at Grigor Mirkovic. And Jesus, if you can't tell a scared witness from an accomplice, God help you."

Xavier gave her an inscrutable, reflective-shades look. *These cops,* Rory thought, *with their smoked glass and mirrors.* It creeped her out.

"Is it true you called one of our officers

an asshole yesterday?" Xavier said.

Rory slumped.

"You got a problem with cops? Because the court might find that interesting."

"No problem with cops."

"Just with detectives?" Xavier said.

"Say again?"

"People remember you dating Seth Colder."

The chilly air tingled on Rory's face. "Good for them."

"Interesting that you both split town around the same time."

Like she wanted to stick around after the accident? "Breakups don't involve a victory parade. People just drive away and don't wave good-bye."

Her voice was cool, but inside, a filament had begun to heat.

Xavier seemed bemused. "Curious that he hasn't been back."

Rory had a million things she could say, and not one she wanted to mention to this woman. And one question she dared not ask: *What happened to him?*

"Did Colder ever tell you why he quit the force?" Xavier said. "Because some folks in the department would still like a clear explanation."

"I was working halfway around the world

when he left the force. I heard it third-hand. I haven't talked to him about it."

And why did Seth matter? Was Xavier just trying to provoke her? "Why did you come out here?"

"To give you a heads-up. Townie to townie. Detective Zelinski plans to apply for warrants on you. Search warrant for the premises where you live, and an arrest warrant for conspiracy and felony murder."

Rory held as still as the trees. Inside, the filament shattered into flailing streams. *The Thing.* If this were a horror movie, Xavier would have been torn to shreds.

"He doesn't have probable cause," she said.

"The courthouse is a mess. It'll take twenty-four hours for him to get the application before a magistrate. So figure you have till tomorrow this time before he comes up your driveway with cuffs. If you'd like to avoid a scene, I suggest you turn yourself in before then."

Rory kept her face blank. "Is that all?"

Xavier got back in the car. "It ought to be enough."

Rory walked the rest of the way back to the house. The blue Southern California sky, perfect and empty, seemed to drain the energy from her. Chiba walked at her side, head down, panting.

She climbed the steps to the porch and fumbled with her keys. She had to do something. But what?

The voice, coming from the sidewalk behind her, was quiet. "Rory."

She stared at the keys. They hovered an inch from the lock. She could get inside and shut the door in four seconds, maybe five. She could slam the door without saying a word.

The silence behind her was freighted. She turned around.

He stood on the sidewalk, hands at his sides, waiting.

She said, "Hello, Seth."

18

He looked the same, and not. Taller, weirdly. His shoulders had that same tilt, not exactly a pose, but an attitude. A stance that said, *Yeah, right. Prove it to me. I'm not buying your bullshit.*

But the smile, the fearless grin that had always taken the sting out of the attitude — that was missing. His sandy hair was short. He had lines around his eyes that hadn't been there two years earlier. The planes of his face, of his physique, seemed more sharply defined. He'd lost weight.

He looked uncertain. She thought if she snapped her fingers, she might blow him out like a candle.

Seth Colder, the center that did not hold.

"Knew it would be sometime. Didn't think it would be today," she said.

"Can I come in?"

"Tell me why."

"Better if I do that inside."

She looked at the keys, for someplace to rest her gaze other than on him. *Not now,* she thought. Not like this: unprepared. Two years she hadn't seen him, spoken to him, written to him. And yet, yesterday in the courtroom, she had found his image welling up in front of her. She felt like she had god-damned conjured him here.

Chiba padded to his side, tail wagging. Seth scratched the ruff of his neck. His gaze stayed steady on her.

She unlocked the door and let him in.

His walk was familiar. A long, slow stride. His jeans were scuffed, his Caterpillar boots covered with dust. She didn't recognize the denim work shirt or the white T-shirt beneath it.

She shut the door. "How did you find me?"

He kept walking, a tactic she remembered. It gave him time, it drew out the suspense, and it drove her mad. The tilt of his shoulders remained. He held himself tightly. He looked around at the house.

Too much like the cop he had been. Everything was evidence.

"Seth."

He paused by the mantel to examine a photo of Rory's parents. He had an eerie ability to hold himself stationary, and so silent that he seemed a black hole, swallowing light.

That stillness had always been a trick. And it was a useful trick for a cop. Open a conversation, pose an awkward or aggressive question, then shut up. Let the other person grow anxious in the silence. Until they finally filled it and revealed all kinds of things. But beneath the silence Seth had always run hot, and sometimes ragged.

"Why are you here?" she said.

Where have you been? How can you look so good and so bad at the same time?

"I saw the siege on the news." His voice, always deep, had a new edge. "I saw you."

She didn't answer. He glanced at her shirt. It was an old cross-country T-shirt that said, *My sport is your sport's punishment.* It was stuck to her with sweat.

"You —" He cleared his throat. "You ran long this morning?"

"Six miles."

He nodded. "Glad you're — good to know you're running. Great. A hundred percent great."

The last time she'd seen him, he was on his knees in the middle of the road, covered in glass and blood, much of it hers. She had a crack in her femur and a compound fracture of the tibia. He had a gash in his forehead. He'd cut it on the frame of his pickup when he climbed out through the window. Climbed without looking, without thinking about broken glass. That was him back then: rash. Throwing himself into things wholeheartedly, foolhardily, was his modus operandi. That's why he'd answered a police emergency call in the first place, with her in the truck. He had turned his entire existence into a police emergency call.

She hadn't spoken to him since that night, since the minutes after the crash when he tried to rescue and comfort her. Worse had come, she had heard, though Petra had only vague details. *Nearly killed,* Petra had said. End of his career in the Ransom River Police Department.

Where have you been? The question caught in her throat. She wasn't going to ask. Not when she had been the one who bolted town without telling him good-bye. Not when she'd gotten over him. She took a tall glass from the cupboard, filled it with water, and poured it into Chiba's dish. The dog put his head down and drank noisily.

Seth said, "Where'd you run?"

"The river trail."

A wistful smile crossed his face. The river. The old times, the *back before.* The smile quickly ebbed, as if caught in an undertow.

The place had dark memories too.

"How are you, Aurora?"

She set the glass on the counter. How much courage did it take for him to ask that question?

"I'm broke," she said. "I just got canned. The charity I worked for lost its funding. I've got steel screws in my right leg but last week I clocked five K in nineteen minutes. Yesterday I watched Judge Wieland get shot by a vigilante with shitty aim. That guy then got a hole blasted through his chest by a shotgun. One of the gunmen had his head blown out twelve inches from my face. The cops think I was doing a Texas two-step with the guy and that I'm in his rooting section. And just before you turned up, Grigor Mirkovic's pot roasts tried to scare me into confessing I screwed the trial over out of love for the cops." She smiled. "I'm great."

His face was grave. "Grigor Mirkovic's men?"

"For carnivorous worms, they looked good in coat and tie."

He said nothing. Her pulse had picked up. She was on a roll.

"I missed the bar exam," she said. "The hospital wouldn't discharge me in time to take it."

"I realize."

"That cost me the job with the firm in San Francisco."

"I wish it hadn't."

"They said the job offer was contingent on me being up and running with a law license in my back pocket. They couldn't wait for me to take the exam the next winter."

He nodded. Was he telling her he already knew? Or was he urging her to go on — like a man being whipped, saying *Please, sir, may I have another?*

"It blew me out of the water," she said.

She couldn't tell him the rest. It had lodged so far down in her chest, and felt so sharp for so long, that letting it heal over had taken every effort to be still, to let scar tissue tighten around it. It had become a flaw in her heartbeat.

Quietly, he said, "I'm sorry."

But *sorry* didn't cover it. And he knew that. He didn't plead, didn't expand on those two words. He waited, unarmed, for whatever she dealt back at him.

She waited until her breathing calmed. "Where have you been?"

He hesitated. Like he couldn't believe she was letting him off the hook. He gave her a quizzical look. "What have you heard?"

"You left the force and moved away."

"That's all?"

"I heard that you were injured," she said. "In the line of duty."

The quizzical look on his face remained. As did the tilt in his shoulders, and a tightness, maybe an ache. He looked toward the kitchen. Maybe he wanted coffee. She didn't want him to feel at home. She didn't want him to know how goddamned awful it was that he looked so amazing, so present, so alive, so near.

He said, "I saw you talking to Detective Xavier. Who else have you spoken to in the police department?"

"Why do you want to know?"

"It's important, Rory. Please."

Please? Seth had never been good with asking nicely. Not with suspects, not with drunks in biker bars, not with anybody who crossed him. And she assumed that he regarded her as having crossed him. Telling him, *We're done. Period. Permanently,* would seem to fall in that category.

"You don't work for the police department anymore. You're not investigating the courthouse attack. Why should I divulge anything to you?"

"Fair enough."

She calmed herself. "Seth. Why are you here?"

"To warn you."

"About what?"

He took a moment. "Don't count on the Ransom River PD to properly investigate the attack. Don't trust anybody from the department."

"What?" She heard the incredulity in her voice.

He turned, slowly, from the fireplace. "Don't talk to the cops anymore. The department's bent."

For a long moment she didn't move. Then she said, "I'll make coffee. You talk."

19

"The Ransom River PD is corrupt," Seth said.

He stood with the morning light slatted behind him through the kitchen shutters. Hands in his pockets, for something to do with them. Cops on duty never put their hands in their pockets or laced their fingers together. They needed them free to react to threats. Rory guessed that said something about how he saw her.

"There are officers in the department on the take. Some who sell information to outside organizations, and I don't mean the media."

"Which officers?" she said.

"I don't know."

"But you're certain?"

"It's why I quit."

She had the coffeepot in her hand. She stopped. "What happened?"

"The undercover op I was working when

you left — guy got killed. An ATF agent."

He said it without emotion, but it packed a punch.

"That's terrible," she said.

Chiba walked over to him. Seth crouched and scratched the dog behind the ears.

"I'd set up a meeting with the sellers. When the ATF guy and I got there we were ambushed," he said.

She didn't move. "Oh my God."

"I don't know who, but one of my brother cops tipped the sellers off."

He stood and sauntered to the window. The sun striped his face.

"Seth . . ."

He stared out at the trees and foothills.

Rory said, "Detective Xavier asked me about you."

"Did she, now."

"Like a kid poking an animal with a stick. Asked if I knew why you quit. Said people in the department would like a clear explanation."

He looked over his shoulder at her. "Xavier came by to twist your hair over it? Interesting. So they really won't be happy to see me."

"Why would the police department be unhappy to see you? Because you moved away? You're the son of a much-decorated detective."

"They distrust me."

"So the feeling is mutual."

He stared again out the window. "If you let Xavier talk to you again, she'll probably channel some talking points and gossip. Colder's assignment blew up in his face. Colder allowed another cop to get killed. Colder lost his nerve. And so he quit."

Coming in a flat, dispassionate tone of voice, it sounded brutal.

"That's preposterous," she said.

He shrugged.

She felt indignant. "No — Seth, that's . . . Christ, is that what people actually believe? Or is it a snide lie somebody's deliberately spreading about you?"

He tilted his head and for a second, the well-trained neutrality slipped from his expression. He looked at her with gratitude and warmth. Then, as though a painkiller had abruptly worn off, he glanced away.

She swallowed. "The bent cops — they're spreading this story?"

"I don't know. Guy quits the force when he leaves the hospital — people draw conclusions."

"Hospital."

She said it as an opening, but he shut that door.

"Nobody comes out of an ambush pretty." He turned from the window. "So I quit. And then I went looking for work someplace else. I blew town. You'd had it right all along."

"How's that?"

"What you always said. 'Don't look back — something might be gaining on you.'"

Acid rose in Rory's throat. "Did you tell anybody?"

"In the department?" He smiled. "Ms. Mackenzie, you can try to convince the world you're completely cynical. But I am on to you."

Heat spread across her cheeks. Of course he hadn't told anybody. He didn't know who to trust.

"The rot in the department is deep," he said, "and goes way back."

"How do you know?" she said. "*What* do you know?"

"I haven't been ignoring the department these past two years."

"You're convinced."

"You have no reason to trust me, but I'm asking you to."

It felt like a slap. "I trust you." Oh, how her heart twisted. "Do you think the department — crooked cops within the department — are, what, selling information to whoever was behind the courthouse attack?"

"Behind the attack?"

"Nixon and Reagan weren't the only people involved. I'm sure of it."

He walked to the kitchen counter. "Let me make the coffee. You do the talking."

She explained what had happened during the siege, what she'd seen on the courtroom CCTV video, and the accusations Detectives Zelinski and Xavier had made during interrogation.

"How'd it end?" Seth said.

"I said I wanted a lawyer."

He smiled sourly. "Saved and damned in one sweet statement."

"I know."

"They're trying to scare you," he said.

"It's working." She pressed her fingertips to her eyes. "I'm convinced somebody besides those two gunmen was behind the attack. The thing is, whatever they wanted, they didn't get. That means they still want it. And they're still out there."

"A criminal attorney won't be able to help you with that," he said.

"I know. So I'm going to need to turn to another law enforcement agency for help — the FBI? The U.S. Attorney's Office?"

"Are you asking me?"

"Yes." She felt angry now. "Yes, I'm asking you for help. Unless you drove out here just to tell me I'm in deep shit and sayonara."

He didn't flinch. "Hold fire. If things get bad, we'll call in the feds. But for now, we lack proof."

We. "How are we going to get proof?"

"Rory, I know you hate to fight. You'd rather walk away and let idiots scream and swing at thin air. But when you get backed into a corner, you battle your way out."

His view surprised her. She thought she ran, not walked, from hopeless battles. "Is that where I am? In the corner, backed against the ropes?"

"And it's time to come out swinging."

"With what? You have ammunition?"

"Yeah. To start with, I found out Nixon's real identity."

20

From his shirt pocket Seth took a folded sheet of paper. He handed it to her.

She unfolded it. It was a rap sheet that summarized a long criminal career. She inhaled.

"Sylvester Church. Recognize him?" Seth said.

In the mug shot Church had unkempt brown hair and a droopy biker mustache. Down his cheek ran a scar, like the track of a tear. His eyes, gleaming from the flash, were hot and confrontational.

"It's him," she said. "The guy who called himself Nixon. I saw his face when SWAT pulled off the ski mask. He'd shaved the mustache and his head. But it's him."

She was both baffled and impressed. She pored over the rap sheet. "How did you find him?"

Sylvester Lyle Church. Age forty-five. Five foot eight. A hundred ninety-two pounds of larded muscle and cruelty. His sheet went back twenty-seven years. Burglary. Possession of stolen property. Possession of crystal meth with intent to sell. Armed robbery. He had done time in county lockups and state penitentiaries. She counted nine and a half years incarcerated.

"What the hell was he doing in the court-room yesterday?" she said.

Seth had a canny light in his eyes. He seemed to be thinking the same thing she was.

Church was a con. A pro.

She scanned the sheet again. "An ex-convict. With nothing on his rap sheet but crimes dealing with money and profit. Something's missing." She turned it over. Nothing on the back. "Where's the record of his ties to extremist groups — prison gangs? Aryan Brotherhood, Christian Identity?"

"Nothing."

"There's a big hole here. Called motive."

"He had to have motive."

The image on the page gripped her. Church's eyes were wild, maybe with chemical fury. "How did you find this guy?"

"What time do you have to be at court?"

"Nine thirty. Why?"

"Sylvester Church isn't the only thing I

found. Got time for a drive?"

Seth, Mr. Surprise. Why did she ever doubt it? "Let's go."

They drove toward the city center in Seth's new truck, a black Tundra. The sun was gold and sharp in the sky. In the shadows, frost prickled on the grass. Morning traffic surrounded them: school buses, farm trucks, commuters drinking coffee or texting or both. Rory had grabbed a two-minute shower. Her hair hung damp on her shoulders. She held Sylvester Church's rap sheet in her hand.

"How'd you get this? Did you talk to somebody in the Ransom River PD?"

"No. Called some contacts to verify information, but only after I found it myself."

"And what did you find?" she said.

"The two gunmen drove to the courthouse. By themselves."

"You know this for certain?"

"A Chevy Blazer was found parked behind the building."

"You saw it?"

"On the news, like five million other people. Being winched onto a flatbed truck. That's how I know they drove it themselves, and nobody else was with them."

She thought about it. "Because, if somebody had dropped them off, they wouldn't have parked the Blazer and left it there. And if anybody else came with them and stayed outside as a getaway driver, they wouldn't have stuck around when things went bad."

"You got it. Once the sirens got loud, they would have hauled ass. But nobody did that."

"Before Judge Wieland got shot, the gunmen ordered four of us to line up and walk through the door to chambers. I didn't know —" Her voice wobbled. "Didn't know what they planned to do with us. I thought . . ."

For a moment she smelled cordite and heard screams.

Seth glanced at her. "Rory? You okay?"

"They were taking us out of the courtroom, but I didn't know — I was afraid that . . ."

Her voice was getting away from her. It all was getting away from her. She balled her hands in her lap so Seth wouldn't see them shake.

After a long moment she could see clearly again. What she felt was relief, so strong that it nearly made her cry.

"If there was a getaway car parked out back, a big SUV, that's where they were taking us," she said.

"What else did you think?" He shot a glance at her. "Jesus. You thought they were taking you out to kill you."

She shut her eyes. When she opened them, Seth was reaching toward her. It seemed an automatic gesture, an urge to comfort her. But he hesitated. His hand hung in midair.

Instead of a gentle touch, he clenched his fist and thumped it against her shoulder. A play-punch, almost a rewind to their childhood.

It was reassurance, and it worked. The humming terror that had gripped her in the courtroom dissolved. She felt lighter. The four chosen hostages hadn't been headed for execution in the judge's chambers.

"The gunmen wanted to get away with you," Seth said. "That's more interesting."

"And worrisome. They wanted me yesterday. I assume they still want me today."

He turned onto a broad avenue and headed downtown. Orchards gave way to crowded housing developments with maple saplings turning autumn red. They passed a park where morning dog walkers were exercising. The swings on the playground were empty.

"Here's the thing," Seth said. "Experienced criminals like Sylvester Church, guys who take part in grab-and-go robberies, know that a getaway car is necessary but it isn't enough."

She turned, curious.

"In a well-planned heist, the team swaps out their getaway car. They drive away from the scene in one vehicle. Then switch to a second. They either meet up with other members of their team or switch to a vehicle they positioned ahead of time."

"And did Church and his partner have a switch car?"

"It was the first thing I looked for, when I saw their Blazer getting towed."

"You found it."

He continued toward the center of town, poker-faced. "Want to see it?"

"Is it parked in a spot where security cameras can catch it?"

He let out a *heh.* "Clever girl."

"The cops think I'm an inside man. Video showing me checking out the switch car would do my cause no good."

"No video cameras. As Church undoubtedly wanted it."

They passed St. Joseph's Catholic Church, and then First Presbyterian, and the Assembly of God, and the Unitarian church, and the Iglesia Pentecostal. They passed the cross street that led to the civic center and the courthouse. Rory couldn't help looking.

The tree-lined boulevard ran perfectly straight, cutting across the valley like the crossbar of the letter *H.* The courthouse was two miles west, beyond the long procession of traffic lights, corner after corner of them. Green, yellow, red, an electric pulse driving the city.

At the wheel, Seth looked focused and eager. That look was familiar, and yet it masked two years of blank history.

"What are you doing these days?" Rory said.

"Working in L.A. Living in Santa Monica."

She wanted to ask him: wife, kids, harem, any new fetishes? Women whipping him? Jesus, why was she thinking these things?

"You finally open that workshop you always dreamed of, crafting exotic Chia Pets?" she said.

He smiled. "I sit behind a desk in the Federal Building all day. Reviewing cold-case files."

She raised an eyebrow. "You joined the FBI?"

"No. I'm working for a legal outfit, evaluating closed cases, convictions that are being appealed, miscarriages of justice."

"Like the Innocence Project?"

"Specific to federal cases. Why? You want

my card?"

"I guess I'm surprised," she said. The rest was implied: *Seth, behind a desk?*

"It's a job," he said. "It's a paycheck for a guy who ain't gonna run and jump through fiery hoops anymore."

Something in his tone worried her. "Are you okay?"

"Got all my fingers and toes. Some say I even still have my mind."

They passed a strip mall so Californian that in five thousand years, it would be regarded as an archaeological site. Taco Bell, In-N-Out, Applebee's, Jack in the Box, and Burger King. Teenage wasteland. Next door was a big-barn bed-and-bath store — ten acres of fluffy pillows and downy duvets and king-size beds. In fifth grade, she and Seth once bicycled here after school. They bought Jolly Ranchers and a *Sports Illustrated* at the 7-Eleven and sat on the curb sucking their blue Slurpees through straws. To get out of the heat, they locked their bikes and went inside the Beddie-Buy. It was cool and soft and seemed padded, floor to ceiling. The bedroom displays looked magnificent. Like the White House, Rory thought. And she got the idea that if a global catastrophe occurred, they could hide in the store until the army came. They spent hours exploring, working out which bedroom they'd each choose if the apocalypse rolled down on Ransom River. The Beddie-Buy had a Starbucks, so they figured they'd have food and drink for the duration.

"Remember our disaster preparedness day?" she said.

"You were a strange little kid."

"But the only one who would have been prepared for Götterdämmerung."

She now realized how far back her sense of calamity went. She'd always had the notion that she needed a safe house and an escape plan.

"Riss worked there for a while," she said.

Seth actually snorted. "Nerissa, working retail, in a store devoted to beds and bedding."

"Really."

Beyond the Beddie-Buy near a freeway entrance was another strip mall. It had a tanning salon, Vietnamese noodle house, and palm reader. Gas station and car wash. Seth pulled in and drove around to the back.

Behind the car wash was a parking area for half a dozen cars. It was empty aside from a dark blue Chrysler minivan. Seth stopped.

Rory said, "That's it?"

It was dusty and freckled with bird shit.

Dried mud was splashed along the wheel wells and bottom of the chassis. On the dashboard, crumpled McDonald's wrappers and crayons were visible.

"You sure it isn't here for a wash and vacuum?" she said. "It looks like something an overwhelmed mom of triplets would drive."

"I'm sure." Seth turned off the engine and climbed out.

Rory followed. The noise of the car wash blended with the drone of traffic on the nearby freeway. She put her hands in the pockets of her peacoat and circled the vehicle, looking for whatever had tipped him.

Parking permit for a Montessori school. Back window showing a fan of clean glass, cleared by the wiper, surrounded by heavy dust. Tailgate crusted with dried, splattered mud.

"I'm not seeing it," she said.

He nodded at the license plate. "Van's dirty, but the plate's clean."

She stepped closer to the van. He was right: the mud crusted on the tailgate didn't touch the license plate. And the plate didn't look as though it had been wiped; it looked pristine.

"They switched the tags?" she said.

He nodded. "I still have contacts at the DMV. I asked them to run it. These plates come back as belonging to a Fiat 500." He pointed at the corner of the windshield. "The VIN" — vehicle identification number — "comes back to this van."

She shook her head. "Did you drive around town all night, looking at every vehicle on the street for tiny inconsistencies?"

"Process of elimination." He walked around the van. "The gunmen would want to park a switch car close to the courthouse, but not too close. And not in a direct line of sight. They'd want witnesses and the police to lose visual contact when they fled the scene."

"Right."

"And they'd want to park the switch car someplace where it wouldn't draw suspicion. For instance, a quiet residential street — a strange van might be noticed by alert neighbors. And they would want to position it so they could swap vehicles and get going again immediately, and at high speed."

"The freeway," Rory said.

"Yeah. So they'd want a public place, somewhere the vehicle wouldn't stand out, with quick access to the interstate."

"But not the mall?"

"Big malls have CCTV cameras that cover the parking lot and the loading dock. On the other hand, a strip mall might only have an interior camera near the cash register in a convenience store." He looked around. "And none at all surveilling the back side of a car wash."

From where they stood Rory could see the freeway entrance. It led over the hill and soon reached a coagulated mass of other arteries: I-5, the 215, the 405. Get on the freeway, and in less time than it took to watch a sitcom, you could have your hostages headed for Northern California, Las Vegas, or the Mexican border.

"How long did it take you?" she said.

"Three hours. Give or take."

She huddled deeper into her peacoat. His tenacity and devotion were thrilling and alarming in equal measure.

"And it was the license plate that told you you'd hit pay dirt."

"Plus the way the vehicle's parked. It's facing the street. The driver doesn't even have to put it in reverse to back out of a slot. It's ready to roll."

"I'm impressed."

He gestured her toward the passenger-side window but said, "Don't touch it."

She gave him a *Do I look stupid?* look. She

stretched on tiptoe. "Dear God."

On the front seat was a sealed Baggie, full of heavy cable ties. And airline sleep masks. Another Baggie held four cell phones.

"Their getaway kit," Seth said. "These guys came prepared to transport hostages and cover their tracks."

"Burn phones?" she said.

"Prepaid, probably bought with cash earlier this week. Untraceable. And the fact that they're here in this vehicle, not with the gunmen, speaks to the team's determination not to be tracked. I bet they've never been used. Only turned on once to make sure they work. Turned off, so no GPS system or phone company can back-trace their path through the grid."

An employee of the car wash came around to the back to throw a trash bag into the Dumpster.

"I've seen enough," Rory said. She didn't want to be recognized, now or later. She checked her watch. "And I need to get to the courthouse."

"Let's book," Seth said.

They got back in his truck and headed downtown.

"Big question," Rory said. "You found the switch car. Why haven't the police?"

"Last night they were overwhelmed with

other matters. They were securing the crime scene, sending in the forensics techs to process the courthouse. Debriefing the hostages. Rounding up witnesses. Terrorizing you."

"They have to suspect a second vehicle exists," she said. "After all, they taught you to look for one. Right?"

"They're not stupid. They'll find that van and impound it. Probably" — he checked his watch — "about now. A new shift came on at eight a.m."

"What are you going to do with this information?" she said. "I don't see you phoning the PD."

"They don't pay me anymore," he said.

"Seth, why are you playing Lone Ranger?"

His shoulders tightened. "If that's what you think I'm doing, I can let you off at the next corner."

"No. Sorry." She said it so automatically that it surprised her. "I don't mean to impugn your motives. But you got the vehicle identification number. What are you going to do with it?"

"I'm going to use it as the starting point to build a case against the gunmen. And to find out who was behind them and why they're after you." He glanced across the truck. "We're going to use it to get you protection, via federal law enforcement if we need to."

"And you also want to use it against the Ransom River PD?"

"That would be a dividend. The point is, I don't believe they're going to protect the victims of the attack. They're going to protect their own asses."

"Hi-yo, Silver, away."

He rolled along the tree-lined boulevard toward the civic center. "So does that mean you're happy to see me?"

She laughed. That surprised her too.

"I'll take that as a yes," he said. "So I'll presume you want to know how I came up with the name of the second gunman."

21

"You got Reagan's name?" Rory said. "You're kidding me. How?"

"Through the van."

"I thought Sylvester Church stole the van."

"He did. From a used-car lot in Las Vegas. But he didn't hotwire it. Somebody got the keys from the office and gave them to Church. And the dealership is owned by the brother-in-law of a young man named Kevin Berrigan."

"Berrigan's the second gunman?" she said.

"And model citizen. Married, father of two kids under seven, usher at his church. Steadily employed in Las Vegas for the past five years."

"What the hell happened to him? How did he get from *A* to *Z*?"

"That," he said, "is a fascinating story."

Ahead lay the broad, sycamore-dotted lawn of the courthouse. A news crew was camped on the corner, and police cars parked along the curb.

Seth pulled over and stopped. "I'll let you out here."

"You really don't want anybody to know you're in town."

"Nope."

She paused, her hand on the door handle. Traffic passed by. "Thank you."

"Call me."

For a moment he held her gaze. A shadow darkened his lively, renegade's eyes. Maybe he had been thrown back, never thought he'd hear her thank him again in his lifetime. Because he looked like he had heard a ghost.

"Where have you been?" he said.

"Helsinki, London, then Geneva. Working for Asylum Action. A refugee charity — it helped people who were threatened with being sent back to danger zones."

His eyebrows lifted. "Why'd you come home?"

"The corporation that funded the charity pulled the plug. Completely."

"Without warning?"

"New PR team. They retooled the corporation's branding to breast cancer and Formula 1. The Asylum office in Geneva shut down, days before the office in London." She pinched the bridge of her nose. "All the case files are locked in storage. Families are in limbo — some in danger. Nothing I could do. Not a goddamned thing. Besides take the first plane home."

Seth gave her a long, concentrated look. And she knew he couldn't read her. He was trying. But in the past two years she had learned camouflage.

He thought he'd lost her. He didn't know the half of it.

"You might want to think about laying low," he said. "Out of town."

"What do you think I've been doing the past two years? Like I said, Helsinki, London, and Geneva. Yet here I am."

She climbed out. He glanced at his rearview mirror and pulled away.

For a moment she stood on the sidewalk. *Who was that masked man?*

It wasn't the devil-may-care boy who had wanted to protect her when they were kids. It wasn't the idealistic, daring cop who had swept her away. That's not who had just driven off. This guise, she didn't know.

Inside the courthouse, Rory's pulse picked up again. Everything seemed brighter than normal, etched with black borders, and loud. Granular — small sounds pinging and hitting her with the velocity of tiny stones kicked up by a passing car. At the weapons checkpoint, two uniformed L.A. County Sheriff's deputies greeted her.

One held up a hand. "Court's been suspended today. All divisions."

She got out her driver's license. "I'm a juror on the Elmendorf trial. I was told to report."

His expression softened. He checked her ID against a list on a clipboard. "Go on in. Glad you're in one piece, miss."

"Me too. How are the guards who were on duty yesterday?"

"Safe. Fine. They got the day off."

She bet they did. She bet they got their careers off. And she noticed that security had been beefed up all around. Deputies were guarding the exit-only side doors, so that nobody could sneak in with a gun — as the *Justice!* vigilante had apparently done.

"Hope things stay calm out here," she said.

"You said it."

At the door to a courtroom on the second floor, a bailiff verified Rory's ID against another checklist. It was an in-camera session — a closed meeting with a judge. When she saw the people inside, her throat caught.

Helen Ellis and Frankie Ortega were sitting in the front row of the public gallery. Helen looked pale and pasty, but when Rory sat down Helen grabbed her hand and squeezed. Rory squeezed back.

Without his sweatshirt, Frankie looked thin and tough. His right arm was a death-metal tattoo sleeve. Rory was sure people mistook it for a gang tat, but the flaming guitar told her otherwise. He looked like a spooked buck, ready to bound out of sight at the first loud noise. He lifted his chin in greeting. Playing cool.

Rory didn't care. He was alive; he'd been there with her; he was okay. She hugged him, squeezed his bony shoulders, wanted to lift him off his feet.

"I'm so glad you're all right," she said.

He looked abashed. "You too."

Judge Yamashita wore a Peter Pan collar over her judicial robes. She thanked them all for coming. She explained that *People v. Elmendorf* was in recess. Trial was suspended. A new judge would be appointed to take over Judge Wieland's duties.

Behind Rory, Daisy Fallon quietly began to cry.

Yamashita said that once things settled down, both the prosecution and the defense would file motions for a mistrial. She couldn't foresee that any of the jurors before her would have to sit another hour to hear testimony in the case. After the events of the previous day, it was unthinkable that the trial would continue. The case would be declared a mistrial, and the jury would be dismissed.

Her face was kind. "You have suffered a terrific trauma. As has the court. I want to thank you for your service to the justice system. Thank you for turning up this morning. Because of you, the system will continue to work. It will not be brought down by violence and anarchy."

Frankie eyed Yamashita without blinking. Rory didn't know whether he was terrified or catatonic.

"However," Yamashita said, "until the court has officially considered the disposition of the case, the trial remains active and on the docket. And you remain officially its jurors. You can be called back to court at any time. Don't go anywhere. Don't leave town."

Nail us to the floor, Rory thought. *Line us up like ducks in a shooting gallery.*

On the way out Helen Ellis walked with Rory. The older woman seemed to have stiffened overnight, as though gravity had increased threefold and she had trouble pulling herself along.

"Are you all right?" Rory asked.

"My husband wanted me to go to church this morning, talk to the pastor." She shook her head. "We were coming down Cloud Canyon Road past the tall rocks. You know how the morning sun shines through the slit between them and looks like a cross?"

Rory didn't, but nodded anyway.

"Today it seemed so bright, it reminded me of crosshairs. I had to pull the car over. I couldn't drive past it. Isn't that stupid?"

Rory squeezed Helen's hand again.

"You take care," Helen said.

Rory was halfway down the stairs when her phone rang. It was her former law professor David Goldstein.

"My God, Ms. Mackenzie — is what I read in the paper accurate? You were inside that courtroom yesterday?"

"Me and about sixty others."

"How dreadful. Are you all right, dear?"

Bless him; he was all cuddles beneath the starch. "Yes and no. I need your help."

She explained as she descended the stairs to the lobby. Outside, a camera crew had set up camp. She turned her back and spoke quietly.

"I need a criminal lawyer. Somebody experienced," she said. "A gorilla, preferably."

"This is serious," Goldstein said carefully. "Ms. Mackenzie, I am very concerned by what you've told me of the police department's behavior."

"That's why I'm talking to you."

"Leave this with me. I'll get back to you."

"Thank you, Professor. You don't know how much."

"Wait to thank me until we see what the criminal lawyer says."

She told him good-bye and pushed through the door into the sunshine. A few disaster tourists lingered, pointing and snapping photos. The news crew seemed blessedly self-concerned and didn't spot her. She was almost to the corner when she heard a voice calling to her.

"Aurora. Aurora Mackenzie."

On the side street, a chrome-colored Toyota Land Cruiser had pulled over. A woman stuck her arm out the passenger window and beckoned to her.

Rory stopped. It was her aunt Amber.

She thought about falling to the ground foaming at the mouth, or running to the news crew and confessing. To the JFK assassination.

Amber leaned out the window, sunlight bouncing from her eyeglasses, gesturing fulsomely. "Come here, sweetheart."

Better to get this over with in public, when she could legitimately claim to be in a hurry. She walked toward the car.

And her cousin Nerissa climbed from behind the wheel.

A swig of battery acid to wash down the saccharine. Rory neared the car. "Hey, Riss."

Amber reached out the window and grasped her hand in an *I'd like to teach the world to sing* way. "Aren't you just amazing to come back here this morning?"

"What brings you downtown?" Rory said.

Amber's hands were cinched into wrist-support splints. She claimed to suffer chronic pain from carpal tunnel syndrome, though as far as Rory knew she hadn't typed a word in a decade.

"We were so worried about you, honey," she said.

Amber was a hard-wrung fifty-three and looked sixty. Her Janis Joplin hair was dyed a fretful red. Her floral blouse, splashed with enormous daisies and honeybees, seemed to fill the entire car.

"I appreciate it," Rory said.

Riss cruised around the front of the SUV. "You escaped without a scratch. It's a miracle. And everybody's going to want to know exactly how you made it out."

Riss slid her hands into the back pockets of her jeans. Her filmy top floated like a jellyfish across her breasts, almost dreamily. She eyed the news crew on the courthouse lawn.

"You need to decide how you're going to explain it, and you'll want your family at your side," she said.

Her feline gaze was depthless and patient. "I called you yesterday during the siege. I wanted to help you get intelligence to the police. The news crew was waiting. You didn't answer."

It seemed to Rory that a claw had begun to scrape down her spine. "The gunmen confiscated our phones."

From the backseat of the SUV came a childish voice. "Hot. Out."

In the backseat, three car seats were strapped in. Filled with a toddler each. One, a little boy, squirmed and pressed his fists against his eyes.

Amber spoke over her shoulder. "We'll get to Auntie Amber's in a minute." She smiled again at Rory. "You have to tell us all about it. I mean, every word. My dear Lord, it's just too awful."

Rory tried not to look astonished. "The details might be too much for two-year-olds to hear."

Amber ran an ad hoc day-care center in her home, looking after half a dozen pre-schoolers. As far as Rory could discern, she parked the kids in front of her television while she watched soap operas on a second set in her kitchen. Amber wasn't callous or neglectful. She simply moved slowly and found any expenditure of energy to be a massive effort of will.

She laughed. It was a smoker's laugh, a wet, chesty sound. "Been years since something this exciting happened around here." She nodded at the toddlers. "I'm giving these little ones a taste of history."

One of the little ones squirmed, fighting against the sharp sun in his eyes. Another was asleep, a pacifier hanging precariously from her lips. The third looked hot, her cheeks flushed, her brown hair stuck to her forehead in damp curls.

Amber patted Rory's arm again. "You must have been terrified. *Terrified.*"

"It was rough."

Riss leaned against the side of the Land Cruiser. She seemed annoyed to be chauffeuring her stepmother around Ransom River with a car full of day-care kids. And she looked overtly bored, as if hearing about the siege was a waste of her time. But her gaze cut across Rory's chest. She didn't like

Rory getting Amber's full attention.

And Rory wondered at an envy so powerful, it caused her cousin to anger at the thought of remaining safe while others were threatened at gunpoint. As though Riss considered herself Cinderella, and Rory the evil stepsister who had kept her from attending the ball.

Granted, Riss had gotten the short end of the stick when her father left town. She was nine when Lee Mackenzie — jack-of-all-trades, man who hated cages — took off to Mexico to work as a roughneck in the Gulf oilfields. He still hadn't come back. Maybe, Rory thought, that was one reason Riss's startling eyes either tracked or ignored you. Hard eyes, full of suspicion.

The claw scratched deeper in Rory's spine. The danger signs were there.

Amber held on to Rory's arm. "Did the terrorists threaten you? Did they torture anybody?" She patted her chest as though she had palpitations. "Did they do anything dirty to the women?"

Rory said, "No. And I'll let you get going before these kids lose it."

"I can barely stand to imagine it," Amber said.

The little girl with the dark curls lost control and began to cry. Amber patted Rory's arm and released her. Over her shoulder she said, "Okay, Addie."

Riss stepped close. She licked her lips and stared at Rory's feet. Her blue-black hair swung in front of her eyes. "You're good with that deadpan face. When it's my step-mom asking the questions. Not so good when somebody tougher confronts you."

Rory went cold. The little boy in the back-seat wailed.

Riss stared at the ground. "If you won't accept any help or take my advice to talk to the media with me, maybe you shouldn't talk to them at all. Things can go bad real quick."

She looked up at Rory through a waterfall of black hair.

"This is not about you and me," Rory said.

Riss slowly tilted her head, as though Rory had said something absurd.

Riss turned away and got back behind the wheel. Rory's head pounded so hard she barely heard the car squeal away from the curb.

22

Rory stood on the sidewalk outside the courthouse, below sycamores and crimson maples that flickered in the cold sunlight. She felt exposed. She felt like the loose end of a rope that had come untied in a stiff wind and that was unraveling.

She got out her phone and made a call that two hours earlier would have blown her mind.

"Yeah," Seth said.

"Meet me at the corner of Main and Treacher. By the Dairy Queen," she said.

"You sound stressed."

She started walking. "Riss."

"Five minutes. I'm on my way."

It started when they were twelve. It didn't start with Riss.

When they were twelve, Seth had blond hair that fell to his eyes and wore T-shirts with skateboarding logos and a wallet on a dog chain that draped from his jeans pocket. When they were twelve, Rory had learned the hard way never to raise her hand in class. On spring days after school they would go to the river. Upstream of the storm drain, they'd climb the chain-link fence that was supposed to keep kids out. They'd catch tadpoles or skateboard down the concrete banks where the river had been paved over.

The storm drain was three big culverts side by side that ran beneath an entire neighborhood. Eight-foot-diameter concrete pipes that opened like mouths from the side of a reinforced hillside. The winter had been dry, so dirt lay packed along the bottom, with bits of trash and lost things in it. Inside, it was black. The storm drain was a tunnel with no light at the end of it.

One day Seth stood at the entrance and said, "Wonder where it comes out."

"A mile away," Rory said. "Probably."

"Want to find out?"

Her stomach went queasy. "I saw the news once. When it stormed for a week and the Los Angeles River flooded. And this teenager, he got swept in."

Her voice echoed against the walls of the culvert. Seth picked up a stick and poked at the dirt.

"He was swept so fast, like he was surfing. He got pulled into a storm drain. It was three miles long and the water filled it up to the top. He came out half an hour later, drowned," she said.

Seth looked in the culvert and up at the sky. It was so blue they could see jets high up, like silver bullets. Telling her: no rain.

He threw the stick aside and turned to her with a smile. A spooky one. "I brought a flashlight. And walkie-talkies."

"It's not a good idea."

"I'll go first." He got out the walkie-talkies and gave her one. "If there's any problem, I'll call you."

He turned on the flashlight and walked into the culvert. The light tracked ahead of him. She pressed the button on the walkie-talkie.

"Can you hear me?" Then, because she knew it from TV, she said, "Over."

The walkie-talkie fuzzed. "It's dry. Nothing but dry."

"Come back," she said.

She stepped closer to the entrance. She couldn't hear Seth's footsteps. Then, from the walkie-talkie, he screamed.

Her whole body turned electric. For a second she stood shocked to the spot. Then she pressed the walkie-talkie button and ran inside.

"Seth. Seth."

He kept screaming.

"I'm coming," she said.

The light faded to gray. The screaming stopped.

"Seth, where are you?"

She heard a whimper in her voice. Had he fallen into a pit? Did an animal get him? Or a person? A Freddy Krueger?

"Seth."

From the darkness in front of her, the flashlight flipped on. It was aimed up at the ceiling, and it illuminated Seth's face like a monster movie.

"Gotcha."

She jumped, hard. She came down shouting and punching. Swinging like a wild thing, fists pounding his arm. And he was laughing. Laughing so hard he had to grab his stomach.

"Screw you, Seth." Spit flew from her mouth. "You stupid ass-face. Butt-clown. You shit-barfing wiener."

He put up his hands to stop her punching him. "God, you should see yourself."

"It's not funny."

"I got you in here, didn't I?"

She lowered her hands but the fists

wouldn't uncurl.

"Rory. Look. Nothing's dangerous back here. It's just a tunnel. We're safe."

But she still couldn't see the end. Couldn't see light anywhere except from the flashlight. And all that showed was Seth's face.

He waited for her to calm down. "Want to keep going?"

She considered kicking him in the nuts. "No. I don't want to go any farther."

He waited a moment, mischief in his eyes, as though hoping he could get her to change her mind. Finally he shrugged.

"Okay, cool."

They walked back toward the exit side by side. When they stepped into the sunlight they saw the group of kids outside. Three guys were at the top of the concrete bank leaning back against the fence. Standing in front of the storm drain, waiting for them, was her cousin Boone.

Boone was fourteen and in eighth grade and never let younger kids forget it. He was already tall and sometimes he even shaved. And he never looked at you straight on. He might stand right in front of you, like a door, and keep you from walking around him, but he always looked at something off to one side, with a slitty-eyed look. And if you were the thing off to the side he was looking at, watch out.

He was standing on Seth's skateboard. "What do we got here?"

Threads of cold water seemed to run under Rory's skin. They were two miles from her house. Four miles from Seth's.

"What were you two doing in the culvert in the dark?" Boone said.

"Nothing," Rory said. "Get off Seth's board."

"Frenching? Or did you get in her pants, Colder?"

The cold threads crawled beneath Rory's skin. "Shut up."

Boone gave a sideways look at his friends. "That's pathetic, Colder. Could you find anything in there?"

There was no good way around him. And Rory knew if she did get around him, there was always his stepsister. Riss didn't have to be there in person to be behind him. Riss was sneaky and would find a way to get you later. The question was, how much later.

Seth said, "Looking in your pants and finding nothing. I bet you're used to doing that, Boone."

It was like a punctuation mark on the day. A sharpened pencil stuck directly into

Boone's face. Her cousin finally looked at them.

Rory had seen dogs' eyes when they were angry. Boone's eyes looked like that.

Boone was strong and when he got angry he just unloaded. It seemed to him that everything and everybody deserved it. Fail to keep him happy, and you got it. People, computers, even a toilet once, that he smashed with a hammer. He was going to beat the shit out of Seth.

Seth didn't wait for it. He threw himself at Boone and shoved him off balance.

Boone tripped backward and stumbled off the skateboard and fell on his butt. "Shit."

Seth grabbed the board. "Rory, run."

She was already scrambling up the far concrete embankment. They heard Boone's friends laughing. That was only going to make it worse.

They reached the top of the embankment and got halfway up the chain-link fence, clattering and clanging, before Boone grabbed Seth by the back pocket of his jeans and ripped his hands loose. Seth dropped back to the ground.

Rory got to the top of the fence, ready to swing over. Boone pulled Seth up, hauled back, and punched him.

It wasn't like in the movies. It was an

unruly swing, just energy and anger. It spun Seth sideways. Rory's legs turned to spaghetti. She hovered, tentatively balanced, halfway over the fence. Boone held on to Seth, yanked him around, and got ready for the shit-kickery.

She grabbed the fence tight. *"Boone."*

He gave her one of the sideways looks. And she booted him as hard as she could in the head.

His head snapped and his hands dropped. That was all the time Seth needed. Rory screamed, "Hurry!"

They got across the fence and onto the frontage road, and that's when Rory found out how fast and how far she could run. They didn't stop for fifteen minutes. Her throat hurt and the light seemed like it was spinning. They ran through the side gate at Rory's house and slammed it shut and bent over, hands on knees, panting.

"You okay?" Seth said.

She nodded. "You have a big red mark on the side of your face."

He touched his cheek and shrugged. He smiled. "He didn't follow us."

She stood up straight. She had a stitch in her side but felt crazily great.

And scared again. "He doesn't have to."

23

Seth picked her up beneath the giant soft-swirl ice cream cone of the Dairy Queen. Rory slammed the door of the truck and he pulled back into traffic.

"What happened with Riss?" he said.

"She threatened me. Vaguely. In her borderline aggressive way."

"With?"

"Trouble. A media backlash if I don't let her . . ." She rubbed her eyes. "Exposure. Humiliation." She breathed. "Or maybe I'm just losing it."

"You're not losing it."

She looked at him. "No. I'm not. What does she want? More of me."

It took twenty-four hours. Twenty-four hours after Boone shit-punched Seth, and Rory left her cousin with a shoe print on his head.

When the bell sprang the kids at East

River Middle School, Rory loaded her backpack at her locker, surrounded by noise. The energy on a Friday afternoon was like helium balloons ascending, a thousand at once. The walk home was a mile through flat suburban streets. Rory's dad was in the Sierras for the Forest Service and her mom wouldn't be home from the high school until after five p.m. The day was sunny.

Across from the campus was a lemon orchard, the trees dark green and heavy with fruit. A dirt path ran through the orchard, but that shortcut was reserved for the cool kids. The dirt path was where wicked magic changed the rules of school. Get fifty feet into the orchard and the vice principal couldn't touch you.

Rory never took the dirt path, though the thought thrilled and scared her. She would have been challenged before she walked three steps. Seth could take the path. He could let his jeans sag, let the dog chain drape from his pocket and his hair fall into his eyes, and get away with it. Seth moved between worlds. Even then.

Boone always took the dirt path. Riss hardly ever did. She usually stayed after school for performing-arts rehearsals or drill-team practice. Amber would pick her up later.

Rory took the sidewalk along Treacher Avenue at the edge of the orchard. She was a block from school when four girls walked out of the trees and surrounded her.

Chelly Stasio said, "We know what you tried to do with Boone."

"What are you talking about?" Rory said.

Britiny Glover stepped toward her. "It's disgusting."

Linda Rich got behind her and grabbed her backpack. "You got your diary in here? You talk all about how Boone is your dream lover?"

Rory spun and tried to shake Linda off, but the fourth girl, Crystal Glass, shoved her.

She stumbled and they pushed her again, into the orchard.

"You're a perv," Linda said.

Rory knew she was in trouble, that if they maneuvered her deeper into the trees, she was toast on a stick. She didn't want to be toast. She didn't want to fight, because four against one was great odds, if you were the four. She didn't want to run. Run, and she'd be known forever at school as a coward.

The girls were Riss's followers. They sat at her lunch table. They walked to class together. Rory had no doubt that Riss had put them up to this.

Linda was the tallest and the loudest. She looked like some kind of sizzling firecracker. She simply walked forward and butted into Rory.

"Your cousin. Your own *cousin*. Eww."

Rory pushed her. "Stop it. You don't know what you're talking about."

"You got him to go into the storm drain," Linda said. "You tricked him in there and then you pulled down your pants, you perv."

"That never happened. That's a lie. Boone tried to steal Seth's skateboard."

Linda pointed at her. "Blame Boone — you wuss. Look at you. You're about to cry. Crybaby."

Rory's face was burning. "It's a lie, you dumbasses. And if you believe it, you're idiots." She thought, *Well, that makes me deader than dead to the popular kids.*

Linda grabbed her backpack and wrestled it from her shoulders. Rory hung on to the strap. "Stop it."

The other girls tore it from her hands. Linda danced back, unzipping it. She threw out Rory's math book and lunch box.

"Don't," Rory said.

Linda found her English notebook. She waved it in the air. "Eureka. The mother lode."

Rory reached for it. "Give it back."

"Ooh. This must be really good stuff."

Clutching the notebook, Linda turned and ran from the orchard. Chelly and Crystal ran after her. Linda laughed and said, "Let's see her get an A in English class now." Britiny took the backpack, flung it into the trees, and chased after them.

For thirty seconds Rory stood breathing hard, needles of humiliation prickling her skin. *Don't cry.*

She stumbled through the orchard and picked up her math book. Found her lunch box. Kept going, looking for her backpack, and heard a girl call, "Rory?"

She looked up sharply. On the sidewalk, Petra lay down her bike and ran into the orchard.

"I can't find my pack," Rory said.

Petra knew something had happened, but she said, "Let's look."

They found it in a sticky patch of mud. Rory wiped it off and slung the pack across her shoulders. She swallowed the lump that clogged her throat. *Don't cry.*

And don't tell. Telling would do no good. Her mom would turn purple, and her dad would phone Aunt Amber — she could hear the phone conversation, the black storm in her dad's voice, yet another warning that Amber needed to *lay down the law* to Riss and Boone.

It would backfire. Rory's parents would fight her corner. They'd go Conan the Destroyer on anybody who hurt their only child. But when the backlash came, they wouldn't be around.

She pulled the cuffs of her sweatshirt over her hands and wiped them against her eyes. No, telling would only deepen her problems. A hard breath caught in her chest. She would just have to hold it in, all of it.

She walked with Petra back to the sidewalk. Across the street on the soccer field at school, the drill team was practicing. Riss had stepped out of line and stood at the fence, staring at her.

"Let's go," Rory said.

Petra picked up her bike. Rory climbed on behind her and hung on, all the way home.

24

In her third-grade classroom at West River Elementary School, Petra was writing on the blackboard. The chalk broke and her nails hit the slate. At the sound, the kids squirmed and said, "Eww."

She brushed chalk dust from her hands. "Ooh, indeed. You know what that sound is? It's a horse's hooves raking the ground. The horse that belongs to the Headless Horseman."

She picked up *The Legend of Sleepy Hollow.*

But before she could read from it, a car alarm rang. The classroom overlooked the parking lot, and twenty small heads swiveled to see the culprit.

"Class. Back here." Petra made a spinning motion with her finger. And she glimpsed a Camry with its flashers blinking.

Dammit.

A minute later she was speed-walking

across the parking lot. She raised her key fob and clicked the remote. The alarm kept blaring. She clicked again. The lights were having a seizure. She jogged up to the driver's door and hit the remote one more time.

The alarm shut off. The lights stopped flashing. The car looked fine.

The voice behind her was low and chesty, a big man. "Alarms are so sensitive. Sit on the bumper, they go off."

She turned. A guy in a suit straight out of *Mad Men* stood behind her. Out of *Mad Men,* if he'd been blown up into one of the balloon animals for the Macy's Thanksgiving Day Parade.

A dark SUV crept nearer in the parking lot. Balloon Animal was wearing dark glasses and enough hair gel to grease a seal.

"We need a word, Miss Whistler."

She backed up. How did they know her name? She turned, and another man was standing there blocking her path. She glanced toward her classroom. She couldn't tell whether anybody inside was looking.

Balloon Animal walked toward her. He could barely fit between her car and the one next to it. When he brushed the door she expected him to squeak like rubber.

"You've got a problem," he said.

"Stop," she said.

He kept approaching. "I'll do whatever I want." His face was grim. "This problem you got, it's called Aurora Mackenzie."

Seth and Rory cruised in his truck through a flat commercial zone of mattress show-rooms and used-car dealerships. On the car lot, windshields shone with the sun, prices painted in red *wow-kapow* letters across the glass. Rory held her phone to her ear and talked to her law school professor David Goldstein. She spoke for a minute and thanked him. Hung up.

"He's found a criminal attorney who'll see me today," she said.

"Where?" Seth said.

"Century City."

That was a forty-five-minute drive over the hill, across the San Fernando Valley, and down the Sepulveda Pass to the busy busi-ness corridor in west L.A.

"I'll drive you to the meeting," he said.

"This isn't your problem." She gave him a sideways glance. "Don't you have work to-day?"

His smile was low and chilly. "I am work-ing."

"On what?"

"Conspiracy, fraud, perverting the course

231

of justice. If the Ransom River PD screws with you, I'll read 'em the entire penal code and sprinkle the charges over the department like confetti."

"Who'll be the client?"

He grinned, still chilly, and looked at her.

"Me? No. I don't want to be used as a front for a vendetta."

His face turned stung and uncertain. "That's not what I'm after."

"I'm not bait, Seth."

"Duly noted."

"Sorry." She was fuming. She forced herself to calm down. "I feel like I've been rubbed raw with sandpaper."

"I know." He drove in silence for a minute. "So Riss is pissed off that you were chosen Hostage for a Day. What happens if you ignore her?" he said.

Rory ran a hand through her hair. "Doesn't work."

She'd tried it when she was twelve, after Riss's posse roughed her up in the orchard and stole her notebook. She went back to school and pretended nothing had happened. And the next day, she was called to the office.

The cafeteria staff had found her notebook on a lunch tray. The school secretary told Rory to be more careful with her things.

The look on the secretary's face caused her stomach to hum. When she opened the notebook, she saw why. It was vandalized. Her English class poem was covered with graffiti. She saw her own words: *iridescent* and *chimera.* They were crowded by *Boone.* By hearts, and *I love you* and . . . She stared. *Let me suck you.*

And half the pages were torn out. Her muscles turned to yarn.

She began to find pages around campus. Stuck to her locker with chewing gum. Taped to a mirror in the girls' room. They were covered with swear words. And *perv.* And *virgin.* And drawings of dicks. And of her, naked. Bent over. She knew Riss had goaded her posse to do it. Riss was too smart to risk doing it herself.

In Seth's truck, she watched the used-car lots stream past. "Ignoring Riss, staying under her radar, playing dead — it all just fans the flames."

What happened if she ignored Cinderella? Prince Charming would show up.

That Memorial Day Rory's family had held a barbecue. Burgers and hot dogs on the grill. Rory helped her mom slice beefsteak tomatoes. Sam wore an orange paisley shirt and capris, and she rattled the ice cubes in her tea and joked with her friends in the kitchen. Outside by the BBQ, jovial banter surrounded her dad. Amber sat in a lawn chair on the patio, nursing a beer. Riss and Boone watched TV in the den.

It was never spoken of — the awkwardness of Uncle Lee's absence. He was Will Mackenzie's baby brother, the rascal who always got into trouble and almost always wriggled out of it with a smile and a contrite shrug. And he'd left town. For work, Amber insisted.

Sam would nod, tight-lipped. She and Will mentioned Lee only in murmurs. They stopped if Rory came into the room. Her dad would look furtive and her mom would smile in a way that seemed painfully sweet. But then, her mom never let anybody speak ill of the family. If somebody slighted Will or Rory, she wanted to "tear them a new one." Will called Sam his little wolverine. So nobody badmouthed Lee. Nobody ever used the word *abandoned.*

Because Lee hadn't abandoned his family, Rory thought. He was working in Mexico. He sent Amber money. He wrote Rory postcards. *Greetings from Yucatán.* The postcards showed aqua seas and jungles with ancient stone pyramids. She imagined him digging for treasure in Mayan ruins.

234

She finished slicing the beefsteak tomatoes and set out the ketchup and mustard and stood on tiptoe to watch the brownies baking in the oven.

Her mom smiled and wiped a smudge from Rory's cheek with her thumb. "Looks like mustard, sweet pea. And it's on your shirt."

Wiping the back of her hand across her face, Rory went to change.

When she walked into her room, Boone was standing at her corkboard. He nodded at the postcards tacked to the board. " 'Wish you were here.' "

"What are you doing in here?" Rory said.

He looked at the floor next to her, with the slitty-eyed look. "You owe me an apology."

"Sorry I called you a sack of flaming dog poop."

"When did you do that?"

"Just now."

He turned and looked directly at her.

She pointed at the door. "I have to change. Excuse me." She was ready to push him out. Shaking inside, and suspicious, but ready.

He walked to the door. But instead of leaving, he shut it. "Apology, Aurora."

"Boone, get out."

"Say you're sorry."

"Fine, I'm sorry," she said. "Now get out."

He crossed his arms. "I don't believe you."

Rory grabbed the knob, but he leaned back against the door with all his weight, so she couldn't open it. Distantly she heard women's laughter and Led Zeppelin. Her dad was in charge of the music.

"Okay, I'm really actually truly sorry I kicked you in the face," she said. *Not.*

"That's a start," he said. "You were pretty ballsy. But only because you had a boy there to back you up. Let's see how brave you are when nobody's here to help you and you don't have to hit me at all."

"What are you talking about?" A quaver lurked in her throat.

"A dare. It won't hurt."

She didn't like that. "Boone, get out of my room."

She tried to shove him aside and open the door. He moved her back, not hard, but firmly.

"Get away," she said. He blocked her path. "Boone."

He raised his hands, like he was patting out a fire. "Shh. Rory, it's just a game. Stop being a wuss." The sneaky smile had gone far, far away. "You kicked me. So you kiss it and make it better."

She felt a crawly sensation down her arms

236

and legs. "That's all?"

"Yeah." He stepped closer.

She just wanted him to leave her alone. "Fine." She stood on tiptoe and pecked him on the forehead. His shirt was warm. He smelled like sweat and spearmint gum.

"Better?" she said.

"Now it's my turn."

She stepped back. "Boone, you said."

His hand went to the hem of her T-shirt. "It's no big deal."

She shoved his hand away. "No."

He stepped closer and looked at her directly and tugged again on the hem of her shirt. His left hand slid beneath it and stroked her stomach.

"Boone, stop it."

"It's only fair. You touch me, I touch you." His hand flattened against her skin. His palm was hot. "It's not like it's going to hurt. Everybody does this. Everybody in the world."

"No, they don't." She squirmed. "You're my cousin."

"Shh," he repeated. "Just show me your tits. Let me touch them and we'll be even."

"No."

"What are you scared about? Doctors look at tits all day long. Babies suck on them. In public, at the food court at the mall. Why are you making this a big deal?"

"Stop it."

She shoved at his hands but he moved against her and he was bigger, he weighed more, and he kept nudging her back, toward her dresser, toward the wall.

"Cousins aren't supposed to do this," she said.

"That's weaksauce. I'm your *step*-cousin." He tilted his head and smiled a weird smile. "Okay, I'll let you touch me first."

He pulled his hands off her and unzipped his jeans.

She shoved him away, hard. And that's when she saw that her closet door was open. Standing inside it, staring at her like a mannequin, was Riss.

"Shit," Rory yelled.

Boone turned to his sister. The look on his face said, *You spoiled the game.*

Riss stood for a long, still second, her eyes unblinking. She took one step toward Rory.

"You are such a freak," she said.

There was a knock on the door. An adult called, "What's going on in there?"

Rory ran for it. Behind her, Riss muttered, "And a loser."

Rory threw the door open. In the hallway stood one of her mom's work friends. The woman wore an expression of surprise and a teacher's suspicion of kids doing bad things behind closed doors.

"Sorry, I thought this was the bathroom," she said.

"No. We're going outside now."

Rory looked pointedly at her cousins. Boone slouched past her and down the hall, avoiding the teacher's gaze. Riss glided from the closet, like a reanimated doll, and sauntered past Rory.

Rory's heart was beating like a rabbit's. She felt like she was going to vomit. In a bright haze, she told the teacher, "Bathroom's down the hall."

She walked back to the kitchen and through the happy chatter. She went outside to the patio and got herself a soda from the cooler. Her dad was flipping burgers, telling the neighbors that the Lakers weren't worth a good piss this season.

Amber sat in the lawn chair, beer in one hand, cigarette in the other. Rory took her soda to the avocado tree that shaded the back wall. It was a perfect climbing tree, with sturdy branches and smooth bark. She put the soda in the notch and hoisted herself up.

The leaves formed a canopy. She sat in the tree and popped the top on her soda but couldn't force even one swallow.

Her mom was laughing in the kitchen. The sun bounced off the patio windows, reddish. In the family room, Riss and Boone had slumped onto the couch to watch TV. Riss was peering out the window in Rory's direction.

Below the tree, Pepper barked up at her.

"Not now, boy," she said.

Riss kept staring.

Later, after everybody went home, Rory discovered that Uncle Lee's postcards had been ripped off her corkboard. All that remained were the tacks. She decided to ask for a lock on her door. And her window.

At school the next week, Rory got used to feeling like silence wasn't safety. Something was waiting, some jack-in-the-box, ready to spring. Later, she saw a documentary and learned about the Bouncing Betty, a kind of land mine. That's how she felt walking around school.

It was Friday when Riss found her, between periods, at the water fountain. Rory felt her looming as she bent and drank. Slowly she straightened and wiped her lips. Riss had on the mannequin face.

"That's it. Close your mouth. Close it tight," Riss said.

"I don't know what you're talking about,"

Rory said.

Riss didn't exactly smile. She looked more — dismissive. "Is that your new plan? Amnesia?"

"I don't want to talk about this."

The look got sharper. It was a sneer. "Actually, amnesia is good."

Rory turned and headed for the science pod.

Riss caught up with her. "Nothing happened." She walked alongside, staring at her. "Because if you ever claimed that it did, you'd be wrong."

"Sure, Riss. Whatevs."

"You'd be lying."

Rory looked straight ahead and headed for her classroom.

"Bad things happen to liars," Riss said. "Because they deserve it."

Stop it, just stop it, Rory thought. But she didn't say it. The only thing that would make Riss go away was getting to her science classroom.

"Liars get in trouble," Riss said. "But not just them. Things happen around them. It's called karma."

Don't look at her.

"Like, you know when people talk about you, your ears burn? When liars talk, it's *their* stuff that burns."

That was when Rory first thought that Riss was crazy.

Riss lowered her voice. "You know how your dad was cooking hot dogs? How'd you like it if your real dog got cooked? Pepper on the grill."

Rory stopped. She turned and glared at her cousin. Riss pulled back a few inches.

"Don't you dare even talk about hurting Pepper," Rory said.

Riss held back, but only for a second. "I'm not. *Karma* is."

"I hate you," Rory said.

"Liar. Liar, liar." Riss backed away. "But you're not going to say anything about Boone. Because you don't want your world to get burned up by your lies."

The bell rang.

"If you tell, I'll know. If anything happens to Boone, I'll know. If your dad does anything, or your mom, or the school, I'll know. And you'll pay. You won't know when. But anything you touch gets taken away. You poison it. If you touch it, you kill it."

She walked away.

25

Seth drove slowly along in traffic. "You need to stay away from her."

"I need to put an electronic ankle bracelet and a muzzle on her. But that ain't gonna happen."

"Is she after publicity?"

"I never know," Rory said. "She's certainly after a way to break out of waitressing at a cocktail bar where she dresses up as a naughty Catholic schoolgirl. And she's still after me. Why she's so gung ho on the trial, and the attack . . ."

They rode in silence a moment. They both knew that Riss loved to pull tricks from her sleeve. Rory knew the only thing that would really protect her from Riss's desire to lash out: getting out of town.

"Tell me about the second gunman," she said.

"Kevin Berrigan."

Seth slowed for a corner and turned

toward the foothills, headed to Rory's neighborhood.

"Salesman for a tool-and-die company in North Las Vegas. Steadily employed. On his first marriage. One kid in first grade at his local public school, the second in diapers at home. And not just an usher at church, but a Eucharistic minister," he said. "But it seems he had a taste for something besides communion wine."

"Gambling."

"Poker to begin with. And bets on the sports book. Basketball. That's how he got into trouble."

"In debt to bookies?" Rory said.

"At first." He stopped for a light at a railroad crossing. "Then in debt to the loan sharks he used to pay off the bookies."

"So what the hell was going on with him?"

"What would be your wildest guess?"

In the back of her mind she noted that Seth had slipped into an old pattern — of playfulness, of trusting her to engage with him. He crossed the railroad tracks and accelerated.

She watched live oaks go by. "The courthouse attack wasn't political. And it wasn't personal," she said. "The two gunmen couldn't have been more different, at least on the surface. One career criminal. One upstanding citizen with an Achilles' heel. Did they know each other well? What's the connection?"

"None that I've found so far. Other than that they charged into that courtroom side by side, shotguns loaded."

She turned to him. "No connection between them at all?"

"So far. It'll be there."

"But neither of them have any apparent extremist ties. They're not related to the victim. Neither was ever arrested by the defendants. They didn't meet in line at the neighborhood pharmacy and decide jointly to go off their meds and take a psychotic road trip."

"No."

The trees blurred past.

"In that case, I think it was about money," she said.

Seth nodded. "So do I. Maybe they were after the five mil in gold bullion from the start."

"Possibly. But that sounded like a crazy-ass demand they made up on the fly," Rory said.

"Unless they planned to take selected hostages to a remote location and then demand the bullion as ransom."

"That's more plausible. But it's still off

the wall."

"Because attacking the courthouse to begin with is such a ludicrously high-risk strategy as to be insane."

"Bull's-eye."

The truck hummed along the road. The radio was playing at low volume. Foo Fighters, "Long Road to Ruin."

Rory felt a seed of excitement, tiny and fragile. "Money. But not money they expected to get from the people in the courtroom. They weren't attempting to extort cash from the government or from a wealthy hostage. They were being paid to attack the court."

"That's my assessment too."

She considered it some more. "But so much of this still makes no sense. Sylvester Church — okay, he was a career criminal. Maybe he did it strictly for the paycheck."

"Yeah."

"But Kevin Berrigan? What, he found this opportunity on Craigslist, decided that raiding courthouses paid better than selling equipment to Jiffy Lube? That's not plausible." She shook her head. "He was doing it under duress."

Seth turned onto the winding road that led to Rory's neighborhood. The mountains looked etched in the sun, gray and brown and rocky above foothills blanketed with orchards.

"Berrigan was forced to do it," she said. "To pay off his gambling debts."

"Yeah."

"Jesus."

The road curved past a windbreak of eucalyptus trees. Christ, what kind of people could force Berrigan to attack the courthouse? Who had that sort of power and could inspire such fear?

"Vegas loan sharks — I don't see it," she finally said. "What's their interest in a courthouse attack? Where's the upside? There is none."

"So it wasn't Vegas loan sharks."

Sunlight flashed across the black hood of the pickup. She said, "It was the person who bought Berrigan's gambling debts from the Vegas loan sharks."

"That's my guess."

Somebody who was still out there.

"How deep was Berrigan in debt?" she said.

"I don't know the number. Six figures minimum."

"Minimum? Then this isn't about money." She ran her fingers through her hair. "It's about big money."

"Wrong." He looked sober. "It's about

huge money. Because even a career criminal wouldn't take on a near-suicidal mission unless he was promised colossal bucks."

"And the pressure on Kevin Berrigan had to be tremendous. He wouldn't have done it otherwise. He had to believe that attacking the courthouse was his last resort."

It was nuts, she thought. And yet it had happened. "Sylvester Church — from what you know of him, did he do *anything* for reasons other than money? Family, pride, anything?"

"Boring and unimaginative guy. Too lazy to work, too greedy to get a regular job. With Church it was always all about the cash."

She half turned in her seat. "So how much was he promised?"

"Sadly, in Southern California you can hire a killer to shoot your ex for a few thousand bucks. But if you want a guy to attack a high-security, high-visibility location against armed opposition, you have to pay significantly more."

"Six figures, would you guess?" she said.

"High six. Maybe seven."

Her mind raced. "So the moneymen expected an even larger payoff at the other end."

"Enormous."

"What on earth could the people behind the attack have been after?"

Seth's face sobered. "Find that out and we'll get the cops off your back and make you safe."

He turned onto Rory's street. They cruised around the big curve by the eucalyptus grove.

"Oh no," she said.

Outside Petra's house a police car was parked at the curb. Two uniformed officers were in the driveway. Petra stood talking to them, hunched and miserable, wiping her eyes.

26

Seth pulled his truck to the curb. Rory jumped out and ran across the lawn toward Petra and the cops.

"What's going on?" she said.

Petra walked toward her, arms crossed, head low, strawberry blonde hair hanging lank around her face. Rory opened her arms. Petra walked straight into a hug and sagged against Rory's shoulder. It was an unfamiliar and disconcerting reaction.

She was shaking. "Thank God you're okay."

"Me?" Rory said.

"Mirkovic's men."

Rory tightened her grip. "What happened?"

"I'm fine. They didn't hurt me."

Seth approached, as did the two uniformed officers. One of the cops rested his hand on the telescoping baton tucked into his utility belt. He eyed Seth and Rory and didn't look tender.

"Two unknown men set off Ms. Whistler's car alarm in the parking lot at the elementary school," he said.

Petra wiped her eyes again, and her nose. "When I went to shut the alarm off, two balloon animals in suits got out of a Suburban and tried to scare the shit out of me."

Rory turned to the cops. "I think the same men confronted me on this street when I was running earlier. Detective Xavier saw them."

Petra was flushed. She tucked her hair behind her ear, and Rory saw that she'd lost one of her bangly Indian earrings.

"They said I had a problem named Aurora Mackenzie," she said.

The breeze rustled the plum trees. Seth put a hand on her elbow. "Seriously?"

"They said the justice system took a hard knock yesterday, and that victims like Brad Mirkovic and his family are suffering because of it."

"Sons of bitches," Rory said.

Seth said, "And they specifically mentioned Rory's name — as a problem?"

The officers turned their gaze on him. "Excuse me, sir. Who are you?"

Rory said, "He's with me."

Petra took a breath. "I'm fine, Officers.

Thank you for escorting me home."

"You're sure you'll be all right, ma'am?"

She nodded. "Thanks for giving the house a look-see. I appreciate it."

The cops sauntered back to their patrol car. Petra waved as they drove off.

She was still waving when she said, "Mirkovic's men said you have some explaining to do, Rory. They said you need to be prepared to tell them what they want to know."

"Petra, I am so sorry."

Petra turned and looked at her. It was a harsh, desolate look. "They said being around you is dangerous — look what happened to people around you in the courtroom yesterday. They said if I wasn't careful I could get hurt."

"Jesus." Rory's face heated. "I don't —"

"You should leave town. Go someplace. I mean it. Split."

"I can't."

"Bullshit."

"It's the trial. I was just officially informed by a judge that none of the jurors can leave the area." She glanced at Seth. "And the police department told me the same thing last night. So if I head for the hills, and they find out —"

Seth said, "Which they will. They're crawling all over you."

"— they'll put out a warrant on me and drag me back. To jail."

Petra said, "Then let them arrest you. Maybe that's better. Maybe you'd be safer in police custody with a twenty-four-hour guard."

Seth said, "Not on your life. You'd be in worse shape in a cell. Mirkovic's network could cause you trouble inside. You're better off under . . ."

"What?" Rory said.

"Under my protection."

She slid past that. "I do not want to end up in police custody."

She heard a bark. Inside the house, behind the screen door, Chiba stood wagging his tail.

"Did Mirkovic's men say anything else to you?" she said.

"Yeah." Petra looked like wax. "They said they'd be back. They said you'd better have answers for them when they come knocking on your door."

27

The chilly breeze rattled the leaves. Rory took Petra's arm and led her toward the house.

"You should get out," she said.

"We both should. Could you stay with your parents?" Petra said.

Rory shook her head. "I don't want to drag them into this."

The very thought of bringing Mirkovic's men into her parents' orbit caused a hollow feeling in the pit of her stomach. She opened the door. Chiba barked and sat and wagged his tail. Seth followed them in.

Petra said, "I'll go someplace for the weekend. Santa Barbara. Could you at least stay at a motel?"

Rory looked at Chiba.

"Take the dog to your parents' house," Petra said. "Then hide."

"Hide." Rory slammed the door so hard it shook. "Like a cornered rat?"

She stalked across the hall and the kitchen and through the living room. She scraped her hair back from her face with her fingers. She stopped by the fireplace.

Petra darted in and scooped ceramic figurines from the mantel. Her Hello Kitty goth collection. She held them to her chest, out of Rory's reach.

"The hell I'm going to hide," Rory said.

Seth stood back from them, absolutely quiet. But his face was strange.

"What?" Rory said.

He shrugged. His expression was expectant. She spread her hands.

"What time's your appointment with the lawyer?" he said.

She checked her watch. "An hour. Why?"

"Did the judge and the cops say not to leave the Ransom River city limits? Or did the judge say not to leave the jurisdiction?"

She knew what he was going to suggest and shook her head. "That won't fly. The judge did *not* mean jurors could stay in Santa Monica."

"I'll take the sofa," he said.

"No, Seth. Not your place."

"Think about it."

She'd done a lot in the past two years, but thinking about Seth Colder's bed was not at the top of the list. Not every night. Not when she was sober. Or alone.

Petra looked embarrassed to be there. She said, "Friday after school I'm going to hit the road. Rory, please. Get out of this house at least."

"It just makes me crazy," Rory said. "Petra, this is your home. The whole thing is infuriating."

Before she could throw something breakable, Petra picked up a bowl of fruit from the coffee table. It was filled with oranges. She offered them to Rory.

Rory grabbed the whole thing and pitched it at the wall.

The bowl clanged and clattered to the floor. Oranges rolled in all directions.

"Not quite what I had in mind," Petra said. "But that's okay."

Rory turned to Seth. "What am I going to do? Knowing the names of the gunmen isn't enough. What can we do with this information? Where do we go from here?"

"I'm working on it," he said.

Petra rubbed her forehead. "Mirkovic's men said something else to me." She looked distraught. "They said you seemed to take your oath as a juror kind of twisted. That you were willing to pervert the course of justice and wouldn't come clean with them, but you sure liked to get homey with your fellow jurors."

"What did they mean?" Rory said. But she was afraid she knew.

"That they'd seen you in court, being friendly with the others in the jury box. Especially the people who sat on either side of you. They said they were going to find out what was going on one way or the other. Somebody could talk, they said." She was fraught. "It could be you. Or not."

Rory stood for a long moment, feeling ensnared. She thought about Frankie Ortega and Helen Ellis.

One of the oranges rolled slowly across the floor. Chiba trotted over, picked it up with his teeth, and dropped it at Rory's feet. He joined the others in staring at her.

The lawyer's office was on the sixteenth floor of a black glass skyscraper at the corner of Santa Monica Boulevard in Century City. Outside the floor-to-ceiling window were the Los Angeles Country Club and the Santa Monica Mountains, a vista of emerald fairways and hillsides jeweled with million-dollar homes. Sitting across from the lawyer's desk, Rory's stomach churned. The view alone told her that this visit was going to be costly. A secretary in patent stilettos brought coffee on a silver tray, and the coins rang louder in her head.

A second later Jerry Nussbaum came in. "Ms. Mackenzie."

He stood as tall as a point guard, with the wingspan of a vulture. Rory stood and shook his hand.

"David Goldstein tells me you need my help." He sat down behind his desk. "That means I listen."

At three hundred fifty bucks an hour, Rory figured, he'd better. And she'd better talk fast.

"I'm a juror on the Elmendorf murder trial. And the Ransom River police apparently suspect that I have some link with the gunmen who attacked the court yesterday. They're threatening to prosecute me. They haven't been specific, but they're tossing around terms like conspiracy and felony murder."

"David sketched the basic scenario for me." Nussbaum took out a legal pad and a fountain pen. "On what evidence are they basing these suspicions?"

"CCTV video recorded during the siege. The gunmen seemed to choose me deliberately. And later I talked to one of them. One on one."

"That's it?"

"That's apparently enough."

He wrote with quick, sharp strokes. "We'll want to see the video."

"I've seen it. If you want to play conspiracist, you could make anybody in that courtroom look like an accomplice. But the cops homed in on me telling the gunmen, 'We have to help him,' after Judge Wieland was shot. They assert it's evidence I was working with the gunmen."

" 'We.' "

"Right."

Nussbaum looked thoughtful. "Take me through it."

It took her twenty minutes, and by the end, again, her heart was thudding, her hands knotted in her lap. Her coffee sat untouched on the table beside her.

When she described the tactical assault on the courtroom, Nussbaum shook his head. "Since 9/11, Homeland Security has had buckets of cash to dole out to local law enforcement — grants to first responders who want to go paramilitary. Every truck stop in America now has a fully armed SWAT team."

He wrote more notes. "Is there anything else? Anything you want to tell me that could influence the situation?"

The defense attorney's gambit. He would provide her with a zealous defense, and, if it came to it, force the prosecutor to prove her guilt beyond a reasonable doubt. He would not ask a client if she was guilty. He just wondered, hypothetically, if she had anything else she might like to divulge.

"Three things," she said.

Nussbaum's face was alert and open. He looked ready to hear.

"I didn't do it," she said. "I did nothing except get called for jury duty. I never saw the gunmen before yesterday."

He nodded. He didn't indicate whether he believed her or not. He may or may not have considered her truthfulness relevant at the moment.

"Two, I think they were paid to attack the courtroom."

That caused surprise. "How's that?"

She laid it out. He took more notes and began to frown. He didn't know what to make of her theory.

"Three. I stopped talking to the cops when they came down on me. I told them I was getting a lawyer."

His expression turned rueful. "Kiss of death."

She smiled, but without any humor. "God bless the USA."

He carefully capped his fountain pen and set it on the legal pad.

"And four. I just got laid off. Let me come in and work here to defray my bill. I'll do anything. Staple documents. Lick envelopes. Play a crazed hostile witness while you prep for cross examination."

Nussbaum hesitated. When he finally spoke he seemed to have both stress and a smile in his voice.

"You're admitted to practice in New York, you said?"

"Yes. And I'm taking the California bar exam in February."

"Then, Counselor, when this matter is resolved we may have a desk for you in the library. In the meantime, we'll work out a fee agreement."

"Thank you," Rory said. "How much trouble am I in?"

"I wish I could say you weren't in any trouble at all. You shouldn't be."

She nodded. For a moment, he looked like he was contemplating the lawsuit he'd file on her behalf six months from now, for malicious prosecution.

"But if the Ransom River PD wants to take this all the way, you're in big trouble. They can twist the evidence and implicate you on the slimmest of pretexts. Face it: They have the power. They can make your life hell."

"I don't know if they actually believe what they're alleging, or if they're trying to rattle me, or just want a scapegoat to pin the blame on."

"We'll have to address all three possibilities."

"I'm scared witless," she said.

"If the police, or the media, or anybody else wants to talk to you, refer them to me," Nussbaum said.

"What can you do?"

"Guard your back. Be ready if they arrest you or try to take you in for more questioning."

"Nothing, in other words."

Nussbaum's expression was melancholy. "Keep your mouth shut and your head down. I'll deflect the incoming missiles."

"Good luck with that," she said.

28

Rory got back to the house midafternoon. It felt strange to be home at two p.m., instead of in a buzzing office, or in a drafty warehouse filled with documents, or in an old Range Rover, carrying a backpack and refugees' files. Two p.m. meant *Judge Judy* reruns and commercials for companies that bought your gold jewelry at ten cents on the dollar. Two p.m. was the time of loose ends.

And she had a bad feeling that she herself had become a loose end of the very worst kind. She pinched the bridge of her nose.

She checked her messages. She'd applied for twenty jobs so far: with Amnesty International, Human Rights Watch, and law firms in New York, L.A., San Francisco, and even, as a safety application, Ransom River. For a numbing second she saw herself at the checkout stand at Beddie-Buy, thirty-five years old, worn out, holding a silent competition with Riss to scan customers' throw pillows the fastest. Then she checked e-mail and perked up. A San Francisco firm wanted to speak to her. A phone interview: the first elimination round in job jujitsu. But it was a start.

The knock on the front door made her jump like a cricket. She ran upstairs, peered out the dormer window, and saw Seth's truck parked in the driveway. He was directly below her, standing on the porch. She ran back down and let him in.

"How'd the meeting with the attorney go?" he said.

"If you enjoy eating bile, it was amazing."

For a second he looked disappointed, as though he'd hoped she might simply welcome him in and be glad to have him there. But the world had moved on from those days.

"The gunmen. I've been thinking," he said.

She led him into the kitchen and put on a fresh pot of coffee. She avoided looking at the television, as though it might flare to life of its own volition and suck them through the screen into an episode of *Dog, the Bounty Hunter.*

"My brain's fried. Feed it to me," she said.

"Church and Berrigan. Here's the point I

keep coming to. Not only was the attack not personal, but it was never supposed to develop into a siege."

Rory had two mugs in her hands. "What do you mean?"

"The gunmen were there to grab four hostages and *take them away*. But the attack went wrong."

She set down the mugs. "Because the bystander counterattacked. There was chaos. That slowed them down."

"They were supposed to get in and out with you and the other three 'chosen' hostages. But they blew it. They didn't move fast enough. The cops arrived before they could escape with you and the others."

"That makes sense," she said.

"That's why the gunmen ended up barricaded inside. That's why you ended up against the window. That's why they wasted time inventing demands that sounded ridiculous: because there weren't supposed to be demands." He paused. "Just an abduction."

"Me."

It jumped into clear relief against the confusion and mayhem of everything that had happened. "It was a kidnapping that went bad."

The chill drip of adrenaline, of threat and

fear, began working down her arms to her fingertips.

"Why?" she said. "To cause a mistrial? Certainly not to influence my vote. Nobody in the history of jury tampering has attempted to rig a trial by kidnapping a juror *from the courtroom.* Not even Tricky Dick Nixon and his pal Ronnie Reagan."

"No. Jury tampering generally leans toward blackmail and quiet bribes."

"Nobody does it in front of the judge and lawyers and the press, in the middle of testimony."

"So it wasn't your role in the trial. It was you."

"That is goddamned freaking me out."

He stared at her. She hadn't moved.

"Aurora Mackenzie. The ice sculpture of freak-outs," he said.

"Is that an insult?"

"Hardly. Rory, you could be *on fire* and you'd have exactly the same expression on your face."

That, for some reason, nearly made her crack. She turned to the coffeemaker and poured mugs for both of them.

"The media is playing up the terror angle," she said. "Cop hatred. But the gunmen had the perfect opportunity to execute the defendants, and they didn't."

266

"It wasn't political," Seth said.

"It was about me."

He watched her for a moment. "Your NGO work. Political? Dangerous?"

"Always political. Rarely dangerous. Seth, I spent ninety percent of my time evaluating case histories and court filings and transcripts of deportation hearings. I bought myself a parka because I worked for seven months in a warehouse outside Helsinki, reading bureaucratic reports. I wasn't hired for my razor-sharp legal mind. I was a glorified paralegal. A document drone. That's not what the siege was about."

"Dangerous," he said.

"No." She ran a hand through her hair. "I went into the field only twice. And not to places where the government is going to reach out *to America* and seek revenge against an expat aid worker."

"Where?"

"Once to Syria."

"That's dangerous."

"Before the unrest. I cadged my way into flying with an ICRC delegation. It was safe."

"Like Russian roulette is safe."

"We're talking about a repressive state, not a first-person-shooter video game. I traveled everywhere in an air-conditioned Range Rover. We ate at five-star restaurants.

Watched CNN at the Sheraton."

He shook his head, seemingly disbelieving. "Syria. Then you spun the chamber and headed where?"

"Zimbabwe."

As she said it, the vista rose in her mind. Red earth. A vast bowl of blue sky. Acacia trees gracing the horizon, tall trunks spreading to lacy green canopies. The air thick with the smell of wood smoke from cooking fires. It clung to people's clothing, dense and earthy.

"Again, not personally dangerous to me."

" 'Personally?' " he said.

She paused. "That country . . ." She tried to explain it. "It's beautiful. And completely messed up. We went to a village in the bush, about a hundred miles from Bulawayo."

"Why?"

"Family that had escaped to South Africa and then to Britain. They spent fifteen months in a detention center in northern England — mom, kids, a grandfather, all cooped up in a dormitory behind razor wire — before their request for asylum was rejected. They were judged economic migrants rather than political refugees. They were sent back. We went to see if they were still alive."

Seth was looking at her strangely.

"We found them. They . . ." She had to pause. "The grandfather had died. Been grabbed by thugs, driven out to the bush, and had his legs broken before being dumped and left to crawl home. He didn't make it. The mom and kids were alive. Mom had been raped by soldiers. The kids were ragged, but they had a roof over their heads and were in one piece. We couldn't do anything. We left."

Seth stared at her, hard, for a long minute. "That's it?"

"That's it. We drove back to Bulawayo, hopped a commuter flight to Harare, then British Airways to Heathrow."

"So how come your face is as pale as a sheet of paper, and you look like you're about to break out in hives?"

The view in her mind flared white again, and she smelled the smoke that clung to Sarah's dress and heard the clarion laughter of the little girl, Grace. Four years old, racing her tiny brother. Running hard, with unbridled joy. Smile on Grace's face, full of mischief. She had looked thin.

"It has nothing to do with me. My group was completely safe."

"But?"

She turned away and stared blankly at the television. "We planned to file an appeal on their behalf with the British Foreign and Commonwealth Office. But . . ."

"Rory?"

"Asylum Action lost its funding."

Four years old. She squeezed her eyes shut and swallowed it all. She sensed Seth approaching and hovering near her shoulder.

She shook herself out of it and stepped away from him. "The courthouse attack had nothing to do with their case. Zimbabwe doesn't strike out at aid workers like me after we come home to California. It's preposterous."

"Rory."

"The whole thing's a farce."

"Hey."

She turned. "We live in a sick little world, Seth. But that sickness isn't what's infecting my life right now. So tell me what else you're thinking."

He paused and looked at her like she was an unstable and possibly explosive substance.

Two years with Asylum Action. Two years, and what good had she done?

Two years, and what had Seth done?

"Go on," she said.

"The siege," he said, slowly. "If it's about you, then why? There's only one thing I keep coming back to. It's not just you but your family, and Ransom River."

"What?"

"Rory, you haven't done anything in Ransom River except grow up here, and win a case full of trophies, and get the hell out of town. So how come the gunmen came after you?"

"What could it have to do with my family?"

"We have to find out."

She began to feel angry. "Why do you think it's *my* family? How come you don't think it's something to do with you?"

"I doubt it."

"But we're talking criminals here, and you're the ex-cop. That's your milieu."

He burst into an incongruous smile. "Girl, I gotta love you just for your vocabulary."

"Your stomping ground. Your scum bucket. The slime in which you swim."

He raised his hands, calling truce. "The people who sent the gunmen have to be after huge money. Agreed?"

"Agreed."

"But you aren't rich. Neither are your parents."

"Hardly."

She saw where he was going. She put down her coffee.

"So where's the cash?" she said.

"That is the question."

"Do you have any idea how to find out?"

"Yes." His face darkened. "From the last person who'll want to talk about it. Especially to me."

"Somebody from the police department?"

"My dad."

29

Lucky Colder lived in one of Ransom River's oldest neighborhoods, tucked under live oaks near the Hill — the one that Ransom River was over, the one that separated it from the San Fernando Valley and the crawling energy of Los Angeles. The homes had been built in the forties, when aerospace came to the town. Later, a popular television western had been filmed there. Most of the sets at the Callahan Ranch, as it had been called on TV, were long gone. But the house where the matriarch held sway, standing hands on hips astride the front porch while her seven sons rode out to wrangle cattle and fight varmints, had been preserved as a city park. The show itself lurked in a vault somewhere, waiting for its resurrection as a period piece, retro chic.

Seth drove slowly, almost reluctantly. The trees looked heavier. The homes looked smaller. Flashback City.

"How long since you've seen your dad?" she said.

"Longer than he'd like." He smiled. "Last month."

He stopped at the curb. Exactly where he'd always parked, to the inch. He left the engine idling for a moment, as though he might decide to floor it. The Colder house was tidy, with a covered porch and neat rose beds. An old Chrysler New Yorker was parked in the driveway. A bumper sticker said, SUPPORT YOUR LOCAL POLICE DEPARTMENT. They got out and walked toward the door. A sign was nailed next to it: FORGET THE DOG, BEWARE OF THE OLD MAN.

Lucky lived a quiet life, but it hadn't always been that way. Though Rory hadn't known it as a kid, Lucky had lived hard. Only years later did Seth tell her about his dad's struggle with alcohol and how his parents' marriage had gone to the brink before Lucky got sober. He'd been an AA sponsor for years now. And he had been on his own since Seth's mother died from cancer five years earlier.

Rory asked, "How's he doing?"

Seth's expression said, *Let's find out.* He knocked.

Inside, footsteps creaked toward the door.

When it opened, Lucky Colder stood surprised. His expression was so quiet that it looked wooden, and for a moment Rory worried that he might slam the door on his son. His half-glasses had slid down his nose. He had a newspaper in his hand. He was wearing good slacks and Rockports with a short-sleeved button-down shirt. And suspenders.

Then his face split with a grin. He clapped Seth on both shoulders.

"Dammit, I was all ginned up to debate the Jehovah's Witnesses and send them away in tears." He turned to Rory and shook his head. "But look who we have here. My goodness. What a day."

"Hello, Mr. Colder."

"For God's sake, girl, it's Lucky. Come here." He hugged her, patted her hard on the back, laughing. He smelled of aftershave. Something he'd had on the shelf since 1968. Hai Karate, maybe.

He raised his nose and eyed her through his half-glasses. "My, you look fine."

"So do you, you rogue," she said.

He had to be curious to the point of combustion. Maybe he was secretly alarmed to see her with Seth. But his enthusiasm seemed unpretentious and genuine. It warmed her.

His face sobered. "You in one piece? I saw the news yesterday."

"They didn't hurt me."

"Awful thing. Dreadful." Lucky glanced at his son and back to Rory. "That why you're here?"

She nodded.

He led them to the living room. It was still paneled with fake pine. "Yesterday must have scared the bejesus out of your parents."

Seth said, "Rory's okay."

"Parents' worst nightmare, even when your kid's an adult. Enough to make the toughest bastard pray."

Seth looked at the floor.

Rory said, "Yeah. Mom built a Santeria altar, and by the time I got home Dad had made a giant sculpture of Jesus out of butter."

Lucky laughed, bearlike. "Your dad still with the Forest Service?"

"At a desk more than he's with the Hotshots, but of course."

He cleared newspapers from the sofa. "Sit. Seth, give me a hand with some coffee, would you, son?"

They headed across the hall to the kitchen. Rory sat. The living room was as she remembered. A green plaid sofa. Coffee table with a chunk whacked out of it, a victim of the catapult Seth built to fire ball bearings across the room. Photos completely covered one wall, the frames dusty. Commendations from the Ransom River Police Department. School photos of Seth and his three older brothers. They all had the same sandy hair and dark eyes, but Seth's photos revealed his restless energy.

The only addition was an eight-by-ten photo of Seth's late mother, in a silver frame, on top of the television.

On the entire wall of photos, not one showed Seth with Lucky. And not one showed Seth in a police uniform.

In the kitchen, Lucky grabbed mugs and spoons. Seth lingered near the door. Lucky spoke to him in murmurs, but Rory caught "out of the blue" and "last thing I ever expected," and "mind my own business, but . . ."

Lucky shoved a carton of milk into Seth's hands and they came back into the living room. Lucky handed Rory a mug of coffee. She sipped. It was strong enough to make her nerves ping like a radarscope. Seth ambled to the window and looked out.

Lucky eased himself onto the sofa. "It's good to see you both, but I know this isn't an ice cream social. What brings you here?"

His gruff, blunt, teddy-bear manner had

undoubtedly served him well as a detective. Depending on what he wanted to get out of you, he could be either cuddly or ferocious. When she was a kid, he had terrified her. He'd always been warm and welcoming, but his intelligent glower, the look on his face that seemed to say, *I'm watching you and you won't get away with it,* had been enough to petrify her.

He sat with his arms crossed, his coffee steaming on the table. He seemed to be trying, intensely, not to look at Seth. She realized that he had not come to grips with Seth's decision to quit the force. It seemed to still be a raw scrape, unhealed and stinging.

Seth scanned the street outside and turned from the window to face his father. "This has to be off the record. Nothing leaves this room."

"Of course," Lucky said.

"Rory and I have come to the conclusion that the attack on the courthouse was designed with one purpose in mind. To abduct her."

Lucky's only reaction was to raise an eyebrow.

"I got the gunmen's names," Seth said. "They had to be doing it for money."

Lucky slowly leaned forward. "You'd better lay it out."

Seth explained. Lucky listened and didn't interrupt. After five minutes, he picked up his coffee cup. Seth stood by the window, his shoulders slanted, a challenging expression in his eyes. Rory waited for Lucky to tell him to stand up straight.

But Lucky said, "You okay, son?"

Seth shifted. His face pinched, as though with pain. "Yeah." He paced across the room. His gaze panned the wall of photos.

Lucky blinked and looked away. After a second, he cleared his throat.

"I'll buy it," he said. "Makes sense, what you've come up with. So what do you want from me?"

Seth turned. "Where's the money coming from? And why do they think it has something to do with Rory? That's what we don't understand."

Lucky looked at her.

"They attacked the courtroom, shot people, held sixty innocent folks hostage — it's ghastly," she said. "And if it's about me . . . what the hell for?"

Lucky said, "You're entitled to be mad."

"I want to take a tire iron to somebody."

"And scared."

"I'm terrified."

"But you're not entitled to feel guilty

about it."

Her face burned. "How can I not?"

Seth's cell phone rang. He checked the display and said, "Excuse me."

He headed to the front door. He waited until he was outside before answering the call, saying, "Yeah." He closed the door behind him and walked to the street, talking in low tones.

Lucky couldn't take his eyes off him. Without turning to Rory, he said, "Seth's not telling me something. And not giving me the full story."

Finally he glanced at her. "He brought you to me instead of the police department."

"You're his closest source," Rory said. "And you know the history of this town."

Lucky smiled. It was rueful. "He doesn't trust the department. It's a point of contention between us," he said.

"I can imagine," she said.

His face tightened. "Did he tell you corruption runs through the department like a virus?"

She did not intend to get into a game of *Dad said, son said.* No way. "He didn't use that phrase."

"But he thinks the whole force is bent."

She didn't actually shrug, but Lucky got the gist of her reaction.

"He worked with good people. Gil Strand-berg, Ray Nguyen — guys I knew. So where he got the idea . . ." He shook his head. Looked at his hands.

"Seth had a very bad experience," he said. "The warehouse fire. It was every cop's nightmare. Losing a brother officer — dealing with that's always a killer."

She frowned.

"But with the injuries Seth suffered . . ." He glanced out the front window. Seth was pacing on the sidewalk by his truck. "Everything came crashing in on him at once."

He paused. Blessedly, he didn't actually look at her. She was part of that *everything*. But she didn't know what he was talking about.

He held still a moment longer. If she'd just walked into the room, she would have thought he had been stuck in the gut by a knife.

"Lucky?" she said.

He shook his head. "He had a terrible time getting perspective. It happened so soon after . . ."

The air felt heavy. "After I left?"

"Everything seemed to look like flames to him." His voice thickened. "He looked for somebody to take it out on. He needs somebody to blame. He doesn't know how to forgive. Or at least, he hasn't found a way to let it go. Most of all, he can't forgive himself."

He finally turned his sad, troubled eyes on her. She sat stunned.

"Lucky, I haven't heard any of this. Seth hasn't spoken to me about a fire."

Outside, Seth ended his call and strode briskly toward the house.

Lucky seemed to calculate whether he had sufficient time, and asked, "What's going on with you two?"

"After I figure it out, I'll let you know."

She saw the pain on his face. It was deep and too much for him to explain. Whatever had happened when Seth's undercover operation went wrong, whatever injuries and pain he had suffered, Lucky could barely speak of it.

She said, "What exactly happened to him at —"

Seth walked back in. He seemed to take the emotional temperature in the living room. His gaze flicked between his dad and Rory.

"Sorry for the interruption. That was a contact. I'm trying to get more information on Sylvester Church and Kevin Berrigan. They're working on it."

"Contact?" Lucky said.

Seth didn't elaborate. After an uncomfortable second under his dad's eye, he began to pace again.

Lucky said, "Son, sit down."

Seth paced.

"You're making me seasick. Sit yourself down and listen to me."

Reluctantly, Seth took a seat on the arm of the sofa. "What is it?"

"You think money is behind the attack on the trial?"

Rory said, "Yes."

Lucky set down his coffee. "My advice? Back away."

"Dad," Seth said sharply.

"Leave this alone."

"No."

"No good will come of digging into it."

"Forget that. This isn't a scavenger hunt at a birthday party," Seth said.

"You're talking about 'huge money.' A coordinated attack by heavily armed gunmen on a well-defended building full of law enforcement officers. Multiple casualties already." He looked not just pensive, but fierce. "Back away. You think you can dig into this on your own? That's foolish." His mouth pinched. "That's dangerous. Son, be sensible. Choose your battles."

Rory said, "This battle has chosen me. I

fight or I surrender. And I won't surrender. Somebody else already dug the pit and set me up to get buried in it. And I'm not going."

Lucky looked torn. For a moment resistance tugged at his features. He sat straighter.

"All right. You want to know what the gunmen were after. Where the big money is? There's only one thing that makes sense."

He turned to Rory. "The Geronimo Armored car robbery. When you were kids. That's what it's about."

"Say that again," Seth said.

"The armored car heist. It happened not ten miles from here. The robbers got away with twenty-five million dollars. And that money's never been found."

30

"That heist was almost twenty years ago," Seth said.

"Twenty years ago this February twelfth," Lucky said.

The heist was part of Ransom River's folklore. It was up there with *The Callahans* and the Great West Side Tire Fire, which raged for weeks in a mountain of discarded radials behind the auto-wrecking yard. The heist was bigger than the prom queen's float smashing into the pumps at the Union 76 station during the homecoming parade.

"I remember," Seth said.

"The meteor shower," Rory said.

They'd seen the police lights that night. And the next day they'd heard the buzz in their fourth-grade classroom, boys and girls uneasy and excited, murmuring about *bank robbers.* On the news, reporters stood outside yellow police tape and talked in urgent grown-up tones about a shootout.

Her parents had stared spellbound at the TV. Rory had been transfixed: a *shootout*.

"An armored car was attacked and robbed," she said.

And the rest began to whisper at her. *That night. The tree house.*

Lucky said, "Do you remember anything else?"

"I was nine."

Seth said, "What's special about that robbery, Dad?"

Rory said, "Besides the twenty-five million bucks? I'm guessing that's a megaton of money compared to your average daily L.A. County bank robbery."

"That's massive," Seth said.

Lucky said, "The cash was being delivered to a Federal Reserve processing facility, where it was supposed to be destroyed."

"Why?" Rory said.

"What do you know about the life cycle of money?"

"Little. I don't have any."

"Hold on."

Lucky pushed to his feet and trundled to his bedroom. They heard a dresser drawer open, and close again. He returned with a money clip that held a slim stash of folded bills. His emergency cash, Rory bet.

"Paper money doesn't last long," he said.

"Currency wears out. And the smaller the denomination, the quicker a bill deteriorates." He slid the bills from the money clip. "A dollar barely lasts eighteen months."

The one in his hand looked soft and tired and had a well-established crease in the middle of George Washington's face.

"Same length of life, more or less, for fives and tens." He handed her the single and held up a twenty. "This'll last two years."

He gave it to her and unfolded a fifty. "This'll last longer because it doesn't circulate as much."

He flattened a hundred and held it up so Ben Franklin smiled at her. "This might last seven years."

"Got it," Rory said.

"When a bill gets mutilated or so worn that it's unreadable, the government will replace it with a fresh one from the Bureau of Engraving and Printing."

He continued to hold up the hundred-dollar bill.

"I'm not sure what I'm supposed to be looking at," she said.

Lucky turned to Seth.

"Is this a quiz?" After a moment Seth said, "It's an older currency design."

Lucky nodded and set it on the coffee table. "A classic."

He showed them the last bill from the money clip. The difference was immediately apparent. On the new bill, Franklin's portrait was much larger, and set to the left. The colors of the bill were more subtle and elaborate.

"Anticounterfeiting measures," Lucky said. "It's an ongoing battle between the Treasury and counterfeiters worldwide. The government's rolling out another model as well, with three-D security ribbons that make it look like the Liberty Bell's jumping up at you when you tilt the bill. Plus a second security thread, a portrait watermark, and images that change color when you turn the bill. The bell goes from green to copper." He looked canny. "A U.S. hundred is the most-counterfeited bill on the planet."

Seth said, "Why do you still have that old one? You're a skinflint, Dad, but not that tight."

"I'm still waiting for you or your brothers to earn it."

Seth smirked, not exactly amused.

Lucky said to Rory, "I told my boys the first one of them to memorize the Bill of Rights would earn a hundred bucks. Not surprised the older boys never got around to it. But this one here" — he nodded at

Seth — "I did think a young man who wanted to be a police officer might care about civil liberties. Or at least about knowing the Fourth and Fifth Amendments."

Maybe it was intended as a joke, but Seth reddened and looked out the window. Lucky's lips drew tight.

He tucked the bills back in the money clip. "When paper money wears out, the federal banking system replaces it. Branch banks set aside bills that are worn or damaged. Eventually, they're collected and replaced with shiny new Federal Reserve notes. Damaged bills — dirty, torn, defaced — are sent to sites where they're shredded."

Rory said, "And the cash from the heist was on its way to the shredder."

"The processing site was in eastern Los Angeles County. But the method they used to deliver the cash was prey to security flaws."

"Geronimo Armored," she said.

"A secure courier was always contracted to collect the cash from the branch banks. Geronimo Armored scheduled their collection runs so they could pick up large volumes of cash and take it to a company depot. The depot would bundle it up and then transport it to the processing site to be destroyed," he said. "But on the occasion in question, somebody got wind of the huge collection and attacked the armored car en route to the Geronimo depot. Outside a branch bank in Ransom River."

Seth finally looked at his dad. "It was ambushed with inside information?"

"Like almost all big armored heists," Lucky said.

Rory said, "Wait. If the money was on its way to be destroyed, wasn't it worthless?"

Lucky shook his head. "Branch banks set aside bills they *think* are too old. But the feds might disagree. Sometimes it's obvious a bill's too far gone, but other times a bill's just soiled. The ones who decide whether a bill will be destroyed are the inspectors at the Federal Reserve processing facility. Plenty of bills are deemed usable. They're sent back into circulation."

"So the robbers gambled that they'd get legal tender," Rory said.

"Yes."

Seth said, "How did the robbery go down?"

"One of the Geronimo guards exited the bank with the money on a dolly. The other guard opened the door to the armored car so he could load it. That's when the robbers attacked," he said. "But it went bad. The Geronimo guards fought back. One robber was killed. Two were captured and imprisoned. Both guards were injured."

Lucky stopped, his eyes gleaming.

"And?" Seth said.

"The money disappeared and has never been found."

"Twenty-five million dollars," Rory said.

Lucky nodded.

They were quiet for a moment. A clock ticked. Lucky's face was flushed. Seth had gone back to avoiding his father's gaze. But this time, Rory thought, it wasn't because his dad was poking an old wound. It was because Lucky was exposing a crusty scab of his own.

"Does that mean it's an open case?" she said.

"A cold one," Lucky said. "The convicted robbers have never spoken one word to the authorities about what happened to the money."

"It's still out there," Seth said.

"Yes."

"So somebody got away with it."

Lucky nodded somberly. "But they never spent the money. The serial numbers of those bills were recorded, and they haven't shown up again. Plus nobody has ever tried to collect the reward. And that reward is big."

Rory said, "And you think that robbery is connected to the attack on the courtroom yesterday."

"Hunch. Intuition. Call it an old detective's gut acting up. But yes. Ransom River, something so risky and outrageous — that's what I think."

Seth said, "Were you assigned to the case?"

Lucky's mouth pulled to one side. "Every detective on the force was assigned to the case one way or another. This was national news. Our fifteen minutes. It had everything people wanted in a heist. Guns, money, a getaway. A dead man. It was a big deal."

"You investigated the currency angle?"

"At the time I was in Crimes Against Property. That put me on the task force assigned to hunting down the stolen money."

"But you never found it."

Lucky stared at his coffee. "Maybe the getaway driver's up in the Cascades with D. B. Cooper, using it as kindling for his campfire."

Seth rubbed a knuckle across his chin. He ambled back to the window, stared at the street, and thought about it.

"Why now?" he said.

"Why do I think people are after the money now? Because the robbers are getting out of prison. They've waited a long time for that cash. And with new greenback designs getting phased in, the old bills get more and more distinctive. Soon they'll be too distinctive."

"But the older currency is still good," Seth said.

"Yes. Until it goes into the shredder, every bill that's been issued by the U.S. government since 1861 remains legal tender. But with each day, passing the cash from the heist gets more difficult. Soon those old-style bills will look so unusual that they'll stick out like a sore thumb. And remember, the serial numbers were recorded. A strange-looking bill — especially if it's a hundred — passing it will become nearly impossible. If anybody's going to get rich, they need to find that money ASAP, before it becomes so risky it's useless."

Seth said, "Twenty-five million. I can buy it."

Rory said, "I can't. Because a heist that took place when I was in fourth grade has absolutely no connection to me."

For a second, Lucky's expression was zealous, as though he was about to spring a trap, or hit her with the last, triumphant bit of evidence. But his ardor dimmed. He looked almost sad.

"It does," he said. "Nobody could prove it, and nobody would talk. But rumor has it, the man who got away was your uncle Lee."

31

"Lee?"

"Lee Mackenzie. None other. I'm sorry, Rory," Lucky said.

She felt stunned. "That's crazy. Lee isn't a bank robber."

"He was a person of interest in the investigation."

Seth turned from the window. His face was dead solemn. Her heart sank.

Uncle Lee — sweet, crazy Uncle Lee, who was half-assed at everything he did. She really knew nothing about him. Except that he had been in jail several times and had scooted across the border to Mexico and stayed there.

She closed her eyes. "What did the police know about him?"

"Nothing tangible," Lucky said. "A few bits of hearsay, mostly from unreliable characters. His previous run-ins with the law were . . . let's call them small-time but aspirational attempts at criminality."

"Aspirational. Meaning he was looking to get into things in a bigger way?"

"He liked money," Lucky said.

Rory put her elbows on her knees and leaned her head against her hands. "Person of interest — so, a suspect. But you had no evidence against him."

The silence was pounding. She looked up.

Lucky had shed his jolly exterior. She saw the stony resolve he must have had as a cop. The teddy bear had teeth.

"Lee got busted three or four times over the years I was a detective," he said. "Fencing stolen property, one time using a stolen prescription to obtain Vicodin, I think it was. Things like that. He pled out, got probation the first time, did a couple of months in county lockup for one of the other charges. Small-time stuff."

"So why, if none of the others involved in the robbery would talk . . ."

"Sometimes it's what *doesn't* get said, as much as what does."

"Oh God."

"Nobody had heard about Lee being involved with the heist. The other robbers were from L.A. But they had Ransom River connections. They ran in the same circles. And Rory, there's one big stonking clue in all of this."

She knew but hated to say it. "No. Lee left town before the robbery. I'm sure of it."

"Your uncle left town right *around* the time of the robbery. And he hasn't been back."

She wanted to argue. It was the thinnest of links. But she also suspected that Lucky had more evidence than he'd revealed. Maybe much more.

And worst of all, she could believe it.

She could believe Lee would be involved in the heist. But there was one thing she couldn't believe: that her uncle was behind the courthouse attack, or any attempt to hurt her. That still made no sense.

"How am I going to tell my parents?" she said.

Lucky simply looked at her. Almost, it seemed, with pity.

"You don't have to tell them," he said. "It won't come as a surprise."

Her limbs went cold. She felt like she was shrinking inside. And then she felt stupid. Blind.

Of course her parents suspected. How could they not? And the low conversations, the mutters in the kitchen that stopped abruptly when she walked in, the awkward glances and forced smiles that came from mentioning Uncle Lee — the entire Mac-kenzie way of doing emotional business took on new shades of gray.

The night of the meteor shower, the night of Freddy Krueger, she and Seth had hidden in the countryside for an hour before she snuck back into her room through the window. She'd paused, listening, but the house was quiet. In the morning, at breakfast, she said, "I heard a noise last night."

"It was nothing," her mom said.

"There was a van out back. A guy got out."

Her mom's smile looked like a jack-o'-lantern. "It was a man from your dad's work. He was drunk. He just needed to sleep it off."

And her mom stood and took her dishes to the sink and left the kitchen.

A random fragment of memory bloomed, full color. Her mom, coming into her room to tell her good night, after the Memorial Day barbecue. After Boone and Riss had gone home. After the postcards from Uncle Lee had been ripped from her corkboard.

Sam had strolled in, smiling. Rory was sitting on her bed with a book in her hands. Sam bent, kissed her on the top of her head, smoothed down her hair, said, "Don't read too late." Rory had nodded, feeling roiled

298

and disturbed. Sam stepped back, and her gaze snagged on the corkboard. The bits of postcard stuck beneath the tacks, all that remained. Rory waited for her mom to say something. She herself did not want to mention her cousins. Did not want to start a *thing.* Just let it all stay quiet. *Shh. Nothing to see here.*

But Sam stared at the corkboard for a pensive moment and forced a smile again. "Sleep tight, sweetie."

Turned and left.

What had Sam thought? That Rory had torn down the postcards herself? They never mentioned it aloud. It was one of those things that just floated past, a piece of emotional junk that the family presumed would degrade and sink to the bottom.

No more postcards arrived from her uncle after that. The supply on the corkboard was never replenished.

Sam didn't know, however, that Rory had another postcard from Uncle Lee, one she kept in her desk drawer. It was particularly colorful and adventurous, and Rory had kept it as a special, secret message from her uncle. So Boone and Riss hadn't been able to rip it down. As far as she knew, the postcard was still there, in her old desk or in a box in her closet at her parents' house.

The shrinking, sinking sensation intensified. Lee hadn't withdrawn from his family. He had run.

She felt Seth and Lucky staring at her.

She exhaled. "So what do we do?"

Lucky said, "I'll ask the department to pull the file on the Geronimo Armored robbery."

"No," Seth said.

Lucky sat back, stung. "I haven't been put completely out to pasture. The department has a cold-case crew — some of us old-timers look at open cases from time to time. And this is a big one."

"Don't," Seth said. "Not yet."

"You got to trust somebody, son."

"Dad, I trust *you.*" For a moment Seth looked hurt. Then he crossed to the sofa and put a hand on Lucky's shoulder. "Just let me think about this for a while."

Rory stood. "Seth's right. Don't excavate the file yet."

Lucky seemed regretful. "If your uncle's involved, you won't be able to keep it buried forever. And you won't be able to protect your folks. Or your aunt."

"I don't want to. I want to find out the truth. And if Lee's involved, the chips will have to fall where they may. But let me talk to my parents first."

She nodded at Seth, indicating she was ready to leave. To Lucky she said, "Thanks. I appreciate your help. And your honesty."

"Sorry to be the bearer of bad news," he said.

"It is what it is. Nothing to do with you."

At the door she gave him a hug. He squeezed her and thumped her on the back, then turned guardedly to Seth.

"Good to see you."

After an awkward pause, Lucky gave him what Rory's dad called the Great American Buddy Pat: a hearty cuff on the shoulder.

The phone rang as Seth opened the door. They were halfway to the truck when Lucky called to them and came outside.

His expression was cool. "I know you want time to think about having me talk to the department. But time's up."

Seth said, "Who was it?"

"Another old-timer. Detective who still punches the clock. He pretended he was calling just to chat, but he gave me a heads-up. The detectives who interviewed Rory last night —"

"Xavier and Zelinski?" Rory said.

"Them. They wanted him to feel me out, find out what you're up to. And find out what's going on between you two. Word's spread that you're here, son."

"What the hell?" she said.

"Watch yourselves," Lucky said. Then he looked at her. "Just a second. Rory, Seth'll catch up with you."

Seth looked wary, but Rory nodded and said, "I'll be in the truck." She walked toward the pickup and heard the men's voices behind her.

Lucky said, "I know you're going after the truth. And I know it's futile to try and stop you. But don't get Rory killed."

"Dad."

"Listen to me, Seth."

Rory forced herself not to turn and stare. Lucky lowered his voice. But she heard it, as clear as glass.

"She loves you," Lucky said. "And you love her even more. You couldn't live with her death on your head."

In the sun, as Rory approached the truck, her reflection warped and winked back at her, distorted and semitransparent. She saw beyond it. She saw that by returning to Ransom River, Seth might put himself in danger. And she saw why he had returned despite that risk: for her. The sun jumped from the windows and stung her eyes.

32

They rolled through flat farmland striped with rows of strawberries. Irrigation sprinklers rainbowed the air in the warm autumn afternoon. On the stereo the Black Keys pounded out hard blues. Rory stared out the windshield.

You love her even more.

She didn't want to bleed in front of Seth. She listened to the music.

"Lee," she said. "That night."

"Freddy Krueger," Seth said.

"If that was him . . . Goddamn it."

In her hermetically sealed memories, her uncle had delighted in seeing her. She remembered a man who always had a moment, a smile, a laugh for her. He could have ignored her, as adults sometimes did, and paid attention only to her parents, but he was generous with his affection. She clearly remembered her sense of soaring when Lee came through the door. He was fun. He was young. He tickled her. He made her laugh.

Maybe he just never had a job, so he always had the time. Maybe her parents were too busy being responsible to engage in lighthearted mischief with her. But that didn't seem right either. They'd delighted in her too. A warmer, calmer enchantment, but one that was solid, that always bore her to safety.

Even if her uncle had been part of the gang that robbed the Geronimo Armored car, what could that have to do with an attempt twenty years later to abduct her?

"Why would anybody want to grab *me?*" she said. "I know nothing about the money from the heist."

Seth watched the road. "You're a bargaining chip."

"But who's trying to drive the bargain?" She shook her head. "Not Lee. Presumably, if he was the fourth man on the robbery, he's the one who got away with the money."

"That's the bottom line, literally and figuratively. If he got the money and got himself over the border, he's the big winner."

"And the surviving members of the gang, who are about to get out of prison, want their cut. So they use me . . . I still don't

304

—" She stopped, her lips parted.

"What?" Seth said.

"Oh my God. It makes sense now. What the gunmen whispered in the courtroom." She half turned in her seat. "They mentioned 'payment' and 'consequences.' And then they very clearly said something about 'drawing him out.' "

Seth flicked her a look, sharp. "You thought they were talking about a witness to Obrad Mirkovic's murder."

"I did." She rubbed her forehead. "Everything's come at me so fast, I haven't kept track of it all. They mentioned 'losing' and 'the girl.' "

"If you're the girl, and they were after the money . . ."

"Then Lee is the one they want to draw out."

Slowly, as though far gone in thought, Seth nodded. Rory's pulse began to pound.

"If they want a bargaining chip to draw Lee out of hiding, why go for his niece?"

"Instead of his immediate family."

"Maybe they have a lingering sense of loyalty to Lee? Or to Amber?"

"Rory." He looked jaundiced. "We're talking about people who sent gunmen to storm a trial during open court. Loyalty and consideration played no part in it."

He was right. She said, "You're not going to sit back and wait for me to tease the family history out of my parents. Are you?"

"No. I'm going to find out about the men who carried out the heist. One's dead; two are in prison. I'll chase down their records, see if there's anything we can hook onto." He looked serious. "Couple of cons, about to be released after twenty years inside, thinking their partner Lee took off with millions while they paid the price — that's motive."

"No kidding," Rory said.

"But talk to your folks."

"That'll be fun. Like running my hand through a can opener."

He looked pensive. "I never knew your uncle. Were you his pet niece or something?"

"You mean, if I were to be taken hostage, would he surface to rescue me? What made me special?"

"Yes."

"He played this magic trick where he pulled a coin out from behind my ear. And he always called me Aurora. He explained that Aurora meant dawn. The sun coming up. He said that was me."

Seth eyed her. "He adored you."

"I thought so."

"And you adored him."

"I was a child."

"All the purer."

They drove past an avocado orchard. The trees flashed green in the sun. The hard blues on the stereo faded.

Seth said, "About calling the cops."

"You're not going to let your dad talk to his old buddies on the force?"

"He doesn't want to believe there's corruption in the department. It's not that he's naïve; it's that he trusts the people he worked with. But I don't know who those trusted people might talk to. And I don't want somebody bent to get word that you're digging into this." He glanced at her. "So about *you* calling the cops to discuss this matter further."

"They can talk to Nussbaum from now on."

"You know why they gave you twenty-four hours to come clean?" he said.

"So they have time to get mints for my pillow at the jail?"

"They're working on a 'first forty-eight' theory."

"Yes. If they don't solve a crime within the first forty-eight hours, the likelihood of doing so plummets."

"I know you've been to law school."

"Law school doesn't teach that stuff. TV does."

"This is the flip side. The department is under enormous pressure to close this case. Believe me, the detectives who interviewed you, the uniforms, the lieutenant who took the lead on the siege — they're all being stepped on to show results."

"Within forty-eight hours."

"Which gives them a huge incentive to claim they've done just that."

Her stomach tightened.

"The chief of police is pressuring them. The mayor is pressuring the chief. The county's pressuring the mayor. Fox News and Court TV are pressuring all of them and asking why nobody's been dragged to jail yet."

"They're demanding red meat," she said.

"And guess who they'll throw to the dogs. Tomorrow morning, they'll haul you in on some flimsy pretext to show they've 'solved' the case. They'll perp-walk you into the police station with the cameras rolling."

His expression soured. "They'll ruin your reputation. But arresting you will only put the investigation into a holding pattern. They're not stupid."

"Just ruthless," she said.

"You don't understand how ruthless.

Once they get you inside, their purpose will be twofold." He glanced in the mirror. "First. Frighten you into confessing."

"I won't do that."

"Rory. You're a suburban girl who reads Toni Morrison. The last place you bought espresso was a lakeside café in Geneva, where the graffiti is in *French*. They will try to frighten you into confessing to any goddamned thing they want, by putting you in lockup with violent felons."

She swallowed.

"And once you're in lockup they will not protect you. I guarantee this. No matter what happens to you, the guards won't stop it."

"You know too much about how this kind of pressure works," she said.

He eyed her. "What do you know about jail? Have you ever been arrested?"

"Yes."

His surprise was immediate. "When?"

"College. A Free Darfur protest. We chained ourselves to the admin building. Campus police hauled us into the station."

"How long were you locked up?"

"Three hours."

"You haven't been to jail."

She waved him off.

He said, "At the very least they'll lock you

in a cell full of informants. Thanks to the drug war, there's a whole dirty shadow economy of jailhouse snitching in return for reduced sentences. And yes, a snitch will be happy to lie and say you've confessed, in exchange for a plea deal."

She sank in her seat.

"Or maybe the cops will use you as bait to draw the real bad guys into the open. They'll spread the word that you have valuable information. Then see if somebody tortures or kills you for that information, so they can watch who the torturer passes the information along to. Phone calls, jailhouse visits, that way."

"Bait. Fun. Shit."

He gave her a sharp look.

"Sorry. Jesus. Is this America?"

The playing fields of Ransom River High School scrolled past. Beyond them, through thickening haze, the foothills looked blue-gray in the afternoon sun.

Rory felt a black spot growing in her heart. She needed to act. "Would you mind turning around?"

"Where do you want to go?"

"To speak to the person who's been bugging me about the siege. My aunt Amber."

"You think she's involved?"

"In the past fifteen years, you know how

many times she's asked about me?" She made a big round zero with her fingers. "Yet last night and today she's all over this thing. Calling me, leaving messages, flagging me down outside the courthouse."

"Rory, excuse me, but if Amber's the woman I remember . . ."

"Not a criminal mastermind? I know. It doesn't mean she's clueless. And she would lose nothing by throwing me to the wolves."

"And maybe gain millions she thought she deserved all these years?" Seth said.

"Bingo." She pointed at a freeway on-ramp. "She lives out near Pedregosa Ranch. You mind?"

"Not at all." He glanced in the rearview mirror. "But I'm going to take an indirect route."

"Why?"

"Because somebody's following us."

She didn't turn. Her security training from the NGO and Peace Corps days kicked in. *Don't look.* "Who?"

"Wrecker with RANSOM RIVER AUTO SALVAGE written on it, about a hundred fifty yards back."

She glanced in the side mirror. The truck was behind them on the busy road. Her voice grew cool.

"That," she said, "is Boone."

33

"How long has he been following us?" Rory said.

"At least two miles. I saw him when we turned out of Dad's neighborhood."

"Which means he tailed us there," she said.

"He's been following longer than that." Another glance in the mirror. "I saw that wrecker last night near the police station."

She turned to him. "You were at the police station?"

"Nearby."

She didn't know what to say. She looked in the side mirror again. Maples blurred past. The wrecker cruised along steadily, seven or eight cars back.

"What is he doing?" she said.

"Watching you."

The black spot in her chest felt cold. "He's either scouting on behalf of his mom, look-ing for something they can sell to the tabloids, or . . ."

"Or what?"

"I don't know. But it's something bad."

"Do you want to ask him?"

"No."

"You can confront him. Politely, if you want. I'll pull into that Taco Bell and you can wave him down."

"You in the mood for confrontation?" Rory said.

"He hasn't stolen my skateboard this time. I don't need to do anything. But if you want to see what happens when you call him on this game, I'm up for it."

"You haven't spent any time around him in the past decade. I don't recommend you start now."

"In that case, I'll lose him."

He pulled into a left-turn lane. The light was red.

Traffic was skimpy. He checked the cross street. There were no oncoming vehicles within two hundred yards. He jammed the pedal down and ran the light, swinging the truck sharply around the corner.

Rory's grabbed the window frame. "Dammit, Seth."

"Oops." He accelerated up the street. "Color blindness comes on suddenly sometimes."

He glanced in the mirror. "Yeah, the wrecker's stuck behind cars at the light. Boone can't get around without looking like an absolute maniac."

The truck gained speed. A block farther on they reached the Westside Shopping Center. Seth practically skidded into the vast parking lot. He got among the rows of parked cars and accelerated, revving the engine. He zeroed in on the farthest corner of the lot and squealed around a corner to the alley on the back side of the mall. He floored the pickup past Dumpsters and loading docks, blew past delivery trucks that were unloading merchandise. In his wake trash blew into the air.

Rory held on to the frame of the cab and braced herself. Her mouth was dry.

Not this again. "Seth."

It wasn't fun. It wasn't exciting anymore. She gritted her teeth. "You don't need to do this."

He raced to the end of the alley, braked sharply, and rounded a corner to the exit. He bounced out onto the street and punched the accelerator again.

"Do you see him?" he said.

Rory could barely see anything through her nerves and anger.

"Rory."

She looked in the side mirror. "No."

"Do you see any vehicles at all following us?"

He took the next corner hard, swinging wide into a residential neighborhood.

"No. For God's sake. Stop," she said.

Seth raced to the end of the block, screeched around another corner, and kept going. Ahead was a city park, with playgrounds, a wooded picnic area, baseball diamonds. Seth sped into the parking lot, floored it to the far end, and swung the pickup behind a maintenance shed. He rocked it suddenly to a stop and pulled the parking brake.

He glanced around. His face was calm but his eyes were bright. "We're completely out of sight of the road. If he doesn't pull in here in the next thirty seconds, we're clear."

Rory gripped the frame of the truck. She was pressing her feet hard against the floorboards and leaning back against the seat, like she was braking. Like she was falling and bracing herself against a calamitous stop.

She opened her mouth to speak and thought better of it.

Seth glanced at his watch. "We lost him."

She unbuckled her seat belt.

Seth had his hand on the gearshift.

"Rory?"

She opened the door and climbed out.

"Where are you going?"

She bent and put her hands on her knees. After a second she heard Seth's door open. She straightened and walked to the maintenance shed. It was a faded wooden structure painted dull red. Seth rounded the truck toward her, his face concerned but wary.

She put up a hand. "Don't."

He slowed. "You all right?"

"Are you out of your mind?"

She leaned back against the shed. She locked her knees so he wouldn't see them shaking. From the playing fields came the sound of a bat connecting with a baseball, then cheers and laughter.

She glared at him. "You can't help yourself, can you?"

"Do you think Boone just happened to be behind us? Do you think it was innocent?"

"This isn't Operation Ratchet, Seth. It's my *life*. And I don't want to think about what Boone was doing following me," she said.

"You'd better."

"I don't understand why you behaved the way you just did."

"I wanted to get you out of a threatening situation."

"If you wanted to have a car chase, you could have let me out first."

"In the middle of the street? Alone? With somebody after you?"

A vast and heavy silence descended on them.

Seth tried to hold her gaze and couldn't.

He looked angry. Maybe at himself. Maybe at her. Maybe at the situation. His hands were clenched, like he wanted to punch something. And the pain was back in his posture.

"I'm sorry," he said.

She could barely see straight. Her heart was pounding. *Sorry* — for what? This? For all of it?

"Rory?"

"I heard you." She leaned her head back against the shed and closed her eyes. "I heard."

She wanted to tell him. She felt such a swell of emotion that she nearly was lifted off her feet and pushed toward him.

Don't look back. Something might be gaining on you.

She opened her eyes. He had drawn close to her — closer than he'd dared come all day. He looked familiar, and beautiful, and such an obstacle. She held herself against the wall. She wanted to kiss him. She

317

wanted to tell him everything.
She said, "It's over, Seth."

34

Then

"I need to tell you about my job."

They were lying on the beach in Malibu on a hot Saturday afternoon. Under a pale blue sky, sunlight fried the surface of the Pacific. Sand was stuck to Rory's shoulders. Seth's hair was wet and tangled. He rolled over.

"I'll need to be gone for a couple of weeks at a time," he said.

Only a few people on the Ransom River police force knew he was undercover. The rest thought he had quit the force for a regular job.

"And some people think I've become a small-time hood. You get to be one of them — in public."

Operation Ratchet, it was called. Later, Rory called it Operation Fucking-You-Up. It was an investigation into illegal gun dealing in Ransom River and northwest Los

Angeles County.

"Fine," she said. "I think you're a hood. I don't know you. I never saw you. We didn't have this conversation. Who are you?"

"When I'm on duty I can't see you. I can't call you, and you can't call me."

He had a separate cell phone for when he was working. A separate driver's license and credit cards, with another name. He had a cover legend.

She said, "Okay. I'll play." She should have known better. She'd always been lousy at games.

And later, at his apartment, he got dressed — not in jeans and a T-shirt, but in a black suit and blue dress shirt, sunglasses, and a Rolex. She drove him to a storage locker. By the time they arrived, his grin was gone. His face looked like glass — smooth, blank, and sharp-edged.

In the storage locker, instead of his old Yamaha bike was a Mercedes. He didn't look at her after that.

It thrilled her. It thrilled her so much, she didn't see that it was a game she was destined to lose.

Seth's real and covert lives first collided on a Thursday night on Sunset Boulevard, to the soundtrack of indie rock. The club was Hollywood loud, shiny with tourists and hustlers and wannabes. He and Rory should have been anonymous. They should have been far enough from home.

The club was dank, except when it turned dingy. Seth sat with his back to the wall, as always. He had one hand on Rory's leg and the other on a cold bottle of Carta Blanca. The band was a second-generation knock-off of Joan Jett and the Runaways.

Seth saw the guy come in. He set his beer on the sticky table and leaned over to kiss Rory's neck.

"Get out," he said. "Look shocked."

Her lips parted in surprise. He ran his fingers into her hair and held her close and murmured in her ear.

"Get up and leave. And act like I just grabbed your ass and asked for a three-way with you and the singer."

"What . . ."

"Catch a taxi to the Beverly Center. I'll pick you up there."

She shied away from him. He pulled her back.

"Slap me. Give me a dirty glare. Stare all you like as long as you look royally pissed off. But leave." He squeezed her to him. "Go."

They had discussed this. If he told her to split, it was because somebody from his other life had shown up. She didn't need to pretend to be disoriented or upset. She disentangled herself from him with a flat slap across his cheek.

She stormed toward the door and shot that dirty glare back at him. He was leaning forward, hands loose around his beer bottle, talking to a man who looked like a human knife, ready to stick you.

Standing behind the man were two others. They looked like they expected at any second to fight off weaker, stupider people.

Rory walked out of the club into a thumping night, cold air, headlights, neon, billboards. Her palms were sweating. She was nearly sick, and blinking with amazement. She walked three blocks before she flagged down a taxi.

She slammed the door and the cab pulled into traffic on Sunset. A strange electricity swept through her.

The voice in her head sounded like Seth's. *That was some mad shit.*

She smiled and couldn't stop and, for the first time, understood what caused Seth to grin that pirate grin. It was the blood; it was a thrilling sting in her muscles that said, *Yeah. This.*

He picked her up thirty minutes later at the Beverly Center, and they didn't talk about it, didn't remark on the encounter, though he told her, "You did good." They went back to her cheap student apartment in west L.A. and made crazy love. And while they clutched each other and she bit his shoulder and they stood against the wall, in the dark, desperate and wild, she thought, *It's dangerous.* It hit her and didn't seem strange — *What he does is dangerous. His job could get him killed.*

The people he dealt with were criminals. Real, in-the-flesh criminals, not dumb kids caught joyriding. Not ne'er-do-well relatives nabbed with too much dope or stolen stereos, people like her dear, misguided uncle, who was born with an excess of charm, joy, and poor judgment. The criminals Seth dealt with sold guns to other criminals and to criminal organizations in the U.S. and Latin America: automatic weapons, in bulk, at discount, and they didn't take well to bad-faith negotiation. They would kill a snitch. What they would do to an undercover cop, she didn't want to imagine.

And Seth was worming his way into their business stream. He was trying to bring down the people at the top of the supply chain.

He held tight to her legs and hoisted her

against him and shut his eyes. But he said, "God, Rory . . ."

It's dangerous.

She tightened her arms around his shoulders, loving the sound of her name on his tongue.

It was only later that a new fear began to seep into her thoughts.

He's dangerous.

The kick she'd felt in Hollywood lingered. It was a tangible rush: the Sunset Boulevard Express. But gradually, things got off-kilter.

It went wrong like a gear loosening and getting out of balance. Seth not coming home. Not answering her calls. Not returning her calls even when he was off duty, because he was exhausted and stressed out. The job engulfed him.

To infiltrate networks that were selling significant firepower to criminals in Southern California — and exporting arms by the truckload to even deadlier criminals in Mexico — Seth became another person. And the person he became was troubled and frightening. Undercover work, he claimed, was like creating a character in a video game. But that life was lonely, isolating, and psychologically perilous. Righteous justification powered him. As did the thrill.

But the longer he played the game, the deeper he went. The more dim and distant the exit signs became.

And to most other cops on the police force, he didn't exist.

Before being accepted as a probie undercover officer, he'd had to go through psychological testing, to ascertain whether he could live a lie without losing his mind. He aced it.

It worked, he told her, because he stuck to the rules. He never went into a situation without knowing exactly what he was after: evidence of the crime he was investigating. He couldn't go fishing or lure innocent people into committing crimes. He had to slide into a target's world and watch events unfold. To assuage Rory's worries, he explained that he had clear guidelines from the PD. Most important was to remember that he was first and always a police officer. And his training provided him with principles for situations where his actions were, unavoidably, ambiguous.

Except it didn't. He was intense, inventive, and young. That made him rash.

And, as Operation Ratchet drew closer to the point where arrests would be made, he withdrew into himself under the pressure.

Then came Rory's second ride on the Sunset Boulevard Express.

35

Seth pulled away as though she'd back-handed him.

"No," she said. She saw that he had misconstrued her words. "That's not what I mean by *It's over.* I mean the past, every-thing —"

"I get it."

"No, you don't."

Her phone rang. She let it.

"I mean what's done is done. Let it go. I don't want to get caught up in an endless loop, repeating history," she said.

"Don't worry. That's not going to happen. I'm clear on that now."

The phone kept ringing. The sun felt un-naturally bright.

"Can we stop for a minute and back this conversation up?" she said.

Seth nodded at her ringing phone. "I imagine that's relevant."

She looked at it. Local number. Familiar.

She answered. "Amber?"

"There you are, honey. I was worried for a sec."

"What's up?"

"I just got a call from Boone. He said he saw Seth Colder here in town."

"That may be the case. I didn't see Boone — is he downtown?"

She eyed Seth. He became alert.

"I just wondered if you knew Seth was around. I thought you might want to know. Because. So you'd be prepared, in case."

"In case?" Rory said.

"In case you ran into him. I didn't want it to be a hurtful surprise," Amber said.

"That's thoughtful of you. I appreciate the heads-up."

"We all know what a . . . troubling time you had, honey. I don't know what he could be doing here. Do you?"

"I'll figure it out. Thanks, Amber."

She hung up. Seth stared at the keys in his hand.

"You willing to get back in the truck?" he said.

He didn't say, *Have I blown it all over again?*

It happened three days before she was scheduled to take the bar exam. Seth came home and stripped off the clothes and jewelry and washed off the cologne of his assumed persona but couldn't shed his apprehension. Unease hung in the air around him like an almost-visible cloak. And with the bar exam looming, Rory was under serious pressure. Three years of education, tens of thousands of dollars in student loans, and her job hung in the balance.

He was jumpy, far focused, quick to anger. She was short-tempered and touchy. She should, maybe, have cut him some slack. But life didn't come with a Rewind button.

She couldn't say whether it was a mistake, a slip, or bad luck. Or even a tip-off. Later, she knew, people had made inquiries. They'd grilled Seth. Still, nobody knew for sure.

She and Seth had dinner in the San Fernando Valley, a Mexican restaurant across the city limits from Ransom River. The place had twinkly white Christmas lights strung around the walls and garish paintings of matadors. The food was cheap and plentiful, and the beer was colder than snow.

And it had a jukebox. Seth was standing next to it, one hand braced on the wall, choosing a song to buy for his quarters. His back was turned. Rory held on to her Diet Coke, wondering if he was turning his back on her as well. Whether he was losing his grip on his own life. She was watching him so intently that she didn't see the door open. She didn't realize she had been approached until the man was standing next to her table.

It was the human knife.

He was short and wore a white turtleneck and a tweed jacket with leather elbow patches, as though he were a history professor. But his eyes were like a doll's: round, all pupil, no expression. One of his goons stood behind him.

"Imagine seeing you here," he said.

She stared at him, quietly. Every synapse in her body shouted, *Run.*

"Excuse me?" she said.

"You must have changed your mind about my friend Hollis."

He didn't look at Seth. Neither did Rory. She was trying furiously not to say the wrong thing. The next words out of her mouth needed to be the right ones.

She held the man's lifeless gaze. "Could be."

"How long you two been seeing each other?"

"I'm sorry, I didn't get your name."

"I didn't offer it."

At the jukebox, Seth dropped in his coins.

"Sweet Home Alabama" began to play. He turned around.

He didn't even hesitate. He walked back to the table. And his walk was not his walk; the look in his eyes was not Seth Colder's. He approached smoothly, like a cobra.

"Dobro," he said.

The man smiled. It was a waxen, humorless grin. His eyes stayed round and predatory.

"So you managed to corral her after all," Dobro said.

Rory had never believed in guardian angels. If anything was hovering over her shoulder, breathing down her neck, it didn't have wings and a halo. She hoped her heart wasn't pounding so hard it was visible through her chest wall.

Seth put himself between her and Dobro. Not to protect her, she thought — Dobro didn't seem overtly aggressive. No, Seth was *claiming* her.

"The beer's good," he said. "Enjoy yourselves."

The man's waxwork smile remained. He looked at her. "Your mister's not being polite. What's your name, sweetheart?"

"I'm the goddess Wanda," she said. And she smiled at Seth, coldly, a flash of teeth. "You better treat me like a goddess if you wanda get anywhere with me."

Dobro snorted. He said to Seth, "We'll see you around."

He and his man walked to the bar. Seth sat down. His face was blank, but his eyes were wired. He drank a long swallow of beer. "Sweet Home Alabama" rocked from the jukebox.

Across the room, Dobro and his man took barstools and watched Rory and Seth in the mirror behind the bar.

Seth said, "Eat."

Rory couldn't have eaten if she'd had a gun to her head. "How long do we have to stay here?"

"Until we're finished."

But when he finally put cash on the table and they strolled outside into the hot evening, Dobro followed them.

"Where you going, goddess?"

Seth was holding her hand. Under his breath he said, "Ignore him. Get in the truck."

The sun had dropped behind the hills in the west. Red twilight drenched the sky. Dobro slouched toward them with his muscle in tow.

"Where you going in such a hurry? There are things I'd like to discuss."

Seth dropped her hand and became electrically alert. "We'll set it up."

Dobro walked past him and slid a hand around Rory's shoulder. His doll eyes were black in the dusk. "There's no rush, goddess. You can do better than this guy."

He laughed, a whinnying sound. Rory felt things teetering, like a vehicle about to tip, barely balanced.

Seth's voice was flat. "This dance is mine," he said, and reached for Rory's hand again. "Let's go."

Dobro squeezed her shoulder and only gradually relinquished his hold. He took a cigar from his pocket, and a gold lighter. He said to his man, "Bring the car around."

The man left. Dobro nodded Rory toward the truck. "You go on."

Unsettled, furious at being belittled, she headed toward Seth's pickup. She glanced back. Dobro was watching her.

He turned to Seth. "We need to rethink our arrangement."

It was all he got out. Seth punched him hard in the face.

Dobro reeled back under the force of the blow. He raised his hands toward his face and Seth hit him again, in the diaphragm. He doubled over. Seth kicked his knees out from under him. Dobro hit the asphalt and Seth booted him in the gut.

"Come near her again, I'll take you apart," Seth said.

He hauled back and kicked him in the kidney. Rory couldn't move.

Dobro tried to rise and Seth planted a boot between his shoulders and crunched him back to the asphalt.

"So much as look at her, I'll clip your nuts."

He backed away. Dobro pushed to his knees. His gaze was deathly. Seth turned. For an instant he looked surprised to see Rory standing in the middle of the parking lot.

She got in the truck.

Seth climbed behind the wheel and burned out of the parking lot. Dobro remained on his knees.

Rory couldn't bear to look at Seth. All she could see was the expression on his face when he had turned around after kicking Dobro.

Fury. Calculation. Electricity.

He accelerated along the street, a broad suburban boulevard lined with downscale retail stores. Mattress showrooms with huge banners across their plate-glass windows. Tanning salons, McDonald's, auto-parts stores, garish billboards. Rory's vision went out of focus, constricted, shoved the crimson sunset to the edges.

"Dobro won't come after you. Don't worry," he said.

She didn't answer.

"He'll want me, but he'll think twice." He glanced at her. "You were sharp back there. You gave him nothing."

The truck raced past a gas station and a strip mall.

She said, "You beat him up to preserve your cover."

He took a beat, as though the remark caught him by surprise. "I preempted any move he might try to make against me."

"By kicking the shit out of him."

"He was openly challenging me." He glanced at her again. "He is not a good guy."

"And if you'd left it alone? Driven away?" she said.

"Rory, don't."

She turned, slowly, to glare at him. "Don't tell me you were being my knight in shining armor."

"He followed us to the restaurant. He has obviously been probing me for weaknesses. He thought tonight he had found one."

"You scared the hell out of me back there," she said.

"Me?" He turned, baffled. And beginning to look angry.

"Seth, you calmly beat that guy to a pulp."

"Do you know who that was?"

"Of course not."

"He is a midlevel nobody. He preens like he's the shit, but he's a gofer."

"So?" The edge in her voice was sharp.

"So now he won't come back on me. Word will get around. He stepped out of line, and I pushed back."

Rory's pulse beat in her temples. "You mean if he'd been a bigger fish, you would have let him get away with it?"

"I would have taken a different tack. Rory, he was pissing all over me and threatening you. I had to act. I spoke in the only language he understands."

"So cops can commit assault and battery if it fits with their cover story?"

Shaking his head, he pushed it through a yellow light. "Get real. Things could have been very dangerous back there."

"Then why haven't you called it in to your handlers?"

"For Christ's sake." His face looked cold. "Why don't you make a checklist for me. Mackenzie-approved tactics."

Her hands were trembling. "That's not the problem."

"Don't tell me I'm reckless. I'm not."

He was, bravely reckless. Sometimes he

seemed to taunt fate — to seek a cut from the Reaper's scythe, to prove to himself he was invincible.

"That's not it," she said.

"Then what?" he said.

They crossed the Ransom River city limits. The boulevard emptied. Plowed fields and lemon orchards spread out on either side of them. Black furrowed ground, trees huddled thickly together.

What was the problem?

"You enjoyed it," she said.

She turned in her seat. She had jumped in the truck in such haste that she hadn't bothered to buckle her seat belt. She reached for it but paused.

"You enjoyed beating that man up," she said.

He looked at her with reproach. His face was white.

"Seth," she said, "what's happening to you? What the hell is going on?"

"What's *going on* is that this investigation is at a critical point." He shook his head. "Don't do this. Not now."

"This investigation is dragging you into a pit. A deep one. And I don't know what to do."

"You do nothing. The job will take care of itself."

"How?"

"I can't tell you operational details. You know that."

Compartmentalization. She knew that too well.

"And then what?" she said. "Can you tell me when it'll be over? When you'll come back to me, as yourself?"

"Soon."

"You've said that before."

"Rory, why are you doing this?"

"Because you're scaring me."

He looked at her, and in his eyes was resentment and hopeless fatigue — as though explaining everything would simply drain him to the bottom.

"*I'm* scaring you. Me. But that guy back there" — he nodded in the direction of the restaurant — "Dobro? He'd sell his sister to Somali pirates for cigarettes. And he touched you, Rory. He laid his hands on you."

Because I was with you.

"And what do you mean, come back? I'm right here. I've been beside you since fourth grade."

"That kid I knew. The nasty bastard I saw at the restaurant, I don't."

"That nasty bastard is who I'm supposed to be. *When I'm at work,*" he said, enunciating each word with chipped care. "Because at work *I am an undercover cop.*"

But she knew, despite his vehemence, that he wasn't being honest. He thought he was. But he couldn't see it. He'd been swallowed by the job, the life, the importance of staying in the role. He had lost himself.

And she saw again his face, as he turned away from Dobro in the parking lot.

He had smiled.

That rakish grin, the *devil's got me* smile. He had felt fulfilled and justified and goddamned *happy* at kicking a man to the ground. For her, he thought.

The truck raced toward the foothills, the night falling, orchards giving way again to homes and the vast asphalt prairie of a car dealership. She squeezed her eyes shut.

"I can't do this anymore," she said.

"Fine with me. Let's let it lie."

"No." She turned to him. She had to be looking straight at him when she said it. "I'm done."

He paused a beat. He knew what she'd said. He had to. He was, it seemed, waiting for her to take it back.

"Seth, that's it. I'm finished."

"What are you saying?" He shook his head again, as though he didn't believe her. "No."

"We're done," she said.

"Because of Dobro?" He sounded incredulous.

"Yes, because of Dobro," she said, "and if you can't see that — Jesus, Colder, if you can't understand that, you're farther gone than I imagined."

He held the wheel. The sun had dropped below the horizon and the sky was a bleeding red, fading to black.

"That's it," he said.

"Yes."

"Like that."

It seemed obvious, pure, easy. She knew already she was regretting it, that this would be a bleeding wound, sharp and deep, but she was so livid, so full of fear and righteous anger, that she could feel nothing but her own triumph in saying it to him.

He didn't look at her. His gaze was on the road, but she couldn't tell whether he saw anything at all.

"Then it's done," he said. "That's it; the cord's cut."

She nodded and watched the neighborhood race by. Her heart was pounding.

"I won't pretend with you," he said. "If we're finished, that's it. We're not friends. We're nothing. No smiling and acting like it's amicable."

She said nothing. He drove.

"I'll take you home," he said.

She bit back, *That's mighty nice of you.*

He drove on, in acid silence. Rory didn't want to be near him. She didn't want to breathe the same air as him. She was exhausted and ready to cry and was not about to let Seth Colder see even a hint of that.

When his phone rang, she didn't move. Normally, he might have asked her to dig it out of his back pocket. She heard him pull the phone out, peripherally saw him glance at the caller ID. He answered, "Colder."

The truck rolled straight down the road at fifty miles an hour. He said, "Where?" He stared out the windshield but his face was set in a thousand-yard stare.

"When?" he said. "Where's the nearest patrol unit?"

His tone of voice chilled her. He glanced at the clock on the dashboard.

"Nobody's closer?" He listened again. "I don't want to risk —"

He frowned. Rory could hear the person on the other end, an official and urgent voice.

Seth glanced around outside. "I'm two miles away. And I'm not alone."

He looked reluctant. He didn't glance at Rory. He listened to the urgent request

coming through the phone. He finally acquiesced.

"I'm on my way. But send a patrol unit
ASAP."

He ended the call and dropped the phone
on the dashboard. "Domestic disturbance,
shots fired. It's at an address that's linked
to the operation. It's an emergency." He
barely gave her a look. "I'll drop you at the
Outback — you can get a cab home. I'll give
you the fare."

"Don't bother," she said.

Ahead, the road curved and spoked into a
V. A column of eucalyptus trees lined the
shoulder. Seth accelerated into the curve
and signaled, planning to veer left at the
fork.

"Something bad is going down. I need to
get there," he said.

His voice was stretched tighter than bal-
ing wire. He was already gone, into a head-
space where he felt secure when everybody
else felt like screaming. He had something
to aim for, something he could help with,
when Rory had become a hopeless cause.
In the failing light, his face was pale and
planed with injury.

He held the wheel hard and angled around
the curve. The trees picket-fenced on the
right, like figures in a strip of film that was

coming off the reel. Seth signaled and crossed the yellow centerline, angling for the fork in the road.

The other pickup was black, and fifty yards ahead, and headed straight at them. No lights.

"Seth."

Rory pressed herself back in the seat and jammed her foot to the floor as if she had a brake pedal. But she didn't.

Seth spun the wheel. He threw it hard to the left and tried to get out of the other truck's way. The eucalyptus trees swung past. Then the black truck was there.

The impact was loud and brutal.

The black pickup T-boned the passenger side of Seth's truck. The frame buckled. The windshield squealed and cracked. The window by Rory's face shattered. The grille of the black pickup bore straight at her, crushed the side of Seth's truck, sent her flying.

They skidded sideways, pinned to the black pickup, as if skewered there. It felt like being borne along by a freight train. The black truck kept coming, filling her with noise, with heat, the metal and energy crushing everything as it came on. The cab of Seth's truck crumpled to half its size.

They skidded, tilting, until the other

truck's front wheels locked and flattened and dug into the road. Crushed together, they swerved off the asphalt and hit a tree. They stopped ugly, with a heavy metallic crunch.

Rory seemed to be floating. She was on her back, staring through strange twisted branches of metal at the sky. She saw stars. She blinked and her eyes felt stabbed with pain. A horn blared, long, loud, helplessly.

The stars seemed overcome with a violent yellow light. A bus had stopped next to them. Its headlights were shining in her face. She realized she was lying faceup on the dashboard of Seth's truck.

She realized she was hurt.

Her eyes were tearing, but every time she blinked, the pain sharpened. She raised a hand and saw blood.

She turned her head. Glass crunched beneath her.

"Rory."

She stopped moving for a second and took inventory. "Rory, hold still." A swell of pain began at her feet and rolled upward through her.

"Rory, babe, hold on."

Seth was talking to her. She heard other voices. A man, two men, maybe from the black pickup, or the bus. Moving around outside.

More glass crunching. With a wrenching squeal, hands pulled the entire windshield out of the frame in one shattered piece of safety glass. The truck rocked beneath her. Seth appeared, kneeling on the pickup's hood.

"Rory, babe. Can you talk?"

She moved her hand, and the sharp sensation, stinging, got her arms too.

"Aw, Jesus, hold still — it's glass spall." His hand hovered in front of her face.

The other voice: "Can we help?"

"Call an ambulance," Seth said. "First aid kit's in the back. Hurry."

He scrambled around, crouching on the hood, trying to position himself so he could see her, could do something.

"Hold on," he said. He brushed glass from her face with trembling fingers. "Hold on."

She saw his face. He was bleeding too. His voice was bleeding. The sky, however, had turned blue. It had bled out.

36

Rory pushed off from the wall of the maintenance shed. On the park's baseball diamond, players cheered a home run. She walked to Seth's new Tundra and got in and closed the door. She buckled her seat belt. Seth climbed behind the wheel and fired up the engine. He studiously avoided looking at her.

"Seth . . ."

"Later. After. We don't have time for explanations right now."

It was an out, and a defense mechanism. But she nodded. *Later.* He pulled out of the park and headed back toward the center of town.

"I need to go to Amber's," she said. "Something's going on."

"You want to go alone?"

"No way."

"I'm not sure she'll talk to you if I'm hanging around."

"Then you can take me home to pick up my car and follow me over there. You can wait outside. Up the street, out of sight."

He drove cautiously along a residential street toward the freeway. Autumn leaves shivered in the breeze.

"Look for Boone. And look for a newer silver SUV," he said.

"Excuse me?"

"Late-model silver SUV. It was at the stoplight behind the wrecker." Seth swung onto the on-ramp and raced onto the freeway. "Boone isn't the only one tailing you."

The view out the tinted windows of the SUV was busy and wrong. Traffic, stores, suburban sprawl. Supermarkets and a mall and not one single view of the black Toyota Tundra pickup with the ex-cop and the girl.

The driver looked around. "Where'd she go?"

"You lost her."

"No."

"She's gone," the passenger said. "And why was the wrecker following her?"

The engine of the SUV rumbled. The air-conditioning was blowing, though the day outside was cool.

"Did they make you?" the passenger said.

The driver shook his head. He hoped not.

They'd been anonymous so far and wanted to keep it that way.

"This is getting out of control," he said.

"We need to stop this. Need to step things up. She should be sucking her thumb and writing journal entries about her terrible ordeal, not out driving around with Mr. Macho. This is not normal."

"Talking to an ex-detective is very abnormal."

"If she thinks he can keep her out of county lockup, she's stupid."

"I know. Figure she'll be arrested in the morning. She won't keep quiet. She'll talk. She'll tell the department everything she's figured out."

They looked at each other. With every minute the girl was loose, she could figure out more and more pieces of the thing. And she looked pretty close to obsessed about doing that. Once she put it together, it was game over.

"We're running out of time. We have to move the schedule up."

"That's a risk."

"This entire thing's a risk," the passenger said. "We have to take the chance of exposure. Otherwise the rewards might go up in smoke. We gotta move."

The driver got on the phone.

37

Amber Mackenzie's house could have
been a set for the old TV western that had
filmed in Ransom River. *Rustic* described
it charitably. In the hills at the edge of
town, high above eroded gullies, it was a
dismal home, with patchy grass and bare
dirt along the foundation, where flowers
should have bloomed. Behind it rose rocky
ranges and the blue-green peaks of the
national forest. Rory crested the hill and
coasted down the road to the driveway. The
lawn was strewn with Barbies and Big
Wheels.

She parked her Subaru and walked to the
door. A garden hose snaked carelessly across
the broken sidewalk. She heard Seth's truck
rumble to a stop a hundred yards back, just
beyond the top of the hill, and reverse
around a corner so he could get out and
watch the house past scrawny bottlebrush
trees and a neighbor's Winnebago.

Rory knocked. Inside, a television softly buzzed.

The door opened. Amber stood surprised, her splinted hands at her sides.

"Aurora. My word." She pushed open the screen. Her frantic red hair hung over her shoulders. "Come in, honey."

The house was stuffy. Though it was autumn, a fan was blowing in the living room. Five children sat on the carpet, huddled in a semicircle around the television. SpongeBob was loudly educating them about subaquatic life.

Amber led Rory into the kitchen, just off the front door. "What's going on?"

Rory nodded at the kids. "Can you talk?"

"I'm keeping an eye on them."

Amber pointed. A mirror hung on the hallway wall, catching the toddlers' reflection.

She crossed her arms. "If you're worried I told your parents Seth's in town, don't be."

"That's not it." Though the thought of how her father would react to seeing Seth made Rory blanch. "I'll deal with Seth. Don't concern yourself with that."

Amber scratched an arm. The kitchen counter was clean but cluttered. There were loaves of Wonder Bread and juice boxes and four children's lunch boxes lined up next to a pack of Virginia Slims and Amber's lime green pill container. Through the container's transparent lid Rory saw pills organized in tiny compartments labeled M–Sun. The pills looked like a mix of M&M'S and jelly beans.

"What's your worry, then?" Amber said.

"I want to know what's going on."

"I don't understand."

"Why have you been so eager to talk to me?"

Amber flipped her hair over her shoulder. It was almost coquettish. "The courthouse siege is big news. I'm no different from the rest of the folks in town. And honey, face it, I've got an inside track."

"Open curiosity, that's it? Okay, here I am. What do you want to know?"

Amber smiled uneasily. After a moment she turned and opened the fridge.

"Iced tea?"

"No, thanks. Take your shot, Amber. Ask me whatever it is you're dying to know."

Amber took out a pitcher and shuffled to the cupboard for a glass. She poured and reached back into the cupboard for a box of pills. She popped one from a silver bubble pack and washed it down with tea. It was OxyContin.

Rory glanced at the hallway mirror. The

kids in the living room were mostly goggle-eyed and glazed in front of the TV. One little boy was playing with a Hot Wheels car. The little girl with the sweet brown curls, who had been in Riss's car outside the courtroom earlier, climbed to her feet and looked around.

"Rory, I think you've gotten the wrong idea," Amber said. "I don't know who's been putting notions in your head, but this is nothing more than an aunt's concern and natural human curiosity."

The OxyContin remained on the counter. Rory wondered if Amber had a license to operate a day-care center, or whether she got around that by claiming to be a neighborly figure who helped out with part-time babysitting.

Rory picked up the OxyContin box, put the bubble pack back inside, and set it on an upper shelf in the cupboard. She put the lime green pill organizer beside it and closed the cabinet door tightly.

"I've got an idea about what's going on," she said, "and I'm not the only one."

Amber's face had gone crimson. "I'm disabled. I have chronic pain. It makes it impossible for me to hold down a normal job."

"I'm sorry."

"Everything's always been so easy for you, Miss Bright Bulb. Well, not everybody has life served up to them on a silver platter." She held up her hands. "This comes from trying to hold my family together, keep a roof over my kids' heads, put food on the table. What would you know about any of that?"

Rory thought of the shotgun shack in Zimbabwe, and little Grace, and the sticks Grace's mother collected for her cooking fire before men with tire irons kicked down the door.

And Rory thought of Lee. He'd been a single dad to Riss when she was a baby. Riss's mother had died in a car wreck in Topanga Canyon, drunk on Southern Comfort, when Riss was six months old. After that, Lee could have treated his responsibilities as a chain to be severed with bolt cutters. But he didn't dump Riss. He held her tight. Amber had once said, *They were a package deal. A gorgeous man and his precious baby girl. How could I resist?* All Rory's life, against every high tide that threatened to erode it, she'd clung to the notion of Lee as caring father. He'd given his daughter a home with a new mom and a brother. He'd made a family for her.

But the truth shone ugly in the light of

noon. It stood in front of her in the gloomy kitchen. Lee had brought a family together, and he'd left it, maybe in a getaway car.

A small voice came from the hallway. "Miss Amber?"

In the kitchen doorway stood the little girl with flyaway curls the color of cocoa. She was barefoot, bouncing up and down on her toes. Her T-shirt had a bumblebee on it.

Amber said, "What is it, Addie?"

"I'm thirsty."

The little girl looked about a year and a half old. Maybe younger. Rory wasn't an expert. Her eyes were bright blue, inquisitive, and fearless.

"Miss Amber's talking right now, honey."

"Please."

Rory said, "I'll get her a drink."

Amber waved at the juice boxes. "Not those. Get her a sippy cup with water, else the rest of them will want drinks and then I'll be a half hour changing diapers."

Rory found a sippy cup in the cupboard with the OxyContin. Little Addie bounced after her.

"Me. Let me pour."

Amber shushed the child. "Adalyn, no."

Rory said, "It's okay."

She picked up the little girl and held her over the sink. Addie was light and wriggly and she focused with pure concentration on the water that braided from the faucet. Rory put the plastic cup into her small hands and Addie stretched, serious and wobbly, to hold it beneath the flow. She filled it nearly to the brim.

"Good job," Rory said.

She set the girl on the counter. Addie carefully held the cup still, watching the water as though it might jump to life and make a run for it. Rory steadied the cup and pushed the top down securely.

"There you go," she said.

Addie smiled. It was a smile of discovery and wonder, and it gave Rory a pang. She briefly thought about how, once, she might have had a child this age. If she and Seth had stayed together. If things had worked out. If, if, if.

Everything's always been so easy for you, Miss Bright Bulb.

After the wreck, after the paramedics and police and road flares and ambulance, after the ER and surgery, Rory regained consciousness in the recovery room, woozy and sick. She opened gritty eyes and saw her leg encased from toes to thigh in a blue fiberglass cast. She breathed. Pain ripped her abdomen.

She closed her eyes. The surgeon's voice woke her again, strong and close.

"Aurora. We stopped the bleeding. But you lost a lot of blood."

She focused, to speak coherent words. "I have to be out of here tomorrow. Bar exam on Tuesday."

He floated into view. Blue scrubs, pale arms. Blurred face. "We'll see how long you need to stay here."

"Where's Seth?" she said. "Is he okay?"

"Who's Seth?"

The million-dollar question. "Seth Colder. Was driving the truck."

"You were the only person admitted after the accident," he said.

He paused. "Ms. Mackenzie," he said, and his voice was gentle. "I'm sorry, but there's more."

He told her the extent of her injuries. Slowly, she felt the night close in for good. She was hospitalized for two weeks. She missed the bar exam. She lost her job with the law firm in San Francisco.

She lay drugged and vague and silent, staring out the window. Petra visited, brought flowers and booze and brushed Rory's hair from her forehead with her fingertips. She held tight to Rory's hand, listening and saying, "Oh, girl." Rory's parents spent every free minute with her. Sam would glide in while she slept, and when Rory opened her eyes she'd see her mom above her, gripping the railing of the bed as though trying to hop a train. She looked beatific and tormented.

"There you are," she'd say. "You rest, sweetheart. You get better."

It took days before Rory found the courage to ask, "Where's Seth?"

Sam gave her a cool look. "He's not here."

"Where is he?"

"He told your dad you'd broken things off. He said you two had called it quits for good."

"So he hasn't come to the hospital?"

Sam said nothing.

Rory turned to the wall.

Rory smoothed Addie's hair.

Amber said, "You get on back to Sponge-Bob, Adalyn. The grown-ups need to talk."

Rory lifted Addie from the counter. The little girl scrambled into her arms like a monkey and hugged her tight around the neck. She smelled like baby powder and bananas. Rory set her down and she giggled and ran from the kitchen, water sloshing in the cup.

Amber sobered. "What do you really want?"

"I want to know what's going on," Rory said.

In her jeans pocket, Rory's phone vibrated. She had a message from Seth.

Before she could read it, she heard a vehicle pull into the driveway. Amber leaned back against the counter and crossed her arms. A few seconds later the front door opened.

Boone stood in the hall, staring at them.

"Come in, son," Amber said. "It's a family reunion."

38

Boone had grown into a tall and good-looking man. His brown hair brushed his collar. He had Amber's fawn eyes. He wore a shirt from Ransom River Auto Salvage. The matching tow truck was parked in the driveway.

But his frame was stringy. Possibly from the energy he spent smoothing his charm over the anger that boiled below the surface. Possibly from his bursts of temper. Given his plea bargain for handling stolen property, Rory thought it was possibly from the effort of keeping his hands to himself. He liked stealing things. If he couldn't have them, he liked ruining things. Especially while he was drunk. Given his love for whiskey and fried food, she wondered if his slimness was thanks to cocaine or meth.

And he still looked at people sideways. He sauntered into the kitchen and took an apple and a beer from the fridge. He leaned back against the counter, polished the apple against his shirt, and stared at the window behind Rory.

"Surprised to see you here, cuz, considering how you've been trying to avoid me."

"It's been a busy day. How's everything?" Rory said.

"Having fun figuring out what the hell's going on in town."

Amber said, "Good to see you, sweetheart."

He took a bite of the apple, leaned over, and kissed her on the cheek. "What's Aurora after? She want to know when Dad's coming home, so she can greet him at the airport with banners and confetti?"

Amber's face darkened. "Boone."

One of the kids in the living room began to cry. In the hallway mirror, Rory saw two toddlers struggling for control of a stuffed bear. Addie sat watching them for a second, then wobbled to her feet and waded over, the sippy cup trailing from one hand. She patted one little girl on the cheek. It was random and ineffably affecting.

Boone was now staring at Rory's feet, as though he could set them on fire.

She said, "You know what, I've clearly come at a bad time. I'll catch up with you later."

"Really?" Boone said. "I think now's a perfect time."

The screen door cringed open. Perfume filled the air.

For a moment Rory held still. Thinking: *Hey, Seth, where's your warning message?* He could have at least honked his horn, or run to the kitchen window and beat on it, shouting, *Get out of there — it's coming.* She turned.

Riss stood in the doorway. She tilted her head. "Well, rah-rah, sis-boom-bah."

In the living room, the children's crying intensified. "Mine. *Mine.*"

Riss leaned against the doorframe, blocking it. "Aurora walks in and a houseful of kids start crying? It's like an exorcism movie. *Be afraid.*"

"I'm on my way out," Rory said.

"What are you doing here?" Riss glanced at Boone and Amber. "What's going on?"

Amber raised a hand. "It's nothing."

"She just drops in for the first time in history, and it's nothing?"

Amber said, "Leave it, Riss."

Boone finished the apple and threw the core in the sink. "Strange, though, isn't it?"

Rory said, "It's been a strange couple of days."

He wiped his hands. "And what do we

361

have to do with it, princess?"

Oh, boy. Rory's fingers began to tingle.

"Seriously," he said. "You haven't been to this house for ten years, and you show up this afternoon? What's that about?"

Rory's throat felt tight. Boone wasn't fourteen anymore. He was thirty, and six feet tall, with gnarled muscles along his tattooed arms. But the feeling in the air carried more than taunts, more than resentment. He looked anxious. And Riss looked predatory. Rory got the sensation of being circled.

It was how they behaved when they had something to fear. When they sensed that something they'd done risked being exposed.

Amber had retreated to a corner in the kitchen. She looked distraught. Her glasses caught the light. "Boone, you don't need to talk like that."

He popped the cap from his beer and drank from the bottle.

Riss let the screen door creak shut. *"Talk like that?"* She imitated Amber's voice. "It's a legitimate question. I'd like the answer too."

In the living room, the toddler tussle escalated. A little girl started sobbing. Rory saw two kids in a heap on the floor, tugging on the stuffed bear. The little boy kicked his feet and screamed. Addie put her thumb in her mouth and ran to a far corner.

The little boy wailed, "Let *go.*"

Sighing, Amber pushed off from the counter and walked slump shouldered into the living room. "Hey. Hey." She pulled the kids apart. The crying continued. She took the battlers by the hand.

"Nap time." Her face exhausted, she led them down the hall to one of the bedrooms.

The sound of crying became muffled. Rory felt the weight of her cousins' stares.

Time to go.

But Riss remained in the doorway. "Amber's not in any shape to talk."

Rory's eyebrows went up. Since when had Riss abandoned *Mom* and started using Amber's first name?

"She's up to her ass in diapers and snot. You may jet around the world drinking champagne, but some of us have to work for a living," Riss said.

"Your mom's been hounding me to talk to her. But she's clearly busy now. I'll catch up with her another time."

Rory stepped toward the door but Riss settled herself against the doorframe and casually put one foot against the other side of it. Boone sidled from the kitchen into the hallway.

He towered over her. "Did you come here to brag?"

"Excuse me?"

"Did the high-and-mighty Samantha Mackenzie send you here to lord it over Amber?" He reached out with a finger and flicked the collar of Rory's peacoat. "Got that in Europe, I bet. Ooh la la. Lived the life of Riley, didn't you?"

"I lived in the wild and hunted my own food. You should see me wield a crossbow." She pointed at the door. "Excuse me."

Riss didn't move. Her eyes were bright and hard. "What did Amber say to you?"

And there it was. As blatant as Riss ever got.

"Nothing." Rory put up a hand. "Riss, please. Don't."

Boone closed in behind her. "Don't what?"

In the mirror, Rory caught a reflection. Little faces gawking at the grown-ups. Addie, thumb in her mouth, stood watching them.

Don't say anything else. Just get out.

Riss stared at her. The limp breeze from the fan lifted her black hair and her filmy blouse. "Do you actually suspect Amber?"

Rory nearly jumped. *"What?"*

"It's not her."

"I don't —"

"Everybody knew. Everybody heard. It was never a secret. Anybody could have been the source."

"What are you talking about?" Rory said.

"I told you to watch yourself. That if you weren't careful, things could boomerang on you."

The hallway began to feel cold. "Riss."

"I offered to help you with the media. But damage control ain't my mission."

She held still a moment longer, then shrugged and stepped aside.

Rory slammed open the screen and stormed out.

She jammed her Subaru into gear and gunned it out of the driveway and up the road. The sun raked her face. She drove a hundred yards, crested the hill, and passed the neighbors' Winnebago. She pulled over beneath a canopy of heavy oaks, in dappled sunlight. On a cross street Seth sat in his truck, phone to his ear.

She shut off the engine and sat gripping the wheel. Why did she let them get to her? And what had Riss done?

She got out of the car. Pacing, she pulled

her phone from her pocket and went on-line.

Seth ended his call and climbed out of the pickup, his face full of concern. "Rory?"

"I made a mistake," she said.

She searched for *Aurora Mackenzie* and *juror.* It took her ten seconds to find it: a post on a gossip zine.

MIRKOVIC TRIAL JUROR HAS TROUBLED PAST.

Seth approached. She shoved the phone into his hands to keep from hurling it through the windshield of her car. Immediately she grabbed it back and read.

Rumors are swirling about Aurora Mackenzie, one of the jurors taken hostage in the attack on the Ransom River courthouse. The former star athlete has drawn praise for signaling the authorities during the attack, about conditions inside the besieged courtroom. But when she was sixteen, Mackenzie was besieged by rumors serious enough to cause high school officials to withdraw an award she was slated to receive.

"Jesus, this?" she said.
Seth leaned in to read over her shoulder.

"The sports awards ceremony? What the hell."

It happened her junior year. That season she won every dual meet, won the conference, won CIF. She went to State for the first time, broke 18:30 and finished in the top twenty. Afterward she fell to her knees, arm around the girl she outkicked to the chute, and puked on the grass. It was the best moment she'd ever lived.

She was going to be named Ransom River's Athlete of the Year. At the ceremony, the cafeteria was packed. Rory had on her girly dress, coral chiffon with spaghetti straps and sequins. The cheerleaders were up front, dancing. Then the vice principal approached with the cross-country coach and said, "Miss Mackenzie, we have a problem."

When she followed them outside, Coach took out a cell phone. "I was forwarded this text message half an hour ago. The teacher who sent it to me got it from two girls in her history class. They said it came from you."

On the display a message read, *OMG. EPT pos. Can't deal. R.*

Rory said, "I don't understand."

The vice principal said, "You shouldn't have sent that message. It's been forwarded to half the girls in your class."

"But I didn't send it. What . . ."

EPT pos.

The warm hum in her chest turned to a sharp ping, like the flat line on a cardiac monitor. They thought she was pregnant.

"It's not true," she said.

Coach said, "Do your parents know?"

Things deteriorated from there. Rory insisted she didn't send the text. She wasn't pregnant. Somebody had faked the message to start a rumor about her. Coach looked disappointed. The vice principal finally shut down the argument, saying, "When you joined the cross-country team you signed the honor code. You swore not to bring the school into disrepute. Given this situation, we feel it would be inappropriate for you to receive Athlete of the Year."

All the heat leached from Rory's body. She clamped things down and walked back into the cafeteria, into a blur of stares and whispers. She took her seat and clenched her coral chiffon skirt in her pale fists. She sat like clay while Athlete of the Year was awarded to Ransom River's star tight end, Boone Mackenzie.

Afterward, Riss ran squealing across the cafeteria, pom-poms raised, and threw her arms around Boone's neck. As Boone spun her around, she spied Rory. Her gaze was eager: searching for pain, for lash marks. She looked triumphant.

Now Seth covered Rory's phone with his hand. "This is bullshit."

"Riss warned me something would happen if I didn't play ball with her."

"It's crap-ass gossip."

Mackenzie was stripped of the Athlete of the Year Award, Ransom River High School's highest accolade, because of an honor-code violation. Sources familiar with the incident say rumors of sexual misconduct were rife, and that Mackenzie's affair and pregnancy were common knowledge on campus at the time. However, Mackenzie continued to train and compete, and four months after the incident she won the state cross-country title. The cross-country coach left the high school soon after.

"Well, isn't that peachy." Rory leaned back against the car. "They're implying I had an affair with Coach and then had an abortion. Ain't that just a pie full of turds with whipped cream on top."

"Especially considering Coach DiMezza was a woman."

She tried and failed to laugh. She rubbed her forehead. "The cops will eat this up. Honor-code violation. Scandal. It's fuel for their theory that I'm a rotten apple."

"It's a hit piece, but the truth's in there. You won State the next season. You had your vengeance."

And Boone got kicked off the football team for punching a coach.

Seth looked at her warily. "You okay?"

"You can stop asking me that every ten seconds."

He raised his hands in surrender. "Tell me what happened at Amber's."

She exhaled. "Riss and Boone are creepier than ever." She glanced around the side of the neighbor's Winnebago. From this angle she could see down the hill to Amber's kitchen window.

"You texted me," she said.

"Got a lead on the people in prison for the heist."

"You didn't see Riss and Boone drive up?"

"I did. They didn't see me."

"Good. They know I'm on to something."

She saw movement inside the kitchen window. And she stopped, dead.

Her cousins stood by the counter, talking, close together. Too close.

Seth turned to follow her gaze. He went still.

Riss and Boone weren't touching, but they looked hungry. They stood inches apart, conspiratorial, intimate, like a single organism. Symbiotic. They were talking in low, staccato bursts.

Boone put a hand on Riss's waist. Riss, lips moving, pressed against him. Her left hand slid around his back. Her right pressed flat to his chest. She spoke. He watched her face, as though being hypnotized, or receiving a dark blessing.

Riss tossed her hair. He nodded. Then he grabbed her around the haunches and lifted her onto the kitchen counter. He clutched her with both arms and pushed her hair back from her cheek and buried his face against her neck.

"Oh my God," Rory said.

39

Rory found her parents at their acreage. Her dad had converted the shed into a man cave, a workshop and second garage built around the sacred, tarp-covered red El Camino. The big door was half-open.

"Mom? Dad?"

The late afternoon sun was heavy orange and losing heat. Her mom was digging in the garden beside the shed. She stood up and took off her gardening gloves. Her smile evaporated.

"What is it?" she said.

"Everything."

Sam's face drew in on itself. As at all moments of tension, her drawl lengthened. "Is it the courthouse attack?"

"And everything else. Please. Both of you." She called: "Dad, come here."

Will Mackenzie came out of the workshop with his phone in his hand. "Honey, you're pale."

"We have to talk."

"I know." He held up the phone. "That was your aunt Amber."

Rory dug her nails into her palms. "What did she say? I don't know how she's spinning this, but it's bound to be full of lies."

"Really? You haven't spent the entire day joined at the hip to Seth Colder?"

He looked hurt and betrayed. She said, "Dad —"

"Aurora. Don't deflect." His face had reddened. "Why?"

"I'm not here to talk about Seth, and if you —"

"Rory, no." Her mom put a hand over her mouth. "I thought you were over him. This . . . oh, Rory."

Will Mackenzie slowly drew himself up. "Why is he here?"

"Stop. Please." Rory put up her hands. "This is not about Seth. It's something much worse."

Samantha shook her head. She looked on the verge of panic. "Honey, if your head was clear, you'd see that not much is worse than hanging out with Seth."

Rory felt heartsick. Their resentment and anger at Seth had seemed reasonable at the time of the accident, in the heat of the moment — no parent wanted to see a child lying injured in a hospital bed. Seth had provided an easy target for their fear and frustration. But this was off the scale.

She walked inside the shed, went to the workbench, and turned off the small television her dad kept tuned to ESPN. Her parents followed her in, looking baffled and wary. She paced.

"Riss and Boone," she said. "There's something wrong with them."

Will drew a breath. Sam went perfectly still.

Rory stopped and looked back and forth between her parents. "You know what I'm talking about, don't you?"

"No," her dad said.

"They're sick. And they're involved in something very bad." She clenched her hands close to her sides. "I don't even know where to start."

Sam's face was tight and pained. "You look like you're going to cry, honey. Just start wherever."

"This is going to sound awful," Rory said. "But it's important. Please, just listen. Don't say anything until I finish."

Will stood in the doorway of the shed, the evening light catching him from behind. He looked like a soldier about to throw himself on a grenade to muffle an explosion.

"Boone and Riss are involved with each other. Romantically."

That was the wrong word, but one that might lessen the blow. Her parents didn't react. They looked like abandoned puppets.

"I think they're in love with each other," Rory said. "Or as much as they can be. They have a relationship that passes for love, in any case."

"Stop," Will said.

"No, Dad. You have to listen to me."

"Where is this coming from?"

"From what I saw today."

"What you *saw?* What were they doing?"

"They were embracing. And not like brother and sister."

"They aren't brother and sister," Sam said.

Rory looked sharply at her. "You're not surprised. Are you? You don't doubt me."

Will turned and looked out the door at the countryside, as though he could disconnect from the conversation.

"Dad, don't," Rory said. "This is real."

He shook his head. "I don't want to hear it."

"You have to."

"Why are you bringing this up now? Don't you have enough to worry about?"

"Because it's all connected."

That brought his head around.

"They're not brother and sister. I know we all treat them that way, but they aren't related. They grew up under the same roof, but they're from completely separate families. Riss doesn't even call Amber 'Mom' anymore," Rory said.

That got her dad to relax, maybe a millimeter.

"Riss's connection is with Boone. And it's far closer than friends or cousins or siblings." When her parents didn't look at her, Rory added, "You'd recognize it. They see themselves as two against the world. They always have."

Sadly, slowly, Will nodded.

Sam said, "There's nothing we can do about them. And" — she rubbed a hand across her eyes — "there's nothing we *should* do."

"Sam," Will said.

"It's not illegal. It's sick. It's sick because *they're* sick. I'm not talking sexually. I mean they are difficult and troubled people. You know it, Will. You've always known it."

Rory said, "This has been building up for a long time."

Her nerves tightened. And then, as if bursting from deep water into the air, she realized: *Don't be afraid.* She had done nothing wrong. How many times had she coaxed refugees to speak up, to tell the truth at an asylum hearing? She had told them it would be empowering.

Believe your own truth, she told herself.

"When I was twelve, Boone tried to undress me and fool around."

Sam went rigid. "What?"

"At our barbecue, over Memorial Day."

Sam's mouth opened. Will turned toward Rory at last. His face closed with anger.

Rory spoke slowly, forcing herself to tell the story in clear and dispassionate detail. She didn't spare anything. She told them how she and Seth had hopped the fence near the storm drain. Sam didn't roll her eyes and Will didn't reprimand her. And what had she expected, disappointment over a minor bit of mischief when she was in seventh grade?

Yes. The perfect daughter had never thought it possible to show scrapes and scuffs or admit anything less than one hundred percent sunshine all the time.

"You haven't heard the worst of it," she said.

Will sat down on an old secondhand sofa. He said nothing.

"When I found Boone in my room, I thought he was alone. But Riss was hiding in the closet. Watching."

"Dear God," Sam said.

"She just stood there, absolutely silent, until I backed up and saw her."

"Boone didn't . . ."

"No. He didn't touch me." The memory still made her skin shrink. The closeness of his face, his smell of sweat. "One of your friends knocked on the door. That ended it."

She saw the relief on Will's face. She said, "Except for what Riss did next."

She told them about Riss threatening Pepper. The little dog had been like the fourth Mackenzie, for years — a stalwart and kooky presence. The idea of Riss wanting to hurt him seemed to cut her mother deeply. Will's face went the color of cornmeal.

"They're dangerous," Sam said.

"Riss has been threatening me again. And Boone's been following me," Rory said.

"Christ," Will said.

"Why?" Sam said.

For a second Rory held back. Her suspicion was inchoate, almost ghostly. But it was growing: that her cousins knew about the heist. They knew their dad may have been involved. They'd grown up hearing the lore of the missing millions. They must have.

"Because they've realized I think they're involved in what happened at the courthouse yesterday," Rory said.

Instead of profanity, her parents reacted with silence.

"I told you that I thought the gunmen had an ulterior motive. That they were working with somebody or some group on the outside."

Sam said, "Boone and Riss? That's . . ."

"Preposterous," Will said.

Rory said, "I don't think so."

She waited a beat. When her parents stopped squirming, she said, "It's about Uncle Lee. And the armored car heist."

If the silence in the shed had felt heavy before, now it seemed electric.

"That's why I went with Seth today to talk to his dad. That's what I've been checking into," Rory said.

Shock and alarm crackled from her parents. Will looked stunned. Sam looked faint. She joined Will on the sofa. Rory took her hand. It was cold.

"I'm convinced the gunmen were after me," Rory said. "But on its own it makes no sense. The heist is the only thing that does. The only damned thing."

Her parents said nothing.

"So tell me. Tell me the truth, straight up. Is it possible that Uncle Lee stole the money?"

The words hung in the air.

"The night of the meteor shower when I was nine. That van, and the drunk in the street — was it Lee?"

Her dad stood and walked to the shrouded El Camino. He put his hands on the hood and leaned on his arms and stared blankly out the shed door at the oaks shuddering in the evening breeze.

After a long silence, Sam said, "Tell her."

For a painful few seconds, Will didn't move. Then he walked to the workbench and sat down on a stool.

Rory held still. "Dad."

Finally he looked at her. "Lee had lots of trouble with the law. But he never did anything violent or dangerous. Not that I ever knew of. He was always just falling for get-rich-quick schemes, and believing the wrong people, and . . ."

Sam sat up straighter. For a moment Rory thought this was news to her mom, that she didn't know what Will was revealing. Then Rory realized that was impossible. Her parents were too close. And they'd lived the last thirty years together. Sam knew.

Rory felt a weight in her chest. How had

her parents found out? Had they figured it out after Lee disappeared? Had the difficult truth slowly sunk in over the years? When Lee had been writing Rory postcards, had he been letting her parents in on the secret?

Will paused. As if summoning an effort to overcome decades of pain and inertia and shame, he said, "That night. It was late. Dark."

Rory's breathing caught.

"Lee showed up here. After the robbery. He wanted help." He paused and looked at her with despair. "And I gave it to him."

40

"Lee turned up at the kitchen door. Middle of the night. He pounded on the kitchen window. He woke me up. And when I let him in, I saw him . . ."

The pain on her dad's face was seemingly fresh, as though Lee were in the kitchen, not twenty years' gone.

"He was injured and desperate," Will said.

"Injured?" Rory said.

"He'd been wounded in the getaway."

Rory could hardly inhale. "He was the getaway driver?"

Will looked at her with kindness and gentle regret, as though he hated to prick the bubble she lived in. "I don't know. I wasn't privy to their plans."

She flushed.

"I just know that once the armored car guards started shooting, it all went to hell. And when it ended, Lee was the only one still standing. He managed to get back in their vehicle and drive away."

"And he came here? To the house — to you?" Rory said.

Will nodded. Sam shifted.

"What did he say? What did you think?" Rory said.

Sam looked at her. "We were horrified."

Rory sensed a wire stretching tight between her parents. Will clasped his hands and spoke in low, measured tones that sounded broken. Like a doctor reciting a dying patient's list of injuries.

"Lee said nobody was supposed to get hurt. There wasn't supposed to be any violence."

"It was armed robbery," Rory said.

"He said he thought it would be a victimless crime."

Sam stood and scratched at her arms and took up pacing. "The fool."

Will eyed her. "It's absurd, but that's what he said. Victimless crime. It was old money — useless, worn-out bills that were going to be shredded anyway. It wasn't really theft, more like Dumpster diving. And that's not a crime."

"You're kidding," Rory said.

Sam shook her head. "You didn't know Lee's powers of reasoning. Or unreasoning. He could talk anybody into anything."

Rory thought: *But I did know. He talked me into believing in the adventure.*

Will said, "He lived in a fantasy world. But it fell apart. It fell apart in violence. And he should have seen it coming a long way off. We all should have."

He stared at his hands. "Lee'd been . . . fading from our sight for years. We didn't know who he'd gotten involved with. I should have. It was bad."

Sam said nothing. Rory sensed that this was an old, old refrain.

"Lee turned up that night . . ." He rubbed his face. "Bleeding, covered in glass, shaking, begging me for help."

"What kind of help?" Rory said.

"Every kind. Medical, to start with."

"He'd been shot?"

"In the arm." He absently touched his shoulder. "And gunfire had shattered the window of the car and he had glass embedded in his face. Shards in his eye. He was in agony."

Sam said nothing. The word *agony* didn't seem to register with her.

"I was . . . *shocked* doesn't begin to cover it. I tried to get him to sit down and make sense. At first he wouldn't tell me what he'd done. Kept saying, 'This thing happened. I need to go.' I wanted to drive him to the

ER but he refused. He wanted me to take care of the glass myself. I didn't understand, and I . . ."

"Will," Samantha said. Her drawl was like an undertow. "You got the first-aid kit and pulled the glass out of his face. And then you asked if he needed a lawyer."

"You knew what he'd done?" Rory said.

Will nodded. "Of course. And he tried not to tell us at first, just weaseling around. 'The thing.' 'What happened.' But it was crystal clear that something very bad had taken place. And he was neck deep in it."

"Did you call him a lawyer?" Rory said.

Will shook his head. "He refused. And before I could even suggest it, he said, 'And I'm not turning myself in either.' " He paused. "Lee didn't just need medical help, or a place to hide out while the cops drove around the boonies looking for the getaway car. He begged me for protection — for himself, and for his family."

"Oh God," Rory said.

"He wanted me to protect him from the cops. And he wanted to protect Amber and the kids from the whole thing."

"Amber didn't know?" Rory said.

Sam's look was scathing. "Maybe, maybe not. Even when she was compos mentis, Lee didn't take her into his confidence. They had a marriage based on . . . fantasy, not real life."

Will cleared his throat. "Rory, you can't imagine the shock. It was like the whole world just split apart at the seams. Here was my brother. My flesh and blood, the kid I'd grown up sharing a room with, this guy I loved —"

His voice broke. Rory felt a knot in her throat. Sam looked implacable.

Will coughed and went on. "I felt — torn. That's the only word to describe it. Just ripped in half. What was I supposed to do? Let my only brother go to prison for decades? I wanted to — I wanted to . . ."

Sam stood up and crossed to the workbench and wrapped her arms tightly around him. He drew a rough breath and fought not to break down. After a long moment Samantha locked hands with his. Will took a breath and wiped his eyes.

"He wanted to get away. And I helped him."

Rory felt frozen.

"He wanted to get out of the country. He wanted to go to Mexico. He wanted me to help him get across the border," Will said. "And I was his brother, Aurora."

Rory understood now. The jumbled pictures from her childhood began to assemble into a coherent pattern.

"You thought I'd never figure it out," she said.

Her mom said, "Desperation makes people strangely certain."

"Mom. Dad. The van out back. The staggering drunk. Seth and I saw it. We saw *him*. And all these years . . . you said *nothing* happened."

They seemed ready to capsize. Will said, "We couldn't tell you. How could we? It wasn't fair to you. It wouldn't have been safe for you to know."

"Mexico," she said.

Will nodded.

"The postcards. The letters. It was more than abandonment."

Sam's eyes looked flat. "He abandoned his family in all kinds of ways. Long before that night."

Will said, "Lee was crazy. I mean he was manic that night. Scared and desperate and — I'd never seen him so . . . single-minded about anything. 'Get me to Mexico. I'm going. I need your help.' "

"What was his plan? To wait until the case went cold? Or until the statute of limitations ran?" Rory said.

"Plan?" Sam laughed, a brutal sound.

"I promised Lee I would not let his family

suffer," Will said.

"You drove him over the border?"

Rory heard herself: Her voice was wooden and distant. Will looked at her.

"You're not denying it," she said.

"Rory." His voice was kind. It was *Honey, there's no Santa Claus.*

She put a fist over her mouth. "The money," she finally said.

"Lee didn't take that," Will said.

"What do you mean?"

"He did, I mean. He robbed the armored car. And he drove away from the scene with . . ." He spread his hands. "Millions. But he didn't take that money to Mexico."

Rory looked back and forth between her parents. "So where is it?"

41

Her parents didn't answer. They held on to each other in a drafty shed in an empty field, inside walls that had been patched and repainted at least three times, facing a forty-year-old car that was meant to be Rory's inheritance. The light through the door had faded to dusky grays and blues.

"Dad. Twenty-five million dollars was stolen in the robbery. What happened to it?"

Will spoke quietly. His eyes were distant. "It was a sight to see."

"Lee had it with him when he showed up here that night?"

Will nodded.

"Jesus," Rory said. "In the back of that van? Mounds of cash?"

"It was in duffel bags and stacked in bricks on the floor. It was bound up in plastic. Bunches of bills with bands around them. They'd been counted and prepared for transport to the Federal Reserve processing facility."

"You saw it."

"Did you know that each denomination of bill gets wrapped with a different color of paper?"

"No."

"Currency bands, they're called. The fed and the banks have standard colors they use. I remember some. Violet, that's for stacks of twenty-dollar bills. Brown's for fifties. Mustard's for hundreds." He looked surprised. "A strap of hundreds with a mustard band, it's ten thousand dollars. A hundred hundreds. Not even an inch thick. Weighs almost nothing. And that van was piled knee-high with them."

Sam didn't look at her husband. She'd heard this story before.

"Hundreds, deep enough to swim in. I couldn't fathom it all."

"Dad . . ."

He met her gaze. "Lee wanted me to drive him over the border with the cash. He said he'd give me a cut." His mouth drew tight and he shook his head viciously. "That was . . . a bad moment. I told him I'd drive him anywhere he wanted to go. Family — blood — that's one thing. He was my brother. I wouldn't turn him in."

"But . . ."

"I know what you're thinking, Aurora. I knew from the second you applied to law school. You'd learn every last detail about criminal law. You would understand about what it takes to become an accessory after the fact. I was willing to break the law to protect my brother. I couldn't . . . couldn't . . ."

He took another breath. Sam rested her hand on his arm.

"I couldn't take the thought of him behind bars for life. As much as I hated him and felt angry at him and just . . ."

Sam squeezed.

"In the heat of the moment, I told him I would take him across the border. That I would protect his wife and kids. I would not let them go hungry or suffer problems while he was away. It was a snap decision. A gut decision. I was . . . Rory, it was god-awful."

"I'm sorry, Dad."

Sam's eyes flashed. "Don't be. This wasn't brought on by your father."

Will said, "I said I'd drive him to safety. But him. Not the money."

"Why?" Rory said.

"Lee could repent. Lee, I could explain to the police if it came to it. I was willing to . . ." Again he broke off.

Sam said, "He was willing to risk himself for family." She looked at Will with strength and a devotion that nearly made Rory tear up.

"He was willing to put himself on the line to save his brother. But he was not going to risk himself for dirty money," Sam said.

Rory said, "You knew it would be one thing if the cops learned you'd helped your brother evade arrest. But it would be another matter entirely to get caught driving him across the border with twenty-five million stolen dollars in the back of your car."

Will looked grateful that she'd said it. "I told Lee he was worth more than all that money. Family was worth everything. The money was just paper."

"Did he fight you?"

Sam hesitated a moment, her eyes flashing, then stood and walked to the window. "Damn, I want a cigarette," she said.

Rory turned, taken aback. "Since when?"

"Haven't smoked since I was twenty, but give me a Marlboro and I'd light it up right now."

Will cleared his throat. "Lee had no way to get across the border without me. He didn't want Amber involved. He had no contacts left he could trust. He went ballistic about leaving the money behind, but I told him I wouldn't touch it. I wouldn't turn it in. I would act as though I'd never seen it. But he had to leave it. Period."

"And he did?" Rory said.

"He had no choice."

"What did you do with it?" she said.

"I took the keys to the van with the stolen cash in the back, and I drove it up into the national forest and I buried it."

"Underground. Twenty-five million bucks."

"With a Forest Service backhoe. I dug a trench in a gully on the far side of one of the back bowls in the forest, and I dumped that cash ten feet deep. Covered it up, put rocks back over it, returned the terrain to as normal as I could."

"That's it?" Rory said. "You planted daisies on top of the cash and drove home and kept quiet?"

He nodded.

"For twenty years?"

Her dad said, "For all of us."

His eyes brimmed. Though he tried to remain expressionless, his face crumpled. "I did what I thought best. And everything has gone horribly wrong."

Then he broke down. For a painful minute, his choked crying filled the shed.

Sam held his hand like a vise grip and

rubbed the back of his neck.

Rory wanted to ask questions. Stopped herself. Her mind was galloping in a dozen strange directions. One of them being: "Regard me as your attorney right now. This conversation is privileged."

Sam gave her a look that was surprised and grateful. She nodded. Rory said she might want to talk about the robbery to her own attorney but wouldn't speak to anybody else. Her parents nodded their assent.

"Where is he?" Rory asked.

Sam said, "We haven't heard from him in many years."

"You don't know?"

"He's not sailing the Riviera, or living a life of poverty as a Franciscan monk; that's for sure."

"You never tried to find him? Didn't ever try to get him to come back?"

Will said, "Lee wanted to disappear. For good. 'Cross the border' — once he stepped over that line, he didn't plan on coming back. Ever." He shook his head. "So no. I never once have tried to dig up his whereabouts. Don't you either. I know you wanted to. You had some romantic idea that he was living a Disney pirate's life. It's my fault I let you think that. But he left. He's gone. Don't try to bring him back."

He looked at her, broken. "I told Lee I would never touch that money. A man had died stealing it. It was heartbreak and ruin. It needed to stay buried."

"I understand," Rory said, though she didn't.

"He tried to claim he'd done it for Amber and the kids. He said . . . said they'd need it. They couldn't survive on their own. I told him to forget that. Feeding his kids off of blood money would poison them."

"And what did you do?" Rory said.

He wiped his eyes. "I told him he needed to take care of his family. But I told him I wouldn't let them suffer. They'd be okay."

Sam stood up. "Your dad's been sending them money for twenty years, Aurora."

The acid in her mother's tone was not diluted by her genteel southern drawl. Rory felt another layer of protection peel from her past.

"Lee's never paid a cent?" Rory said.

"Your dad has put every penny in Amber's pocket," Sam said. Her anger sounded clarifying. "Who's after the money now?"

Will took out a handkerchief and blew his nose. "Is that what's going on? It's all about that stolen cash?"

Sam's voice was sharp. "Two members of the gang survived and went to prison."

Rory said, "You're thinking logically. But you can forget Lee's partners. It isn't them."

She stood up. She rubbed her palms on her jeans. She checked her gut.

"It's Riss and Boone," she said.

If her parents were shocked, they didn't show it. Her mom looked stony. Her dad's emotional temperature shifted abruptly, hot to cold.

"They have to know about the robbery," she said. "Amber must know about it, and she must have told them. Don't you think?"

Her dad raised a hand. "You sure about this?"

Rory nodded.

After a second, he said, "Tell us."

"Boone followed me this afternoon," she began.

By the time she laid it all out, Rory felt drained. Her parents looked spent. Sam went to the fridge and poured herself a tall glass of water from a pitcher. She drank the whole thing, staring out the window of the shed, before she said, "Things like this make me understand why somebody would want to run away."

Rory heard the remark and felt it like a sharp rock in her shoe.

"Mom. Dad. You've always told me to get

out of Ransom River. Is this the reason why?"

Will looked at her, caught out, off balance. "We have plenty of reasons for encouraging you to spread your wings."

Sam gave Will a tough look. "Boone and Riss have always been jealous of Rory. Always. Of Rory and our family life. It's been obvious since they were children. Amber encouraged it."

Will looked like he might protest, but Sam cut him off. "Even though you pay Amber a monthly stipend. It's never been enough to stanch the envy."

Will and Lee had grown up poor. Lee had then taken the crooked road, seeking wealth. Will had struggled and worked like a mule to build a stable life for himself and his family.

Rory said, "You pay Amber a stipend. Not riches. Am I right?"

Sam said, "You think we have riches to spare?"

"You gotta be frickin' kidding me."

Will stood up. "Tell me you're not referring to what I think you are."

Rory put up her hands. "We have no riches to spare. Except you could fire up a backhoe and dig out twenty-five million dollars any weekend you felt like it."

"I will not touch that money."

Sam spread her arms, like an umpire calling a batter safe. "Cut it out."

Rory closed her eyes.

Sam said, "We can debate the ethical implications of that money later. Right now we have a huge problem. If Rory's right, her cousins are involved with a massive criminal enterprise that involves murder."

Rory said, "It still makes little sense. Twenty-five million dollars is Godzilla-size motive. But why try to get at it through me?"

Will said, "They hate the fact that their dad . . ."

Sam turned on him. "What?"

"Them thinking their dad loves Rory . . . it twisted them somehow."

" 'Somehow'? I'll say," Sam said. "What if it's twisted them so hard, they don't care if Rory ends up dead?"

42

Rory walked out of the shed feeling disoriented. The mountains seemed to loom, shadowed and sharp.

"Where are you going?" her mom called after her.

She slowed and turned. Her parents stood in the barn-wide door of the shed.

"I won't talk," she said. "But I have to think."

Their eyes, dark with the evening sun, looked hollow.

She walked like a zombie toward her car. She couldn't absorb everything she had just learned. *Revelation* was the English word for "apocalypse." Unveiling. She'd just seen it: a curtain ripped open. Blasphemy, bright and shocking, revealed as truth.

And what roiled her were her mom's words. *What if it's twisted them so hard, they don't care if Rory ends up dead?*

In the hospital after the wreck, one

evening she'd lain dozing in the half dark, curled awkwardly on one side. She came awake to the sound of humming above her. A soprano voice hovered by the bed rails. Exhausted, she listened with her eyes closed. If her mom wanted to lullaby her, no harm done. A hand touched her hair, brushed it off her face, and pressed to her cheek as if checking for fever. The humming turned to soft singing. And the song wasn't a lullaby. It was the Amy Winehouse tune "Some Unholy War." Fingers pressed to her neck to feel her pulse.

She turned and saw Riss staring down at her.

Her cousin withdrew her hand. Her pupils were wide in the dim light. They were wide like a cat's, eyeing a bird.

Rory's heart thumped against her ribs. "What are you doing?"

"You poor kid," Riss said. "You are just a mess."

"Why are you here?"

"Seeing for myself."

Riss set a get-well card on the nightstand and looked Rory slowly up and down. She shook her head.

"Sorry sight. Sorry, girl. So sorry," she said.

She leaned over the bed. Rory shied away

and said, "Hey —" But Riss put a finger to her lips. She bent and kissed Rory on the forehead. Then she put her lips to Rory's ear.

"Karma's a bitch," she said. "I warned you."

Rory could hardly swallow. She felt for the nurse call button. She didn't want to meet Riss's eyes but didn't dare look away.

"You have to learn to listen. Or it won't get better," Riss said.

"Get out," Rory said.

Now she found herself in her car, hand on the keys in the ignition. She didn't remember climbing in. Her phone was ringing.

She didn't recognize the number. She answered and was surprised to hear her neighbor's voice.

"It's Andi Garcia. I was driving past your house earlier and saw the gate open. I didn't think much of it except now I'm near the Cloud Canyon freeway off-ramp and your dog's running loose."

"Chiba?"

"Big dog, part husky?"

Rory turned the key in the ignition. "Is he on the freeway?"

"He's chasing squirrels. There's a lot of traffic."

"I'm coming."

"I called him but he ignored me."

"He's a rescue dog. He has hearing loss from neglect when he was a puppy." She put the car in gear. "I'm on my way. Five minutes."

When she screeched up Cloud Canyon Road to the freeway, she saw Andi's car parked on the off-ramp. She didn't see Chiba. She pulled over and jumped out, her stomach in knots, and scanned the countryside. The air had grown chilled and blue with sunset. Some cars had their lights on.

This off-ramp was three miles from her house. What was Chiba doing way out here?

Then she saw her neighbor, chubby in crimson capris, in the grass beside the off-ramp, about a hundred yards beyond her parked car. Rory hollered and waved.

Andi pointed at the freeway and cupped her hands to her mouth. "He's in the median strip."

Rory ran up the ramp, her leg stiff. She saw Chiba about two hundred yards beyond Andi. He was in the center of the freeway on the wide grass strip between six speeding lanes of traffic.

"Oh no," she said.

Traffic was thin, but the light was bad. There was no good way to capture him either on foot or in the car. Running across the roadway would be dangerous, but so would stopping her Subaru in the center of the freeway. Not to mention illegal.

Dammit, what was he doing here?

Chiba jogged along in the grass. He approached the pavement as though preparing to run straight back across the road, oblivious to the threat. Oh God, the dumb, lovely dog.

A Volkswagen came ripping along, doing the speed limit, and braked hard. The driver hit the horn and Chiba brought himself up short. The VW continued past.

Andi jogged up, out of breath, cheeks pink. "What do you want to do?"

"Can you drive around to the on-ramp on the other side of the freeway and wait there, so if he bolts in that direction you could catch him?"

"Sure." She headed for her car.

Rory ran back to the Subaru, opened the hatchback, and got the leash. She hurried up the ramp again. Glass and gravel crunched beneath her feet. She paused on the hard shoulder while trucks and station wagons roared by. The wind smelled of eucalyptus.

A school bus blared past. Behind it was a gap of several hundred yards before more traffic.

Rory sprinted into the road. Three lanes of scored concrete had never seemed so wide. Headlights rose on her left. The cat's eyes in the road to her right began to glow white. A horn honked. And kept honking, growing louder. She didn't look. She just ran.

She reached the median strip. The horn Dopplered past her. A driver shouted, "Idiot!"

Heart going like a sewing machine, she clapped her hands and whistled. "Chiba."

The dog turned. He immediately dug in and raced toward her. She ran along the grass strip to meet him. He lurched up to her. She grabbed his collar and held on tight.

"Boy, what are you doing here?"

He was panting and shaking. He whimpered and tried to put his paw on her shoulder. He was terrified.

She clipped the leash to his collar. He moaned and twisted and jumped.

"Chiba. Shh."

She tried to calm him. On the far side of the freeway Andi Garcia coasted to a stop on the on-ramp and got out. Chiba shivered and barked, turning in circles at Rory's side.

An eighteen-wheeler rolled toward them. The driver blew the air horn. The noise was horrendous. The truck blew past with heat and thunder and a draft of wind. Chiba panicked.

He was a strong dog, too strong for Rory. When he broke, seventy pounds of pure muscle in flight, he tore the leash from her hands and raced into the roadway.

"No —"

Across the freeway Andi covered her mouth.

The Jetta didn't honk. It did brake. The lights flashed red and it slowed hard, straight, like a black beetle sweeping past. Screeching, laying rubber.

Rory gasped.

She heard a hard thump. The screeching stopped. The Jetta rolled slowly for a second, then changed gears and roared away.

"Oh no, oh no . . ."

Rory ran across the roadway, smelling exhaust and burned rubber. She heard one of the worst sounds in the world. Chiba, crying.

She ran to his side. He'd been hit. On the hard shoulder he lay half-limp amid dust and broken glass. He cried pitiably and tried to stand. His back leg was bloody.

She put a hand on his side. He whimpered and looked at her. His eyes almost broke her heart.

"It's okay, boy. It's okay." She was nearly crying.

She scooped him into her arms. He moaned but didn't thrash. His back legs were limp. Groaning under his weight, she stood up.

"Come on, boy. It's okay."

Nearly staggering, she hurried toward her car. Chiba hung his head, panting. Blood dripped from his back leg to the asphalt. He trembled and whimpered. Traffic whirled by.

Her arms burned with the effort of holding his warm, furry weight. She huffed to her car. Awkwardly she got the hatchback open and laid Chiba in the back. He cried, his chest heaving in and out. She got a beach towel and wrapped it around him.

"We're going, Chiba. It's okay, boy."

She stepped back. When she slammed the tailgate, the window reflected the jangled flash of a red police gumball light.

She turned. Parked behind her Subaru was a silver SUV. The gumball light was propped on the dashboard, spinning. Like an unmarked car. Like the car Seth had seen tailing them earlier in the day.

A man stood in front of the vehicle.

He wore civvies. He was stocky and stolid

and had a face that looked sandblasted. He was Neil Elmendorf, Officer Lucy Elmendorf's husband.

And he had Rory's car keys in his hand.

"What are you doing?" she said.

"You got a big mess here," he said.

"My dog's been hit. I have to get him to the vet."

"You could get cited for all kinds of violations."

She was breathing hard. "Ticket me. Shoot me with a radar gun and call it reckless driving. But God, please — I have to get him help."

He curled the keys tight in his fist and locked his hands behind his back. "Lucy nearly got executed yesterday."

Christ, what is this? "I'm glad she's okay. Please, what do you want? For the love of God, my dog needs help."

"I got shoved to the floor by those assholes and couldn't get to her. Had to watch while they made her write out a false confession. Thought they were going to put a double tap through her head. You know what that felt like, for a husband to be that helpless?"

He was heavier than she was. He looked fit. She was breathing like a guppy and jacked enough to leap up and knee him in the head, but she doubted she could take him and get her keys back.

"Arrest me. Take me to jail. But for Christ's sake do it with the lights flashing, and alert the K-9 unit that you're bringing in a casualty. Come *on.*"

"What did you know about the attack?" he said.

"Nothing."

In the car, Chiba whimpered again, and barked as though in agony.

"Did somebody pay you off to convict Lucy?" Elmendorf said.

"No. Jesus Christ, no. I had nothing to do with the attack. Now cuff me or chain me up and drag me behind your SUV, but goddamn it, don't let my dog die."

The gumball light spun, round and round. Elmendorf's face twitched. And Rory realized: *He's not a cop.*

She backed up a step.

"If you did have anything to do with it, I'll find out. And you'll pay," he said. "Keep your dog on a leash. Unless you want Animal Control to pay you a visit."

He threw her keys, a careless swipe. They landed on the off-ramp.

She ran and grabbed them. Five seconds later she was racing toward the vet's.

43

Chiba lay on the stainless-steel examination table, panting and trembling. Rory leaned over and held him. She stroked the fur on his back.

The vet prepared a syringe. "This will ease his pain."

Chiba had broken ribs, severe bruising, and a mess of abrasions along his side and back leg. The vet had shaved his fur and picked gravel out of the scrapes and gouges. He was in agony but was going to make it.

The vet looked at Chiba with compassion. "Credit German engineering for good brakes. That Jetta must have slowed to around twenty or he'd never have survived."

"Credit cowardice for the jackwipe driving off and leaving him," Rory said.

With a tap on the door, Andi Garcia stuck her head in. Rory waved her neighbor in and gave her a grateful hug.

"Thank you. You probably saved his life."

Andi crept to the exam table and smiled at Chiba. He looked up and whimpered.

Rory said, "The gate at Petra's house has a slide bolt on the inside. It shouldn't have been open."

Andi looked at her sharply. "I don't think it swung open on its own. There was a guy."

Cold, Rory said, "What guy?"

"The one standing there pushing it open."

"Young, brown hair, blue uniform shirt from Ransom River Auto Salvage?"

"That's him. You don't sound happy about it."

Rory looked at her dog. "I'm not."

"You think he let Chiba out on purpose?"

"How long between the time you saw him pushing open the gate and the time you found Chiba running loose on the freeway?"

Andi thought about it. "Maybe fifteen minutes."

Chiba had enough husky in him to run long distances — miles and miles without tiring. But not three miles in fifteen minutes. Not when enjoying an unexpected bout of freedom. He would have stopped at every bush and fire hydrant. He would have meandered. He never would have gotten so far on his own.

Andi said, "Did somebody let him out on the freeway?"

The vet frowned. "Who would do a thing like that?"

Rory phoned Seth. "It's Riss and Boone, and they're after me. I need your help."

"Where are you?"

She told him. "I need a place to stay tonight that'll take a dog."

He was quiet for a moment. She was asking something big and open-ended. She expected to hear him mention his apartment or a hotel. But he said, "I don't want anybody to follow you to my place, or my dad's. You need to go someplace unexpected."

"What do you have in mind?"

"In town. Dogs are no problem. Just follow my instructions for avoiding a tail."

The sun had fallen below the western hills and infused the sky with a rose-washed light. Over the mountains, clouds gathered. Rain was coming. Rory drove slowly along a crumbling one-lane road into the Callahan Ranch, as it had been called on TV. Live oaks and sycamores formed a canopy overhead.

The property was now a city park that closed at dusk. But the swing gate off the main road had been open when Rory drove up. Seth Colder, she suspected, owned a collection of lock-picking tools. She drove through and closed the gate behind her.

A mile up the glen, she eased over potholes and around a bend and saw the desiccated remains of the Hollywood set. There was a barn and the old three-story house with the porch and widow's walk, now preserved as a landmark. The interior scenes for the show had been shot on a soundstage in Burbank, but this classic old building had stood in for the headquarters of the mighty Callahan clan. Nobody had lived here for eighty years. Rory didn't know if it had electricity or running water.

Headlights off, she followed Seth's directions and drove past the house. Seth came striding toward her. In his denim jacket and boots, he looked the part of a Callahan son. Stick a cowboy hat on his head and send him to the back forty.

He pushed open the big barn door. She eased the Subaru inside and parked it next to his truck. She got out and opened the hatchback. Chiba, drugged and drowsy, feebly wagged his tail.

Seth crouched beside the tailgate. "Hey, boy. You've had a hell of a day."

In the corner of the barn was a faucet above a basin. When Rory turned it on the pipe creaked and groaned but filled the basin with water. Seth lifted the dog carefully from the car and carried him over. Chiba put his head down and drank. Seth rubbed the fur between his shoulders.

"Thanks." Rory looked around. "Security guards? Park ranger? Night watchman?"

"Hasn't changed since we were in high school, or I was on the force. Nobody'll check on it unless there's an explosion and fireball."

"I'll try to restrain myself."

Chiba finished drinking. He stood unsteadily, back legs shaking. From the corner of the barn Seth pulled a little red wagon. Rory laid the beach towel in it and Seth set Chiba inside. The poor dog was too whacked-out to realize that he was going against instinct, being pulled rather than pulling a sled. They walked outside and Seth shut the barn door.

The night was descending, the glen cosseted in oaks gone black in the twilight. It was amazingly quiet.

"Where are we camping?" Rory looked at the big house. "I do a poor imitation of Constance Callahan, standing there with my feet wide, spitting tobacco into the dirt and fighting off outlaws."

Seth smiled. "I'm willing to watch that."

She stopped, unsettled by his smile. Jesus, it was the old smile, the one that slid across his face when taking on a challenge.

"She was also expert at throwing a hatchet," she said.

He turned and walked up the glen. "It's getting cold out here. Come on."

The caretaker's cabin was a hundred yards farther up the way, under the boughs of the live oaks. The ground crunched with acorns beneath Rory's feet. Seth let them in. It was cool inside. Chiba raised his head, curious. Seth shut the door and bolted it.

The shutters in the living room were closed tight. A hurricane lantern sat on the coffee table, guttering with amber light. In the fireplace split logs burned, bright orange.

Seth shrugged off his jacket. They arranged a bed for Chiba. Seth opened a backpack and tossed Rory a sandwich and a bottle of water.

"Thanks," she said.

He dropped to a knee in front of the fire and jabbed at the wood with a poker. Sparks spewed, red and dying.

"I checked out the guys who were involved in the heist," he said.

Rory sat down cross-legged in front of the

fire. "And?"

"They weren't part of organized crime or L.A. street gangs. They were semipros who dreamed of the greatest heist of all time and got in way over their heads. One died at the scene. One guy was shot in the head and survived, but with permanent brain damage. He lives in a secure facility for the mentally incompetent. He has no family, nobody who would go after the money on his behalf."

He sat down. "The third guy is in San Quentin, serving out his sentence as a jailhouse preacher. Jesus' biggest fan."

"You believe that?"

"It doesn't matter. These guys were the logical starting point. But they're not the ones after the money."

"Was this a thorough investigation?"

"It was a couple of phone calls and some computer voodoo thanks to a backdoor password I have for the system. I wanted to see if we were missing a red light flashing under our noses. But we're not."

Though she hadn't eaten much all day, she was hardly hungry. "Riss and Boone," she said.

Seth's face was grave. "If your cousins are involved, it means Lee was the fourth man."

The blasphemous shine of her parents'

revelations flared in her mind.

"Riss and Boone are involved," she said.

In the firelight, Seth's face was aglow. His dark eyes seemed to capture and amplify the flames.

"And they're not doing this on their own," she said. "So who did they get in bed with? Somebody from Lee's past?"

"Maybe. Somebody who has connections to career criminals in Vegas — people who can pressure a gambler to take on a suicidal mission? That's some real grease. Who's got that?"

"Let's see. There's the Mafia. There's the Crips and the Bloods, though this doesn't seem their style. There's Lucy Elmendorf's husband, but he's crazy, not connected. There's even Grigor Mirkovic, who's connected and who doesn't mind sending goons to terrify me and Petra. But disrupting the trial destroys his chance to see Lucy and Jared Smith imprisoned for his son's murder. There's the Illuminati. The Vatican. The Mormon Tabernacle Choir." She rubbed her eyes.

Seth said, "Whoever it is, the question remains — how did Riss and Boone find them?"

Chiba set his head on Seth's knee. Seth looked calm and in control. He looked so much like himself, and yet so much older, as though a sadder soul had settled deep inside him and taken on his form.

He caught her watching him.

"About what my dad said earlier," he said.

She looked at the fire.

"I'm trying to get you out of this, not in deeper," he said.

"I didn't hear a thing."

He picked up the poker again. "Are you really that scared of me?"

"I haven't been scared of you since fourth grade."

"Then why won't you look me in the eye?"

He might as well have swept sparks from the fireplace directly into her face. She turned, deliberately, slowly.

"We going to do this?" she said.

He held completely still, though the light from the fire played over his features like winged birds.

"I mean, we going to spill everything, open our veins, see what pours out?" she said.

"I take it back. Are you really that angry at me?"

"I'm not angry. That night, that final night, *that* was angry. I blew up," she said. "I shouldn't have."

He said nothing for a moment. "You're

talking about . . ."

"Before the wreck."

The wood in the fireplace popped. The moment expanded. It was the first time either of them had openly said the word *wreck.*

"I was a mess," Rory said. "And I was scared for you."

"It was about me?"

"No." She raised her hands. Gathered her thoughts. Then thought, *Screw it. Let everything flow.* "I hated what was going on with your job. I hated what I saw you doing. But I didn't hate you. Seth, I loved you."

Seth held her gaze. He seemed unsure whether to rip these scars open. "So . . ."

"And I know it seemed final. I know I told you before the wreck I was done. Period. So I understand why you stayed away afterward. I respect that."

He sat there. "Say that again."

"I respect your reasons for staying away from the hospital. I'd said good-bye." Her face was hot, and not from the fire. "But it hurt. It hurt like a son of a bitch."

A flash in his eyes, then metallic calm. "Your dad kept me away."

It felt like a rock hitting her in the back of the head. "My dad."

"Barred me from seeing you. Had a note put on the board at the nurses' station. I couldn't get on the ward."

The breath left her chest as though she'd been punched. "No."

"Yeah."

"But the police report cleared you of any fault —"

"Rory, from the time we were kids your father has never trusted me."

Her hands hung limp on her lap.

"He was always kind to me," Seth said. "He welcomed me into your house. But I knew."

She stood.

She had acquiesced at the time. In the hospital she hadn't asked for Seth. Hadn't called him, even limited as she was. She'd been in a fog of pain, confusion, and exhaustion.

She walked across the room. Put a hand on the wall. Seth was right about her father's attitude. She hadn't wanted to admit it. And now she wondered if her dad simply hadn't wanted her spending so much time with a cop. A cop's son.

No more.

"Seth, I wanted you there. I wish —"

"Babe, it's way too late for that."

She looked away. The ruddy reflection of

419

the flames rolled across the walls and ceilings, shadowed and jittery. And she abruptly needed to know all the rest.

"The police report on the accident," she said. "The truck that rammed us was sideswiped by another car."

The mystery vehicle never stopped, and nobody got the license number. Black older-model SUV, no tags, driving over the limit with its lights off.

Seth said, "It was one of Dobro's people."

"Jesus. They tracked you from the restaurant?"

"Lured me. The emergency call was a setup." He seemed to steady himself. Maybe to anchor himself, in case he was about to get blown away. "I should have let you out of my truck before responding to the nine-one-one call. Immediately. I made a mistake."

She shook her head. "No. We're done with this."

"What —"

"It was the best choice you had in the situation," she said. "There were no good choices, but it was the least bad thing to do."

Seth paused, his face pained. Chiba shifted and looked up at him.

He nodded. "But if I could turn back the

clock . . ."

"I know." She held his gaze. "What happened after I left?"

"I went back to work. I was determined to finish the operation. The op was everything."

Because he had nothing else left, he meant. And after the wreck, she knew, he would not have been detached and coldly calculating. The man's emotional wiring didn't work that way.

"Tell me. Please. I need to know," she said.

He took his time. "We joined forces with ATF to set up a sting. I had the connections and they had the firepower. We arranged to purchase a shipment of stolen automatic weapons. The ATF guy and I were going to close the negotiation with the sellers."

"Dobro."

Seth nodded. "The people he was working with. The purpose of the meet was to sample the merchandise. Saco — the ATF guy — and I were going to get a look at the weapons, check quality control, finalize the deal. With SWAT and a federal tactical team nearby to back us up."

She walked over and sat down beside him.

"The meet was at warehouse down past the railroad depot, beyond the industrial park."

She knew the neighborhood. Corrugated metal, towers of crushed cars, and trash caught against cyclone fencing.

"We'd done recon. We had blueprints of the building, aerial photos of the property, talked to guys who'd worked there before it closed. We knew every entrance, every exit, every blind spot inside the warehouse where somebody could lie in wait. We had an escape plan, and a backup plan, and a shit-hits-the-fan plan." He looked at her. "What we couldn't do was take a walk-around before we went in, like a pilot checking out his plane before a flight. So we met the sellers' man and followed him inside."

The fire heated Rory's face. She knew her expression was stricken.

"They were outside, hidden," he said. "When we walked in, they chained the doors shut from the outside and set the warehouse on fire."

"Oh my God."

"They sacrificed their own man to ambush me and Saco. They sent him up in flames to lure us into a trap."

She put a hand over her mouth.

"The ground-floor windows had security bars countersunk into brick windowsills," he said. "We ran upstairs to a catwalk. Found a two-by-four and rammed it through a second-floor window. It was a real drop to the ground outside — but by that point we were willing to risk it. Heat and smoke. And loud. The fire was goddamned loud."

Rory felt a stinging behind her eyes.

His gaze drifted. "We didn't get out. The sellers' man — weaselly guy, and not ready to martyr himself for the organization — tried to go out the window before we cleared away all the glass. Big shards, I mean, they looked like shark fins, and they were still in the frame. I took the two-by-four and tried to smash them out, but wasn't fast enough. The catwalk collapsed. The floor dropped out from under us."

He stared at the fireplace. "Saco's backup was on the way. He was live-miked, so they heard; they got on scene but had to break open the doors. By then the place was fully involved. As firefighters say."

He cleared his throat. "The floor fell away as the sellers' man tried to get out the window. He got his head and shoulders through and then . . ." He exhaled. "Nothing below his feet anymore. He was impaled on a shard of glass. Saco and I went down with the catwalk."

His voice was nearly flat. "The fall, and falling debris, killed Saco," he said. "The

ATF team got to me. But there was nothing they could do for their own man." He picked up the poker and jabbed at the fire. "We'd been set up. The sellers knew we were cops."

"Who'd be willing to kill cops, and their own man, in a fire?" Rory said.

"Not your average criminal. Not even your average psychopath. I had a lot of time to think about it. I wasn't clearheaded at first — morphine makes your mind sing, but not in tune. But talking to my handler, and the ATF guys, SWAT — they raided the sellers' operation after the fire. Got a few of them on lesser charges than we wanted. The sellers knew I was a cop. But not because of anything I'd done to tip them. Nobody made me. Somebody had told them."

"You think it was somebody in the Ransom River PD?"

He nodded. "Once I was finally —"

Again he cleared his throat. "When I got back on the street, you know, home from the hospital, I took a look at things. What I found was bad. The sellers knew ahead of the meet that I was a cop. They didn't know Saco was ATF. It was me. And that's why they ambushed us, and why a brother officer died when the warehouse was set on fire."

His voice dropped. "My own department sold me out."

He tossed the poker aside.

Rory was close enough to smell the fresh cotton and clean detergent on his shirt. To see the curve of his cheek. He stared unblinking at the fireplace.

She was inches away. She could practically feel the rise and fall of his chest. He seemed both stone and evanescent.

She raised a hand, as though to touch his arm, and stopped. She had run after the wreck. As soon as she could hold a phone, she'd called a contact from her Peace Corps days and begged — almost physically begged — for any leads on jobs overseas. She had left him exposed, emotionally, and hadn't thought twice.

"I'm sorry, Seth."

He held still, his hand resting on Chiba's side.

Here was her life, sitting before her. Her past, her way through the world, every misadventure and discovery and moment of joy, laughter, and rage.

Please tell me you're okay, she almost said. She couldn't move her lips. A bolus of emotion rose through her.

"What have you been doing the past two years? What's your life?"

He seemed surprised. "Ex–Ransom River undercover cop. Self-exiled townie. Desk job. Long time on the road back. How have you been?"

Alone.

There had been work. Important, tiring, and endless work reading pallets of bureaucratic files while sitting in warehouses. Work that could save families' lives. Work that seemed to pull through her hands like cotton candy sometimes, when families like Grace's fell through the cracks.

And there had been men. Lovers. One-night stands. Friends with drunken benefits. Mostly young, mostly fleeting. Mostly because she felt numb. A pit had yawned opened in her life, and falling into it seemed inescapable.

That's what she'd told herself at the time. It was easier. It was okay. Nothing got under her skin anymore. She didn't want it to. She wanted companionship. A laugh. Somebody to lay down with and hold on to until the sun came up. She had trouble now, seeing their faces.

"I've felt like I was cut loose from my moorings," she said.

His shoulders canted unevenly. The rakish smile, the brio and daring, seemed long gone.

The flames, skittish and hungry, heated a keen impatience in her. The orange light burnished Seth's hair, illuminated his face. She could see the fire in his eyes, reflecting.

She leaned forward and kissed him. Not caring about the wisdom of it, knowing only that she would have turned to ashes if she didn't do it.

He took her face in his hands, his palms warm and callused against her skin. She closed her eyes and felt the scratch of his beard, tasted the salt of his lips. She snaked her fingers into his hair, thinking this was all she wanted: his mouth on hers, his skin against hers, his hand caressing her cheek. She didn't tell him how long it had been since she'd felt at home, and surprised by longing. How long it had been since she could trust that her longing would be returned, and held safe, and never betrayed. That it had been two years — that she hadn't felt this way since the last time she was with him.

He pulled her to him. His back was taut and hard. He kissed her again, and then his mouth left hers and found her cheek, her neck, her shoulder. She let her face fall forward into his hair. He smelled like fire smoke and Old Spice.

She shoved him down and climbed on top

of him. Her heart pounded. She kissed him, hard.

He seemed to hold motionless, suspended. "Rory . . ."

"Don't speak."

He put his hands on her shoulders. "You sure?"

"If I were sure I'd play lotto. Run for president. Stage a coup. Hell, what's the problem? You've become a priest? Tell me now."

"No problem. Not a priest."

She fell on him.

They rolled nearer the fire and grabbed each other. Rory breathed. "Not in front of Chiba."

"Thank God."

He pulled her up and headed to the bedroom. Shut the door and kissed her, walking to the bed. She felt rabid. It was familiar and strange and she felt a yearning like a coil of pain, drawing her in. He pulled her sweater over her head and started on the buttons of her blouse. His hands on her skin. And she was dry throated at the last moment, facing him, even though he should have been known territory. The room was dark. He got a lighter from his jeans pocket and she took it and lit a candle on the night-stand by the four-poster bed. Her fingers trembled. Seth wasn't a new lover. He was the flame.

He held her face in his hands and kissed her hard. She thumbed the top button on his jeans. She knew that she could surrender and swing into lovemaking as they had for the years they were together; it was their lives that had been sabotaged, not their choreography. They both knew the moves. They could do them with their eyes closed.

He looked goddamned amazing in the orange flame. He tasted familiar, and new, and felt like a lifetime she'd missed. She ached to hold him against every inch of her skin. She drew his shirt over his head.

He went very still. She ran her hands around his back. And she stopped, cold.

"Seth."

He didn't move, didn't speak.

Her hands were pressed flat against the curve of his back. She looked up at him abruptly. She stepped back, worry flooding through her. He briefly tried to hold her, then let go. Like surrendering.

"It's a scar," he said.

She resisted the compulsion to tell him to turn around. Scar? The rough skin she'd felt covered his back.

"The warehouse fire," he said.

All the pieces came tumbling down on

her. "Why didn't you tell me?"

His smile was crooked, and sadder than anything she'd ever seen.

A hospital stay. The long road back. His dad talking about tough times and seeming unable to look Seth in the eye when asking him how he was.

She saw now the way Seth tended to stand with his shoulders uneven. It wasn't a cocky pose. It was from damage and pain. She took a breath.

"It ain't pretty," he said.

For a second, she heard it as, I *ain't pretty.*

"Why do you think I would care?" she said.

"People do. At the beach. Moms with kids, men who stare . . ." He shrugged.

She backed up a step. Unbuttoned her blouse and let it fall to the floor. Unzipped her jeans and kicked them off.

She stood in front of him in the flickering light. He saw the surgical scars. The knee, the hip. Across her abdomen.

"Exploratory surgery," she said. "Internal bleeding."

For a moment he glanced away.

"Seth. Look."

He turned back. Breathed. "You're beautiful."

He reached toward her. She raised one

hand — *wait* — and put a finger to her lips. The flames guttered. Her nerves were about to pour from her body.

Tell him.

The small voice inside her head grew sharp teeth and a demanding tone. It grew a frown and tough little feet and began to kick at her.

"I was pregnant."

His eyes widened.

"I was going to tell you. I was going crazy. Sick and thrilled and scared to death. I was going to tell you that night."

His lips parted. He didn't move. "You lost . . ."

"They say I probably won't have kids now."

He squeezed his eyes shut.

They stood in the dim flicker of the candlelight. Two years hovered between them. Then he stepped toward her and held her.

"I gotcha," he said.

They fell together onto the bed.

44

The morning air felt cool. Outside the cabin hung a pearly sky. It had poured overnight, and mist seemed to fizz from the ground outside. It clung to the live oaks and gave the park an eerie feel.

Seth said, "Do you always chow down like this at breakfast?"

He was sitting across the table from her, wearing a green flannel shirt with the sleeves rolled up, leaning on his elbows.

She drank her coffee. "You're asking, when I'm satisfied."

His mouth lifted into a half smile of confident amusement. Other men had to practice that look in front of a mirror. He said, "You don't smoke, so I need some way to judge."

"This is a guy thing, this need for a performance rating. 'How good was I? Scrambled eggs good? Rice Krispies good?'" She waved a toaster pastry at him.

"Pop-Tarts good. Oh, baby."

Until then, hearing his laugh, that wonderful sound, she didn't know how lonely she'd been. Her face must have shown something like gratitude and raw longing, because he reached out and wrapped a hand around her head, reeled her to him, and kissed her.

A wave of feeling slapped her. It made her think she was crazy, that she was scorched, fried, emotionally nuked, because Seth was a live wire, hot and ungrounded, and still so guarded that in a dozen ways he seemed a stranger. This was like stepping into a pool of water with her hand on an electrical switch. But she didn't care.

He had dressed that morning before she opened her eyes. He'd gotten up and stoked the fire in the living room, had led Chiba out and fed and watered him. The dog adored him and wouldn't have cared if Seth looked like a gargoyle. He was a guardian and trying to present a face of stone to the outside world. He didn't want anyone to see his scars. But she wasn't anyone.

She straddled his lap. She kissed him long and good. She felt upside down and, momentarily, spectacular.

His phone rang. She kept kissing him, waiting to see how long he could stand to let it ring. Finally she said, "You pass the test. Answer it."

He checked the display and said, "Work."

She climbed off his lap. He stood and went outside.

While he paced in the mist beneath the oaks, she gathered their things and phoned Nussbaum's office to arrange a meeting.

When Rory went outside, Seth finished his call. He helped her load her belongings in the Subaru.

"I have to go in," he said. "I'm going to stop by Dad's, then head back to L.A."

"I'm going to Century City later this morning." She needed to tell Nussbaum what she'd learned about the heist, and she preferred to do it in person.

The sky looked smooth, silky white. The air seemed to brush like velvet along her skin. The morning felt close, quiet, almost smothered. Seth whistled and Chiba managed to jump in the back of the car. Seth scratched his ears and shut the hatchback. Rory stepped into his arms.

He said, "If Detective Zelinski pulls any stunts, if he so much as dangles handcuffs in front of you, call me."

She smiled. It was a gallows smile, but still. "Bring your lock-picking tools."

She climbed in the Subaru, backed out of the barn, and saw a flash drive on the floor in the foot well on the passenger side.

It wasn't hers. She picked it up. The flash drive was clipped to a white nylon lanyard. Written on the lanyard in black ink were the words WATCH THIS.

Seth pulled past her, honking as he went. She turned the flash drive over in her hand.

The only time her car had been unguarded and unlocked was when she left the engine running while she rescued Chiba from the freeway.

Elmendorf had left the flash drive in the car.

The muffled sky put a damper on everything. Lucky Colder poured water into the coffeepot and turned on the radio, an old habit he kept up even though the news was on the television too. Radio felt more like the old days, workdays. It felt like time spent in a patrol car, and with his compadres on the force. He turned on the coffeepot.

As the coffee brewed he listened to the local news report. The staticky sound was both soothing and a siren call. After a moment, he picked up the phone and punched a number.

It was early, but the shifts changed at eight. The switchboard put him through.

The woman who picked up sounded crisp

and awake. "Xavier."

"Detective. It's Lucky Colder."

She paused just a blink before saying, "What can I do for a fellow Ransom River officer?"

"It's about a case file. The Geronimo Armored car robbery."

Another brief hesitation. "Yes?"

"I'd like to come in and talk to you about it. There's some evidence in the file we were never able to connect with the robbers. I think we need to take another look at it. It may be pertinent to a current case."

Cautiously she said, "Go on."

He didn't know what to make of her reserve. "Mindy, this could be important."

"Then tell me, Lucky." She sounded more natural. "Please."

He talked to her for several minutes. When he replaced the receiver, he felt reassured. He had done the right thing. He knew Seth didn't want him to contact anybody in the department, but keeping this to himself, leaving Rory out there exposed, didn't feel right.

The coffee brewed. He poured himself a mug, feeling better. Feeling confident. Hopeful, almost.

45

Rory drove down the glen. The sun was burning off the marine layer. Blue sky overwhelmed the clouds and colors bloomed to life. Her skin seemed to tingle as well. She had no reason for her heart to drum, except that the moment came on her like a portent.

There had been times in her life when the oncoming vehicle was around the bend and she hadn't spotted it coming. Hadn't heard the two gunmen approach outside the courtroom door. But at others, she'd felt a thickening vapor in her chest, as though ghosts were rising and touching her, testing, as though to see how she would react to joining their ranks.

But right then, the road ahead was clear. The radio was playing Florence and the Machine. She couldn't explain the premonition she was having. She knew she was in deep trouble, but it didn't look like it was on the next several hundred yards of road. So why did she feel like some support beam had silently cracked, some fault line begun to fracture, deep down and thoroughly?

She drove. Maybe it had to do with Riss and Boone.

Baseline assumption: Her cousins were involved in the plan to attack the courthouse. She had no proof, and they would protest, but she had to start with that hypothesis. Ignoring it would be another bush-league mistake, and she was done with those.

The plan, as far as she could see, must have been to take her from the courtroom along with three other people chosen at random. Taking multiple hostages would camouflage the fact that she was the actual target. And attacking her in a public place was the only way they could make it look like she was a chance victim. They could have ambushed her at Starbucks, but the gunmen would have had to shadow her until the lucky moment when she walked into a building where other people could also be captured.

The courthouse attack eliminated those variables. They knew she'd be there. They knew the layout of the courtroom, and even where she'd be sitting. The sheer audacity of the attack, its absolute seeming madness, would convince the authorities it had to be political, or terrorism, or psychosis. Because nobody who wanted money would try to kidnap a bunch of civil servants and a laid-off aid worker. Right?

It was bizarre in its brilliance.

And then what? The desert, maybe. Or the national forest. Maybe they'd shoot the other hostages. Maybe they'd free them by the side of a backcountry road, blindfolded and cuffed. But in any case, they would have held on to Rory and taken her to a far and nasty place. Church and Berrigan would have been paid. Or killed.

And the bad guys behind the bad guys would have taken photos of her and recorded her screams and sent them as messages to force her uncle to reveal the location of the stolen money. Or they'd send the torture photos to her father and mother, to get them to contact Lee.

But instead the courthouse attack went wrong and Rory was freed — under intense publicity and public scrutiny. They'd seen their plan fried.

But Rory was sure they hadn't abandoned it. They would regroup and come at her again, from a different angle.

And soon.

She drove through the rural borderlands of Ransom River. In the quickening sunlight, orchards slid by like cards being shuffled. The leaves of the lemon trees looked emerald green. She put down the window. The smell of fresh earth and sweet fruit filled the air.

The phone rang. It was Nussbaum, and he was on his way to court for an urgent appearance. He said they'd need to reschedule their meeting but could talk while he drove to the courthouse.

"That heist, the armored car robbery," he said. "You're on to something."

"Tell me."

"The Geronimo courier was attacked as it made its final cash pickup, at a branch bank in Ransom River."

"The robbers knew how to hit when it was fully loaded with cash?"

"Indeed. The gang had two vehicles. One was a supercharged Audi Quattro getaway car. The other was an apparently old wreck of a van that actually had a 350 Chevy hemi engine and could hit one-forty on a straightaway."

"That was their switch car?"

"Right."

"Where'd they get the cars?" she said.

"One of the robbers, guy nicknamed Gully

Crooks — his actual name — was an auto mechanic. He hooked the gang up with the vehicles."

"What happened to Crooks?"

"Shot dead by the Geronimo guards during the robbery."

Rory checked her mirrors. Traffic was light. She didn't see any vehicles she'd seen thirty seconds earlier. "Where'd you get this information? You didn't call the Ransom River police, did you?"

"Trust me, Rory."

"Sorry. I have the heebie-jeebies."

"Understood. You want to hear the rest?"

"Absolutely."

"Geronimo Armored was an established secure courier in Southern California. They had contracts with a number of commercial banks for cash transport."

"And was this fact advertised?" she said.

"Not widely. But it was known within the banking and security communities. And to the Fed, and of course to law enforcement. I think you see where I'm going."

"The robbers were waiting for the armored car. They knew its route."

"That's the assumption the police and FBI made."

"And I'm guessing that a well-established secure courier company was professional enough that they didn't follow the same route on each cash pickup. They changed things up so nobody could predict which way they'd come and go."

"That would be my presumption as well," Nussbaum said.

The wheels of her Subaru droned on the concrete. Orchards and strawberry fields striped past. In the distance, tractors rolled and pickup trucks rumbled across the farmland. Along the rows of fruit and produce, workers bent to pick berries.

"But the robbers knew," she said. "They had inside information."

"They must have."

"Who?" Rory said.

"The FBI spent months investigating. To no avail."

"They cleared the Geronimo armed guards of involvement?"

"They were looked at with painful scrutiny. But the Bureau could never connect either guard to the robbery."

"Somebody else from Geronimo?"

"That's the most promising angle. But again, nobody could ever pin it on an employee."

"The bank in Ransom River."

"It was an Allied Pacific branch. The fibbies and the local police grilled everybody from the bank. Employees, their spouses, boyfriends, cats, parakeets, dogs, and the fleas on their dogs. And I mean grilled. Repeatedly, with tongs. Nobody ever came up with anything. That's why this is considered a cold case."

"But the FBI was convinced there had to be an insider connection."

"As am I."

"So, is this insider still around?" she said.

"And itching to get his or her fingers on the money?" Nussbaum said.

Rory's mind jumped around, trying to put it together. "You think if we can find the insider, we'll find who was behind the attack on the courthouse?"

"Well, that would be ideal. But I doubt *we'll* be the ones to find this phantom after twenty years."

Don't be so sure of that, she thought. "Then why did you tell me about this?"

"So you'll watch your back even more carefully than you already were."

Great. She glanced again in the rearview mirror. If any of the vehicles behind her were on her tail, she couldn't tell.

"I have more to tell you," she said.

She explained about her cousins and her uncle. Nussbaum listened without interrupting for five minutes. When Rory finished, he asked follow-up questions and said, "You're convinced?"

"I have no proof, and maybe I'm losing my mind entirely. But yes, I'm convinced."

Nussbaum paused and sounded pensive. "The sins of the father descending to his son and daughter."

"How biblical."

"Rory, this is dangerous. Your cousins — it sounds as though they have few limits."

"If they ever did, the fence has been torn down."

"If the courthouse attack was their grand plan to recover the money from the heist, it's gone awry. And when a plan goes to hell, people can react desperately."

"You're saying they might try again. I already know. That's why I didn't stay at my place last night, and I was on my way to your office. You have security, right?"

His voice toughened. "Go someplace public but out of the way. Someplace your cousins would not expect you to go. Don't speed; don't let yourself be put in a position where the local police can stop you and bring you in."

"On it," she said, trying to sound tougher than she felt.

She ended the call and held tight to the wheel. It seemed to vibrate beneath her grip.

In the back, Chiba had settled low, his chin resting on the lip of the windowsill to watch cars and fields and clouds go by.

Inside dope.

Who was out there, what ghost, trying to get that cash? It must have been eating away at the insider's soul. Money lost. Millions, a dream, an obsession. Worth sending people once more to grasp and grab and die over?

The sins of the father descending to his son and daughter.

Rory didn't believe in guilt by association or genetics. But Lee's sin had been taken up and nurtured by his daughter and stepson. The sin had been buried, with shame, by his brother. And that sin had now been poured out on her.

Everybody who was involved now was the child of somebody who was there at the start. What goes around had come around, hard.

Reason it out. Go back to square one. Somehow the robbers had been tipped off about the timing of the Geronimo Armored cash pickup. Who knew about that?

Because the cash being collected and transported was such a massive amount, local law enforcement might have been informed ahead of time. Maybe the Los Angeles County Sheriff and the California

Highway Patrol. And the Ransom River Police Department.

The radio switched to the news. Rory reached to turn it down and stopped with her hand hanging in the air.

"Judge Arthur Wieland, who was shot by gunmen in the attack on the Ransom River courthouse two days ago, died this morning at West River Hospital."

The rest was lost in her shock.

She pulled to the side of the freeway and stopped. She felt ill. Judge Wieland, a personable and dedicated man with a no-nonsense style and occasional flashes of wit — Jesus, left to bleed in pain, when he might have been helped, might have been saved, if he'd gotten to the hospital in time.

Her anger, at the uselessness of it, felt dry and thorny. In the back of the car, Chiba barked at her. Traffic blew past, rocking the Subaru.

"Motherfuckers," she said.

The phone rang. She ignored it. It stopped and started again. Finally, with a feeling of dread, she answered.

"Ms. Mackenzie? Detective Zelinski."

She leaned her head back against the headrest. "I just heard about Judge Wieland."

"I suggest that you come into the station."

446

"Why?"

"We have more questions for you. I suggest that you don't wait for your attorney."

"You know I'm going to wait for my attorney."

"A failure to attend could be construed as flight."

"That's absurd."

"In which case your description would go out to all law enforcement agencies, with orders to arrest you on sight. And then an apprehension would have to be considered hot pursuit."

He was telling her they'd regard her as a fugitive, a dangerous one, and would take her down with force. Eagerly and without reservation. Ah, power — what fun to wield it, and so casually, with such enthusiasm.

"You don't have to tell me twice," she said.

"I'm starting the timer," Zelinski said.

With an acid feeling in her stomach, she called Nussbaum's office again. He wouldn't be back from court for hours, and his phone was turned off. She left an urgent message for him to call her.

"Tell him I don't want to go to the police station alone, but if I don't show up there, I'm going to find myself on a WANTED poster," she said.

She called Seth. His phone went to voice

mail. She tried again. Same thing.

She called information and got Lucky Colder's number. Punched it in. Rested her forehead on the steering wheel as it rang.

"This is Lucky," he said.

"It's Rory, Mr. Colder. I'm looking for Seth."

"I haven't seen him this morning."

"He's on his way over to your place. When he gets there please have him call me."

"Young lady, you don't sound so hot."

"Judge Wieland just died."

His sigh was harsh enough that she could hear it through the phone. "What a waste. A damned outrage."

"And the police are looking for a scapegoat. They say if I don't turn myself in they're coming after me."

"Rory, then you need to turn yourself in. It's the safest thing."

"Tell Seth Nussbaum's in court. And we need covering fire. Tell him to contact the FBI and the U.S. Attorney. If I don't hear from him in the next ten minutes I'll call the feds myself, but it'll be better if he greases the wheels for me."

"Of course I'll tell him. Where are you now?"

"On the freeway out by the pass. Turning around. It'll take me twenty minutes to get downtown."

"I can meet you at police headquarters myself."

It was a kind gesture. "You're chivalrous. But it's most important that you make contact with Seth."

"Okay. But if you need me, you holler."

"Thanks, Lucky."

She put on her turn signal and pulled out, headed for the police station. *Your description would go out to all law enforcement agencies.*

Great: a BOLO to the Los Angeles County Sheriff and the California Highway Patrol. And of course to the Ransom River Police Department. The same outfits that would have been informed about the Geronimo Armored delivery could now hunt her down instead, and make her the delivery, trussed and bound. She drove, her hair swirling in the wind.

Oh God.

"No," she said, so loudly that Chiba raised his head and gave her an inquisitive look.

Who had tipped off the gang before the robbery? An inside man. Somebody from the Ransom River Police Department.

She tried to rid her mind of the thought that had just overcome her. She tried to think it through, telling herself she was

449

imagining things. But as the miles un-spooled, the road seemed to carry her along to an appalling conclusion.

"No," she said again.

When her phone rang, she grabbed it hoping to hear Seth's voice.

"Ms. Mackenzie, it's Detective Xavier."

Good cop, bad cop. Tag, you're it. It never ended.

She said, "I'm on my way to the station. If Detective Zelinski wants me there any faster, I'll have to break the sound barrier." She wrung her hands on the wheel. "And I'm bringing my dog."

Xavier paused, maybe startled. "Forget Zelinski. Get to your place right away."

"Why —"

"Don't worry about Zelinski right now. There's been a break-in at your house. Somebody tried to start a fire."

"What?"

"We got a call that there's a fire at your residence." She rattled off the address. "And there's a woman in distress on the front porch. It sounds like your mother."

"Oh my God."

"I'm on my way there now," Xavier said.

She accelerated. "Fire department? Paramedics?"

"Backup will be coming. Get home ASAP."

■ ■ ■ ■

Twenty minutes later Rory rounded the bend toward the end of her street. It was a workday, a school day, and the street was empty. She hadn't been able to reach her parents. She saw no hulking black SUVs, no police cruisers.

No fire.

No sign of her mother.

Detective Xavier's unmarked Chrysler was parked at the curb outside the house. Rory pulled up behind it and cut the engine.

"Chiba, boy," she said, "I'll be right back."

She got out and stood for a moment, listening. For what, she wasn't sure. The street was eerily quiet.

"Detective Xavier?" she called.

From a distance, a woman called back: "Here. Coming."

A second later Xavier rounded the corner of the house. She had a phone in her hand and was shaking her head.

"Everything's quiet. No signs of a break-in or fire," she said. "False alarm."

Rory leaned against her car and rubbed her eyes, trying to calm down. Xavier's lips were pursed.

"Call went through the department

switchboard. Caller asked particularly for me. Gave the address. Hinted that it had something to do with you, like they knew you live here."

Rory looked at the house. "You walked around?"

"All the way. No sign of anything wrong."

"Somebody's yanking both our chains."

"You got any idea who?" Xavier said.

Chiba barked and looked at Xavier with delight.

Rory said, "The call came to the police department switchboard — the caller never identified themselves?"

"Woman. Said her name was Candy Graves. I just got off the line with the department. Nobody in the phone book by that name." She put the phone in her jacket pocket. "Want to tell me what kind of game somebody's playing? 'Cause I don't like being made a pawn."

An old game, Rory thought. *With new rules.* She debated and decided in favor of disclosure.

"It could be my cousin Nerissa."

"Cousin." Xavier looked nonplussed. "This is a family feud?"

Rory nearly barked, louder than Chiba, with disgusted laughter. "I think she and her brother Boone also took my dog yesterday and let him out on the freeway off-ramp at Cloud Canyon Road."

A veil fell over Xavier's expression. She looked fatigued. Like a cop's lot was full of this bullshit, winter, spring, and summer.

She nodded at the house. "When I did my walk-around, the phone kept ringing. Off the hook. I heard the answering machine pick up and a woman's voice leave a message. She sounded distraught."

"Who? Did you hear her name?" And was it for real, or another game?

"Didn't hear a name. After the message ended, the phone started ringing again right away, like maybe you'd come home in the preceding seven seconds. Somebody wants to talk to you awfully bad."

Rory glanced anxiously at the house. "Will you wait while I check it out?"

"I have work to do. Real crimes to investigate. Possibly involving you." She turned. "And you need to get down to the station. But if you can listen to the message before I put my car in gear, I'll still be here."

Xavier turned and walked, albeit slowly, to her car. Rory jogged to the porch, keys jangling, and unlocked the door.

She walked in and found Boone waiting inside.

46

Rory stopped, shocked still.

"Cuz," Boone said. "You aren't much of a hostess."

From the hallway, three men in black suits stepped into view.

"We got no coffee, no nothing," Boone said.

Three men, all wearing dark glasses, black suits with pressed white shirts, two with skinny black ties — the carnivorous worms. One wearing a broad and garish purple paisley tie, swarming with shapes, nearly leaping from his chest like crimped heartbeats.

It was Grigor Mirkovic.

She spun to flee back through the door. Outside at the curb, Detective Xavier climbed into her unmarked car. The first suit, the night crawler of a man who'd followed her the previous morning, blocked her path.

She lunged and cried, "Detective —"

He grabbed her around the waist as though she weighed no more than a sack of laundry and pulled her back.

"Xavier," Rory shouted.

The detective hesitated.

"Help!" Rory yelled.

For a second Xavier didn't move. She didn't look toward the house. She sat with the door open, hand on the windowsill.

Rory screamed, *"Help me!"*

Xavier closed the car door and started the engine. She put the unmarked car in gear and calmly drove away. She took Rory's breath with her.

Xavier had heard her. She hadn't waited. She'd driven off and left Rory here with these men.

Xavier knew. She knew Boone and Mirkovic and his men were in the house. She had lured Rory into a trap.

Rory shouted and kicked and grabbed for the doorframe, trying to pull away from the Nightcrawler.

He swung her into the air and silently shut the door.

With a grunt he set her down. Rory turned again to bolt. The second suit approached her from the front and the Nightcrawler clamped her arms from behind.

She fought. "Let go."

The sound of Xavier's engine faded to nothing. Rory's chest heaved and her mouth went dry with disbelief.

The suits closed around her, a cage of human meat, and nudged her toward the living room. She looked toward the kitchen, hoping against ridiculous hope that the door was open and maybe a freak lightning storm would strike these guys and fry them where they stood. Boone loitered there, leaning against the wall. A hot light burned in his eyes.

The men dragged her past the answering machine and the cup of pens and a letter opener that might have let her grab something sharp. She looked at the phone and the Nightcrawler grunted, "Don't bother; we cut the wires." She tried to dig her heels into the floor but the Nightcrawler hoisted her off the ground. They slogged her into the living room and set her down before Mirkovic. He sat on a lounge chair, reclining, his legs crossed, his hands resting on the arms of the seat like a medieval liege being presented with a disobedient peasant.

"What are you doing here?" Rory said.

The Nightcrawler held her arms tight, bent back.

Up close, Mirkovic's face was heavily

lined, with the rough skin of a heavy smoker. His eyes were hard and watery. They looked like teary gray marbles. His hands, resting on the arms of the chair, were thick, scarred, as though he'd cut them punching the shit out of men with steel teeth. The ring on his pinkie, for all she knew, may have come from a heavyweight champ he brained with a crowbar.

He looked implacable and ready to uncoil like a whip. "It's time to have a serious talk."

"What do you want?" she said.

"Justice."

His voice was accented, and he seemed uninterested in pronouncing words in a familiar way. It was up to others to understand him.

"And to deliver punishment," he said.

"I don't know what you mean."

She saw no flicker of interest on his face.

"I know you," Mirkovic said. "Aurora Faith Mackenzie, juror number seven."

Don't lose it. But a sound like a loud dial tone took up all the space in her head.

Mirkovic said, "You sat in the jury box staring at the defendants. You looked so enamored of them."

Get it together. Get it all the way to hell together. "No."

"And I saw you looking at me." His gray

457

marble eyes were flat. "In the court, you look at me like I am an insect. A bug that smells bad, and you wish should be removed from polite society. Not like now. Now you are showing me respect. This is better."

She tried to breathe. She tried to stand straight. If she hadn't been so afraid of peeing her pants, she would have spit in his face.

"Your job disappeared. I know this. I see all the research for voir dire. Yes. This surprises you?" He remained so still that it was like being spoken to by a mummy. "Before the charity went broke, you were aid worker. I know this too."

The Nightcrawler said, "Huh. Overseas? Like, the Peace Corps?"

"Exactly like," she said.

Mirkovic eyed his goon. The Nightcrawler shut up.

Mirkovic said, "Aid workers, I know them. They come to Serbia, Bosnia, Kosovo, all of former Yugoslavia. Like lice. Infesting the countries. We saw the UN vehicles and your pious pity for towns that should have accepted defeat."

He held up one hand, index and middle finger extended. Suit Two took a gold cigarette case from his jacket, placed an unfiltered cigarette in Mirkovic's waiting fingers, and lit it with a silver lighter. The room filled with gray and acrid smoke.

Mirkovic took a drag, squinting. "This disgust, it is one reason I come to United States. To escape the hate of you aid workers. I come to America, nobody cares. I am European immigrant, hard worker, a self-made man. I don't have to put up with aid workers looking down their noses and talking shit about my country. America likes my bootstraps and my can-do spirit."

The smoke trailed up from his cigarette and fractured into drifts. "And then they put you on the jury. To judge the killers of my son."

It wasn't a conversation but a lecture. The suits stood like fence posts, listening attentively. But she figured they'd soon get to the inquisition.

"They put you, this woman who hates self-reliance, on the jury. They put you, this person who cannot accept how power works, to judge the beasts who shot my son. What do you know about vengeance?"

The ash grew long on his cigarette. "You would see my boy as a thug, and judge the police officers helpless? Or you would knead your hands like a granny and worry that these police will feel frightened in prison with street scum, and give them a slap on the wrist?"

Slowly, he raised the cigarette to his lips and took another drag. He exhaled through his nose.

"Is a joke," he said.

Like a zipper slowly coming undone, she understood it wasn't about her deliberative skills as a juror. He didn't think she was in on the courthouse plot.

He knew she wasn't.

He eyed her with the dead bright eyes of a shark. The smoke hazed the air around him like a nimbus.

She knew all the rumors about Grigor Mirkovic. His businesses involved not only nightclubs but construction — concrete and rebar, particularly. Perfect covers for burying people he had killed in cement. But his off-the-books businesses were hijacking, theft, drugs, prostitution, gun running. There were rumors of human trafficking from Mexico. The royal flush of organized-crime poker hands.

"You hired the gunmen to attack the courthouse," she said.

She didn't think it mattered if she confronted him. He wasn't here to let her buy her way out of the situation. He didn't care if she knew, not at this point. He was the one Boone and Riss had made a deal with.

He wasn't going to let her go free.

Mirkovic tapped ash onto the wood floor. "You are not so stupid after all."

"Why did you do it?"

Now, at last, he smiled. It was the empty and chilling smile of a great white showing its teeth.

"Delay will not become rescue," he said.

The zipping sound intensified in Rory's head.

The smile stayed on Mirkovic's face, humorless and bright. His new American teeth were large and very white.

"Share the joke, then," she said. "Give me that much."

Behind her, the Nightcrawler smirked. She wondered if she'd just earned some twisted kind of respect, for not peeing on his shoes. Boone lurked at the back of the room, saying nothing, but his hands clenched and unclenched, and he bounced on his toes, like a boxer dancing around the ring.

Mirkovic said, "It was the only way to capture you without anybody getting wise that you were actual target." He shrugged, as though it made perfect sense. "You would look like a random victim."

"And Judge Wieland?" she said.

"Quick and clean, get you and the others from the courtroom — it has been done

461

before many times, in places where you and your aid worker friends like to sit in Internet cafés with your cappuccinos, flirting and pretending you are tough."

Rory had a weird and awful feeling: the sensation that the ties that bound her to life had just been cut with a sharp and shiny knife. That she had spun around the sun almost thirty times and learned to speak some Thai and swum in near-Arctic seas, she'd nestled in her mother's arms and made her parents smile, and she'd taught girls to read. That she'd loved the best friend she had ever had, shared his heart, and at least held the flash of a life they created together.

She felt herself giving it up. Not flying apart, but letting the cord spin free, letting everything spill out.

Maybe this was the final cut in the rope. Maybe there was nothing beyond the horizon. She had nothing left to fight for. And at least she'd come home.

She felt a weightless and sun-bright terror that seemed to throb through the air in the room. But she wasn't going to beg. Whatever happened, she was free.

Fall seven times, stand up eight.

If they were going to take her, it wouldn't be on her knees.

"You hired Sylvester Church and Kevin Berrigan," she said.

The suits straightened. Yeah. They had no clue that she knew the gunmen's identities.

Mirkovic continued to smoke.

"You're after the money from the Geronimo Armored car heist. You think I can help you recover it," she said. "You think you can dangle me from the end of a hook and force my uncle to turn it over to you."

Mirkovic stared at her through the haze of cigarette smoke. "Who told you this?"

"Nobody. I figured it out myself. But I am not the only person who knows. Not by half."

"Okay. So you tell all your friends this on Facebook. So what? Nobody believe you. Nobody know I am sitting here enjoying your hospitality." He flicked the cigarette carelessly to the floor. "Now shut up."

Suit Two stuck out a toe and ground out the cigarette on the wood.

Mirkovic said, "Where is the money?"

"I don't know."

He raised his index finger. Behind Rory, the Nightcrawler took hold of her hand and twisted.

She gasped at the pain. "I don't know."

"You know. All your life."

She shook her head. The Nightcrawler twisted her hand harder. She bent, trying to curl away from it, but he held her fast. Her mouth opened with the ache.

Mirkovic's expression didn't change. "Where is your uncle Lee?"

"Mexico," she hacked. "Last I heard from him."

"Where in Mexico?"

"Beach. Yucatán."

"Jokes not funny," he said.

"I haven't heard from him in years. I don't know how to contact him."

"It's okay. Somebody will."

The pain in her hand was spiking like nails. "Nobody knows where Lee is. Nobody's heard from him in twenty years."

"You think I am greedy? You are the one who won't tell me where the money is even to save your life. That is so greedy it is foolish," he said.

She leaned forward as far as possible to ease the near-breaking pain in her arm. "I don't *know.*"

She wasn't one to pray. But right then, she practically begged any deities to *make her forget.* Erase the knowledge that her father could pinpoint exactly where the cash lay buried. Cut it from her mind. Because the pain the Nightcrawler was inflicting was sharp but transient. She was already frightened. If he took up tongs, or got the disposable lighter from her pocket, she didn't know what she'd say. *Forget. Forget.*

He said, "Of course you know. You left your palm print."

She twisted her head to see him. "What palm print?"

"Must we do this?" he said.

"What palm print?" But her hand had begun to sting, and not from the Nightcrawler's grip. From a memory. *Then. That night.*

"On the side of the van," Mirkovic said.

He shifted, as if his efforts at patience and forbearance were tiring him. "For many years it was an unknown print. But we have now cold-case investigations, and AFIS. The police can check old evidence and look for new prints that have entered the criminal justice system in recent years. Comparison prints."

Boone said, "You got yourself arrested at some protest." He laughed. "What's so funny about peace, love, and understanding? I'll tell you what." His laugh died. "Power to the people, Rory."

She felt like her feet had been kicked out from under her. And she thought: *They don't know where or how. Don't tell.* If she did nothing else, she had to keep her parents' names out of it.

She said, "Maybe I touched the van weeks earlier. In a garage someplace, when I was with my uncle."

"Not possible."

"I didn't go with him on the damned robbery."

"You stumbled on the heist. Or overheard where the money is buried. Or your dear uncle Lee confided in you." Mirkovic waved her objections away. "Enough. This is business. I am businessman. Money out of circulation slows the economy. It harms the business cycle, like credit crunch. It is a crime," he said. "And all that old, worn cash will serve my interests perfectly. I do business in Mexico, and in my Mexican businesses, crisp new dollars stand out. Much better to use old bills."

Plus, nobody across the border would be monitoring the serial numbers of the stolen millions.

"You see, this is brilliant solution to many problems. Especially when your usefulness to me is over. I am not wasteful. You will have a second experience."

Second experience. She felt a chill.

"But for the sake of saving time, I ask you

once again. Where is your uncle?"

"I don't know. Nobody does. I think . . ." She sagged. "I think he may be dead."

"That would be most unfortunate," Mirkovic said.

"Nobody's heard one word from him in years."

"He can reappear. Incentives are amazing." He flicked a finger. "Get the camera and equipment."

The pain in her arm momentarily disappeared beneath a rush of adrenaline. Equipment to do what to her?

"I'm telling you, Lee has vanished," she said.

Mirkovic shifted in his seat. He uncrossed his legs and leaned forward. "This money, you think it's yours."

"God no."

Boone jumped forward, pointing. He barked, "She sure as hell does."

Boone was amped. His pupils looked as small as fleas and heat seemed to pour off him in waves.

The Nightcrawler must have been surprised by Boone's outburst, because he let up on Rory's arm and half turned to face her cousin. It was an automatic defensive move, which told her that none of them

467

trusted him. Whatever Boone was on — meth, gin, lifelong resentment — was building up the pressure, like a bottle of butane dropped onto an open flame.

He took two steps toward Mirkovic and the suits moved smoothly and instantly to keep him back. Boone raised his hands, stepped away. Wiped his nose.

He pointed at Rory. "She wants the money. If she hasn't already took half of it and spent it all."

She smiled. "Well. Boone Mackenzie. Thank you for finally making this easy."

At that, Mirkovic eyed her with interest. Like cataloguing an insect for unsuspected potential to surprise him and maybe hurt somebody.

"I'm glad you finally stopped slinking around, trying to kill my dog and hiding behind your mom and your hatred of my family. Thanks for stepping forward at last," Rory said.

"Not Mackenzie anymore. It's Renfro."

Renfro was his birth father's name. He jinked a shoulder and stepped back and turned sideways to Rory, his half-shaded, slanted look. "She better tell us where it is. Take the video and let's get going."

Mirkovic said, "In due course."

Boone's mouth pulled down, like a thorn

had caught against his lips. "Always getting postcards from my dad."

"What, you think he put secret codes in his messages to me when I was a kid? *X* marks the spot?" She smiled again. A strange, cold calm descended on her. "You should never have torn them up, Boone. Maybe you destroyed your only chance to find all that cash."

His eyes popped. The blue butane flame flared and he looked at her at last. *Oh shit,* was all over his expression.

Mirkovic said, "Where is the money?"

"No idea," Rory said. "I knew nothing about it before yesterday. If I'd known where it was, don't you think I would have bought myself a first-class ticket to the other side of the world? You can't actually believe I'd be in Ransom River, scraping pennies out of the sofa and hoping to get a job at the Dairy Queen. Nobody in my family would still be here. We'd have bought an island in French Polynesia and installed ourselves as the ruling dynasty. I'd be that princess Boone always thought I was, and I'd be grinding the heel of my glass slipper into photos of his face every morning after coffee."

Boone looked at her like he'd never seen her before. "She's nuts."

Maybe, Rory thought. Maybe she was having an out-of-body experience. Maybe she was already reincarnated as a woman who didn't give a damn about her own life anymore but was ready to spill it all to get these assholes in police custody or six feet down. And she'd do anything to keep them from thinking her parents were the key to finding the money.

She let her hair fall in front of her eyes. Torqued forward under the Nightcrawler's grip, she glared up at her cousin. "If I'm nuts, I'm still ten times more connected to humanity than you are." She turned to Mirkovic. "What did he tell you? Did he approach you, or vice versa? Did he tell you he and his stepsister want to set up housekeeping together? How are you going to keep this quiet once they build their triplewide trailer on a Ransom River hilltop and hang a chandelier on the porch, next to their Lamborghini — the one up on blocks?"

Boone recoiled. "Shut up. You are a freak."

Rory laughed. The sound spilled brightly from her lips and fizzed into the air, so sharp and desperate that it seemed to disperse the smoke from Mirkovic's cigarette.

Mirkovic looked at Boone. "Close your mouth."

Boone pointed at Rory, aggrieved. "See what I've had to live with all my life?"

"You and your stepsister are no business of mine. But you will not stay here. You will not spend any money in Ransom River." The flat calm returned to Mirkovic's face. "You said you would move to another country."

"I will, I will. Rory's wack."

Mirkovic's gaze lingered on him. "Then we get going." Slowly his head turned toward Rory. "You will take us to the money."

Boone said, "Let me work on her. We got a deal."

Mirkovic glanced at him. "You do not need to remind me." To Rory he said, "Family business does not concern me. But your cousin is correct — we have a deal. Boone insisted."

"Insisted on what?" she said. The laughter had all spilled out, but the chill remained and was taking root. She dug her fingernails into her palms to keep herself angry.

"You will make a video so your uncle understands he must surrender the money to me immediately. It will be your star turn. Everybody in California wants this." He uncrossed his legs. "And then Boone will have his after-party with you." He shrugged.

"It is price I pay to get the economy going."

Boone said, "I need ten minutes with her."

The Nightcrawler said, "This isn't a playground. You'll have time afterward. Mr. Mirkovic has other appointments today."

Boone swiped a hand across his nose again. "Fine. Take her upstairs."

He nodded at the staircase. As he did, his phone rang. The Nightcrawler tugged Rory backward across the living room.

Eyes on Rory, Boone answered the call. "No time to talk."

Rory heard a woman's voice on the other end.

"Soon," Boone said. "Go on to Mom's and get the baby."

He was talking to Riss. Rory nearly stumbled. The baby?

"Don't matter what Mom says. She won't be able to stop you. Pack Addie up and get ready to roll. I'll be there soon."

Mirkovic sat forward. "Boone. Hang up."

Boone casually put away the phone. "Business."

Mirkovic said, "The child is a distraction."

"Riss won't leave her here with Amber. It's a point of pride."

Addie.

Little Adalyn, who had let Rory help her pour a cup of water, and who had wrapped

472

her soft hands around Rory's neck and laughed. The light in the house turned sickeningly hot. Addie wasn't a day-care kid. She was Amber's granddaughter.

Riss's child.

Addie was Riss's daughter. And there in front of her was Boone, acting proprietorial about the child. Boone. *Boone?* Getting ready to turn his world around — by torturing Rory, grabbing the stolen millions, and taking off with his stepsister and the little girl.

He tilted his head at her. "Stop looking at me like that."

He booted Rory's knee out from under her, so she dropped in the Nightcrawler's grip. He nodded toward the hallway. "Move."

The Nightcrawler swung her around, and she glimpsed Mirkovic's face. Why was he staring at Boone so sharply?

47

The Nightcrawler shoved Rory along the hallway. Boone strutted ahead to the stairs.

Addie. Earlier, at Amber's, Riss hadn't even looked at Addie. She'd come straight into the house and laid into Rory. She hadn't spared a breath for her own child.

And Riss wanted to take Addie as a point of pride? Take her into what? A sinkhole seemed to open in Rory's chest, dank and septic. Riss would take Addie into a nightmare. A diseased life with parents who cared only for each other and who inevitably cut everyone else out of their twisted existence. Fear overwhelmed her.

The Nightcrawler breathed into her hair. She stumbled along the hallway.

She had a lighter in her pocket, the disposable one Seth had handed to her when she lit the candle at the caretaker's cabin the previous evening. She could find something flammable and set the house on fire with

Boone in it. She'd get out. Somehow. She was thinking on the fly — she'd dropped out of Girl Scouts before they got to the arson merit badge. But chaos was better than organized torture.

Boone stopped on the stairs and turned to the Nightcrawler. "Give her to me. Wait down here."

"She isn't a blow-up doll," the Nightcrawler said. "I need to supervise."

"She's not going to cause trouble," Boone said.

"You kidding? She's nothing *but* trouble."

Sounded like a plan.

She could set the bed on fire. Or Boone's shirt. The books on the shelf. She bet Hunter S. Thompson would burn like a rocket sled.

She wasn't thinking linearly, but ideas popped in front of her eyes like bleach bubbles. The stolen cash. Grigor Mirkovic, who was willing to turn the trial of his son's killers into a piece of theater for the chance to obtain millions in dirty bills. It was astonishing. She wanted to ask him: Why? Did he care so much for money that seeing justice done for his son took second place? Or did he truly consider the trial a farce and think he was putting the court system to more productive use?

She struggled upward, bent forward as if she were bowing. She said to the Nightcrawler, "Let go so I can climb the stairs."

He barked. It may have been a laugh. "Honey, you crack me up." To Boone he said, "Get the bathtub filled."

Rory's knees loosened.

The Nightcrawler steadied her. He said to Boone, "And get the camera. In case of accident."

Boone laughed. "In case?"

They were going to drown her. And in her own house, where it didn't matter if she left forensic evidence on every square inch of the floors and walls and ceiling.

The Nightcrawler said, "If she doesn't tell us what we want to know, we'll need proof that noncompliance is painful. It'll also be something we can edit to make it look like she's still breathing. Get that ex-cop to give up the information if he thinks he can save her."

Boone reached the top of the stairs. "No, let her go. She won't cause problems. She won't utter a peep."

She felt the lighter in her pocket. They'd have to put her in front of the camera. They'd want to keep themselves out of frame. She'd have a moment. She simply had to be fast. She couldn't let Boone get started with whatever it was he thought would turn her mute.

He opened the door to her bedroom. "Bring her in."

Rory climbed the stairs with the Nightcrawler breathing heavily behind her. They would have to pass her desk. It was covered with paper. It could be the point of origin.

Boone walked through the door. The Nightcrawler brought Rory in behind him.

Boone turned to her. "Hush, now. Don't let your friend get any more hurt."

Slumped on the floor in the corner, bruised and battered, was Petra.

48

Petra lifted her head, slowly. Her eyes were puffy, her lip split and crusted with blood. Her hands and feet were tied to the foot of the bed with an electrical cord. "Ro. Sorry."

Tears rushed to Rory's eyes. She spun on Boone so fast that he actually shrank back. Her teeth were bared.

"Let her go," she said.

"You got no say anymore."

He went into the bathroom and turned on the taps. From downstairs, Suit Two called to the Nightcrawler.

"Hadzic. Come here a minute."

The water gushed into the tub. Boone said, "I got this. She won't act up. Not when her little bed partner's licking her wounds."

The Nightcrawler looked like he doubted the wisdom of leaving the room.

Rory dug her nails into her palms. "Don't hurt Petra again. I'll do whatever Boone wants. Just don't hurt her."

Boone sneered. He may have thought it was a smile. He may have thought a sneer and a smile expressed the same feeling: pleasure at other people's pain.

Rory held still, trying to look compliant and submissive and beaten. Trying not to feel compliant and submissive and beaten. *Keep it together.* She did an inventory sweep of the bedroom. Floor, desk, bookcase. Window.

Suit Two called to the Nightcrawler again.

The Nightcrawler said, "I'm going to lock the door and take the key with me."

He walked out, shut the door, flipped the key from outside, and thumped down the stairs.

Petra said, "They said if I screamed they'd slit your throat."

Boone pointed at her. "Not a peep out of you. This isn't your show."

Rory backed toward the desk. Boone grabbed her by the shirt. She gasped. He pulled her off balance against him and began backing her toward the bathroom.

"Twenty years, cuz. Twenty fucking years; did you truly think you could get away with it forever?"

He shoved her backward through the bathroom door at the sink. She hit the counter and knocked over bottles and containers. They clattered to the floor and into the sink. The bathtub was halfway full, the water pouring out in great gulps, loud and turbulent.

Boone pointed at her. "Don't move."

He took out his phone and smoothly thumbed the controls. He was breathing audibly. She cringed back against the counter.

Still looking at the phone, he said, "Tell me where the money is or you get waterboarded. Like the witches of Salem. Full-immersion baptism."

She pressed herself back against the counter. A bottle of rubbing alcohol had fallen into the sink. She could smell it.

"Okay," she said. "I'll tell you."

He glanced up, alert.

She had a hand on the bottle. The other in her jeans pocket. She picked up the bottle and with one ragged motion flung it on Boone's face and shirt.

"What —"

She flicked the lighter and threw it at him.

The flames lit silently. They were nearly invisible, ghostly white and violet wraiths that jerked and picked at his shirt and hair and face.

He shouted in pain and crashed backward toward the door, pawing his skin. Eyes shut, arms frantic, he hit the wall. Rory ran at him, pulled her right arm back like she was spiking a volleyball, and smashed his head against the doorjamb.

She ran past him into the bedroom. She grabbed a pen from the desk, pulled off the cap, and jammed the pen into Boone's ear. He shrieked in agony.

"Petra, the window," she said. "We're getting out."

The roof was steeply raked — the eaves over the living room. The drop to the lawn was probably fifteen feet. She had only a second. She pressed her back against the heavy bed frame and lifted it, groaning, a couple of inches from the floor. Though the electrical cord was twisted tightly around Petra's wrists and ankles, it was knotted only where it had been looped around the foot of the bed. Petra slid the makeshift rope underneath it and was free. She shook loose from the cord and stumbled to her feet.

"Quick," Rory said.

Petra staggered to the window and forced it open. Boone was canted against the bathroom wall, eyes streaming, ear bleeding. He'd stopped spinning and attacking himself, so he was probably no longer on fire. Rory picked up her brass Thai Buddha. She swung it with everything she had and slammed him in the face with it.

The blow shook her arm. He yelled and bent double and brought his hands to his face. *"Bitch."*

Petra wobbled onto the sill and crabbed her way to the roof.

Boone swung at Rory. She slammed him again with the Buddha. He staggered back into a shelf and knocked it down. Knickknacks and photos toppled across his shoulders.

He had dropped the phone to paw at his eyes. She scooped it up.

"Petra, get to the tree," she said.

Footsteps pounded up the stairs.

She wound up as if she were preparing for a hammer throw, and she swung the Buddha at Boone one more time.

Karma might be a bitch. But Buddha packed a punch.

The statue connected with a dull thud. Boone dropped to the floor. He couldn't see. His face was battered. He reached out blindly and tried to grab her. She jumped on his knees. He screamed.

She picked up the desk chair and shoved it under the doorknob. From the hall outside the room, the key rattled in the lock.

She climbed out the window. The huge old avocado tree that shaded the house was twenty feet along the roof from the window-sill. Petra was halfway there, hands against the shingles, sidestepping toward it.

Rory hurried. Her running shoes slipped on the shake tiles. "Climb down the tree and we'll get to my car," she said.

She heard the Nightcrawler shout at Boone. "Move the chair."

Petra reached the end of the roof. She needed to jump to the tree, and fast, but struggled for balance.

Rory caught up with her. "Come on."

She held tight to Petra's hand. A large branch was three feet away, but Petra could barely see through her swollen eyes.

Shaking, she said, "I don't know if I can."

"We jump or get killed," Rory said.

Without even a breath Petra threw herself at the tree. The branch shuddered and the leaves shivered and she grabbed hold and shimmied aboard it.

Rory leaped a moment behind her.

Back at the window, Boone shouted, "Those *bitches*."

She steadied herself on the swaying branch and shot a glance at the street. Her hopes crashed.

The Subaru's hood was up. That had to mean one of Mirkovic's men had ripped the wires out.

"Shit."

She nodded the other way, toward the orchard behind the house. "We have to run. Hurry."

Petra grabbed the trunk of the tree and stepped onto the top of the fence. It creaked and swayed under her weight.

On the roof, feet scrabbled across the shingles.

"Go," Rory said.

Petra dropped the six feet to the dirt beyond the fence. Rory swung out and threw herself over the fence after her. She landed hard and went down. Her right leg twanged with pain.

Petra hauled her to her feet. Behind them, they heard the sound of men in pursuit. They ran into the orchard and toward the hills.

49

Rory held her arm around Petra and ran across the cool earth beneath the avocado trees. Petra panted and stumbled to keep up. Rory was running as close to flat out as she could but felt Petra dragging, her stride uneven. Petra's face was battered and she held one arm against her ribs as though she'd been kicked. Hard, and probably repeatedly.

"Run," Rory said. "I have you. Just run."

Petra nodded. She sounded like she couldn't get a breath. Shame tightened around Rory's chest like a chain. Petra had been drawn into this mess because of her. Hurt because of her.

She chanced a glance back. Across the field, Suit Two was climbing over the fence, headed this way. Distantly she heard an engine rev. It had the heavy rattle of Boone's wrecker.

Mirkovic's men probably didn't know the

terrain. But her cousin certainly knew this orchard went on for half a mile, and that a dirt road bisected it not far ahead.

She fumbled Boone's phone from her back pocket. She dialed 9-1-1.

"I'm in the orchard behind Miravista Road," she told the dispatcher. "I heard gunshots from the Whistler house. Hurry. Men are chasing two women into the orchard behind it."

She didn't wait for the dispatcher's reply. She hung up, kept running, and thought, *Crap — what's Seth's number?*

She punched it in. The display jumped around as she careened over the uneven ground. Petra stumbled and nearly went to her knees. In Rory's ear, the number began to ring.

And ring. She pulled Petra along.

Seth's voice mail kicked in.

"Get to my neighborhood," she cried. "Get the feds. Mirkovic and his men are after me and Petra. Boone too, on wheels. Seth, please . . ."

She grimly held the phone. There was something else. She had seen a glance between Mirkovic and the Nightcrawler — when Boone mentioned the baby. It was a quick connection, a message wordlessly understood. They were thinking: *Get the kid.*

If they got little Addie, they would have leverage over Boone and Riss.

And she'd seen something worse in Mirkovic's eyes. Something visceral and territorial. *The kid.* When Boone said Addie's name, Mirkovic got a look that said, *Mine.*

Rory had seen the way Mirkovic reacted to Boone. She felt with nasty certainty what Mirkovic must think: Boone was a loose missile, a heat seeker. Promising Rory to him as a hunting trophy had failed to keep him on their leash. They wanted something to hold over his head until they could dispose of *him* . . . and on the phone he'd given them the answer. The baby.

Riss would be the most potent bargaining chip. But Mirkovic wanted the little girl too.

"Seth," she said, her voice rough, "get somebody to Amber's. One of the kids is Riss and Boone's little girl. I think Mirkovic's going to go after her. This whole thing's coming apart and they're desperate. They'll use anything and anybody to get an edge." She fought for breath. "If Mirkovic can't get me, maybe he'll try to use Riss as leverage with Lee. But think what they might do to Lee's grandchild."

Petra stumbled again. She was just about running on empty.

"And the cops. Xavier's on the take," Rory

said. "Seth, get help."

Petra straightened, limping, her face contorted with pain. "What you said . . ."

"It's all true." Every awful word.

Petra slowed. "Go on. Go to your aunt's house. I can't go any farther."

"No way." She tightened her grip on Petra's hand and pulled.

"Run. Get help. I'll hide," Petra said.

"I can't leave you here alone."

Petra dropped to a walk. She was going with everything she had, but she was at only half strength to begin with, beaten and bruised. "I can't. You go."

Near panic, Rory put her hands on Petra's shoulders. "They'll find you. Look around. There's nobody out here. They're trained men and they'll track you and narrow it down until they have you cornered up a tree."

Petra's lip trembled. Rory looked back the way they'd come. She couldn't see or hear Mirkovic's thug, but the trees seemed to shudder. *He's there.*

She needed to get to a populated spot. Even Boone wasn't such a wild dog that he'd kill her in front of an audience. Not before he got the money. They needed a store, a post office, someplace public.

But Petra looked spent. A sob welled and

fell from her lips.

Rory nearly lost it. "I'm sorry. Oh, honey."

She squeezed Petra's hand and pulled her along. They reached the dirt road that cut through the middle of the orchard. Rory listened, heard no vehicles, slowed, peered right and left.

Nobody. No help either.

She paused, looking around. Which way? And then she tried to take an overhead view of the landscape. The orchard, the river . . . and past it, fields and eventually a shopping mall. A mile, maybe.

"Give it all you've got and we'll make it to Rock Creek Plaza."

They stepped from between the trees onto the dirt road. And Boone's wrecker turned the corner about a quarter of a mile away and headed toward them.

Petra jumped. "Oh God."

"Run."

She didn't look back, just peeled out, nearly dragging Petra across the road and into the trees on the other side. Boone's engine gunned, throaty and loud.

The phone rang in her hand. She was running too hard to get a look at the caller ID. She put it to her ear.

"Rory? Where are you?"

It was Seth. Her spirits leaped and her

heart beat harder.

"Orchard behind the house. Heading north. Petra's hurt. We need help. Now."

Petra turned and looked back. *Bad idea,* Rory thought. Lot's wife tried the same thing and it went poorly.

"Boone's in his truck, after us," Rory said. "Closing."

Seth sounded like he was driving. "Help's coming. I'm on my way."

"We'll reach Old Ranch Road in a minute," she said.

Petra said, "He's coming . . . Oh, Rory . . ."

Rory said, "Did you hear that?"

"Keep going," Seth said. "Just keep going. I'm coming."

Petra said, "No — Boone's driving off. Where's he going?"

Around, Rory thought. Getting out of the orchard so he'd have a clear run at them. He knew they were headed for the road and the safety of civilization on the far side of it. If he could get there first, he'd cut them off. They'd be pinched between him and the suit who was pursuing on foot.

Ahead, the trees ended. They ducked beneath low-hanging branches and emerged from the orchard onto a wide straight road that ran into the foothills. It was absolutely empty. No traffic, no broken-down cars, no hitchhikers, not even roadkill.

Nothing but a low, throaty note on the air, the sound of a big engine heading toward them.

Across the road, a hundred yards away, was Ransom River. The caged section of concrete and cyclone fencing that ran toward the long and dark storm drain.

"We'll cross the river," Rory said.

"How?"

"We'll climb the fence and ford it. Petra, the fence runs for two miles. They can't get across it in vehicles. If we hurry, we can lose them. We can even hide in the storm drain — they won't know where we've gone."

"Are you kidding?"

"Dead serious." She put the phone to her ear. The line was still open. "Seth, are you listening?"

"It's a risk," he said. "I'm still a mile away."

Petra looked close to crying but nodded. Rory stuck the phone in her pocket. They ran to the fence, grabbed hold, and pulled themselves up, digging the toes of their shoes through the diamond mesh. The steel pressed painfully into Rory's fingers.

The noise of Boone's rattling engine grew louder. The suit stepped from the trees and

walked toward them, as calmly as a man
processing to Communion.

50

Rory balanced unsteadily on top of the chain-link fence. Below, the river was running fast. Already swollen from the autumn rains, it was choppy and several feet deep. And the overnight downpour had worsened it. She blanched.

Petra nearly gasped. "It's dangerous."

Rory looked back. The suit walked toward them at a measured, inexorable pace.

"So's he."

They jumped like they'd been juiced with high voltage and landed on the concrete riverbank.

In the distance, Boone's wrecker appeared.

Rory and Petra scurried down the steep slope of the riverbank. At the edge of the water a rusted tricycle lay upside down, wheels clawing the air. Near the storm drain, a shopping cart seemed to be fording the river. White plastic bags clung to it like wet ghosts. They ran to the lip of the concrete. The water gushed past.

This ain't no swimming pool, Rory thought.

Across the river, up an even steeper concrete bank, another high fence waited. But beyond it, beyond the gravel frontage road that paralleled it, were fields, and beyond the fields was hope: Rock Creek Plaza.

Rory stepped off the concrete lip into the river.

The current grabbed at her legs. The cold bit. She braced herself.

"It's manageable. We can do it."

Petra grabbed her hand. Beneath the cuts and bruises her face was pale. They forged into the river. It swiftly covered their knees and whitecapped off their thighs.

Behind them, the wrecker whined up and ground to a halt. The door slammed. Rory glanced back. Boone ran to the fence and glared down at her. His face was strawberry red, his eyes slitty from the alcohol fire. The suit loomed beside him.

Rory got Boone's phone. The call to Seth was still active. "We're crossing the river a hundred yards upstream from the storm drain."

"I'm close. I'm driving up the frontage road on the far side. I'll get there."

She felt the two men behind her. Two, not four. Mirkovic and the Nightcrawler hadn't come. *Addie,* she thought.

Boone rattled the fence as he started to climb. He yelled and dropped back to the ground, swearing and shaking his hands. He shouted, "Seth ain't gonna save you, Rory."

Petra said, "He didn't hop the fence."

"His hands are burned." The diamond mesh must have hurt him too much.

The door to the wrecker slammed shut. The truck's gears ground and the engine whined.

Rory struggled to keep her feet beneath her in the brown churn of the river. She stuck the phone in her pocket. The concrete was slippery. The current forced them gradually downstream, but they didn't fight it.

Downstream, the storm drain swallowed the river. Rory got a good look at it: three culverts, eight feet high, a line of concrete tunnels that dropped from bright sunlight and frothing water to rough echoes and blackness. The river funneled into the drain in a roil of white water.

She leaned forward. Her pulse throbbed in her temples. *Don't lose your footing. Fall, and you'll be swept away.*

She looked over her shoulder. Boone was backing the wrecker up.

Petra slipped. Her feet tangled with Rory's. Rory slid to her knees. Reflexively she put her hands out to brace herself. The water, cold and powerful, sloshed over her.

"God," Petra cried.

Torn loose from Rory, she fishtailed away in the current. She splashed and spun and gasped into the water, instantly taken.

The river swept her toward the storm drain.

Seth drove with his foot to the firewall and the wheel jolting back and forth in his hands. The truck bounced over the rough gravel road that ran along the chain-link fence above Ransom River.

The truck bucked over a rise, and four hundred yards upriver, there it was. Seth gunned the truck through dust and kicking gravel to the entrance of the storm drain. The water gushed into it, at least waist high. It was muddy brown. He saw debris bobbing on the current. But he didn't see Rory.

Fishtailing to a halt, he put the truck in park. He flipped the tail of his shirt over the Glock, threw open the door, and stood on the frame of the truck. And he saw Rory on her knees, half-submerged, struggling to her feet. Near her, splashing, caught in the current, he saw Petra.

"Jesus, no."

Rory got her feet under her and splashed toward Petra, seeing the maw of the drain, hearing a roar. They'd come almost a hundred yards downriver in just a few seconds.

Boone's wrecker dropped into gear. The engine gunned.

Petra fought the current, swimming, almost clawing the water, trying to stand. The culverts seemed to suck her toward them. Rory ran, but the river outdistanced her. Breathless, she watched Petra recede toward the storm drain.

And hit the rusted shopping cart.

She crashed into it and got snagged between the basket and wheels, as if wedged in its jaws.

And Rory heard another sound: an engine. She looked up. On the far side of the river, on the frontage road, Seth's truck had stopped on the gravel in a storm of dust. In a second, he was out of the cab and over the fence and careening down the slope.

Upriver, the wrecker rammed the fence. Its big push bumper smashed down a ten-foot section of chain link with a bang and clatter. The suit climbed through the gap.

Petra's face was just above the water. Rory splashed to the cart and tried to pull her out. The current gushed like a broken fire hydrant. If she didn't get a good grip, Petra would slip from her hands like a fish and be gone again in an instant. She slogged to the downstream side of the cart as a backstop. Seth jumped into the river and forged to her side. Together they slid Petra free. Rory braced her against the force of the water.

Seth hauled Petra to her feet. "Go."

Rory put an arm around Petra's waist and together they battled toward the far side of the river. Seth followed, a hand on Rory's back. Rory helped Petra onto the concrete bank. It was slick and as steep as a playground slide. Petra scrambled up the slippery slope on all fours.

Seth said, "Up, Rory. Run."

He turned, putting himself between her and the suit. Mirkovic's man was jogging along the far slope, heavy and relentless. Rory climbed onto the bank.

Boone shouted something. Seth said, "Hurry."

Petra reached the top of the fence and tumbled over.

The sound of gunfire was deep and shocking. Rory gasped and threw herself down against the concrete. The crack of the gun had sounded bigger than a handgun.

Upriver, coming down the far bank, was Boone. He had a matte-black shotgun in his hands. He raised it and fired again.

The shot hit the culvert. Concrete chipped and flew. Seth stood in the river facing him.

Rory got to her feet. "Seth . . ."

Boone pumped the action with one hand and leveled the gun again.

Seth shouted, "Stop, Boone. F—"

He fell before she heard the gunshot.

Seth took the round in the chest, buckled like he'd been hit with a swinging log, and went down. The crack of the gunshot reached her, like a whiplash. Seth fell back into the water. The splash swallowed him.

Rory slid down the concrete and leaped back into the river and flailed toward him. Seth surfaced, his head back, arms outstretched, and the water took him into the culvert. Fast, like night dropping, he disappeared.

Off balance, she careered toward the spot in the river where he had been standing.

Petra shouted, "No — Rory, no."

She kept running.

Behind her, Boone shouted, "Stop."

The water gushed into the culvert, choppy and brown. Rory didn't seem to be breathing. Chunks of concrete blew from the side of the culvert. Another gunshot pocked the air. Rory jumped sideways, flinching, hands covering her head.

"Stop," Boone shouted.

She stopped, thigh deep in the river, and slowly turned. Thirty yards away, on its trash-strewn banks, Boone stood facing her. He held the shotgun level and steady.

"Petra, go," she said.

Petra hesitated.

"It's our only chance," she said. "Get out of here, get help. Get to the sheriff's station. *Go.*"

Petra paused only a second longer before climbing into the cab of Seth's pickup, slamming it into gear, and taking off downriver along the frontage road.

Please, Rory thought. *Please get the sheriffs here.*

In the river, a branch sliced past. In such a swift current, Seth was already a hundred yards gone down the dark throat of the storm drain. She could barely see because her vision was throbbing so hard.

Boone marched toward her. The suit flanked him. Rory reached into her back pocket and raised Boone's phone. They couldn't tell it was wet and ruined.

She shouted to be heard above the rush of the water. "Cops are on the way. They've heard everything."

Beneath his rage, uncertainty crossed Boone's face. Then he raised the shotgun.

Rory held his gaze. She spread her arms and fell backward into the churning water. It carried her into the darkness.

51

The water swarmed over Rory's head. The world dimmed brown, and sound muffled to a bubbling throb. The river pulled her, racing, through the concrete drain.

She surfaced, grabbed a breath, and looked back. The orb of light at the tunnel entrance bobbed and shrank. Boone was running toward it, looking as small as a dart.

She tried to stand. The water came up to her waist. She was going faster than she could run. *Holy Jesus.*

On the roof of the culvert a shadow passed, and she heard a splash. She glanced back. Boone was outside the ever-shrinking tunnel entrance, but she didn't see the suit. She had the strange visceral sense that an alligator had entered the water.

She swam. "Seth," she called.

He had fallen faceup. Head above water; that was his only chance. If he'd rolled . . . Fear, sharp and black, opened like jaws in front of her.

The light zeroed to nothing. She bobbed up, tried to breathe without swallowing the cold dirty water. The current surged and tossed her against the wall of the tunnel. "God —"

She'd never seen the other end of the culvert. The exit could be barred by grids of rebar. She could get swept against it and have no way to get out. The urge to fight back upstream was almost overpowering. Lizard brain screaming: *Air. Light. Idiot.* The darkness felt smothering.

She still had Boone's phone in her hand. Her fingers were shaking from the frigid water. She mashed the keypad.

The display lit up, weak blue light. The walls of the tunnel jumped into freakish relief. The tunnel ran straight, on and on.

The display shorted out and the tunnel went dark. Behind her came splashing. Like something hunting, beneath the surface. The suit.

She started swimming hard.

When the storm drain spit her into daylight, she gulped air as though she was starved of it. The river smoothed and rolled, a heavy brown snake. High above its concrete banks, the sun seemed to bleach the world to a white sheen.

She saw no sign of Seth.

Spinning around, she took a step back to the culvert. Could she have missed him inside? No.

She looked downriver. Scanned the banks. It was a dry day. If he'd climbed out, she should be able to see a trail of wet footsteps.

From behind, a heavy object hit her. It felt like sodden meat. She hollered and spun. Saw a hand. A man's hand. It trailed away.

As it sank she saw a navy blue jacket. Cuff links.

The suit rolled. His skin was fish pale. His mouth gaped, full of water. His eyes were blank. He kept rolling. Facedown, he swept away from her.

"God. Oh Jesus."

Shaking, she pawed through the water to the concrete bank. Her legs felt like they might at any second snap like reeds and drop her flat.

She climbed onto the bank and stumbled along, scanning both slopes. She swiped an elbow across her face. She tried to inhale and couldn't. She was alone.

She ran along the sloping bank for three hundred yards, until the water roared into yet another storm drain. Branches and trash had snagged near the entrance. The water frothed away inside. The suit surfaced and hit the logjam and bounced off and was sucked into the culvert. She turned away.

Seth was gone.

She held there for a long minute, trying to convince herself she was wrong, that there had to be a way to find him, that if she only wished hard enough she could turn around and he would be standing behind her, smiling, saying, *Gotcha*.

The wind kicked up. She began to shiver.

Addie.

Shakily she grabbed the fence and climbed. She felt as small and wobbly as she had at twelve. She swung over the top and dropped to the gravel on the outside. She ran.

Though she was cold her second wind came quickly. She'd run only a couple of miles. She was wet, and her jeans were chafing, her shoes splashing water, but she could run. She had to.

Boone had to be on his way to Amber's house. As did Mirkovic.

But she knew something that she hoped Boone had not considered. On the far side of the hill, her parents had their acreage and work shed. The El Camino was parked under a tarp. The Elco that her dad fired up every month, and kept tuned, and which had a spare key in a magnetic case stuck inside a rear wheel well.

She picked up her pace, fast on the downhill. She reached the shed winded and unlocked the combination padlock. She scraped the door open. Inside, the car waited in dusty sunlight. She pulled off the tarp.

She knelt by the rear wheel and found the magnetic key case. The driver's door creaked when she opened it. Inside, the cab was close and hot. She turned the ignition. The starter made a grinding noise.

"Come on."

Through the windshield the hood looked long and sleek and as red as a fire alarm. She feathered the gas pedal.

The engine guttered to life. *Yes.* She gave it more gas. The exhaust coughed and the power of the V-8 rattled through the steering column.

She eased the car from the shed. A minute later she was roaring down the dirt road, spewing a tornado of dust behind her.

52

Rory bombed up the hill in the El Camino. Past the crest, Amber's house sat dispirited in the sunshine, as though poised for a long downhill slide. A Big Wheel lay upended on the lawn. The bare patches of dirt looked like mange. The road and driveway were empty. No SUVs, no wrecker. She half swerved to the curb, jumped out, and ran to the door.

She opened it without knocking. "Aunt Amber?"

The television was droning. She rushed past the kitchen. "Amber."

At the end of the hall, Amber stepped from her bedroom. "Rory?"

"You need to get out. Now. How many kids are here?"

Amber looked uncertain. "You're sopping. What on earth?"

"How many kids?"

Amber tucked her unruly hair behind an

ear and cocked her head. "Just Adalyn. Only one boy comes on Friday, and he stayed home today with a cold."

Relief washed through Rory.

Slowly, vaguely, Amber said, "What is going on? The sheriffs phoned a while back and asked if I was okay. Said, stay inside with the door locked, and they'd send a cruiser to keep an eye on the place."

"Great." Except that Amber hadn't locked the door. How much OxyContin had she taken? "Where's Addie?"

Amber pointed to the living room. "Why you asking about Addie?"

"Because I know, Amber."

She let the words sink in. Amber's eyes sharpened, turned bright. Rory hurried to the living room.

Near the burbling television Addie crouched over a clutch of trolls and ponies. Her brown curls framed her face. Rory knelt and put a gentle hand on her back.

"Hey. We're going for a ride. You and me and your grandma."

Addie looked up, curious but accepting. She stood and let Rory hoist her into her arms.

Amber shuffled toward her, eyes watery, fiddling with a bead necklace. "If the sheriff's sending a car, how come we need to split?"

"Because the sheriff's not the only one coming."

Amber stood in the hallway, pale. "Who?"

"Mirkovic and his men." For starters.

In the backyard, trees bent to the wind. Shirts flapped on the clothesline.

Amber pressed a hand to her chest. "Lord God Almighty."

Rory walked past her. "Where's Addie's car seat?"

Addie said, "Ride in Amber's car?"

"My car, honey," Rory said.

Amber looked at the little girl. "She's legally mine. I adopted her."

"Riss doesn't care about the law. Let's go."

"Riss surrendered her parental rights. She's mine." Amber put a hand on Rory's arm to stop her. It was cold and trembling. "Mirkovic wants her?"

"Riss told you he's the father?"

"It was a onetime thing. Not planned. That club Riss works at, Butterfly Bombshell, Mirkovic owns it." Amber looked at Addie. "Riss . . ."

"Riss told *Mirkovic* he's the father?"

Amber nodded and looked at the floor. "He's coming because . . ."

"He heard your son say something that

convinced him he's *not* the father."

Amber shuddered and her lips quivered. She apparently believed Mirkovic had fathered Addie. Or she'd been trying to believe it, though part of her suspected otherwise. And she didn't want to know the truth.

"We need to go." Holding Addie tight, Rory ran to the kitchen.

"Don't judge us," Amber said.

Rory's skin was prickling. She picked up the phone. "The sheriff's phoned here? That was the last call?"

"Why do you need to know if they was the last people to call?" Amber saw Rory's face and took a step back. "Yes."

Rory pressed Callback.

Amber said, "If Mirkovic thinks Riss lied to him about the baby . . ."

Amber's tone said the rest: He'd seek revenge for her duplicity. Rory hugged Addie against her hip.

On the phone a woman answered, "Sheriff's Department."

"A man's been shot at the top of the Ransom River storm drain."

She tried to explain it clearly. Even to herself she sounded garbled and uncertain. "He was swept into the drain. Get rescuers out there."

She tried to flatten her voice, but an image filled her mind: Seth, going down, hard. The flat crack of the gunshot reached her like a second blow.

"Your name, ma'am?"

She gave it to her. "And you're sending a cruiser to my aunt's house. Send it fast. It's an emergency. I'm getting her and her granddaughter out of here. We're going to drive to the minimart on the farm road."

She peered out the window. Heard nothing. Saw nothing but blowing dust. "I'm driving a red El Camino."

"Ma'am, do not leave the residence. Lock the doors and windows and sit tight."

"It's too dangerous."

A blunt cool ring of metal pressed against the back of her head. A voice said, "Shh."

She stilled. A man's hand reached around from behind and took the phone.

Pressing the barrel of the shotgun to her head, Boone stepped into view.

53

Boone's face was flat. "Not a word."

Rory didn't move. Boone hung up the phone. Then ripped the jack from the wall.

Amber looked waxen. "Son, what are you doing?"

"Get the baby, Ma."

"What happened to your face?"

From the corner of her eye Rory saw him point at her. "She *did this* to me. Get the goddamned kid."

Rory held Addie tight against her hip. "We're getting out of here, Boone."

"You could say that. But not with her. She's mine."

Confusion seemed to pop from Amber's eyes. She stood as though paralyzed, her face slack, the color draining from her skin. "No. Boone, not . . ."

And Rory realized she was seeing raw, inchoate fear.

"Mirkovic's coming," Amber said. "If he

finds you with Addie, what'll he do?"

Rory's nerves began to crackle. The barrel of the shotgun nudged against the side of her head. She smelled gun oil and cordite.

Boone pried Addie from her arms. The little girl stiffened. She didn't cry, but she knew something was wrong. Amber continued to stand like a piece of melting plastic.

Rory said, "The sheriff's department heard. They know. They're on their way."

"They're quick," Boone said, "but not *this* quick." He snicked the gun into Rory's hair again. She flinched.

He laughed.

He stepped back, propped Addie on one hip, and aimed the shotgun at Rory's chest. Addie held out her hands to Rory, fingers opening and closing.

Boone spun her away. "Forget her," he said. "Who's my girl? Give me a kiss."

He began to tickle her. Awkwardly he dug his fingers into her ribs. She squirmed and flinched.

"Laugh, baby," he said.

Addie twisted and squealed unhappily. "No, Uncle Boone, stop."

"Come on, it's funny." His smile was half-cocked, fading.

Rory heard the back door open. In the hall behind Boone, a shadow moved. Riss slid into view.

Engrossed in trying to make Addie adore him, Boone couldn't see her. The hairs on Rory's arms and scalp stood to cold attention. Riss inched silently into half light. She watched Boone with the child. And as Boone's laughter scathed the room, her face darkened.

She glided forward, eyes unblinking. "What are you doing?"

He turned, startled. "Where you been?"

She walked up and took Addie from him. The little girl whimpered and looked at Amber.

"Nana."

Amber held on to the counter like it was the rail of a sinking ship.

Riss said, "What's Rory doing here? And looking like a drowned dog." She glanced at Boone. Got a full view of his face. "What the hell —"

"She burned me. The bitch *burned* me." Boone hitched the gun in his arms. "And she tried to get away."

Amber put a shaking hand to her lips. "Riss, Boone . . . what have you done?"

"Shut up," Riss said. "Where's Mirkovic? Where are his men?"

Rory found her voice. "They're coming.

And they aren't bringing brownies and punch."

Riss eyed her with calculation.

"Mirkovic's coming for Addie, and he's furious that you lied to him," Rory said. "We need to get the hell out. All of us, right now."

Riss looked at her, now more incredulous than suspicious. "You don't get a say." She cocked her head at Boone. "Get something to restrain her with. We got to give her to Grigor."

Boone's lips parted. "She burned me. She tried to kill me. I'm not giving her back to him."

Riss's eyes flared. "Afterward, Boone. *After* the money gets located." She shook her head. "Did you get her on video?"

"We will," he said.

Amber said, "Riss, you told Mirkovic Addie's his child. But . . ."

"For fuck sake, it was a lie," Riss said.

Rory said, "We need to leave. Right now. Mirkovic's men won't trust Boone anymore, because he let me get away the first time. They'll take me. And because they don't trust him they'll also take Addie."

Riss scoffed.

Rory said, "And maybe you, Riss."

"Hell no."

"Lee's *your* dad," Rory said. "A Mackenzie through and through, right? Who's going to make the biggest emotional impression on him?"

Riss went quiet.

Christ on a flying monkey, would these people not understand what she was telling them?

"Riss, the sheriffs are coming," Rory said. "They'll arrest you."

And Riss smiled. A slow, *I've got you* smile. Rory's stomach dropped.

Riss turned to Amber. "Thanks for phoning to tell me the sheriffs were so concerned about you. I called them back. They were relieved to know we're on the way to your brother-in-law's house and won't need them to stop by."

Amber said, "Riss. No."

Addie twisted in Riss's arms and stretched a hand toward Rory. Riss roughly pushed it down.

One play. That's all Rory could think of. One more play. Now.

"I'll take you to the money," she said.

Riss turned. Boone turned.

Rory said, "It's yours, every dollar."

Boone's eyes brightened. Riss seemed to calm to the smoothness of agate.

"You know where it is?"

516

"I found out."

"How?" Riss said.

"I'll tell you on the way."

Boone said, "I knew it, you liar." He pointed at her. "She knew all along. Your dad took her with him when he hid it."

"No," Rory said.

Riss raised a hand. "We're not going anywhere until you tell me how you know."

Boone said, "Let's move. She can prove it real quick. She takes us or she doesn't. Proof."

But Riss didn't move. She held Rory in her sights, as Addie fussed and reached for Amber. She held the little girl like she was a slimy object.

She shook her head. "How did you know this was about the money?"

"The courthouse siege," Rory said. "The gunmen mentioned it."

"No way," Riss said.

"They were amateur hostage takers, not top-notch mercenaries."

"That doesn't mean they'd talk about the money."

"Their plan went balls up five minutes in. They started talking about *everything*," Rory said. "Mirkovic had promised them huge rewards to get them to take the risk. They wouldn't do it for a flat fee. They refused to attack the trial unless they got a percentage of what Mirkovic was aiming to recover. He told them it was a mammoth stash of cash."

"That prick," Riss said.

Rory remembered what Seth had told her about convincing people a false identity was the real deal in undercover work: Mix some truth into your lies.

"Your dad's postcards," she said.

Riss's face hardened. Boone said, "What?"

"Your dad sent postcards to me when I was little. You ripped them off my corkboard and tore them up."

"What are you talking about?" Boone said.

"Your dad sent me postcards from Mexico after he fled the country," she said, slowly, articulating each word. "You destroyed some, but I had a drawer full of them."

Riss's face slowly turned crimson.

"After the siege, I put two and two together," Rory said. "Who else could they be after, these people? Me? I'm broke. My parents? They're a teacher and forest ranger living in an old ranch house. No, they wanted something from Lee. And there was only one thing that made sense. The robbery happened right around the time he left. The money was never recovered. I figured he wouldn't take that secret with him — he'd want somebody to know. And the only thing that connected him to me was the postcards."

Boone stepped forward. "Where are you hiding them?"

The gun loomed in his hands, the barrel long and black. She tried, harder than she'd ever tried anything, not to let tears creep into her voice.

"I got them from my parents' house and gave them to Seth," she said.

Riss shook her head as though clearing her ears. "You're fucking with me."

"No."

Boone's parted lips turned into a fishy gape. "Seth."

She turned her glare on him. It took nothing. She was half a breath away from losing it.

Riss said, "Wait. Wait a second. You're saying my dad wrote you the location of the money and you never went to look for it? That's beyond bullshit."

"Of course he didn't. But he always wrote in rhymes, or puzzles. When I was little I thought he was sharing his adventure with me. But yesterday I reread them. They're map coordinates, longitude and latitude. He was leaving clues."

"Why you?" Riss said. The *Why not me?* was in her voice like lye.

"Because he knew they'd always be there. I would collect them. My parents wouldn't move. They'd hold on to them — on to all my stuff — like treasures."

Riss glared. She stepped forward and slapped Rory in the face. Amber gasped. Addie jerked and began to cry.

Rory's face stung. She took it. *Don't lose your shit.*

"The cash is in the mountains," she said.

"You goddamned princess," Riss said. "Where?"

"The national forest. I'll take you to it." She pointed out the door. "But we need to leave right the hell now, before Mirkovic gets here. 'Cause if he does, he'll cut you two out of the deal like that." She snapped her fingers.

Boone nodded. "Yeah. Come on. We're the ones who can cut Mirkovic out of the deal. Move it, girls."

Rory stood firm. "You, me, and Riss. We'll go."

Boone waved toward the door. "Everybody in the truck, come on."

"No," Rory said. "Let your mom take Addie someplace else."

Riss's expression turned sly. "Why?"

"Besides the fact that Mirkovic is *coming here right now,* we can't take Addie. She

can't even hold still in your arms. We're going to the forest to dig up twenty-five million bucks. We don't want a crying baby
drawing attention to us."

Boone was halfway to the front door. But
Riss hadn't moved.

"You're not as clever as you think you
are," Riss said. "Go. Addie's coming with
us."

Bringing the little girl along, she pushed
Rory to the door.

They walked outside and headed to the
wrecker. It was parked seventy yards up the
hill, where Rory hadn't been able to see it
from the house. The wind had picked up.
The screen door flipped back and smacked
against the wall, battering, like ruined ap-
plause. Across the road, half-hidden in a
grove of live oaks at the edge of a gully, was
Riss's Toyota Land Cruiser. She must have
coasted over the lip of the hill with the
engine off and parked it out of sight before
she snuck in the back door.

Boone held Rory by the hair, shotgun
jammed into her ribs. Riss followed, shov-
ing her between the shoulder blades.

"You don't have to push. I'm taking you
there," Rory said.

She listened for Mirkovic's SUV parade,
but the wind blew through the oaks and

eucalyptus, a hard brushing sound that overcame all else.

She felt, despite everything that had happened, a depthless surprise, like a gut punch, that her own family was this greedy and animalistic, that, unchained, they grabbed for everything without regard for life, for love, for others. They were a cheap documentary on the power of hatred and need, come to life.

The crumbling road stretched black and empty down the hill, all the way to the floor of the valley. It cut like a gnarled cable through dry scrub and empty fields. The city lay distant, beneath a beige haze, like a cataract. The sharp blue-gray ridges of the mountains rose beyond it, rocky and isolated. Boone gazed at them eagerly. His thirst for the money seemed ready to turn him inside out.

Riss shoved Rory again. Rory felt some swirling approach of danger, of violence, of cold endings. She pinned her eyes on the truck.

"We need tools. And bags," Riss said.

Not in a million years was Rory going to suggest where to find shovels and a bag big enough to hold a body.

Boone pushed her into the passenger side of the wrecker's cab. He climbed in behind her and clambered across her lap, pivoting over the shotgun as if it were a vaulting pole. A thread of sweat rolled down her back. Boone dropped into the driver's seat. He laid the shotgun across his lap, aimed at her stomach, his left hand awkwardly clawing the trigger. With his right he turned the ignition.

Leaning forward, he peered past Rory out the passenger door at his stepsister. "Follow us in your car. It'll take two vehicles to carry everything."

Riss backed away, nodding. Addie squirmed and sniffled in her arms.

Boone stomped on the clutch and ground the shift into first gear. He checked the rearview mirror and turned his head to look out the driver's window.

Where, Glock raised and aimed at his face, stood Seth.

54

Rory let out a breath that was beyond shock, beyond disbelief. Seth was standing on his own feet, eyes clear and focused, hair disheveled. Shirt damp. Gun shining. Her heart beat hard against her ribs and her voice rose in her throat, a cry of joy.

Boone sat astounded, right hand on the wheel, left on the trigger of the shotgun. Seth held the Glock in a two-handed grip, chest high, the barrel aimed square at Boone's face.

"Federal officer. Don't move," he said.

Rory blinked. Felt a firework detonate in her chest.

"Put your hands on the dashboard," Seth said.

Boone stared straight at him. His hands didn't move.

Head pounding, Rory pitched out the passenger door. She hit the asphalt and scrambled to the back of the wrecker, out of the line of fire. Down the road, near the El Camino, Riss had stopped on her way to the garage.

Seth was two inches from the driver's window. His Glock was one inch from the glass.

He called to Rory. "Is Riss armed?"

"Not that I saw." Her voice sounded tinny.

"Riss, don't move. You and Boone are under arrest."

Boone still had not put his hands on the dash. Rory knew he was gripping the shotgun. But swinging that long barrel around to shoot at Seth would take a second he didn't have. If he tried to raise it, Seth had him dead.

Amber cried, "Boone — do what he says."

The wind rose, and dust scudded across the dead lawn. Amber sank to her knees, hand in front of her mouth.

Without turning his head, staring unblinking at Boone, Seth said, "Rory, come here."

She rounded the back of the wrecker. Seth held like a stone. He was standing awkwardly, working to hold his firing stance.

"Get the gun from my back pocket."

She approached. *How?* she thought. *Why?*
"Petra?" she said.

"Safe."

She saw no blood. But he winced every

time he breathed. He was wheezing heavily and fighting not to double over. And she saw, at the collar of the wet shirt that clung to his chest, the black body armor he wore beneath it.

She lifted the tail of his shirt and took a handgun from his back pocket. It was heavy.

"It's a Beretta. Unsafety it," he said. "Chamber a round."

She ticked the switch on the side of the gun. Racked and released the slide. It snapped into place with a nasty click.

"Get back," he said, voice tight, eyes on Boone. "If anybody moves toward you, or me, or reaches for their pockets, fire."

"Addie," she said.

He cut his eyes at her. Some message in that look. Maybe — she thought — it meant *Don't shoot in Addie's direction, but let Riss think you will.* She backed away, both hands on the Beretta, finger outside the trigger guard, weapon aimed at the asphalt.

And Riss began to back down the road toward the El Camino, parked at a crazy angle to the curb. "Don't shoot me."

She looked calm. She looked unearthly. Her black hair flew in the wind like a dark corona. On her hip, Addie huddled and pressed the heels of her small hands against her eyes, fighting the dust.

Facing the wrecker, Riss kept walking backward. She gazed at Boone with the confidence of a trapeze artist flying toward the partner she knew would catch her.

"Riss, stop," Rory said.

Riss continued to back down the hill another ten yards, until she reached the El Camino. She swung Addie away from her hip and set the little girl in the bed of the car.

Riss raised her hands. "I'm unarmed. Don't shoot."

She stood in the center of the asphalt, her arms up in a position of surrender. But her eyes shone with defiance, and her gaze was riveted on Boone.

"No," Rory said. With a start, she headed toward her. "No."

Boone hesitated only a moment. He released the clutch and gunned the wrecker.

Riss bolted.

The wrecker lurched forward. It aimed straight downhill at the El Camino and the toddler sitting in the bed.

"Addie," Rory shouted. "Oh God."

She ran. Just ran, Jesus, ran toward Addie. *Get there, come on* — a human being could accelerate faster than a heavy truck over the first few yards. She was running flat out ahead of the wrecker, but it was gaining.

She felt only shredding fear.

Addie stood up and saw the truck looming toward her. She had no chance, not one in a million.

Rory threw herself into the bed of the El Camino, grabbed Addie by the arm, and tried to yank her to safety. She heard the engine, felt the heat.

She heard gunfire just before the truck hit them.

The report from Seth's Glock came hard and flat. The sound was swallowed by the blare of the engine under the hood of Boone's wrecker.

Rory turned her back to the truck. Addie was hanging half-in, half-out of her grasp, her eyes round and scared, her little feet swinging. Rory looked at her, wishing — *please save her* — and the wrecker T-boned the El Camino.

Packed with power and momentum, the blow sent them flying across the bed of the Elco. *Hold on.* She wrapped her arms around Addie to shield her. She heard another gunshot, barely, beneath the roar of the engine.

Barreling along on a downhill trajectory, the wrecker began to shove the Elco sideways down the road. The trees passed by.

The grille of the wrecker stared Rory in the face, hot and roaring. She held Addie and grabbed for a handhold, crawled toward the tailgate. The wrecker pushed the Elco toward a bend in the road. It kept rolling, bumping, and headed for the drop-off into the gulch beyond. Some part of her brain shouted: *Jump.* Then they were in the air. She balled up and hit the ground.

The pain came first from scraping the asphalt. Then hitting her head. Her elbows smashed into the road, and her knees, and she rolled, Addie rolling with her. The truck kept coming. From the ground, it was all she could see, looming, implacable.

She said, "Baby . . ."

The wheels of the wrecker veered. The truck turned and rolled past her face, inches away.

She lay stunned and gasping. Addie was sprawled across her chest. The little girl took a herking breath and broke into terrified sobs.

She saw the road, old asphalt grainy with stones. She was bleeding. Addie had blood streaked across her Hello Kitty shirt, but Rory thought it was her own. She saw the blue sail of the sky, nailed to the sun, spinning.

Above Addie's sobs, she heard the El

Camino slide over the lip of the gulch and roll, thudding, downhill. The wrecker drove into a tree.

She curled tight around Addie. "It's okay. You're okay," she said. The little girl put her head to Rory's shoulder and shook. "We're okay."

She raised her head. The truck had rolled sixty yards downhill and run off the pavement straight into the trunk of a eucalyptus. The engine was still roaring, the rear wheels spinning, but the grille was crushed against the tree trunk, the hood crumpled up, steam shooting from the radiator.

At the open driver's door, Seth let go of the wheel and dragged Boone from the driver's seat. Her cousin fell heavily from the cab and hit the dirt like a bag of flour. He lay motionless. Seth held the Glock with both hands, aimed at Boone, and checked the surroundings for more threats.

His gaze lit on Rory.

In the background, Amber began to wail.

Rory held on to Addie. She cringed to her knees. Her right side was scraped as pink as raw sausage. It was a wall of pain.

Addie's sobs were full of fear but loud and strong. She was okay. She was scared but warm and whole.

Boone lay twisted and still, bleeding

severely from the neck and chest. His shirt was sopping red. Rory held Addie's head tight to her shoulder so she couldn't see.

Rory looked down at her right hand. She still had the Beretta. Looked up. All around. Riss was gone.

Seth frisked Boone. He climbed into the cab, turned off the engine, and grabbed the shotgun. Climbed out, ejected the shells, rested the gun against his shoulder. With every breath, every movement, pain poured across his face. He had saved them.

Amber's wailing intensified. She tottered toward her son. "Boone . . . what did you do to my boy?"

Seth pointed at her. "Stay back."

"You shot him," Amber said.

Seth took out a badge wallet and held up a set of credentials in Amber's face. "Federal officer, Amber. I'm arresting your son. Get back."

From beneath his shirt, moving with difficulty, Seth drew a pair of handcuffs. Boone lay flat, staring aimlessly. Seth rolled him onto his stomach and cuffed him.

Boone coughed and gagged. Seth rolled him back over. Boone didn't move — not a muscle, not anything. Except his eyes. They jumped, seething, as though trying to flee, and to attack.

His gaze lit on Seth. "Fucker. You . . . I can't . . ." He gagged again and tried to spit. "Fuck you."

Boone looked at Rory. She seemed to uncoil, like a spool of razor wire. Every inch of her skin prickled.

"You think you got it all," Boone gasped. "The money, all. But you're screwed. You'll always be a loser."

Before she knew it she was standing over him. The Beretta hummed in her hand. It was aimed at Boone's chest.

He said, "You'll never get away. Riss will . . ." He coughed.

He hadn't once looked at Addie. The gun seemed to sway in Rory's hand, making the sign of the cross over him. Or crosshairs.

"Your own child," Rory said. "You tried to kill her."

Seth's hand covered hers and he pushed the gun down. They locked eyes. She could barely see him. Her rage snaked in front of her like northern lights.

All this. The courthouse attack. Judge Wieland. The *Justice!* bystander. The attempted murder of a little girl. All down to Boone.

She said, "His neck's broken, isn't it?"

Seth said, "He can't fight you anymore."

"Of course he can."

Boone hissed, "Loser. You got no guts, Rory. Riss got away." A hitch caught his breathing. "Bitch," he said to her. "Dick," he added, for Seth. "Gonna top both of you." He spit on the ground, but it came out as drool, clinging to his lips.

"He can fight," Rory said. "But I won't let him win."

She looked at him. And handed the gun to Seth.

The wind brushed the ground and shook the trees. The road was empty, and she couldn't hear any approaching vehicles. But that meant little.

She said, "Mirkovic's going to be coming with heavy metal."

Seth took her words as a blessing to change the subject, or artificial erasure of the tension that bled through the air between them. He got his phone and punched a speed-dial number.

He looked ragged. He held the Glock carefully, ready to fire at new opponents at a moment's warning. Maybe at clouds, or the fabric of the universe.

Into the phone he said, "It's Colder. I need urgent backup."

Rory listened through the brush of the wind, hearing his clear and authoritative tone, the assurance, even with the wheeze from his lungs. Her skin, her bones, were throbbing. She couldn't seem to turn away. She held tight to little Addie and felt the girl's heart beat against her own chest.

Seth finished the call. "Sheriffs and ATF are on the way. Ambulance too."

Rory stared at him. "Who are you?"

"Criminal investigator for the U.S. Attorney." His eyes were earnest and half-crazed. "I'm a federal cop."

He held still, his shoulders canted, breathing with difficulty.

"Broken ribs from Boone's shot?" she finally said.

He nodded. He didn't reach for her, didn't step toward her. He knew he didn't dare. "Paramedics should look you over. Addie too."

The little girl was curled against Rory's chest, gripping a fistful of her shirt. Nearby, Amber stood hugging herself, swaying back and forth.

Rory felt the charge between her and Seth threatening to blow, like an electric arc. "Investigating what — corruption in the Ransom River PD?"

He nodded. That was his new job, with the legal group that worked out of the Federal Building in L.A., investigating old cases and miscarriages of justice.

She half turned, stopped, turned back. "Why, Seth?"

He took her in, and she got the impression he was holding on to her image, drinking in the chance to be close to her, because he feared it would be his last.

"I should have told you when I came back. I was under direct orders to keep it quiet. But I should have told you."

"Undercover," she said. "While undercover."

He didn't actually flinch when she said it. She gave him points for that.

"Need to know, right?" she said. "Protecting the operation, and me, and yourself."

"Yes."

In the distance, far down the road in the cataract of haze, flashing lights worked their way toward them. The wind dipped and a faint siren threaded the air.

Seth held close a second longer. "You saved this little girl." His eyes were dry but yearning. "I love you, Aurora."

When the black SUV crested the hill, sunshine bounced from the hood and windshield. Behind the wheel, Rory saw the Nightcrawler.

Seth said, "Get in the house. Take Amber."

He walked around Boone's truck with the Glock raised, his credentials held out in front of him.

The Nightcrawler swung the SUV around halfway and stopped on the road. He put down his window.

Seth walked toward him. "Federal officer. Get out of the vehicle."

The Nightcrawler didn't react. He seemed oblivious to, or thought he was impervious to, the threat of authority and a loaded gun.

He called to Rory. "Your cousin was a tool. Is he gonna live?"

She shrugged.

"You got some balls, girl. Don't waste 'em."

He stepped on the gas, spun the wheel, and fishtailed back the way he'd come. Seth didn't seem alarmed. He lowered the gun and waited.

A few seconds later the Nightcrawler slammed on the brakes as his car was confronted with two L.A. County Sheriff's cruisers, pummeling up the road toward him. He had nowhere to go.

He tried; Rory gave him credit. He swerved off the road in a wild attempt to escape through the fields. But the eucalyptus hid a ditch beyond the line of trees. He drove straight into it.

When Seth and the deputies reached him,

he was out of the SUV, hands flat against
the hood, feet spread, shaking his head.

55

Half a dozen L.A. County Sheriff's deputies surrounded Boone on the road. The scene was an orgy of flashing lights. Down the hill, a couple of miles away, more lights boomed along the road. Looked like the ambulance. Amber, kept back by the deputies, paced on the lawn, hands clenched in front of her mouth. Rory hoisted Addie higher on her hip and walked toward her.

"Boone's not moving. We got to get him to the ER," Amber said.

"Will Riss come back here looking for Addie?" Rory said.

Amber stopped. Her hands dropped. Her voice dropped too. "When she thinks nobody's looking. She'll do it to make me pay."

"Pay for what?"

Amber looked dumbfounded. "For everything. Her life. God. Sunburn. Nothing's her fault. Everything deserves payback."

Rory nodded. She felt drained. "You'll

need protection. And a restraining order. I know a good lawyer."

Addie wiped a hand across her eyes and huddled in Rory's arms. The pain in Rory's side was coming on stronger, an encompassing throb and burn. She tried to hand Addie to Amber, but Amber backed away.

"No," she said. "Take her."

"What are you talking about?"

"Get out of here. Get *her* out of here. Out of Ransom River."

Rory shook her head. "No. I'm done running from ghosts."

Amber shook her head violently. She waved at the scene. "Riss did this." Her voice rose. "She'll do it again. And again. She won't stop. We aren't safe."

"No. It's time to tell the truth and let the chips fall where they may."

Amber touched Addie's back and looked at her with sadness.

"Amber," Rory said. "I have to ask you something and I need to know the truth. Rock-solid straight up."

Amber turned shining eyes to her.

"Do you think Lee will ever come back for the money?"

"Lee's dead," Amber said.

Heat, light, clarity, like the air pressure lifting, seemed to clear Rory's head. She didn't feel upset. She felt almost relieved.

"You know that for certain?" she said.

"I've never seen a grave, but I'm sure of it."

"Why?"

"I know my Lee. He'd never disappear for good, not even because he'd pulled a job. He would have gone to ground. He might have hid for a few months. I can even see a year. But twenty?" She shook her head. "Impossible."

"You're sure?"

"He was never good at making it on his own. He wanted help from family. He wasn't a ringleader. He was my man, but he was an accomplice," she said. "He needed me."

He needed a woman, Rory thought. "I hate to say it, but —"

"Finding himself a *señorita* to shack up with down in Mexico? Sure. He liked the women, Lee did. Lots of them."

Her face was drawn, and she seemed to be trying to give Rory a message. Rory didn't get it.

"Why are you so sure?" Rory said. "What evidence do you have?"

"He never contacted me."

"Not once?"

Amber shook her head. "He never called.

He never wrote. I know you got postcards on your wall. You really think those came from him?"

Rory shook her head. She already knew that. Those had been emotional lollipops to convince her that Uncle Lee still cared for her.

"He never contacted Riss or Boone either?" she said.

"Not ever."

The sheriffs' deputies had cuffed the Nightcrawler and put him in the back of a cruiser. His sleek wormlike form filled the seat. On the radio, the deputies requested a BOLO for Grigor Mirkovic. They spoke to Seth for a moment.

Rory asked Amber, "When was the last time you spoke to Lee?"

"A week before the robbery. He got up, had coffee and three fried eggs and pancakes and maple syrup with rum mixed in it. He said he was going to L.A. for the week, that he had a deal cooking. Then he stuck a sausage between his teeth like it was a cigar and he swaggered out of there and got in his truck and drove away. I never saw him again."

Rory took a second. "Mindy Xavier."

Amber looked at the ground and seemed to decide that she might as well keep talking. "Lee shared information with her."

Rory parsed those words. "You don't mean he was her informant."

Amber didn't quite look at her.

"You knew she was crooked," Rory said. "Xavier told him the route and timing for the Geronimo Armored courier pickup."

Amber shrugged. She stared at Boone and scratched her arms with worry.

Rory considered it. At the time of the robbery Xavier must have been a beat cop, maybe a rookie. It was unlikely she'd have been privy to such sensitive information. Not through normal channels.

Rory gathered herself. "Lucky Colder."

Amber turned to her, eyes widening.

Rory nodded. "He was involved, wasn't he?"

Symmetry. Lee Mackenzie to Boone and Riss. Will Mackenzie to Rory.

But they weren't the only ones. *An inside man.*

Lucky had been involved in the investigation and still worked occasionally as a cold-case detective. Lucky had tried to dissuade Seth from pursuing this. He didn't want his son digging into it.

The sun caught her eyes. She blinked against a shine so bright it hurt.

Mirkovic knew that her palm print was on

the getaway van. Boone knew. That information could only have come from the Ransom River PD. From the Detective Division.

Behind her, much closer than she'd been anticipating, Seth said, "Where'd you hear that?"

He looked exhausted and was holding a hand against his chest. One of the sheriff's deputies called to him, "Don't act like a hard case. Get those ribs X-rayed."

He raised his chin in acknowledgment but kept his focus on Rory. "My dad?"

She didn't want to tell him. But it was past time for holding back. She felt like opening a vein and letting her entire life, her entire history, her family ties, her loves and fears, spill and wash away for good.

She looked straight at him. "I think your dad passed along information that ended up with the robbers."

"I heard that. Why?"

"It's the only logical conclusion."

Amber hadn't denied any of it. She wasn't telling Rory she was on the wrong track. Rory thought that Amber knew a whole lot more than she was telling. She may have buried it under decades of resentment and disappointment and shame, but she knew.

"There was an inside man," Rory said. "Somebody who knew the schedule for

Geronimo Armored. Seth, this has to have occurred to you."

He didn't answer.

"It wasn't anybody at the bank. The FBI reamed them with a Roto-Rooter tool and got nothing. It wasn't anybody at the Fed — they only knew when the delivery was arriving, not the exact route of cash pickups on the way. It wasn't anybody at Geronimo. That leaves the Ransom River Police Department."

His mouth tightened. "And?"

Rory's face felt hot. Every instinct told her to swallow the words, keep up her guard, bury it. She forced herself to speak.

"Twenty years ago. Your dad was in bad shape."

Seth said nothing. But he knew: alcohol, a marriage going rocky, nights of drinking to oblivion.

"He could have spilled the information to Xavier. He could have slipped. He might not even have remembered," Rory said. She didn't need to say *alcoholic blackout.* "And ever since then he's been trying to make up for those days. Even now that he's retired. That's why he's working so hard on the cold-case file."

Seth's lips parted and he shook his head. But he was going pale.

"Lee's dead, Seth. Amber's convinced, and so am I. He died a long time ago. Maybe soon after the robbery."

"And?" he said.

"The other robbers either died or were arrested that night, but that didn't leave Lee entirely alone. There was somebody else involved in planning the heist."

And Lee, she now believed, would never have been content to abandon the money and live on his wits in Mexico. Walk away from $25 million, forever? No way. He would have tried to recover it. And because he was never good at making it on his own, he would have sought help. He would have turned to the one other person who wanted it as desperately as he did.

"The inside man," she said. "That's who Lee would have trusted to help him get away with the money. But the inside man had a motive to get rid of Lee and keep the entire haul."

"And you think that's my father?"

"I think it was Xavier. But she was too junior to have known the schedule."

Seth looked like he was moments from bending double and dropping to his knees. "No. Rory. That's . . ." The shock turned to hurt. He backed up a step.

Amber shook her head. "I know Lucky.

No way he'd deliberately sell out. No way he'd pull the trigger on anybody."

The wind rose, Amber's dress billowed around her, and her hair fled above her head like Medusa's. Through her wet clothing Rory felt a limitless chill.

By the wrecker, one of the deputies shouted in alarm. Seth hurried over, one hand cradled to his ribs. People clustered around Boone. In a fog, Rory saw Seth kneel and begin CPR.

But she felt herself disconnect from the scene. She felt the ground seem to dissolve beneath her feet.

Amber cried out and ran toward Boone. She yelled at the deputies to *do something.* The ambulance siren rose in pitch. It was almost there. Seth bent over Boone and gave him chest compressions. The sun fell bright on his shoulders.

Holding tight to Addie, Rory stumbled toward the house. She felt as though her world had no bottom, nothing to stand on.

In the kitchen she found Amber's car keys. She went to the garage, started the old engine, put it in gear, and let the road fall away in front of her.

She drove to her parents' house.

56

Rory rapped hard on her parents' front door and opened it. Addie sat propped on her hip. The little girl hadn't spoken since they left Amber's place. She seemed calm, or perhaps frightened mute. But when Rory stepped into her parents' front hall she looked around with bright curiosity. The house was warm, a friendly place. Rory smelled corn bread baking. The stereo was playing Alison Krauss.

"Doggie here?" Addie said.

"No, honey." She'd phoned her neighbor Andi Garcia to get Chiba from her car.

"Can I play with him?"

"Soon."

The autumn sun was failing in the west, dropping toward the dun-colored hills. She walked into the living room.

"Mom?"

Samantha peered out from the kitchen, a spatula in her hand. "Rory? What's . . ."

Addie gazed at her with big eyes. Sam's expression glazed, like ceramic drying in a kiln.

Then she rushed to the living room. "My God, Rory, you're all torn up."

"I'm all right. Where's Dad? We have to talk."

She reached to touch Rory's scrapes and bruises. "What happened to you?"

Rory raised a hand to hold her off. "Not now. Where's Dad?"

"He's out back. What's . . ." She collected herself and smiled at Addie. "Hi there. I'm Sam."

Addie buried her head against Rory's shoulder. Shyly she waved.

Rory said, "This is Adalyn. Maybe she can watch a video and have a snack while we talk."

Rory's heart had lodged so high in her throat she could hardly speak. But Sam got Addie a juice box and corn bread and set her in front of a Disney video. Rory called her dad in from the garden.

When Will saw her standing at the kitchen door, he slowed, gathering himself.

"Hello, sweetheart," he said.

"Uncle Lee," Rory said. "I need the truth. I need all of it. I need it now."

Rory walked back into the kitchen, where

she had a view of Addie in front of the TV in the other room. The little girl had lain down on the floor with her head on a pillow and her thumb in her mouth.

Will said, "Why is Addie here?"

"Later," Rory said. "Lee. He never escaped to Mexico, did he?"

Wind tingled through the chimes that hung from the eaves. Will seemed to withdraw. Sam's eyes were edgy. Rory couldn't tell whether she was close to fight or flight.

"Amber is convinced he's dead. Is he?" Rory said.

Will fought it. His eyes begged her to back off. He raised a hand, almost like he wanted to stroke her hair, to hold her against his shoulder as she had held Addie. Almost as though he wanted to scroll back through the years, to pin time, to whisper in her little girl's ear as he had when she was five.

"I have to know," Rory said. "Boone's been shot."

"Oh dear God," Sam said.

"He tried to kill Addie. He nearly killed Seth. He would have killed me if he could. If he survives, he'll try."

Sam put a hand over her mouth.

"And Riss is out there. She'll try too. She'll come after me. She'll come after me because she'll try to get to Lee. Over the money. The goddamned heist money he stole and brought here to our house. It's a clusterfuck and I can't stop it unless I know the truth. I deserve to know," she said. "Do I call the FBI? Do I hire a PI? Do I go on TV and beg Lee to phone home? 'Cause I'll do that, unless you tell me it's pointless."

Sam said, "Will." Her voice had the weight of a thousand years in it.

One last second. Her dad held off. Then the dam broke.

"No. He didn't . . ." He cleared his throat.

"He didn't get away to Mexico that night, did he?" Rory said.

Will shook his head.

"What happened?"

Sam walked to the window and stared at the lowering sun. It edged her face with shadows. "He died."

Bam, like a cannon shot. "How?" She could barely see. "Where? When?"

Will said, "Don't cross-examine us. This isn't a courtroom."

"No. It's our family's history and our future. It's survival."

Sam slumped. "Rory. For God's sake. Don't make us . . ."

"Did you know he was dead? All these years?"

"Yes," Will said, and his face seemed to

age before her eyes. "Yes."

Something in his bearing silenced her. Anguish. Her hands fell to her sides. When her dad spoke again, it was softly.

"Everything I told you about that night was true. He showed up here, wounded. I was horrified. I never dreamed Lee would get himself involved in something so bad."

He turned to Sam. His eyes were mournful. She stared out the window.

"But he was my brother. I couldn't turn my back on him," he said. "That's why he came here. He knew brotherhood would get him through the door." He paused. "And that's when he turned on me."

"Turned —"

Will walked to the window and put his arms around Sam. She said nothing. She took hold of him. Will exhaled.

He turned to Rory. "How could I ever explain to you — how could I ever go on, if you knew . . ."

His voice trailed to ashes.

Rory whispered, "Knew what?"

Her mom turned from the window. "It was self-defense."

Hot tears leaped to Rory's eyes. "No. Dad."

Sam spoke in low, emphatic words. "He did it to protect you."

Will closed his eyes. "I never wanted it to happen. Never. It was . . ." His lips trembled.

It's not true. "I don't understand." *Not true.* "Oh my God." Rory raised her hands, baffled, begging for a denial, an explanation, angelic intervention.

Sam said, "Lee wanted to get across the border. And he wanted to take you with him."

"Me?" Rory said.

Will gestured at her. "That look on your face, right there. That's how your mom and I felt when he turned up that night."

"Why would he want to take me with him?"

The wind chimes rang. Sam said, "Because he was your father."

57

The light in the kitchen sank to a stinging
red. Rory shook her head. "Lee was not my
father."

Sam stood framed by the sunset. "He was
your birth father. Yes."

"Mom." Rory reached for the counter to
brace herself. The words seemed to be coming at her from a random letter generator,
making no sense.

"I was eighteen. Had just moved here
from San Antonio. I was lonesome and stupid."

Sam looked small, tough, and implacable.
Not a moment's kindness in her voice. Not
for Rory, not for herself.

"Going to school, waitressing, feeling out
of place. He came in the diner and we —"
She paused, and gathered herself, and
forced her voice flat. "You want me to say
the rest? I was gullible, romantic, couldn't
hold my liquor. It was one time. Worst

mistake I ever made." She inhaled. "But the best possible outcome." She eyed Rory and her voice cracked. "Beautiful outcome."

Will reached for Sam's hand. She took it and held it firmly.

Rory put a hand in front of her mouth.

Will said, "Sam told me about it at the outset. She was completely honest."

"I was desperate," Sam said. "Will told me I didn't have to be."

Rory's eyes stung. "Did Lee know?"

Sam's gaze said, *What do you think I am, stupid?* "I wised up real quick. I was an evening's entertainment to him — he was a million laughs back then, and he liked having an audience. But if I hadn't married your dad, Lee would never have remembered my name." She shook her head. "You couldn't have paid me to tell him."

Will said, "We eloped three months after we met."

"And that's what you need to know," Sam said. "I'm Will's wife. He's my husband. You're our daughter."

Her voice choked. Rory's head felt like a melon about to burst.

Uncle Lee. All those years, doting on her, treating her like the princess he always wished Riss was.

"Lee found out," Rory said.

Will said, "Years down the line. He got an inkling. He figured out the timing. He could count."

The sharpness in his voice, like a switch cutting the air, took her aback.

Rory thinking: *Riss. Riss, my sister.*

"Did he confront you?" she said. Knowing she was avoiding the worst part, the hatchet through their lives, the words *It was self-defense.*

"He hinted," Sam said. "Sniffing around the subject. So bit by bit we pulled away from him. That only made him more suspicious. Then one day he flat-out asked me. Asked if he had a bigger litter than he'd thought. That was the word he used. *Litter.*" Her face was flat, but her voice was acrid.

"He was miserable with Amber," she said. "He was planning to leave her. I didn't know it then, but he was planning the robbery with his — his *gang* — and planning to use his cut to get away for good. Mexico, that was his dream. Without a needy wife and that wild little boy of hers. Without that troubled daughter of his. Oh God. Beautiful Nerissa turned out to be cracked from the bottom up. Lee knew Riss was troubled. He was scared of her. And he started . . ." Another tremor in her voice. "He started looking for a replacement. Replacements."

"He wanted me," Rory said, tonelessly. "And you."

Sam straightened. "Lee didn't come here that night for help from his brother. Your dad's too noble to tell you that, but I will. Lee showed up looking for a nurse and maid and bedmate." Her voice gained steam. "Bleeding. Angry, with a gun in his hand. Knowing his life here was well and truly screwed, everything shot, including him. Knowing he'd blown everything, and trying to salvage something by stealing something new."

Will said, "He demanded that Sam go with him to Mexico."

"As if I'd drop my life and go on the run. The gall. The absolute idiotic, fantasist gall," Sam said. "Then he said, 'In that case, I think it's fair I take my daughter with me.' "

Bony fingers seemed to grab the back of Rory's neck.

"Lee tried to force his way into your bedroom," Sam said. "I tried to stop him."

"No." Will's voice was furious. "He tried to take our sleeping child. You threw yourself bodily at him. He had a gun and you threw yourself in front of Rory's door." He turned to her. "Your mother was willing to die to keep him from taking you."

556

The ghost of a memory tightened around Rory's neck. Her, nine years old, climbing in the window and stopping, scared. The nightmare in her mom's unseen voice, the thuds that weren't thunder. Seth nearby, ready to run. The confusion and strangeness she felt as she hung on the windowsill and saw shadows play across the strip of light beneath her bedroom door.

Sam said, "Will tried to pull Lee away from me. Lee attacked him. Punching, kicking, on the floor in the hallway and living room. Will tried to wrestle the gun from his hand."

She briefly covered her mouth. "It was terrifying. It was hell. Hell, here in my home. And my husband was trying to save me and our little girl. And it was his own brother trying to destroy us. Rory, that was the worst part. His own brother." She grabbed a breath but her words would not stop. "Lee wasn't sane. He wasn't even human. He was punching Will and trying to get an angle with the gun. He was ready to shoot your dad."

She looked beyond fierce. "I jumped on Lee. I truly did. I was out of my mind, Rory. And he had a gun," she said. "And . . ."

"He was going to shoot your mother and steal you," Will said. "I had to stop him.

Just stop him. I had to." He took a breath, worked his lips, and then said it. "I punched him in the throat."

Sam squeezed his hand.

"Punched him so hard it broke something. And he went down and . . ."

He turned and walked to the kitchen table and collapsed on a chair. He put his head in his hands.

Sam said, "Will didn't mean to kill him. And it was self-defense. Airtight goddamned righteous self-defense. Don't care if a court would see it that way. It was."

She walked to the table and put her arms around him.

The silence hummed. Outside, the wind chimes clashed like blades. From the family room, Disney music tingled, girlish, giggly.

Rory hung as if in suspended animation. "You didn't call the police."

"There was a van outside carrying twenty-five million dollars in stolen money. A dead man on the living room floor," Sam said. She spread her arms. "Heat of passion, lovers' triangle, a kid in the middle — Rory, don't you know what the Ransom River police would have made out of all that? It would have destroyed us."

It already had, Rory thought.

She said, "You didn't trust the police

department. You thought they'd skim the money and lay the blame on you."

Will nodded.

"You saved me," she said. She didn't think she'd ever said more bitter words. "Saved me. And bore the weight."

"It was worth it," he said.

He looked broken. He looked lost. He seemed afraid to meet her eyes.

"Where is he?" she said.

Will closed his eyes. "Buried in the mountains. In the national forest."

"With the money?"

"Near enough."

The sun winked out behind the hills and bled to red twilight. Rory pushed off from the counter and walked past her parents and out the back door. A chill permeated the air. Her clothes clung to her, damp. Her abrasions and bruises throbbed. She walked to the back of the property, to the avocado tree. She leaned against the trunk. Above her, the tree house seemed to tilt to one side, innocent and lonesome. In her mind she heard laughter, childish ideas, fear. That night. It was a shooting star that tore through her life. She looked at the landscape before her and, for a moment, couldn't identify anything.

In the kitchen, her parents' phone rang. A

second later her dad stepped onto the patio.

"It's Seth. He wants to talk to you."

Her throat was tangled in barbed wire. She shook her head. "Later."

Will spoke quietly into the phone. His shoulders sagged.

Rory said, "Wait. I'll take it."

Listlessly Will handed the phone to her.

"Seth," she said. "Get protection for Lucy Elmendorf and Jared Smith."

Grigor Mirkovic hadn't blinked at destroying the trial of the people charged with killing his son. He spat on the justice system. But he would seek to avenge Brad's death.

"Mirkovic will try to get the defendants before the cops get him. Don't you agree?"

Seth hesitated only a moment while processing her words. "On it."

"Good."

"Rory —"

"Not now." She felt like she was running on a ragged rim, a few seconds from a blowout. "We'll talk later."

She ended the call and turned to her dad.

"Boone didn't make it to the ER," he said.

The chill in the air felt prickly. In the east a blue twilight painted the sky. Rory felt only a pale sense of relief. And underneath it, scratching like a feral animal, another fear. Where was Riss?

Her dad stood on the patio, waiting. She knew he'd wait all night, all weekend, the rest of his life. Over the eastern hills, a white disc of moon began to rise.

"Dad. The money. You remember where it's buried?"

"I could never forget."

She walked back to the house. He followed. When she came through the kitchen door, Samantha simply looked at her, waiting. Her life was in Rory's hands. All their lives were.

Rory said, "I need a map and a flashlight. The moon's up but it'll be dark in the forest."

58

The road ran straight across the hardpan, an asphalt cord that unspooled toward the mountains on the horizon. The desert was cool in the sunrise, the sky a deep and flawless blue. Rory kept her speed steady and her eyes on the vanishing point. She didn't look in the mirror. She knew what was behind her.

Addie was singing in the backseat.

The little girl kicked her bare feet and sang along with a kids' album on the stereo. Dino songs. T. rex: deadly but dead. That's why kids loved dinosaurs. They couldn't hurt you.

Addie was less withdrawn today than she had been for the past three weeks, since the confrontation with Boone and Riss. Physically, she was fine. And Rory had been taking her to an infant-parent therapist, to help her start dealing with the trauma she'd lived through. She no longer clung silently to Rory's side. She was singing. Nonsense words, but enthusiastically. Her eyes were bright.

Rory's bruises had faded to yellow stains. Her right side was a crocodile skin of scabs, but the pain was mostly gone.

Other aches lingered. Petra remained shaken, though she was drawing hope from her third graders. Rory had hated to tell her good-bye. A friend you can trust with your life is a rare, fine thing. After Petra escaped the river that day, she'd bolted down the road in Seth's truck — and found him beyond the storm drain, injured and struggling up the bank. They backtracked but couldn't find Rory. Desperate to get Addie, Seth dropped Petra at a safe location and tore over to Amber's house, where he walked into the fray.

The bowl of the desert brightened, chalk white with the sunrise. Rory put on her sunglasses. In the back of the car, Chiba stirred to watch yucca trees and red bluffs roll past.

The U.S. Attorney had taken over the investigation of the courthouse attack. Detective Xavier had been arrested. Grigor Mirkovic was under indictment for solicitation to murder. Rory had been cleared of all suspicion. She'd been interviewed extensively and would be called as a witness in any trial. But she didn't have to sit tight. The feds knew how to find her.

And she had been given temporary guardianship of Addie. Amber had readily agreed that Rory should take the little girl — for a few weeks, a few months, maybe longer — until Riss surfaced. Rory knew that Riss had the capacity to stay subterranean for long periods. She'd be back, and when she appeared Rory wanted Addie to be far away.

She put down the window. The Mojave hadn't heated up yet, and the air felt brisk. In the far distance, range after range of stark mountains marched to the horizon, purple, brown, sharp, sawing the sky. The Sierras edged into view ahead. She was on the back road to far gone.

And she had cash in her pocket. More cash than she'd ever had. Enough.

Before leaving town, she had phoned the FBI and told them the location of the buried money. She kept her parents out of it. She told the Bureau that one day when she was nine, she and her cousins had gone with Lee Mackenzie to the national forest in an old van. Her uncle, she explained, told the kids it was a fishing trip. Now she understood he'd used them for cover. Left them lakeside for hours, and came back dirty and exhausted.

The Bureau couldn't disprove her story. They couldn't hold her accountable for what she'd seen as a youngster. They followed her directions and found the money.

They paid her the reward.

She put part of it in a trust fund for Addie. She paid her bills and kept enough money to stay on the road for months if she needed to. She donated ten thousand dollars to the school where she'd taught in the Peace Corps.

The rest she gave to Asylum Action. The charity was going to be able to run for at least two years. It would have time to get back on more stable financial footing. The refugees they'd been helping would not, after all, be left in limbo.

The mountains seemed to hover above the horizon, beckoning. She was seeking safety. She was holding tight to a little girl who needed love and care, and who she would ensure never grew up in Ransom River.

She checked her watch. The two-lane blacktop rolled nonstop until the view ran out. But in the distance, at the side of the road, glass sparkled. A minute later she pulled into an old gas station and diner.

Dust swirled around the Subaru when she stopped. It blew against the wall of the diner and against a faded mural of the space age, stars and the moon and a streaking Saturn V rocket.

The black pickup was waiting. Seth climbed out.

He was moving better, breathing better. His shoulders were still canted. If his cocksure grin existed anymore, it was hidden. He was unwilling to reveal himself, even now, even to her.

She parked and turned to Addie. "Be right back, roo." She got out.

"Good timing," Seth said.

"You know I'm fast."

In the dry brush of the wind, the question was plain on his face: *Forgive me?*

Not yet. Not all the way. She was fast, but not that fast. She would absolve him for withholding the truth about his role as a federal cop. Eventually. Soon, even. Because she knew him. She knew who he was, and that she should have seen it. She'd known him all his life.

She handed him the flash drive that Neil Elmendorf had put in her car.

Seth turned it over. "What's this?"

"Bootleg CCTV movie. It's the Brad Mirkovic killing."

"How —"

"Lucy Elmendorf's husband gave it to me. Don't know how he got it. But he had it enhanced. It raises reasonable doubt."

He looked openly surprised. "You want to elaborate?"

"Brad Mirkovic was armed," she said.

His surprise turned to skepticism.

"With an illegal handgun that belonged to Lucy Elmendorf," she said. "Lucy dropped it when she tackled Brad. Brad grabbed it. Without computer enhancement it's almost impossible to see, because it was nighttime. But it's there. Lucy didn't want to admit she was carrying the piece. She thought she was home free via self-defense, so she lied."

"Why would she lie?"

"The gun, I'm guessing, was purchased through a channel that leads back to Grigor Mirkovic's arms dealership."

He curled his fist around the flash drive. "Purchased through Boone, you mean."

Boone's links to Grigor Mirkovic, they now knew, extended beyond the courthouse attack. Boone not only ran drugs through Ransom River Auto Salvage, but was a conduit for Mirkovic's illegal weapons business. Nobody had looked twice at smashed vehicles on the back of his wrecker, or considered that those vehicles might be loaded with contraband.

And through his ties to Mirkovic, Boone had met Dobro, the gun dealer Seth had pursued. Boone told Dobro that he recognized Seth — that his cousin dated him. Dobro took it from there. He contacted Mindy Xavier and got confirmation that Seth was an undercover officer.

Neither of them said the rest. Boone had supplied the vehicle that smashed into Seth's truck two years earlier, injuring Rory.

That was a piece of the puzzle they'd slotted into place and tried to let go of. Boone was dead. They couldn't get much more payback than that.

Rory said, "Lucy Elmendorf can mull her decision to buy that weapon when she lays flowers on Jared Smith's grave."

The wind gusted. Seth nodded and looked up the road. He had sent the authorities to protect Elmendorf and Smith, but they weren't fast enough. Mirkovic got to Smith before the cops did.

Seth put the flash drive in his shirt pocket. The wind brushed sand across the road. They shaded their eyes and avoided any talk of other betrayals. They didn't mention their families.

Lucky Colder couldn't remember much about the days before the Geronimo Armored car robbery. But it was clear that he must have let sensitive information slip to Xavier during a drinking binge. And she had played him, both before the robbery and before the courthouse attack. After the heist he spent two decades saturated with guilt, fearful that a drunken blunder had allowed the robbers to attack the Geronimo Armored car. To make up for it, he devoted himself to the cold-case file. He told Xavier there was an unknown palm print on the getaway van. And Xavier had run it, discovered it belonged to Rory, and contacted Boone and Riss.

Now Lucky was broken, and fumbling to regain his honor. Rory hoped Seth would find a way to help him do that.

"Last chance," Seth said. "You sure you don't want new IDs for you and Addie?"

"I'm sure of nothing. Except that I need to learn how to feed a growing girl. But no, thanks."

Silence scraped between them. A big rig rolled past on the highway, headed north for Reno or Montana. The sun cast shadows across Seth's face.

"I thought you were dead," she said.

"I thought you were dead," he said.

Rory's phone buzzed. She didn't answer immediately. It was a repeated text message, one that came every day about this time. It buzzed again.

"Yet we're both alive. So what about us?"

she said.

"You're running."

"But not away. And not alone."

The wind lifted her hair from her neck. She held out her hand.

He took it. And his smile didn't look like a dare, but like light pouring out. He pulled her in and held her. She hung on, tight.

When her phone buzzed yet again, she took it from her pocket. No caller ID. Despite the fact that she'd changed her phone number once already, the texts kept coming, from seemingly random cell phone numbers. The words were same as before.

I'll find you.

She deleted it. She thought: *No you won't, Riss.*

Seth said, "How far you think you'll get today?"

"Maybe Lone Pine."

"I'll follow."

She smiled. "That'll be a first."

She got in the car and pulled out. She looked, one time, in the rearview mirror. Seth's truck was a hundred yards back. She put her hand out the window, held it up to the wind, and felt the morning air flow through her fingers. In the mirror she saw him do the same.

Welcome home.

ACKNOWLEDGMENTS

As always, I want to thank my wonderful agents, Deborah Schneider and Sheila Crowley, for their support and expertise. I also want to thank everyone at Dutton, especially Brian Tart, Ben Sevier, Jessica Horvath, and Jamie McDonald, along with Kara Welsh, Claire Zion, and Jhanteigh Kupihea at NAL. I'm lucky to work with such great teams. My gratitude also goes to my first readers: Mary Albanese, Adrienne Dines, Kelly Gerrard, Susan Graunke, Tammye Huf, and David Wolfe. My friends Ann Aubrey Hanson and Nancy Freund Fraser deserve special mention for holding my feet to the fire and forcing me to think, hard, about the story I was about to write. And, as ever, to my husband, Paul Shreve: I couldn't do it without you.

ABOUT THE AUTHOR

Meg Gardiner is the author of four Jo Beckett thrillers, as well as five novels in the Evan Delaney series, including the Edgar award–winning *China Lake.* Originally from Santa Barbara, California, she now lives in London.

The employees of Thorndike Press hope you have enjoyed this Large Print book. All our Thorndike, Wheeler, and Kennebec Large Print titles are designed for easy reading, and all our books are made to last. Other Thorndike Press Large Print books are available at your library, through selected bookstores, or directly from us.

For information about titles, please call:
  (800) 223-1244

or visit our Web site at:
  http://gale.cengage.com/thorndike

To share your comments, please write:
  Publisher
  Thorndike Press
  10 Water St., Suite 310
  Waterville, ME 04901